SON OF THE WATER

ISBN: 978-65-5872-604-3 (softcover)

A native of Vitoria (ES), Brazil; Mark Bittercourt acquired the habit of reading and writing while he lived in the USA, but it was when he regressed to Brazil that he took the liking for writing fantastic literature, for he felt idle and presented health problems. He has a bachelor in Biochemistry and Molecular Biology from the University of California; Irvine. Nowadays, he has graduated in English Literature from the Universidade Federal do Espírito Santo.

SON OF THE WATER

MARK BITTERCOURT

Mark Bittercourt, rua Isaltino Arao Marques 65 mata da praia, Vitoria ES Brazil
Phone527999191021

Contents

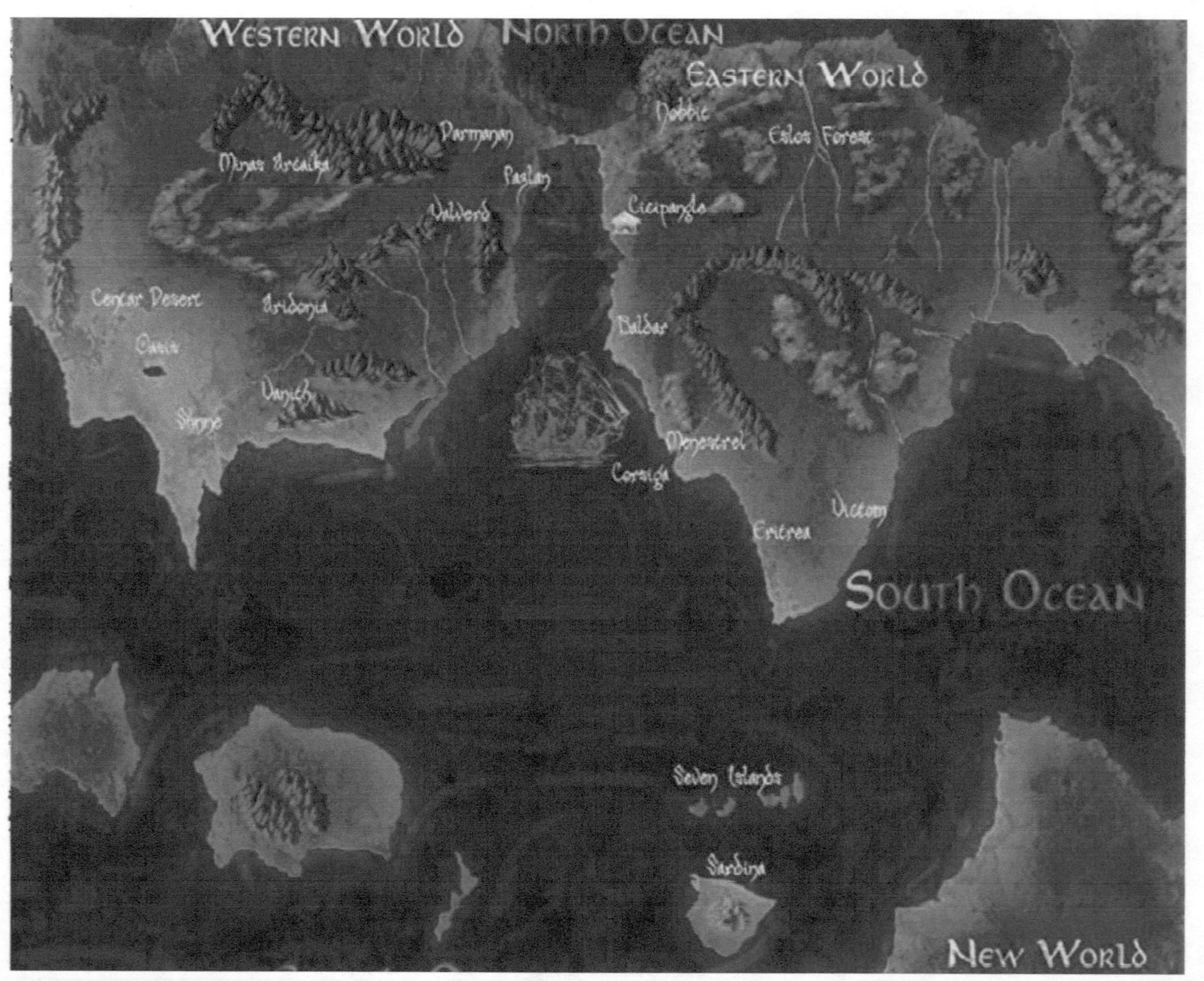

WESTERN WORLD
NORTH OCEAN
EASTERN WORLD
SOUTH OCEAN
NEW WORLD
Nobbie
Eslos Forest
Darmanyn
Minas Arcaika
Paslim
Valverd
Cicipangla
Casper Desert
Iridonia
Oasis
Vanich
Sharpe
Baldar
Peppernel
Coraiga
Eritrea
Victony
Seven Islands
Sardina

CHAPTER 1

The Ubaid Period

The world is not as it seemed twenty hundred seasons later. Several underwater cities across the vast ocean are home to the merfolk. They are underwater dwellers with gills, webbed hands, huge fishlike tails, and muscular builds. Atlantis, their capital, has a majestic structure and organization with many beautiful buildings. Tubular vents suck in oxygen from the shallow waters to the deep waters of the city, where oxygen is scarce. The Atlanteans have large, submerged plantations of green algae placed around cold lights. The algae helps with the oxygen.

Triton III is the king under the water. He stands as the direct descendant of Poseidon, the most powerful of the gods. Triton presented as always kind toward his people, but stood as one quick to wrath and punish with his mighty trident.

Once, he took his family on an expedition to the underground caves. It seemed to harbor strange underwater creatures. The water in those caves ensued as a mixture of salt and fresh water, which created the unique conditions essential to the evolution of fascinating aquatic creatures—for example, the see-through marine frog. The ever-running river waters carved their route into the bedrock. The sea advanced and mixed with the underground lake connected to it.

Triton's daughter, Thalith, disobeyed her father and ventured far into the cave. After a period, she emerged in the harbor city of Menestrel. There, she met a muscular young fellow who was the son of a fisherman. But he happened to be no ordinary man; he came as also the son of the elf-maiden Minerva. He and Thalith fell madly in love at first sight.

Thalith always came to him through the river at night when her parents were asleep. They would swim together, hold hands, and sing songs. She learned his language in a few solar cycles. The dark waters of the river hid her true nature from her lover. On one of those nights, her mermaid songs bewitched him. He could not resist the temptation and made love to her.

Triton grew weary of the underground lake. And so, he realized the proper time for his family to return home came to pass.

Many seasons passed. The fisherman's son returned to the river every night, hoping to see his love, but she remained nowhere to be found. His love had simply disappeared without saying goodbye. Heartbroken, he left the harbor city, searching for a new life. It would be a new beginning far from the river, which reminded him of her.

Meanwhile, Thalith's friends and family became aware she was pregnant. But the child's father remained a mystery. They all knew the mermaid's child could be from no mere man.

Triton became suspicious of all his subordinates. Since no one revealed anything about the matter, Triton punished Thalith. The king-father ordered that she be kept jailed until she revealed who the baby's father was. He let only one servant attend to the princess' needs. Her name was Ninka. They both planned an escape, fearing for the unborn child's life. Since Triton had said he would slay the child once born.

Seasons of planning went by, and they finally had the opportunity. Ninka and Thalith escaped Triton's grasp and fled toward the shores of Menestrel. They knew Triton wouldn't chase them there. Once away from Triton, Thalith gave birth to her baby. The baby boy existed as apparently half human and half merfolk. She took the baby in her arms, hugged him, and laid him down on the warm sand.

"Are you just gonna leave him here?" Ninka asked.

"You know what my father will do to him once he lays his eyes on that child," Thalith responded in a sad and somber tone.

"But you cannot just leave him! Take him to his father, at least!" Ninka replied angrily.

"I do not know where the father stays at the moment. I made sure never to see him again. If my father knew the man's identity, he would have him killed," Thalith replied, looking into the distance.

"If you will not take responsibility for the child, I will." Ninka shed her mermaid skin and crawled toward the baby. Holding it in her soft arms, she turned to Thalith and requested, "Now, leave us. Return to your previous life! He will no longer be angry with you. And in case he asks, say that humans slew your servant and baby as you fled toward the open sea, where none of us are permitted."

Thalith nodded, took a last look toward her servant and baby, and yelled, "Camellus! That's the father's name!" She swam off into the distance.

Ninka sat there, naked and confused about what to do next. She looked at the child and confessed, "Currently, it's only the two of us. First, we need clothes."

She looked along the seashore and saw a run-down cabin. She slowly made her direction toward it and grabbed some timeworn rags to cover her body and the baby.

They spent the night there, and in the morning, they headed toward the nearest city.

"Wow! I didn't know humans could build such things!" Ninka declared as she wandered around with the crying baby in her arms.

Soon, two mature ladies in religious clothing stopped her.

"Do you not hear that the baby seems hungry?" a particular older woman asked.

"Yes, but I have no milk nor any means of feeding the baby," Ninka replied.

The women looked at the sad state in which Ninka appeared and offered their help. They took them to an archaic building. There, Ninka helped herself adequately in the matter of clothing, and they fed the baby.

A single woman asked, "This child does not seem like any ordinary child. Where are you from, exactly?"

Ninka stood, reluctant to say anything, but she soon saw that the worn-out woman meant her no harm. She told them her story and her identity.

The women offered her shelter, protection, and a job for the period she had left. The nuns knew that when a mermaid shed her skin, she had little time left on earth.

As the women walked Ninka to her room, one asked, "What's the child's name?"

"I do not know yet," Ninka replied as she looked at the boy.

"Come on, dear. Don't let this be a thorn in your side. These diminutive ones are a blessing!"

Ninka stopped, looked at the two nuns, and voiced inspiredly, "Thormon! That's it!"

Both nuns smiled.

"Thormon it is, then! He will stay with you for the tiny interval you have left, and once you are gone, we'll make sure we find him a home. If we can't, we will keep him under our wing."

CHAPTER 2

The Jemdet Nasr Period, Dawn of Rebirth

T hirty seasons had passed since Thormon came to the nuns' care. He knew scarcely about his mother. The nuns barely spoke of her, since they had promised Ninka that they would never reveal Thormon's secret.

He appeared poor with almost no belongings but stood brave and always stuck by his friends. The oldest of his friends was Egil, whose interest happened to be cartography. Katrina loved exploring. Thormon, in contrast, as the "middle child," stayed fond of mementos and treasures.

These three inseparable friends had an appetite for adventure.

Egil heard rumors that a band of pirates had buried their treasure on a specific island along the coast. He saw a ship with black sails pass by many times. It always lingered on the deserted island visible from the beach. Egil would write down the places where the ships docked, and then he had an idea.

"Let's go treasure hunting. All we have to do is to build a boat. Once we get to a docked ship, we will find the captain's map in his quarters. What do you think, guys?" Egil pointed toward the island.

Katrina contested, "But, Egil, we are not allowed to leave—or go alone to another island. Are you crazy?"

Thormon rebuked, "Bah! That's never stopped you from sneaking out to the park at night, has it? You can count on me, Egil. If Katrina doesn't want to go, that's more treasure we'll keep to ourselves!"

"All right! If she doesn't want to go, that's her problem," argued Egil. "Wait, guys! I never mentioned I would not go. I just said we weren't allowed to leave. Please, count me in!" Katrina replied.

"What can go wrong? Those pirates are no match for us!" Thormon replied.

They all agreed to take part in the adventure and made their preparations.

The trio would rendezvous at night in the church's backyard. Each night, they would sneak to the carpenter's shop and steal a few wooden planks and nails.

After 15 moon cycles, they had stolen enough wood and nails to start working on their boat. They weren't skilled at building boats, but their willingness stood unwavering. The boat looked slightly funny in the front and square in the rear. It seemed nothing like a proper boat—it looked more like a raft, but it floated, at least on calm water.

"What will we call our grand ship?" Thormon asked.

"How about *Wallabee's Vessel*?" Katrina suggested.

Thormon and Egil looked at Katrina, trying not to laugh at the ridiculous name.

Egil offered, "What about *Pleasant Journey*?"

"Well, that does sound nicer," Thormon admitted.

"All right, but I still think *Wallabee* ensues better. But, you guys did most of the work; thus, you should have the right," Katrina replied.

They hid their craft by the riverbank and waited for the pirate ship to dock on the mysterious island. Every night, one of them would sneak out and stand watch for any sign of the pirate ship.

A few moon cycles followed, but no ship stayed on the horizon. They started to get bored and tried to find a new adventure. Maybe they should find a present for Katrina. Her birthday party quickly approached the set day.

The nuns and priests would take the children to the beach as a birthday tradition. So, on Katrina's twelfth birthday. They gathered around a bonfire and ate marshmallows and barbecued meat.

Sister Lavigne kept an eye on the children while they sang, played, and built sandcastles. At Father Charles's request, they sang happy birthday to Katrina.

Her eyes were as bright as Venus in the dark. They looked like a big family and all the worries about being adopted faded. She stood in the middle, and all the children hugged her.

The priest handed Katrina a gift box with bright papers, courtesy of the clergy.

She unwrapped it and found a lunette and a birthday card.

Father Charles lived as a second-rate poet. But he never missed a chance to write something nice for the children.

The birthday girl finished reading the letter, and a tear of happiness ran down her plump face.

"Come on. Look at the horizon with the aid of the lunette," coveted Thormon.

She took it out of the box and placed it in front of her right eye. She saw the mayor's house, which seemed close with its magnificent halls and wide archways. Furthermore, she turned in another direction, scanning the horizon. She saw the myriad trees covering the hill, the white-capped waves, and a huge ship with black sails. She put the lunette down for a bit and decided to look again.

"What is it? Tell me what you see!" Thormon grabbed the lunette and looked through it. "My goodness! What is that?"

A big, fearsome angel face with wings stretched backward. On the whole, it seemed carved in the dark wood of what appeared to be the front of a ship.

"Give me that! Let me see!" Egil took the lunette from Thormon's hand. "I believe it's what we were waiting for, but what startled you so intensely?"

"Did you see the fearsome angel?" Thormon replied.

"Are you crazy? I think you ate too many marshmallows. No more marshmallows for him, guys," Egil jested with a smile.

Thormon suspected that his eyesight could be superior to his friends.

The ship anchored on the island's far side, and its crew boarded a small boat and prepared to dock.

The three friends were eager to get back to the orphanage.

"Let's hope these pirates stay on the island for a long time," Katrina whispered on their way back to the orphanage.

When everyone came about as sound asleep, the kids put their plans into motion.

"Do you think the map befalls there, Egil?" Thormon asked.

"Of course. I am sure the captain has a map. How else will he find the location when he comes back to retrieve the hidden treasures? It makes sense that the captain probably keeps the map in his cabin in a secret location. Maybe under the bed?"

They came up with different plans and agreed to board the pirate ship.

They went to the riverbank and hid the *Pleasant Journey* under a thicket of brambles.

"What will you do with your share of the booty?" Egil asked as they started their preparations for their pirate adventure.

CHAPTER 3

Setting The Plan in Motion

E gil, Thormon, and Katrina went back to the place where they had hidden their boat.

"Quick, guys. Check to see if it's still intact," Thormon suggested.

"Don't worry. *Pleasant Journey* is seaworthy," Egil guaranteed.

"Y'ar, mates, today we sail toward our booty!" Katrina expressed.

The boys took the boat from its hiding place and put it in the water.

"In any case, it's still above water. I guess we can go," Katrina noted.

They started rowing down the river. "Look, Thormon! Sand!" Egil yelled.

The boat got stuck on a small sandbank, but Thormon used a wooden pole to set it free.

"Guys, you have to be quiet. This is still a secret mission!"

Shortly afterward, they spotted water vortexes.

"Oh no! Do you think we'll make it?" Katrina pointed at the whirlpool.

Egil affirmed, "Of course! We'll keep clear from them. You'll see!"

It wasn't as easy as they thought it would be. It took hard work to steer away from the vortexes, but the boys managed it.

Egil sat down to rest. "Katrina, you help this time." Egil handed his wooden paddle to Katrina.

From then on, it ensued smooth sailing for the rudimentary boat.

The trio approached the remote side of Makake Island, where the seafarers docked the prized ship. They stealthily approached the vessel, always double-checking to ensure none spotted them.

"Guys, I don't see anyone. We can get closer," Thormon probed.

"Don't you think it's a bit too quiet?" Katrina asked.

"Don't be silly. They are all drinking on the island," Egil countered.

They continued rowing, but the deck localized too high, and it seemed slippery to climb. They tried reaching up with their miniature hands, but they failed.

"I think I have an idea." Thormon fell into the cold water with a splash.

"Ha! You're a fool, Thormon," Katrina shouted.

"Shh! You don't want the pirates to hear us!" Thormon angrily uttered while getting back into the boat.

"Stop trying to go up that path," Egil whispered.

Thormon started looking for another route to the ship and spotted a thick rope coming down from the tall ship. "Look! We could go up through there!"

They tied their small boat to the ship, and Egil led them undetected to the deck.

He turned to them and divined, "This is the moon cycle in which we outsmarted the captain of the *Black Seraph of Eritrea*—the renowned ship with the tall, dark sails!"

The children started looking for a direction into the captain's quarters.

"Guys, look! There is someone there," Katrina whispered while pointing to a sleeping buccaneer.

At least ten men were onboard. A few guards were on the mast and the front deck. Some sang and drank rum straight from the bottle, and others slept.

"By the looks of it, they must have had plenty of booze, wouldn't you say?" Egil asked.

"Better for us. They'll never see us coming," Katrina replied.

Thormon whispered, "Let's hope they drink until they pass out— and then we can go forward."

Egil whispered, "No, we don't have time. The crew will be back soon."

Thormon commanded, "OK. Katrina, stay here and keep watch. Egil and I will go forward. Tell us if the pirates return."

"All right—but don't take too long!" Katrina wanted to look inside the cabin as much as the other two did. "Go on! Leave me here!" She bit her lip. "Go get that map!"

The boys rushed forward and found a locked door at the back of the fancy cabin.

Thormon deduced, "It must be the captain's quarters."

Egil tried to force his way in. "The door won't budge!"

A mature, shabby buccaneer looked their way.

"We are done for!" Thormon cried.

For a beat of an eagle's wings, all hope gradually depleted. They thought about how foolish they were for being so unprepared.

Luckily, the children were short, and the poorly lit deck hid their presence. The buccaneer stood drunk.

"My goodness, Egil, things could've turned out badly for us," confessed Thormon.

Egil spotted the small, open circular window and said, "Luck is on our side, man. Look! We can get in through there."

"Wait. What? I don't understand," asked Thormon.

"Look at the window, Thormon. That's our route in!" Egil replied.

"For you, yes. You're skin and bones. I won't fit—and what about Katrina?"

Egil reassured, "Don't worry. She can handle herself better than you can. You putz! Everything will be fine. You worry a lot!"

Thus, the children settled the matter. Thormon waited outside while Egil went in. The porthole stayed closer to the floor from the outside but stood higher up from the inside.

Egil squeezed in through the window, fell on his arm, and broke his wrist. He wanted to yell in pain, but he rolled back and forth on the ground, writhing, biting his lips, and holding his right wrist. His hand would not move.

"What happened?" Thormon whispered through the porthole.

"What do you think, you idiot? My wrist is busted," Egil replied. "It's all because of this stupid plan."

Thormon tried to raise Egil's morale, "Don't be a crybaby. This happened to be your stupid plan to begin with. Hurry up! Suck it up and man up! Are we adventurers or not?" The comment should lift Egil's spirit, and it worked.

Egil stood up and walked over to the desk with tears in his eyes and his right arm hanging. "Now, it's the moment to get what we came for."

CHAPTER 4

The Acquisition of the Map

T he cabin seemed stylish and spacious, and many antiques hung on the walls. Many of the captain's swords were on display. On top of the desk were a gold compass and two silver compasses. One could find a clock tower made with fine mahogany on the wall. Suddenly, Egil entered the stylish and spacious cabin. Many antiques moved, and Egil's heart started pounding.

"Oh, no! It's the captain!"

A big bird on top of a wooden pole peeked in the corner. It seemed like a blue, yellow, and green macaw. Its head feathers lifted, and its eyes opened wide. It looked a bit alarmed, too.

"Hello, pirate! Hello, pirate! Hello, pirate!"

Egil tried to silence the bird, but it kept on squawking, "I am Captain Bobo! Get to work, you lazy bastard! Wash the deck!"

A buccaneer heard the commotion and checked it out.

Thormon quickly hid behind a barrel. The man approached the door and tried to open it, but the captain had locked it.

"Oh, damn it! Barbarosa locked it!" He moved to the side and put his ear to the door.

"Wash the deck! Get to work!"

"Hmm. The stupid bird again. Let me check. That thing doesn't just get up and talk." The older pirate went to the porthole and looked through the circular window. In the empty cabin, there were no signs of an intruder.

Egil hid under the porthole and held his breath.

"Ah! You stupid bird! If I had my will done, you would have been dinner in no time." The pirate went back to the mast. "I bet it must not taste a lot different from chicken."

Thormon returned to the porthole and whispered, "The coast remains clear!"

Egil resumed breathing and decided to get the map and be gone, but there remained no sign of it. He looked everywhere: on the desk, in the drawers, in the barrel, and on the shelves. Everywhere. It came about as something hard to look for with only one hand.

"Maybe the captain doesn't keep a treasure map. I will leave and say I found no map."

Thormon whispered, "Come on, Egil. Don't give up! You can do it! Check for a button or a lever. Perhaps it's hidden in some secret place."

Egil took a deep breath and decided to look around the room again.

What did I miss? If I were a captain, where would I hide my secrets?

Suddenly, he noticed something odd with the tower clock. The ticking rod stood idle.

"Eureka!"

"What is it, Egil?" Thormon asked.

"I found it!" he shouted.

"Shush! Are you crazy? Do you want to alert the pirates?" Thormon replied.

"OK, OK. But I'm smarter than any of these pirates—including the captain!" He opened the glass door and pushed the ticking rod. The whole clock swung forward with a click and revealed a secret compartment. Egil's eyes sparkled with wonder at the treasures that were revealed.

"What is it? What did you find?" Thormon asked.

"What do you think? The booty!" Egil replied.

"We're not here for the booty—just the map. Focus on the map!" Thormon requested.

Egil walked into the secret place and took a look around. He saw a rectangular compartment. It seemed filled with a diamond-encrusted golden ring. Next was a solid gold bracelet, a huge pearl necklace, and an ornamented silver box. There was also a key ring with five keys attached and three maps in a lower drawer. He looked at the maps well, two of which were navigational maps. They were not what he wanted. The third seemed to be a map of the island with marked trails and a detailed description of a hiding place.

"This must be it!" He grabbed the map, folded it, put it under his garment, and left the hiding place.

"Did you get it?" Thormon whispered.

"What do you think?" Egil smiled as he tried to contain his emotions.

"Come on. Let's get out of here!" Thormon expressed with building anxiety.

Egil tried to climb up the circular window. "Shoot, man! I can't reach the window!"

"Try giving me your hand," Thormon replied.

"It stays too high!" Egil replied.

"Try to look for something to climb on. You can do it!" Thormon claimed.

Egil attempted to find something that could work as a makeshift ladder. But the pirates had fixed everything to the ground—and the barrel came about far too heavy for him to move.

"I can't get out, Thormon! Please help me! I don't want to die!"

Thormon extended his arm inside to pull him out. "Try to jump with your arm up. I'll pull you out!"

It stood still too high.

To make matters worse, Katrina came running to warn the boys about the captain and his crew. "We have to leave promptly!"

"We can't! Egil is trapped inside the cabin!" Thormon whispered. Thormon extended his arm even farther. But it proved too far for Egil to touch the tip of his fingers—even with the highest jumps.

"What can we do?" Katrina asked.

"Hold on! Let me concentrate here," Thormon replied.

Time slowed down, and Thormon's perception started to kick in. It seemed as if he existed inside the room with Egil. He started gazing at the hidden compartments while Egil looked for a path out. His mind awareness shifted into high gears as if he felt a change in perception. It led his eyes to focus on what he seemed to be looking for. Something drew his eyes' attention, something silver. The tiny silver keys would have remained unnoticed inside a drawer. That is, if not for his keen perception.

"Grab the keys and open the door!"

The wind befell strong enough that his voice did not reach the drunken men's ears.

"Where?" Egil asked.

"Look inside the half-opened drawers," Thormon answered.

Egil quickly searched the drawers until he found the keys. He grabbed the key ring and ran to the door. He frantically tried the first, the second, and the third; then, the door popped open. He quietly ran over and put the keys back in the drawer. Furthermore, he looked back and ensured everything else stayed in its original place. He shut the tower clock on the wall and left the cabin.

"Let's hope the captain doesn't find out that his map is missing," Egil felt his fear building while closing the cabin's door.

"But how will we lock the door if we return all the keys?" asked Katrina.

"Maybe the captain forgot his cabin door is unlocked?" asked Egil.

"Captains do not make that mistake." Thormon opened the door, went back to the drawer, and took the cabin's third silver key. After ensuring everything remained in place. He closed the drawer, walked out of the cabin, and locked the door.

"Straight away, everything was as it seemed," concluded Egil.

"Not exactly. How will you return that key?" asked Katrina.

Thormon replied, "The captain must have an extra key for himself. How else would he have locked the door in the first place?"

"True!" Katrina confirmed.

"We got what we came for. Let's get out of here!" Egil said while getting on the ropes to descend to the boat.

On the boat, Katrina and Thormon rowed. The tide ensued in their favor, and the pirates were arriving with skiffs on the far side of the ship. The timing came to pass just right for their escape. Before long, they were far away. The wind blew in their hair, and the cold water entering the boat chilled their mood.

"You don't think she'll sink, do you?" Katrina asked.

"Don't worry. We'll get back safe!" Thormon answered.

Egil and Thormon started scooping the water out with their hands.

CHAPTER 5

The Complicated Return

D o you see that thing over there?" Nestor the bald yelled while looking at the kids rocking on the boat.

"What thing?" a younger pirate asked.

"Ah! Never mind. It must be a big turtle or a whale." Nestor turned his back to the ocean.

***

Katrina sat shaking because of the cold water, and a big wave hit the boat, knocking her into the ocean. Katrina sank to the bottom.

Thormon appeared not afraid of the raging ocean.

"Gotta save her!"

He didn't know the swimming technique yet and couldn't remember the last occasion he had dived into the water. He needed to save her. He jumped headfirst into the water. In the dense water, he could see well, but he kept going deeper and deeper.

He wondered why his skin remained intact, not losing heat in the cold water. But his hope did not die yet, so he continued to thrust to the bottom with his webbed feet. There, he saw small Katrina still clinging for her life. She held onto a sharp rock to avoid the currents from dragging her away. The girl seemed pale and numb, yet still beautiful. She persisted with her eyes shut and golden-brown hair flowing in the water.

He approached her, touching her cold arm, and the diluted sunlight shined upon her face. She seemed to be unconscious, but she still held her breath, too scared to accept death. Thormon had plenty of air, and staying underwater wasn't affecting him. His senses were sharp. There, he noticed the beauty of the reefs. Home to exquisite fishes and sea creatures, it almost overwhelmed him. He instantly knew what he should do. The bubble inspired him. He gave her what he had most, and she barely had. He blew into her mouth. Her tight lips surrendered to his pressing mouth, and she inhaled all the air he could offer. The feeling made his heart race and his senses tremble. His mien showed that he felt fantastically alive and did everything to keep her alive and well. He took her hand and swam to the surface.

As they emerged, Egil wildly rowed with one arm, making the boat spin.

Thormon swam to the boat, taking Katrina with him, and Egil helped them onboard.

"How are you guys?" Egil asked.

"We're fine. Don't worry," Thormon answered while holding Katrina in his arms.

"Let's just get back to shore," Katrina suggested faintly.

They reached the beach and left their boat floating on the shallow water. The trio took no heed of its presence after stepping on land.

Thormon grabbed Katrina and carried her to the orphanage.

"How are you gonna explain that wrist?"

"Don't worry. I'll think of something," Egil replied.

They were tired but happy. They walked to the orphanage, dumped their damp clothes into the bin, and put on their pajamas. They tiptoed to their bedrooms and dropped dead on their beds. They were exhausted. It had been enough adventure for one day.

CHAPTER 6

Mending The Broken

"Wake up, you sleepy kids," Sister Lavigne yelled and slapped their weary faces.

Katrina yawned. "What? What time is it?"

Sister Lavigne disapproved, "You lazy, good-for-nothing kids! It's almost night-time! You get up this instant!"

It transpired not that late, but Sister Lavigne liked to exaggerate.

Everything occurred smoothly until a suspicious nun saw Egil's wrist. "What in God's name happened?"

"Uh, nothing. I think it happened when I jumped off the bed," Egil replied.

Sister Lavigne turned around and looked firmly into his eyes. "Could you repeat that, my boy?"

"I jumped out of bed and fell. Nothing else," Egil replied with a mischievous smile.

"Really? You're sure you're not leaving anything out of this fall?" Sister Lavigne had he doubts.

"That's it. I jumped and broke it," Egil replied. Sister Lavigne knew the kids were up to something. But she grew tired of their mischief and decided to care for Egil's wound. She called another nun, and they took Egil to the infirmary.

Egil spent the rest of the solar cycle under the nun's care.

***

"Do you think Egil snitched?" Thormon asked.

Katrina deduced, "I don't know, but since Sister Lavigne didn't punish us yet, I think we are off the hook currently."

"Let's just hope so. Hey! Look! It's Egil."

They rushed toward him and asked a ton of questions.

"What is this? An interrogation? I'm no snitch! You guys know that!" Egil replied.

The kids calmed down and started asking about Egil's well-being. He showed them his cast with pride. It made him look badass!

The girls surrounded Egil and wanted to sign the cast.

The kids decided to put their treasure-hunting quest on hold for a while.

CHAPTER 7

Mischief Revealed

When Egil´s wrist seemed fully healed, they started plotting how to find the treasure on the island. First, they returned to where they left their boat and found it banging on the waves on the beach.

"Wow! I can't believe it's still floating," Katrina said in disbelief.

"I told you, I am a master builder," Thormon replied. They quickly jumped in the water and retrieved it.

"I don't think it can make another trip, Thormon," Egil confessed as he checked the boat.

"Of course, she can! I built it myself!" Thormon replied.

Katrina suggested, "Why don't we make it sturdier? After all, we will be bringing back lots of treasures."

They took it to the orphanage and hid it behind a long-standing oak tree in the backyard. It stayed their goal to make it sturdier. They decided to meet up in their secret place, a massive tree house on the outskirts of the orphanage.

Hundreds of seasons ago, the first generation of orphans had built the secret tree house. The older kid passed down the tree house to the next generation. When the time came to leave, Thormon found that an imperial eagle had built a nest on the top branches. Thormon would feed the two hatchlings in his spare time. He would gaze at the vast landscape. And wonder what scenery he would find beyond the insurmountable Elder Mountains.

They climbed up the under-treated rope.

"Do you have the map with you, Egil?" Thormon asked.

"In any case, of course! Why else are we here?" Egil took it out and put it on the floor.

The map came about as pretty straightforward, but a few details puzzled them.

"Why do you think they edged the whole forest until the ravine?" Egil asked.

After a moment of realization Thormon responded, "They must avoid staying on the island during the daylight at all costs."

"Do you think there's a monster or something?" Katrina asked.

"I dunno. It seems strange," Egil replied.

They talked about the strange notes for a couple of beats from an eagle's wings.

Egil soliloquied, "Let's see how the captain puts the distances between each thing on the trail."

"Look! What are these stars about?" Katrina pointed to the stars on the map.

"Good question," Thormon replied.

The kids suddenly heard a loud knocking on the door.

"Did you hear that?" Thormon asked.

"Oh my! They found us!" Katrina yelled.

"Quick—hide the map! We're going to have much explaining to do," Thormon feared.

They heard a second loud knock and realized it did not originate from their door. They quickly wrapped up what they were doing, climbed down the tree, and ran back to the orphanage. Furthermore, they did not care who or what stood at the door. Their only worry remained Sister Lavigne. If she were to find out what they were up to, they would never again see the light of day!

The banging continued until a nun opened the door. A weathered man looked at the nun.

She looked at the man and said, "Sorry for the delay. We are not accustomed to receiving anyone, especially at this period of the night."

The man complained politely, "Sorry. Ten moon cycles back, some of my wooden planks disappeared. I tried asking around, but no one could give me the culprit. A couple of solar cycles back, I saw three kids taking a boat from the ocean and dragging it back to an oak tree. I decided to investigate." The man grabbed the nun's arm and took her to the oak tree. "You see that boat over there? Probably the culprit made it with my stolen wood!"

Thormon dreaded the turn of events, "They caught us! I know what befalls us."

"Oh my! I never noticed this boat before," the nun confessed.

The man requested with finality, "I would like compensation for my stolen wood. I know that it happens to be one of your children. Call them all down; thus, I can tell you who is the culprit!"

The nun demanded, "Now, Richard. I know you know who did this! Spit it out!"

The kid seemed initially reluctant, but Sister Lavigne pressed him. When he tried to pretend he did not know anything, she gave him a stern look and argued that he would be punished for the rest of the four-season period if he didn't give the names.

"It was Egil, Katrina, and Thormon! They stole the wood! They built the boat! I saw it!" He started crying, lowered his head, and shuffled away, dragging his feet on the wooden floor.

Sister Lavigne took a deep breath and looked up the stairs. "Where are those three diminutive devils? I knew they were up to no good when Egil broke his wrist! Egil! Thormon! Katrina! You small devils, come here this moment! I know you can hear me!"

There ensued no answer.

"You small rascals! You come down here this instant!" Sister Lavigne yelled.

Still no answer.

"Richard, go fetch those troublemakers this instant!"

She waited impatiently and tried to hold her anger inside.

Many beats of eagle's wings later, the trio showed up with blank faces.

Sister Lavigne took an expert look at them and demanded answers, "See this man? He claims that you stole wood from him. Is this true? And don't you dare try to make up any stories. I know you three well!"

They lowered their heads and didn't say a word.

Thormon looked at his friends and started thinking about how to reply.

Katrina and Egil were speechless. Thormon took a deep breath, swallowed, and decided to tell the whole story.

With tears, Katrina turned to the carpenter and confessed untruly letting her imagination loose, "Sir, it's all my fault. I've always wanted to explore the ocean. I happened to be the one who convinced the boys to help me out.

I told them we had to fetch wood and tools from a nearby depot. Please don't punish them. They wouldn't have taken the wood if it weren't for me. I convinced them to do so. Please don't punish them. I am the culprit!" She burst into tears. "I am sorry."

"Oh, my dear. Please don't cry. I'm not going to punish or hurt anyone." The carpenter kneeled and dried Katrina's tears.

Sister Lavigne befell unconvinced, and she also made the boys apologize.

The carpenter looked at the three and gave a labored breath, "You know, children, that wood cost me money. I still need payment for it, and since you have no money, I just can't demand that the sister here pay for it. I was a kid once. Likewise, I know how it is to grant a beautiful girl's wish. I am willing to work out something with you. How about y'all work at my shop for a few solar cycles? I need an extra hand, but I cannot afford one at the moment. What do ya say, kids?"

Thormon seemed a bit surprised by the unfolding of events, but he had no choice but to agree. "When can we start, sir?"

"Now then, kids, let me think. How about the day after tomorrow at the first rays of dawn?"

Sister Lavigne stepped in and commanded, "No! They'll start tomorrow at six!"

"But, Sister, that's still dark!" Egil complained.

Sister Lavigne gave them a cold look and uttered proudly, "You kids are my responsibility! You all will do as I say! You all will be there tomorrow at six! Mr. Hinderman, you can be here tomorrow at six to pick up the kids. They will be waiting for you." She sent the kids off to bed.

CHAPTER 8

Work as Redemption

M r. Hinderman came about early to pick up the kids. He arranged for the kids to work for him every solar cycle for fourteen days throughout the moon cycle. They would run errands for him, such as carrying wood, fetching tools, and cleaning the shop. Also, the trio would sharpen hatchets and pile up the wood boards.

It proved tiresome, but Thormon gladly did it. He always finished first. He seemed keen to learn how to work with wood and make a better boat for their adventure. Learning to build diminutive boats, big boats, ships, and even caravels seemed extraordinary.

The carpenter came to pass as a skilled shipbuilder, who also built chairs, tables, and furniture. Working at the shipyard stayed his priority throughout life. And so they worked the solar and moon cycles.

After their fourteen moon cycles, their debt to the carpenter ended. He confessed, "You kids have helped me out a lot. Now I want to do something nice for you all. Let's fulfill Katrina's wish. What do you say?"

The kids quickly answered, "Yes! Yes!"

The carpenter proposed an agreement, "But this has got to be between us. Do not tell Sister Lavigne. She scares me, too."

They went down to where Mr. Hinderman kept the boat.

"See here?" the carpenter asked. "This area is all wrong. You should level the boards and angle the bottom a bit further."

Thormon listened and fixed the boat accordingly. They even added a small sail and a cargo bay.

Once the carpenter finished everything, they decided to test the boat. It proved sturdy and floated. Mr. Hinderman even made enough room to travel with them.

"OK, kids." Mr. Hinderman got on the boat. "Let's see what this boat can do."

They sailed a bit, but they did not dare go too far.

"Why don't we go closer to that island?" Thormon asked.

Mr. Hinderman chattered leisurely, "In any case, you see, my boy, I have a client named Tartuga, and he said this. The reefs damaged his ship during a desperate escape from a ship with dark sails. Luckily, it managed to reach the shipyard."

"Is the pirate ship still around?" Egil asked.

"No, it's not. It got stuck while giving chase," Mr. Hinderman informed.

"Where did it get stuck?" Thormon asked.

"In the Seven Sister Isles," Mr. Hinderman replied.

"Fortunately, no privateers are lurking around, right?" Katrina asked.

"Now, then, Tartuga did spot a pirate ship with the same description, the dark sails. It headed north to the buccaneer's den port of Sardina. It would seem that the captain buccaneer headed the ship in that direction. It's pretty far. Theoretically, the privateer from the port of Sardina would take several solar and moon cycles to reach the prized island Makake Island. I'd say we're home-free at once, but there could still be further dangers lurking around. I don't want you kids traveling far. Promise me you won't go to that cursed Makake Island. Pirates like to stay there."

After Mr. Hinderman had taught them how to sail and navigate the boat, he docked the boat and wished them good luck.

***

The kids planned what to do and bring to the island for seven moon cycles. Once everything transpired right, they put their plan into motion.

They told Sister Lavigne that they would spend the night at the carpenter's shop to help him out with some work.

Sister Lavigne agreed and let them go to the carpenter's workshop.

"Wow! I can't believe she believed us!" Egil demeaned the nun.

"What an idiot. She is extremely stupid!" Thormon followed suit.

"We better check to see if that miniature rat Richard isn't nearby." Katrina looked for him everywhere.

It came about the occasion to navigate their boat from the shipyard to the island. They said hi to Mr. Hinderman and told him they would do some checking on the boat and take it out into the river. They would pass the carpenter's shop twice, which would suit the story they told the nun. They sailed around the river until Mr. Hinderman left the surroundings.

"Is he still watching us?" Thormon asked.

Katrina replied, "Nope. I think he went to sleep."

"Great! Time to go!" Egil proposed.

At last, they embarked on their journey.

CHAPTER 9

The Adventure Begins

T he boat turned out sturdier and waterproof, and it floated and sailed fine. Thormon became proud of his handiwork and couldn't help but smile as they sailed.

"Look! The island!" Katrina yelled.

A dense fog covered the island. An air of mystery surrounded them. They had to use the small compass that Egil always kept in this pocket.

"Do you think we will get there okay?" Thormon asked.

Egil replied, "Don't worry. We'll be fine. I'm skillful at this. We'll be there in no time."

They followed Egil's directions until they arrived at the island's south coast. They left their boat onshore.

Egil looked at the map and realized the marked track started on the north shore of Makake Island. It seemed localized northwest of the beach, accessible only by the open sea.

"Are you sure we are in the right place, Egil?" Katrina asked.

"No. Don't worry. I know what I'm doing," Egil answered.

"Thus, what ensues now, genius?" Thormon asked.

Egil replied, "In any case, we have two options. We could get back on the boat and head north, but we risk hitting a reef or getting caught by the pirates."

Thormon asked, "And what about the additional option?"

Egil replied, "We can follow the shoreline to the north or cross through the vegetation to the far side."

When Egil mentioned the jungle, Thormon and Katrina turned their heads and stared at it for a while. The jungle looked creepy. In it grew a dense thicket of birches and huge, crooked trees. Cacti and vines with sharp thorns covered the ground. The loud noise of cicadas sounded threatening.

They stared at the jungle and decided after pacing up and down, "To the beach!"

"I've always liked the beach anyway," Thormon confessed with a smile.

They went back to the boat to get the necessary tools. Thormon took the shovel, Katrina had the lamp, and Egil kept the map.

"Don't forget to get our rations!" Thormon yelled.

"You really wanna eat that crap?" Egil replied.

Katrina expressed with a look of disgust, "Yeah, Thormon. That stuff tastes too bland. I don't wanna eat it!"

Thormon said, "What if we take longer than we want to and don't find anything to eat? We'll be in trouble and hungry."

They walked side by side until they reached a bare rock. There seemed no visible trail in sight. They decided to climb it and tried not to slip on the slippery sea rock. Lucky for them, the tide remained out; otherwise, it would be impossible to cross without getting hurt. At times, standing felt hard on the feet. There were irregular slopes, fractured rock, and slippery mold. These made crawling their best option.

"So much for the beach, huh?" Katrina struggled to cross the rocks.

Thormon proposed, "Yeah! Why don't we take this path? Why don't we climb here? It'll be fun. The jungle comes about too dangerous!"

Egil replied, "Nobody forced you, little babies, to come here! You all chose this!"

After taking a sharp left, they arrived at the north beach. They looked down and saw the sand mixed with pebbles and shells, which gave it a rough texture.

"I believe that's where we begin!" Egil deduced.

"Are you sure it's not another climb or a crazy path?" Katrina joked.

Egil explained, "Look! You see the trail marked on the map. It starts there! That's where the pirates anchored. Farther up at a palm tree befalls a trail with footprints and smooth, bare soil. To the left stays the jungle, and to the right ensues the beach."

"OK! You've got the lamp, don't you, Katrina?" Thormon asked.

"Of course!" Katrina replied.

The path started on the outskirts of the jungle. They had to walk in a line because the first part of the trail came about too narrow.

Katrina took the lead and lit the pathway with the lamp held up high. Egil and Thormon were right on her trail.

"Where should our first stop be?" Katrina asked.

Egil pointed out where they should head. "Let's follow the path that leads up the hill. Once we get there, we'll have a better view of the island."

They took the track to a peak where they could see the whole island. Many paths originated from that point. Some entered the jungle at different angles.

Thormon scratched his head and asked, "Where shall we go, Egil?"

Egil looked at the map for a few beats of an eagle's wings, "I think we should take the third to the right, entering the jungle."

"Do you think—or are you certain?" Thormon replied.

"Of course, I'm sure!" Egil replied.

They marched toward the third right in the jungle.

Katrina could not light the route well because insects were swarming the lamp. She endured smacking, hitting, and shooing them off. A few small animals crossed the path, and Katrina screamed.

"Katrina, shut up! We don't know what—"

A deafening shriek paralyzed the kids with fear. The sound went right through them and sent shivers down their spines. It sounded like a tiger's roar. The kids quickened their pace.

"Look! It found us!" Katrina pointed at a tall bush that kept on shaking.

"I told you not to scream!" Egil whispered.

Thormon warned, "Shh! Don't say anything else. Something is not right."

The branches started cracking, and the noise began to get closer.

The kids didn't know what to do. Run away or face the animal?

Thormon with a stern grown-up look finally proposed, "I'll go check it out."

"What? Are you crazy?" Katrina asked.

Egil added, "Don't go! I have a bad feeling about this!"

Thormon walked toward the bush, held up the shovel, and yelled, "Come and get me, you filthy monster scum!"

It seemed complicated to detect anything in the dense brush.

Thormon hit his direction through the wilderness as he went after the thing in the middle of nowhere. Wielding the shovel, he walked and turned his head from side to side, searching for the culprit. He became mad at himself for trying to be the brave one.

Strangely, nothing happened.

"Hmm, nothing." Thormon intended to return, and then another noise sounded. He turned around and searched the bushes.

Nothing.

He walked in the direction of the second noise. He felt almost panicked. "Please don't be anything big! Please don't be anything big! Please don't be anything big!"

He heard the noise again in a small clearing. He approached the spot carefully, tiptoeing across the path. He looked around and saw nothing. He rested one arm on a tree and yelled, "It's nothing, you bunch of wussies."

Something moved again. In this instance, the tall bushes shook all the way from one end to another.

Thormon froze and dropped his shovel. He looked toward his friends and screamed, "Run!" Thormon blasted past his friends, and they picked up their pace.

"What did you see?" Katrina yelled as they tried to keep up. She looked back and saw a big black gorilla-like monster. It had a horn on its forehead and sharp protruding canines and chased after them.

I'm gonna die! It'll get me! Gotta be faster! Thormon thought as they tried to outrun the beast.

"Turn there, guys!" Egil pointed to a vast glade.

They quickly entered, forcing the monster to show its complete form.

The nine-foot-tall monster kept salivating, breathing heavily, and carrying Thormon's shovel.

The kids kept walking backward, too scared to break the gaze.

Katrina screamed in terror as they backed toward the edge of the mound.

The monster came closer and cornered the kids.

"This is it, guys," Egil cried.

The beast stood up, towering over the kids and on the verge of striking.

All appeared to be lost.

Egil tripped on a small rock. He fell backward, grabbing Katrina for support, and she grabbed Thormon. They rolled, slid down the steep slope, and landed in a small cave. Katrina's lamp extinguished upon impact, hiding them.

The monster looked down, but it could not find them. The kids could hear the monster's frustration. It screamed and hit the shovel on the ground until the tool broke. It went around in circles and then moved on.

Thormon noticed, "It couldn't find us in the dark—even though we were close."

"Hmm. Thinking back, the map did say not to venture during daylight," Egil pondered.

Thormon added, "There is something about the dark of the night. Maybe it can't see well in the dark."

"But it attacked us at night," Katrina rebuked.

Egil conjectured, "But think, guys. It seemed a clear night with a full moon, and we had a lamp. Once the lamp went out, and we were in the dark, it couldn't find us."

The children waited in the darkness until a heavy cloud blocked the full moon and dimmed the light.

"Egil and Katrina, hold on to me," Thormon whispered. "I will guide us back to the trail."

"But how can you see anything?" Katrina whispered.

"Just trust me on this one," he whispered.

Egil jested, "Like when you said there was nothing and then went running like a little girl?"

"Just trust me! I can see well at night," Thormon stated.

They didn't say another word and held his hands as he took them back to the trail. They climbed up bit by bit. They were always looking back on their shoulders. The trio expected the beast to appear behind them at any moment.

Once they were back on track, Thormon asked Egil, "Where to?"

Egil stood, slightly surprised, and asked, "But how did you see and know where to go?"

"I told you. My vision seems better than yours," Thormon answered.

Egil declared, "Hmm. I am not certain. But on the topic of where to go, I can't see the map in this darkness. From what I remember, we should follow this track until the northeast beach."

"Give me the map. I can see in the dark," Thormon demanded as he took the map from Egil's hand. Thormon turned it sideways and upside down but couldn't make out any of it. His vision hardly helped on a two-dimensional object. He tried to look like he knew what he came about doing and decided, "OK, guys. To the beach."

Katrina held Thormon's shoulders, and Egil held her right arm. After several beats of eagle's wings, they reached the northeast beach. An immense reef and many sharp rocks in the water surrounded the coast, making it impossible to pass.

Katrina pointed at the reef. "Wow! No wonder we had to walk this far."

"That's why the pirates had to build this trail," Egil realized.

The clouds blocking the moon disappeared, and the night seemed bright again.

Egil took out the map and instructed, "Listen, guys, from this beach, we should follow the sand lane until the ravine. Right about there." He pointed to the faraway towering rocks.

They walked down the beach until they reached a canyon. It turned out to be composed of soaring jagged rocks on either side. A ravine was in its middle, and the shallow water advanced inland. The cartographer marked the final destination on the map, and it wasn't far.

Katrina expressed doubtfully, "Wow! How on earth do we get through to the inside of the ravine? These rocks extend to the deep sea. There is no manner we can flank it."

"It says here that a little bit farther down, we will see an opening in the rock." Egil looked at the map and pointed in that direction.

They searched for the tall rock with the cavity but were unsuccessful. They did not find a cavity with such a description.

"Are you sure you read it right?" Thormon asked.

"Yes!" replied Egil. "Look closer, see-in-the-dark boy."

They searched for an opening in the rock with their hands. They went behind the tall bushes where the pirates piled some bamboo against the stone.

"I think I found something, guys!" Thormon yelled.

They ran over and moved the wooden sticks. Suddenly, an opening became evident.

Egil admitted, "Concealing the passage with bamboo? Pretty clever."

The opening appeared wide enough for the men to carry chests filled with riches. The distant side seemed to come our right on top of a shallow gorge.

They went to the far side of the passage. They advanced farther by wading through the canal. The water reached their knees, but it didn't bother them. They were able to see the seawater-covered colorful pebbles on the ground. The water got shallower as they advanced through. They were in the middle of two parallel natural rock walls.

Katrina stepped on small fish, which scared her. The boys looked back and laughed.

Katrina frowned at them.

They finally got to their final destination: another cave.

"Will this ever end? How extensively farther must we walk?" Katrina asked.

Egil replied, "According to what I read, this opening leads to the treasures. Thus, less whining and more walking!"

The opening led to a long underground cave carved out of bedrock.

Thormon proposed, "Katrina, I believe we can light up the lamp. No monster will see us this deeply in the cave. Besides, if the pirates come here often, we can assume it's safe."

She lit the lamp, and they saw a slope that declined progressively. The passage seemed roomy and took deep turns until opening to a big chamber. On the far side, there was a crystalline lake.

Egil instructed, "Guys, stop! The map markings stop here."

"What? No. That can't be right," Thormon said in disbelief.

Katrina feared, "Shoot! Maybe the pirates retrieved their gold. They got here before we did!"

The kids started arguing, and many bats swarmed above their heads. They dodged and swung their arms until the chaos stopped.

"See what you did, Katrina?" Thormon asked.

A pale salamander swam free from the lake and disappeared on the far side.

Thormon decided to investigate. "Did you guys see that?"

"What? What are you talking about?" Katrina asked.

Without answering, he jumped into the cold water. He walked to the corner and dived.

"What are you doing?" Egil yelled.

"Where in God's name does Thormon endeavor to go in this pond of water?" Katrina asked.

They kept on shouting, but Thormon didn't answer.

Egil tried to sound brave, "I'm going to go after him. Something must have happened."

Katrina advised, "No! Don't do that! Let's wait. What if it's dangerous? Something could happen to you, too. Please don't go there!"

"Now then, if that's the case, we must save him!"

"Don't be a fool!"

Before deciding what to do, Thormon emerged from the water.

Egil asked, "What the hell, man? Where did you go?"

Thormon's eyes were sparkling with delight. He turned to his friends and smiled. "You won't believe what I found. The passage seems located on the far corner of the lake. A thin rock wall separates an even larger chamber from this one. And you won't believe it. It's underwater!"

"Wait! What? How did you find that out?" Katrina asked.

"In any case, I saw a salamander vanish in the water. I decided to follow it, and when I emerged, I arose in a dark chamber. I saw a single lamp with huge storage space for oil, maybe meant to last moon cycles. The pirates probably left it lit on the dry part of the compartment. There were many spread lamps, which I lit, and then presto! I saw ornamented chests with all the booty we are looking for."

Egil and Katrina stared at Thormon.

Thormon pointed to the far side. "You have to go under the water and through a passage. That's where you'll find the booty."

Egil and Katrina were reluctant and asked Thormon if it seemed safe.

Thormon assured them that the water would pose no danger. "Come on, guys! Riches await us!"

They jumped in the water, and Thormon led them to the other side. They dived and surfaced in the next chamber. They climbed to the dry upper part on the far-removed side.

Upon seeing the chests, Katrina lit extra lamps.

The treasure chests were breathtaking. There appeared a golden one, two silver ones, a wooden one, and countless others.

"How are we gonna carry all this?" Katrina asked as she tried to lift one.

Carrying the chest would require at least three grownups. Also, the pirates were smart to lock all the chests.

Egil put his hand on his head and asked remorsefully, "Why didn't I take at least one or two extra keys?"

"If you did that, the captain would have discovered something was amiss. And he would have taken away the chests," Thormon mentioned.

"But, still. I could have gotten at least one key," Egil complained.

Katrina tried to take away the blues, "Come on, guys. We can do this! We'll come up with something. We always do!"

Thormon realized, "But we don't have loads of time. Remember the monster? It can't see well at night. That's why it was written on the map to journey here only at night. We have to leave here before dawn."

"How much time do we have before sunrise?" asked Katrina.

Egil replied, "Dunno. Not too long. The moon came to pass halfway down when I last saw it."

"Let's hurry up, then. Try picking the lock," Katrina suggested.

Thormon grabbed his knife and tried it on all four chests with no luck.

"You're not going to break these locks. I have seen them downtown, and they are tough." Egil started looking for something to hit the chest with. He picked up a rock and started to hit the lock with it—with no luck. He started kicking the chests in a frenzy.

Thormon restrained him and tried to ease his mood, "Calm down, Egil. It's OK! All remains not lost yet! I have an idea! Grab that lamp over there. As a matter of fact, grab them all!"

They grabbed several lamps and brought them to Thormon.

Thormon instructed, "Place them on the wooden chest. I'll add a bit of wax."

Before long, the chest caught fire, and the frame disassembled.

"Wow! You're a genius!" praised Egil.

"He sure is! I am proud of you!" Katrina hugged Thormon.

The fire quickly burned the wooden chest. It revealed its booty. There were five golden rings and a golden ornamented Viking helmet. Also, in the pile was a silver bracelet with big diamonds, a fancy girdle, and a shiny short white sword.

"Oh my! Look at all that treasure!" Katrina yelled.

"We're rich!" Egil added.

"Take it easy, guys. The treasure must be burning hot." Thormon stopped Egil from picking up a ring. "Quick! Grab some water. Hence, we can cool them down!"

Egil took the Viking helmet and three golden rings when the heat dissipated. Katrina took the silver bracelet and the remaining two golden rings. Thormon took the short sword and the fancy girdle.

They started planning their escape back home.

CHAPTER 10

Escaping from Makake Island

H ow are we going to swim back with the treasure?" Katrina asked.
"No problem. Give them to me. I'll put them in this makeshift bag and swim out with them." Thormon took off his shirt.

They put out the lamps and torches and set back toward the next chamber.

Katrina left an archaic lamp lit; so no one would notice anything missing.

They swam back to the previous chamber.

Thormon gave back the items and made sure to cover their tracks.

"Where? How? What am I going to do with this helmet?" Egil asked as he tried to find a path to carry it.

"Put it on your head, buffoon!" Katrina laughed.

Egil put the big helmet on his head, and the loose helmet wobbled as he walked. Each instance, they heard the monsters communicating with each other in deafening roars, they froze and put out the lamp.

Thormon decided to wield the short sword in his right hand, expecting the monsters to show up at any moment. His heart transpired pounding hard. The accompanying kids followed Thormon's lead, equally scared.

They left the cave and entered the dense vegetation of the jungle. They trusted Thormon for guidance in the darkness.

Sunrise seemed imminent, and the moon appeared almost gone. The night seemed almost over, and they had to hurry. Luckily, the most dangerous part of the trail remained behind them. They had only the beach and the coastal climb.

They passed the northern beach and reached the rocks on the shoreline. They had no interval to be careful on their route down. Katrina and Egil tripped and slipped on the rocks several times. The fear of falling or being ape lunch drove them forward.

Dawn seemed at hand, and the first rays of the sun brightened the darkness. The orange horizon felt heartwarming, resulting in a smile. But when the first ray of sun hit their faces, they heard a loud scratching noise. It sounded deep and low at first, and then it became piercing. Daylight had awoken something sinister. The kids looked at the sky and realized the solar cycle had begun.

"We are too late!" realized Katrina.

"They are awake," added Thormon.

"Run, everyone! Run for your lives!" Egil screamed.

They started to run. But each time Egil took a step, the helmet's sound and reflection gave away their location.

"Throw that thing away, Egil!" Katrina demanded.

"No way! It's mine!" Egil tried to run and hold the helmet at the same time.

A male ape cub grabbed the golden Viking helmet from behind and made off with it in a flash.

When Egil noticed that the helmet had gone missing, it appeared too late.

"Wait! I dropped my helmet!" He stopped and looked for it on the sand. "It's gone!"

The others stopped and turned around.

"Don't stop!" Katrina shouted.

"But it's gone!" Egil shouted as he looked for his lost booty.

Thormon looked back and saw the small creature with something shiny in its hand.

"Guys, I think I found it." He pointed in the distance.

The brown, furless thing with a small horn on its forehead and ugly canines showed as it jumped up and down. It looked like it was mocking them. The monster put the helmet on its head, looked straight at the kids, and shrieked.

Egil screamed, "Give it back, you baboon!"

"Shut up! You don't wanna alarm the other monsters!" Thormon tried to chase the slight monster with his sword and said, "Let me handle this, Egil!"

The insignificant ape backed away and screamed.

Egil circled the creature and tried to approach it from behind.

Thormon cornered the beast and pushed it deeper into the bushes.

Egil set out to grab the helmet, but the little monster swung its arm and scratched Egil's forearm. Egil screamed in pain and backed away, but the children kept pushing forward. They weren't going to let the beast keep the pricey treasure.

Katrina saw how much pain Egil felt.

"Stab the beast, Thormon! Kill it!"

Before Thormon could stab the beast, it quickly made its route into the jungle.

Egil ran after it.

Thormon ran after Egil. "Are you out of your mind? Don't enter the forest!"

The creature entered a glade inside the forest with the boys hot on its tail. Approaching the clearing, the two boys stopped and tried to hide behind a tree. Small, primitive huts were visible from afar. There were many apes gathered around in a circle. They jumped up and down, producing funny noises in a ritual for greeting the rising sun.

"What did we get ourselves into, Egil? Let's get out of here!" Thormon whispered.

"But my helmet?" Egil replied.

"Do you wanna die? Do you have a death wish or something? Let's leave promptly!" Thormon whispered.

Before they could make it out, the small creature with the golden helmet warned the backup monsters. A big male ape took the helmet from the cub.

The cub started crying and pointing at the kids.

The larger apes gathered all the warriors they could muster to pursue them.

Thormon and Egil froze in desperation. They looked at each other, resembling helplessness, and retreated at full speed.

"We're doomed! They saw us!" Thormon shouted. "Katrina, run!"

The trio heard the battle cries of the apes from afar. Trees started moving, and birds started flying away. Countless apes stomped on the ground.

The trio rushed to the boat and rowed as fast as they could. The monsters would not enter the water. They just gave a loud screech and threw rocks at the boat. Some rocks hit the boat and the kids. They rowed frantically. But the tide ensured its force, gradually driving them back toward shore.

The monsters waited for the kids. Some even dared to enter the water.

"We need to do something!" cried Katrina.

"Raise the sail! Let the wind help us escape!" Egil screamed.

A gush of wind blew them out into the open sea.

Katrina sighed in relief supposing they were rid of the threat, "Guys, I think we made—"

An immense alpha male arrived on the shore. Pushing and nudging the others aside, it looked straight at the kids.

"Oh, my—"

The alpha male picked up a big rock, aimed it at the boat, gave a horrifying scream, and threw it. The stone hit the mast and broke it in half. Wood and splinters flew everywhere.

Some debris hit Katrina's arm, but her bracelet protected her.

Thormon grabbed Katrina's arm. "Are you hurt?"

"No. Strangely, I'm fine. This bracelet protected me," Katrina replied.

The kids didn't have enough time to figure out what or how Katrina escaped injury. That was because the current kept driving the boat back toward the coast.

The monsters had used up all the rocks and could not keep throwing them, but they did not calm down. They started to fight against each other like wild dogs.

The kids grew further terrified by the beat of an eagle's wings.

"We are done for!" feared Egil looking down.

"No! No! We can't give up!" Katrina looked straight at Thormon with tears in her eyes.

That image broke Thormon's heart. But what could he do? Fear paralyzed them, and the boat seemed to get closer to land.

The monsters were salivating. Their meal increasingly approached them.

Thormon took a deep breath, shut his eyes, and prayed. The first thing that came to his mind remained the beautiful reef corals, in the place where the dim sunshine illuminated all their life.

The vivid memory took his terror away, and he screamed, "I'm not dying today!" He moved to the edge of the boat and jumped into the water.

"Thormon!" shouted Egil.

"He left us!" Katrina started sobbing.

Suddenly, a hand reached the far side of the boat and started dragging the boat toward the open sea.

"Thormon appears to be saving us!" Egil screamed.

Thormon had no idea which direction to take the boat in. But he kept putting distance between the boat and the island. As soon as he saw the others starting to row, he returned to the deck.

"You saved me again! I can't thank you enough!" Katrina smiled as she helped him into the boat.

"You have to tell me how you do it!" Egil looked at the compass.

"Let's worry about that later. First, get us home, Egil," Thormon proposed.

After what felt like an eternity, they could see the shipyard.

"I think we're finally home," Katrina smiled blissfully.

Thormon turned to Egil and said, "How does your arm feel? It doesn't look good."

"Yeah! It would be best if you got that checked out," Katrina advised.

The extended cut on Egil's forearm caused itching. It became swollen and purple, but the bleeding had stopped.

Egil looked at it and snapped, "Damn that helmet, that island, and everything in it! Extreme work for just a few rings." He looked at the three golden rings in his right hand.

"Well, at least we all made it out with our lives," cheered Katrina.

Thormon looked at them, not wanting to say a word about their fortune or misfortune.

As they got closer to the docks, Egil started moaning. He probed his wound with his good hand and looked in agony.

"Dip it in the sea. Salty water appears effective for healing cuts," recommended Thormon.

Egil did, but there resulted in little to no healing—and Thormon and Katrina started to worry even more.

They found a place to dock at the wharf as the sun kept on coming up. The carpenter seemed to be working on his new ship and did not heed the kids. The three kids disembarked and went home unnoticed.

Before arriving home, they had to hide their booty. The tiny rings were no trouble, but the bracelet, the sword, and the fancy girdle were harder to hide. They snooped around and found the perfect hiding spot.

"Get Egil's rings and hide 'em with yours." Thormon hid his booty under a loose board under his bed.

Katrina took Egil's rings and put their booty in a safe box stuck to the wall. She remained the only one who had the key to it.

Egil didn't say anything. He just moaned on his bed.

"Do you think Egil is gonna be OK?" Katrina asked.

"I dunno. I think we should take him to the infirmary," Thormon replied.

"I'm fine. Leave me be," Egil replied.

The kids went to bed after their exciting adventure.

CHAPTER 11

The Consequences of Mischief

A t noon, sister Lavigne woke up Thormon and Katrina.

"Wake up, you lazy sleepyheads! You've been sleeping all morning!"

Sister Lavigne slapped their faces and threw cold water on their heads. They got up with scared looks.

The kids looked toward Egil's bed and saw the blood. Sister Lavigne took a good look at them, but she didn't say a word. The silence scared them more than anything the sister could say.

Sister Lavigne looked at Thormon and asked, "Did you have anything to do with Egil? If you lie to me, I swear I'll cut off your arm, as punishment!"

Thormon looked at the nun with a pale look.

"Did you have anything to do with Egil? Listen to me, boy!" Sister Lavigne shook Thormon.

Katrina lied, "What are you talking about? We had nothing to do with it! Thormon came to pass as deeply sleeping all night long—and so was I. He remains in shock and doesn't know how Egil got injured."

"How do you know injury befell on him, diminutive lady?" Sister Lavigne asked.

Thormon pointed to the bed and said, "Because of the blood."

Sister Lavigne remained quiet for a beat of an eagle's wings. Then she took both kids by the hand and dragged them to the infirmary.

"What were you kids up to this time? How did Egil get such an ugly injury?"

Egil took a good look at his friends and fainted.

The nurse tended to him, and the doctor knocked on the door and asked if he could speak to the kids.

"Did you kids get a fine look at your friend?" He started bandaging Egil's arm.

The kids were in shock.

The doctor looked at them and had a heart-to-heart, "He had his forearm amputated—and he got lucky we tended to it fast. Otherwise, the poison could have spread further, causing death. Do you kids understand? Your friend could have died. Don't you think it's time to come clean? I need to know what happened and how he got that cut."

The nurse called and asked the doctor to close up Egil's wound. He picked up the blazing incandescent blade. Then, he quickly looked at Thormon, Katrina, and Egil and burned the open limb.

Egil's scream could be heard throughout the orphanage.

The doctor took a deep breath, sat down, and turned to the kids. "As I kept saying, your friend could've died, but at present, he'll go through life without an arm—and I don't know what caused such an injury. Maybe you kids know something. This infection can come back, and if we don't know what caused it, we might not be able to save him—and I bet you wish him well."

Thormon and Katrina looked at one another.

Egil seemed still unconscious. But he appeared as if he didn't want them to reveal the truth—or else they would lose all their treasure. They would rather not give up what they had fought for this easily.

Sister Lavigne asked, "How did you get such a wound, my dear? We have to know."

Egil seemed still out cold.

Katrina turned to the doctor and asked, "How long does he have? I mean … will he die?"

The doctor smiled and replied, "No, dear, but we still need to know what happened."

"Is it OK if we talk about this tomorrow? We want to spend some time with our friend. Please let us stay here by his side." Katrina had tears in her eyes.

"OK. But we still need to talk. I'll come back tomorrow, and you kids can tell me what happened." The doctor packed his things and left.

Thormon and Katrina were sitting beneath Egil's bed. Katrina became sentimental, weeping and muttering, "Why? Why?"

CHAPTER 12

Mending the Broken

T he next moon cycle, Egil woke up to Thormon and Katrina watching him. His bandaged arm looked better. The nurse called Sister Lavigne and told her the boy already stood up and stayed good to go.

Sister Lavigne ran into the infirmary. And, without hesitation, she turned to Egil and asked, "At once, boy. How did you get that?"

"I think a poisonous snake bit me while I played in the backyard," Egil answered.

The sister laughed and gazed into his eyes.

The doctor entered the room and coerced Egil "We all know that's no snake bite. It seemed a long, poisonous cut, different from the round, deep twin holes of typical snake fangs. In all my seasons of experience, I have never seen a snake bite do that to a person's arm."

Sister Lavigne attempted to deal with the problem "I suspect you kids have been up to some serious mischief. You kids better come clean! For God's sake, isn't it bad enough that your friend lost his forearm!"

Egil looked at Katrina and Thormon. He took his time looking at his amputated arm and burst into tears.

"We set sail to Makake Island. I believe Katrina already told you how she would like to explore the ocean. Thus, we did. The island appeared inviting. It had a myriad of tall palm trees and a beautiful coastline from afar." He cleared his throat. "We docked on a beach south of the island, where we made a fire and cooked soup in small cans. We were too tired to come back right away. We spent the night around the bonfire. We are not explorers. We wanted to have an adventure. We were eager to explore places and go to different areas. We didn't have a mentor or anyone else to help us understand what and what not to do. Subsequently, we didn't know we had to guard the area. While we were sleeping, a wild ape attacked us. It acted obstinately, and with its greed, it stole my—"

Sister Lavigne pressured, "Go on! Don't hold anything back!"

He continued, "As I was saying, the wild ape took my only heirloom from my backpack. The golden necklace my dying mother gave me. Thormon and I decided to corner the creature with wooden sticks we took from the bonfire."

The doctor expressed "My goodness, kids! Are you mad? It's a wild animal!"

"As I persisted in saying, we were able to make the wild ape drop the necklace and retreat. And as I decided to reach for it, the damn monkey jumped forward and clawed me in the forearm!" He burst into tears.

The nun sat next to him and calmed him down.

"And were you able to retrieve the necklace?" the doctor asked.

"Yes, I retrieved the necklace." He pointed to his satchel.

The doctor opened it and saw the necklace.

Egil elucidated, "I thought the wound was superficial. How could I guess the damn monkey had poisonous claws?"

Katrina said, "Please don't punish him. I am to blame. I wanted to go there."

The doctor smiled and asked the nun not to be hard on the kids.

They all took pity on them, especially on Egil. But the nuns still confiscated the boat to prevent any further unfortunate events.

CHAPTER 13

The Goodbye

T hat winter, Suli and Louarn Thour, traders of goods, came to the orphanage to adopt a child. Sister Lavigne greeted them and walked them around the orphanage. They then told them a trivial bit about each kid. Sister Lavigne asked the adjuvant nuns to gather the kids.

"Ma'am, I believe they are all here."

"OK! Let's go see the kids." Sister Lavigne smiled warmly.

They were introduced to the kids, one by one, and Suli made a list of the children they liked most. "Sister, could we talk slightly more about these kids?"

"Sure! Let's step into my office and talk about anyone you like." Sister Lavigne showed them into her office.

The couple sat down, and when they were about to give the name to the nun, Thormon entered the room: his short-trimmed black hair, light-brown eyes, upright posture, and something about how he held and played a wooden flute caught the couple's attention.

"Why, hello. Did Sister Lavigne give you that flute?" Suli asked.

"No, he made that himself. He seems quite a clever kid," the nun replied.

"Would you mind if we talk to him for a little bit?"

"No problem, but let me tell you, this one conducts himself a bit like a troublemaker."

"Really? What kind of trouble?" asked Mr. Thour.

"To cut a long story short, he built a boat with two other kids."

"Oh, which other kids?" Suli asked.

The nun informed, "I believe Egil and Katrina accompanied him."

Suli mentioned, "Katrina is that gorgeous small girl, and Egil is that poor kid with the amputated arm?"

The nun criticized, "Yes, that's right! This diminutive troublemaker went to an island with his two friends and spent the night there without our permission!"

"Wow! All by themselves? Isn't that dangerous?" Suli asked.

"Of course, yes! A wild beast attacked poor Egil. That's why he lost his arm," Sister Lavigne deliberated.

"Wow! That transpires indeed as a lot of trouble, young boy!" replied Louarn.

Thormon stood there with his head down, thinking the couple would never pick him.

"But, boy, you did build a boat—and that's quite a feat."

"Yes, it stands as something out of the ordinary, but we confiscated it," Sister Lavigne affirmed with a broken smile.

"Really? Where is it?" Louarn asked.

"Come with me. I can show it to you while your wife talks to Thormon." Her obligation rests on informing the adoptive parents of an orphan's good or bad traits. "Introduce yourself to these nice people, Thormon. Mrs. Thour will have a chat with you while I talk to Mr. Thour."

Sister Lavigne and Louarn walked out of the room.

Mrs. Thour asked, "You build things with wood, right? How did you learn such skills?"

Thormon nodded.

"Anyhow, who taught you? Don't worry. I won't tell the nun." Mrs. Thour smiled.

"I learned it from Mr. Hinderman, the carpenter," Thormon replied.

"Hmm. Thus, you had help?" Mrs. Thour smirked slightly. "How long did he take you on as an apprentice?"

"For about fourteen days," Thormon answered.

Mr. Thour walked into the room and said, "Wow! That's not a bad boat. You have a future, boy. I work with wooden goods, and this work seems impressive for a kid."

Thormon smiled.

"How long were you an apprentice?" Mr. Thour asked.

"Fourteen days, honey," Mrs. Thour replied.

"Impressive indeed, honey," Mr. Thour commented.

Sister Lavigne asked, "To go directly to the point of the matter, which kid from the list did you fancy the most?"

Mrs. Thour dropped the list and expressed, "I like him, Lou."

Mr. Thour, being able to read his wife's mien, agreed. "Me too, honey. We'll adopt him."

The man and his wife nodded in agreement.

Sister Lavigne asked, "Really? None of the kids from the list seems appropriate. Are you sure about that?"

"No. It's him. We want him."

"All right, then. Have it your way." Sister Lavigne went to her desk to complete the paperwork.

The parents settled his fate. Thormon seemed happy to have a family. It initially appeared as every orphan's dream. But when he thought about leaving his friends behind, of them not having families of their own, he started to cry.

CHAPTER 14

Life in Baldar

His new parents owned an antique store in downtown Baldar. Thour's market sold all sorts of things, ranging from furniture to weapons. The shop owner placed an abundant collection of items. Each was sorted according to type and value. There were fine statues of wood, stone, metal, and plaster. Also, there were clocks of all kinds, paintings, and tapestries. They had books on almost every subject and parchment. They had many rings, bracelets, necklaces, and girdles. A myriad of impressive armor and weapons could also be found there. Those items seemed sorted, along with wooden and metal furniture.

When the moon cycle came for him to depart, Egil and Katrina ran to say goodbye to him. They hugged Thormon, but they didn't say a word. They just cried.

Thormon's new parents were touched by this goodbye. So, they promised to take Thormon to visit them whenever possible.

They got into the carriage and went off to his new life. His friends watched and waved goodbye as he left.

Thormon looked back at the only town he had ever known. *This means goodbye,* he thought as tears streamed down his face.

"Don't worry, my boy. Everything is going to be fine." Suli wiped away Thormon's tears.

It came about as a long trip to Baldar, and it took a couple of moon cycles to get there. The small houses soon became farms. Then buildings, lights, carriages, and caravans started filling the path.

"Are we there yet?" Thormon appeared mesmerized by all the buildings and people.

"Not yet, son. We still have a couple of places we need to go through before we arrive home." Louarn pointed to a road. "You see that big, white cathedral with a tall tower which supports a big ornamented bell? Do you see the mansions and castles? Those belong to the Landlord Vermundr. After crossing downtown, we'll arrive at our new home. It has a nice iron fence around the property and tall palm trees on both sides. There are trees bordering a flagstone pathway to the house and a big veranda with lush green grass in the front. An archway leads to the big front doors. There ensues a high roof with elegant outer stone walls. Also, thick inner wood walls, and many square windows, which I believe you'll love. In case you want to swim, there's also a beautiful aqueduct with fresh water."

He looked at Thormon, and his eyes shined bright with delight. "I believe you also like animals. Thus, you'll enjoy the company of our fine horses. We also have a stable for them. You can be responsible for that, if you'd like."

Thormon yelled, "We're here!"

"Oh, that's right. Didn't realize I happened to talk that much," Louarn replied.

Suli indicated, "Do you see that garden? Well, that's my herb garden. Maybe you can help me out every so often. I can teach you how to make some medicine. Don't worry—I don't turn people into frogs." She smiled at Thormon.

Suli had always been interested in herbs. She sold her potions for a fair price at the shop. She cultivated many exotic spices in the backyard. They were: borage, caraway, fennel, horseradish, parsley, orpine, salsify, skirret, and sorrel. Also, she made elixirs. Most from anise, blessed thistle, centaury, and ground ivy. Fewer with juniper, lovage, mugwort, nightshade, rosemary, sage, and vervain for medicinal use.

"Oh, where is the shop located?" Thormon asked.

Louarn smiled. "With all my talking, I forgot to show you, but we can go there tomorrow… if it suits you, of course."

Thormon admitted, "Yes! Of course! I heard considerably about it. I want to see it with my own eyes,"

Suli replied, "OK. First thing tomorrow morning, we'll go there, but let's get settled in first."

"I hope you like your room," Louarn added.

Once the carriage stopped, Thormon jumped out and ran around the house. Everything seemed fashioned as new and neat for him. It seemed like nothing he had ever experienced.

His new parents went up to him as soon as he calmed down and took him to his room.

Thormon couldn't believe his eyes. Fifteen beds could have fit in there—and he had it all to himself. He didn't know what to do.

Suli tapped him on the shoulder and pointed towards the bedroom, "That's all yours. You can decorate it as you wish." She smiled. "Welcome home, son. How about a nice bath and then supper? We'll show more of our estate later."

Thormon nodded and smiled. Nobody had ever called him a son or shown him love.

CHAPTER 15

The Magic Staff

T he next solar cycle, bright and early, Thormon patiently awaited for his new father to take him to the shop.

"Wow! Already up? Let's have breakfast, and then we'll go," Louarn rested his hands under his pockets as he planned.

As soon as they finished breakfast, they were off to the shop.

On their route, Thormon noticed that many people were not at ease. Thormon turned to his dad and asked why the folks seemed severely tense.

The father smiled and confessed, "Now then, lots of people have been out of work. Things aren't like they used to be."

A guard stopped their carriage.

Thormon waved hello to the guard, but all he got in return was a cold look.

"Don't worry, son. It's been tough lately."

The guard let them through, and they were off again.

"Dad, how were things before?" Thormon asked.

Louarn pointed at the shop, "We're here!"

It seemed breathtaking. Thormon ran into the shop and quickly started examining the whole store. He lingered in the books and weaponry rows. He didn't know where to start.

"Are there any magical items in the store?"

Mr. Thour smiled and articulated, "Hmm. Magical items? Well, they are hard to come by, and not many people want to partake in such items. A long epoch ago, I acquired an extraordinary silver staff known as the Divine Countenance."

Thormon was a bit confused as he asked, "The what?"

Louarn smiled and replied, "The Divine Countenance."

"Anyway, what did you do with it? Do you still have it? Can I see it? Where is it?"

"Calm down. I sold it to a rich man many seasons ago. To the Count Nevrast of Cicipangle, I believe. You see, this item alone made us wealthy."

"But what exactly did the staff do? It did make you rich, didn't it? Were you able to open portals? Summon monsters? I'm curious."

"Calm down, my boy. I'll tell you all about it." Louarn started looking through the parchments. "Well, it happens to be foretold that the bearer of the staff could call forth a strong wind, which could sweep away anything— from the heaviest animals to the tallest buildings." He scratched his head. "Where did I put that thing?"

Thormon said, "Wow! Why didn't you keep it? You would've been the king of everything. Nobody would dare oppose you."

Mr. Thour smiled and replied, "It turns out to be not that simple. One had a hard time unlocking such power. One has to kill an elder gargoyle from the dungeon of Tenebrae and bathe the staff in the monster's blood. Only that would charge the staff with the supposed limited number of wind summons. I found it!"

"Found what?" asked Thormon.

"See for yourself. Here is Nefrak's ancient testimony. It's a frayed parchment about the staff's first known bearer and his anarchy reign."

"And all of what you told me is in there?" Thormon asked.

"Of course, but it exists only a copy of the original document. You may take it, if it pleases you." Louarn handed Thormon the parchment.

Thormon grabbed the long parchment and ran to the back of the shop. He didn't care anymore about the wonders that the shop had to offer. All he wanted to do turned out to be reading the parchment. He remained mesmerized for a while by the story contained in it.

King Edain the Righteous sent a Myrmidon into the great desert of Centar. In it, he could find the lost city of Tenebra, the fall of Windor the Anarchist, and the destruction of Edain's stronghold.

CHAPTER 16

A Mission For The Grandparents

As time passed, Thormon grew fonder of his parents in love and privilege. He would help at the shop whenever he could, but he didn't like having all the armed men guard the items.

He wanted to be around all the wonders contained there, and it also became an excuse to always be around some of his favorite items: swords and gems. His favorite gem came to be the Star of the Orient, a round, 597.5-carat diamond as big as a chicken egg with brilliant shape, exceptional white color, and eighty-six facets. There remained a particular sword, Gladius, which he dreamed of using.

Louarn noticed Thormon's interest and decided to teach him the skills related to merchantman craft: item identification, appraising, gemology, item restoration, and bargaining.

"I don't want you to go find work elsewhere—like some other young people here."

Thormon became extremely skilled in this new craft and enjoyed every instant, but something seemed to still be missing. He had his parents' love, but he missed his friends. He would write to the orphanage every ten moon cycles, but only Katrina would write back. Thormon would write about the exciting things around the shop.

A customer referred to Suli's elixir as magic, which puzzled Thormon, but he explained in his letters that they were just medicine, according to what his mother said.

He would ask how everyone fared and how the nuns were treating everybody. Since Egil would never write back, Katrina would keep Thormon updated. She mentioned a middle-aged Pazlan couple would adopt her in her last letter. Thormon became happy that she had finally found a family.

As time went by, Thormon became increasingly accustomed to his new life. He would spend half of his day in the shop. He would help his parents clean, guard, and sort items, wax the wooden furniture, and polish the metal goods.

In the mansion, he also spent several beats of eagle's wings watering the plants and helping his mother prepare the soil for herbs and vegetables. He spent the rest of his days playing with the other children around the neighborhood. In the beginning, making friends became harder and harder for him, but he eventually blended in. Thormon knew how to join a group of friends, but he had to prove that he stood bravely and worthy of their esteem, which required an honest smile.

His new friends liked to hunt and practice fighting. Thormon made a wooden sword that proved hardier and steadier than the others.

He entered the group and confronted, "Ormr, I challenge you to a duel! Do you accept—or will you run away?"

Ormr laughed and replied, "I will dispatch you with a hand tied behind my back. Look at you. You're just an imp!"

Thormon smiled and replied, "Thus, this means you are afraid of me. This imp will show you good manners."

There, they heard silence as both kids eyeballed each other. Ormr suddenly swung his sword.

After deflecting two consecutive overhead swings and a left horizontal cut, Thormon thrust his waster at his opponent's torso.

Ormr dropped his weapon and cried out in pain.

The kids looked up to Thormon and welcomed him to the group. All the other kids looked dumbfounded. Ormr had been unmatched until that moon cycle. Ormr became timid and visibly ashamed from then on.

They would also practice archery with crude wooden bows and arrows.

Thormon did well when targeting dummies but intentionally failed when aiming at living animals. He seemingly felt terrible about killing almost any intelligent living being. But he opted not against it. If the cause seemed justified—such as for food or personal defense—no problem transpired.

Logmar and Sveinn became his closest friends. They were

incredibly clever but frail. They would take Thormon to churches, libraries, and even to storytellers. Sveinn wanted to be a gleeman, and Logmar wanted to be a monk. Another kid talked about going to work for some immaculate guy. They were not quite what Thormon liked, but he stayed around them, anyway.

Logmar would help Thormon and his mother copy herbs and potion-making recipes. His mother often mentioned that both kids would do a fine job as cleric inscribers, but Thormon wasn't fond of what life at the monastery sounded like. Thormon preferred action, but Logmar would listen to Suli's stories and tales for several beats of eagle's wings.

Suli had a liking for religion herself. When she came of age, she was courted by a mature man, Camulus, but her family prohibited it and threatened to make her a nun. After seasons of convincing her to join the religious life—and ongoing depression about her beloved Camulus's departure—she became a nun. However, that all changed when the affluent Louarn met her.

Concerning Suli, in her family's eyes, she came to pass as a failure. Not being able to bear fruit hurt her spirit, and she shunned her relatives; but the adoption of Thormon helped dwindle that notion a bit. The boy stayed not her blood, and Auntie Siuma made sure he knew that every instance they visited. She would point out how her children resembled her family and the long lineage of strong men and beautiful women.

Grandpa seemed tremendously different from Grandma. She brooded on the seasons that lay behind and always had a penchant for her family history. Among all the cousins, the most annoying remained Victor, who exceeded four seasons of Thormon's age.

While Thormon was shopping for herbs with his mother, Victor went to Thormon's room and took his backpack. He painted the word "loser" many times with white dye up and down the dark leather, trashing Thormon's only present from his grandpa.

When Thormon got home, David said in disbelief, "Look at what Victor did to your backpack."

"What? What did you do? Why did you do that?" Thormon shouted.

No one answered, and only grins could be seen. Thormon showed his backpack to Grandpa Aurelious.

Aurelious called both grandsons and when he saw Victor, he could see blood in his eyes; hence, he turned to Victor and asked, "Why did you do this to Thormon's backpack?"

Victor held up a big white eraser with a tiny dot in the middle. "Thormon started it! Just look at what he did to my eraser!"

Grandpa asked, "That's it? Are you kidding? This has got to be a joke, right? Thormon must have done something else. There is no way you'd trash Thormon's backpack just for that. Are you crazy?"

Victor looked at his eraser and replied, "He destroyed my eraser!"

Grandpa and Thormon were confused. Thormon marked just a dot.

Auntie Siuma grabbed Victor's arm and pushed him away. "Don't waste your time with such a mutt who thinks he's family."

Before leaving, Victor threatened, "Don't let me catch you alone, you worthless orphan. I will kick your ass!"

Auntie Siuma smiled and walked away without giving Grandpa a chance to intervene. After that, Thormon always avoided Auntie Siuma and her progeny.

CHAPTER 17

The Crossbow

That summer, Louarn came across a crossbow that dated at least seven hundred seasons, according to the design, uniqueness, and eccentric mechanism. The time, mishandling, and overuse broke the archaic crossbow beyond repair. He couldn't think of any manner to repair the thing. He set it aside and worked on its appearance, removing the rust and greasing and polishing the metallic components.

The crossbow drew many customers since the maker crafted and decorated it elegantly and flamboyantly, but their interest faded when they found it useless. One customer attempted to purchase it, but he offered a lower price than what Thormon's father had paid for it. Louarn wouldn't accept anything less than what he had paid for it.

Seasons later, the crossbow remained untouched and undesired on the shelf. Louarn would not admit to making such a bad investment. Frustrated with the crossbow, he took it away from the shop and put it in his workshop at home.

Thormon saw the broken item, and his interest sparkled instantly.

Louarn offered, "Here, you can have it. Do with it what you want. I give up on it."

Thormon's eyes shined with excitement. He started working on it. He took it apart and started to fix each piece, one at a turn.

The crossbow had a complex three-part bronze mechanism, which seemed more stable than regular weapons of the kind, and it was supported within a metallic casing sunk into a hollow section of the wooden stock. The main inner parts of the mechanism consisted of a tumbler, a sear, a trigger, axles, and a bronze catch. The tumbler had two side elements which a bar connected. The maker placed one rapine bird head on top of a side element that extended upward stylishly.

Thormon recognized the pattern and shapes. He knew a scroll contained the information in one of his father's parchment cases. He found the parchment about crossbows at the shop, which helped him understand the device. He made it work after bending metallic pieces, polishing, remaking whole structural elements, and replacing the cracked wooden part. Unfortunately, the aim remained inaccurate. He did a lot of tuning and found out that the decorated rapine bird head served as a counterweight to catch the string as it was drawn back to cock the crossbow. It also seemed positioned as an aid for aiming.

Thormon thought, *I've gotta test this thing.* He went out to the garden.

His mother asked, "Are you thinking of cooking something?"

"No, Mom. I'm gonna test something that Dad gave me to fix."

Thormon started lining up the fruits and vegetables he had picked.

"What on earth are you gonna do?" Suli asked.

"Now then, I think I fixed this crossbow and will immediately test it."

"Thus, you're gonna destroy my crop? And what are you going to shoot with?" Suli asked.

He scratched his head. "I didn't think of that."

Suli laughed and convinced him not to use her crops if she helped him.

Thormon agreed, and they built a dummy.

They took turns shooting at the dummy. Suli showed to be quite a shooter, which surprised Thormon. Thormon missed a couple of shots, but Suli helped him and didn't care much. He couldn't control himself. Thormon became excited that the crossbow worked and beamed with happiness.

Once he finished practicing with his mother, Thormon decided to show his father the fixed weapon.

Louarn voiced, "Wow! The student has surpassed the teacher. Could you teach me the mechanism when you have the time?"

Thormon showed his father the parchments and explained how he had managed to do it.

After much explaining, Louarn finally grasped the idea behind the peculiar mechanism. "Such a beautiful weapon shouldn't be nameless.

It came back from the ashes like that mythical bird."

They named it the Phoenix Reach, and Thormon jumped with joy.

Auntie Siuma knocked on the door, and Thormon knew something seemed amiss. She didn't care enough to bother him, and Victor didn't accompany her. It wasn't a regular visit. She kept on crying.

"Call Suli! Something has happened to Mother!"

"What happened?" Louarn asked.

"The illness began with the sudden onset of a flu-like symptom: fever, headache, muscle aches, and joint pain. We didn't think it looked serious, but then the chronic loss of memory, judgment, and reasoning and changes in mood, behavior, and communication abilities came. She spoke gibberish and would walk right past the house so that she did not find its location or anything else important. After that, intense bleeding from the nose and under the skin started. That's when I knew I had to come here."

Thormon went to look for his mom.

"When did this all start?" Louarn asked.

"About eight solar cycles ago," Siuma answered.

Suli walked into the room with Thormon and asked, "And you took that long to come and tell me?"

Siuma replied, "It's even worse currently. I have to force her to eat, and intense nausea causes her to vomit after feeding."

All three of them grabbed their belongings and rushed to the doctor and the village elders. Maybe one of them would know what was going on.

CHAPTER 18

There is a Chance

The village elder told Arzure to take Guennola to the famous hospital in Cicipangle. Thormon and his parents took Arzure and Guennola to Cicipangle in a carriage. After all, it ensued a long and tiring trip, Louarn sought out the most expensive doctors money could get, but the disease was not recognized or understood by any of them. Suli insisted on taking her dying mother to a well-known herb woman in the city to lessen the suffering of the elderly woman, and they decided to fulfill Suli's wish. Suli got some herbs, but the herb woman didn't know what afflicted the mature lady.

"I believe it's better to take her home. There seems nothing anyone can do for her here. Take these herbs to soften her pain—and let her die in peace." The herb woman gave the herbs to Suli.

Knowing nothing could be done, the family decided it sadly turned out to be the occasion to leave and admit defeat.

As they were going back to Baldar, a shaman bumped into them. He took an expert look at Guennola and instantly recognized the disease as the dark-sun setting. "My, my. She stands in deep waters here."

"What do you mean? Do you know what she has? Please tell us!" Suli inquired.

"Calm down, young lady. I'll help you, but let's discuss what I need to help you first." He put his hands on Guennola and chanted some words. "Hmm. Just what I thought. She'll need a magical elixir of bear's foot, cornelian cherry, and executioner's hood. Only these ingredients can cure her."

"Is that it?" Suli asked.

The shaman replied, "No. I must conduct many ritualistic procedures for the magic to work and require a hefty fee for this toil."

Louarn disclosed, "I will not waste money on this wondrous, superstitious ritual!"

Suli and Arzure asked the shaman about the preparations.

"I have all the ingredients but executioner's hood. It ensues as a rare mushroom, and the only place I know where one could find it befalls on the halflings' haven, far north from here."

Louarn verbalized, "Ha! I told you there seemed to be a catch! Besides paying a large amount of gold, we must also hunt for a mystic mushroom."

With their hopes dwindling, they went back to Baldar.

Grandmother's condition worsened, and nothing could lessen her pain. Most family members were devastated, but the worse hit came about to be Grandpa. He could not sleep with such cruel anxiety.

Thormon proposed, "Grandpa Arzure, we should do something and not just sit here and watch her die."

"But what should we do?" Grandpa replied.

Thormon suggested, "Let's take her back to the shaman. He recognized her disease. He must know something else."

Arzure disclosed, "But even if we took her there, I don't have that kind of money. Only your father could afford it—and there remains still the matter of the missing ingredient."

Thormon had already considered the issue. "I have this valuable ornamented girdle—maybe that could pay for it. I have already evaluated it here. Take a look." He showed Grandpa the fancy girdle. "About the missing reagent, we could get it at the halflings' haven ourselves."

Grandpa looked at the item and sighed, "It seems expensive, but Louarn would never permit it."

"But, Grandpa—"

"Your father will not allow it!" Grandpa retorted, ending the matter right there.

Thormon dropped the subject.

When the Thours were about to leave, Arzure mentioned, "Grandson, come here. I think I know how to get around that problem we discussed earlier. I will tell your father that I will need you here to help me out with some chores. Then we will both go to the shaman."

Thormon smiled.

Grandpa called Louarn and explained that Thormon was needed to help out around the estate.

Louarn agreed right away and thought it would be pleasant for them.

Thormon and Grandpa smiled in anticipation of their quest, which did not match the hopelessness of Grandma's terrible disease.

Suli revealed, "I know you two are up to something, but I don't care. Whatever you can do to save Mom, do it."

After the family left, Thormon told his mother how their plan worked.

Suli seemed a bit reluctant, but she agreed anyway.

Thormon and Grandpa packed their things, mounted their horses, and departed. They were on a mission to save Grandma.

Suli watched with tears in her eyes as they disappeared over the horizon.

CHAPTER 19

Trying To Save Guennola

T he dawn came about with the red sun, and the eastern plains seemed vast. The Elder Mountains were to the right, and the ocean occupied the left immense horizon. The trip to Cicipangle turned out to be a long one, but it remained a safe one, too.

Gazelles jumped and skipped on the grassland, escaping the cheetahs, tigers, and lions. Eagles hunted squirrels, rats, and lizards. A group of dire elks migrated parallel to the trail; they had shaggy fur, and their antlers were almost six heads long.

Arzure had made the trip dozens of times before. Nothing seemed new for him, but for Thormon, everything ensued as a discovery. Many caravans crossed their path, and the timeworn greeted the travelers in every single instance.

Arzure took the opportunity to teach his grandson about life and traveling. "It's always enjoyable to greet strangers, and you should greet and converse about not-so-serious topics with acquaintances. Stick to day-to-day chats that reinforce the social bonds."

"And why should I do that?" asked Thormon.

"You want to avoid giving the impression that you are a snob or a loner."

"I like being around people," answered Thormon.

"It's not only that. Men are social beings; it's our nature."

It turned out to be a fun trip, and they talked about everything.

Arzure's blood and birth were from Eritrea. And his residence turned out to be in Baldar when he grew up to be but a youngling. He had met Guennola at a church gathering. He had always worked as a farmer and never wanted to be anything else. He grew up as a rural man who harvested crops and fed and bred livestock. Arzure's vitality seemed impressive for a man in his seventies.

His grandparents' first encounter happened in a park. As Arzure strolled, the engagement ring he held fell and rolled over to Guennola's foot. She picked it up and returned it to him; it transpired as a classic example of love at first sight. Arzure was engaged to another woman. But he called off his betrothal and started to court beautiful Guennola instead.

Arzure had once seen a centaur, a humanoid with a man's upper body and a horse's lower body. And he did not trust gray and dark elves, gnomes, or petty dwarves. He had no extended contact with halflings, and he did not know what to expect of them. His stories were cut short once they saw the gates of Cicipangle.

"I never told you this, but I don't like this place," the older man disclosed as they entered the largest city in the Eastern world.

Thormon and Arzure went to the herb store. Next, they learned that the shaman lived at the romani encampment. It was settled on the town's western boundary.

Cicipangle avoided the disarray in most cities because Nevrast and his bloodthirsty militia watched the thieves closely.

When Thormon and Arzure found the west road, they had to keep going until nothing but huts dotted the land.

"Look, Grandpa! I think I see them!" Thormon pointed to a large circus tent with red and white stripes in the middle of the camp.

"No. That's not it. It's just a circus. Have you never seen one before?" Grandpa replied with a warm smile.

"Really? What stays inside there?" Thormon asked.

"Well, there are many exotic animals. They have a giant beetle, a mammoth, a red harpy, and a saber-toothed tiger. Also, there was a swamp dragon imprisoned in their surroundings. They have spectacular costumes and diverse entertainers. There are acrobats, animal tamers, clowns, equestrians, and fire-eaters. In addition, horsemen, illusionists, rope dancers, and trapeze artists. They also have bears, elephants, gorillas, lions, panthers, and serpents."

Thormon's eyes shined. "You have to take me there someday!"

"Of course. We'll do that one of these days."

Arzure and Thormon meandered through the encampment with mixed emotions. They were reluctant but fascinated.

A dark-haired man with a goatee and extravagant clothing yelled, "Hey, kid! Come here. I want to show you something."

Arzure and Thormon approached the fancy booth.

The illusionist extended his arm with a closed hand, and then he opened it.

A large ball of fire appeared.

The illusionist handled it with care, retracting and extending his arm. When he blew on it, the fire was extinguished. Next, a small explosion ensued. It produced a shower of thin silvery droplets that originated from his palm.

"How did you do that?" asked Thormon.

"Magic, my boy. I am full of it."

Arzure inquired, "My mysterious fellow, do you happen to know where we can find Shaman Stefan?"

"What? My magic is not good enough for you?" protested the illusionist.

"No, no, my young friend, let's say it transpires as a matter of life and death," replied the experienced man.

"Ah, I see. Follow me then."

The three of them wound their way deep into the encampment. The lights did not reach the forest.

The illusionist entered an archaic tent. Strands of shiny crystals hung on the rectangular entrance tied at the top. The threads hovered over the ground. Shoving the strands aside, they entered the tent. A violet light illuminated the tent. A red glass lamp wobbled from the ceiling. An ornamented music box played a soft, chilling melody.

The shaman closed the music box and spoke as if in a trance. "My inmost thought foreboded that you would try to save Lady Guennola."

"You are right about that, but there occurs also the matter of payment. I want to discuss it with you," Arzure mentioned.

"Go on," the shaman encouraged.

"I would like to trade this girdle for your magic. As you can see, it appears to be not like any regular girdle." The older man took the item from his pack and put it on a low round table.

The shaman took the belt and after analyzing it, returned the item to the table. Shaman Stefan took it and analyzed it. "Why would I want such a fancy accessory for my raiment?"

Thormon and Arzure were speechless.

"Let me see." The illusionist grabbed it and analyzed the girdle. "What if I paid you with gold in exchange for this girdle?"

"Are you sure you want to do this, Sigfrid?" the shaman asked.

"Yes!" People called Sigfrid across the camp as the Great Z.

"Very well. The matter stays settled, then. Bring me the executioner's hood, and you shall have my magical elixir."

"Before we leave, is there any tip on how to get the ingredient besides the halflings' haven?" asked Arzure.

"Sorry, but the answer is no." The shaman rushed them outside and bid them farewell.

"Looks like it seems up to just you and me at this point, Thormon," the mature man stated as they returned to the horses. After getting lost again, they found the route north and left with haste.

As it became darker, the danger increased.

As they passed an outdated bar, Arzure advised, "Be careful, Thormon."

"Why?" Thormon asked.

A strange man approached them and declared, "Please… I want some information. Would you—"

"Run, Thormon! Don't listen to him!"

Arzure and Thormon sped away on their horses.

When they were far away, Thormon looked back and saw the man waving a long knife in the air and muttering a curse.

"I know a thief when I see one," Arzure eased after the danger. "That long knife happened to be no match for the reach of my sword, but its speed happens to be alarmingly fast. I would not want to face that crook alone in the dark. You still need to learn many things about this cruel part of the world."

After that, Thormon kept his crossbow ready at all times. "Where can we rest, Grandpa? I'm considerably tired."

"Not yet. I'll find us a satisfactory place to rest."

They stopped and set up camp at the base of a large tree. Thormon slept like a rock, and Arzure kept watch for several beats of an eagle's wings before falling asleep.

The next moon cycle, they returned to the trail and continued north. The only view along the pathway that came to pass was large, tall coniferous trees. There was no sign of trailing undergrowth vegetation between them. Sometimes, a strong eucalyptus scent filled their nostrils. In early times, the elm trees reeked of a distinct smell. The sun did not penetrate the barks of the tall trees. And the loud, ethereal sound of wind nudging through the tree trunks muffled the sound of any small animals.

Arzure identified all the trees: basswood, beech, chestnut, hickory, linden, and maple. Also, one could find oak, sweet gum, and walnut trees. He would name it and point it to Thormon when he saw one. There were almost undistinguished sounds of howling coyotes, the commotion caused by rapid sprints of the fat dormouse, and the eastern chipmunk. They were the only distractions on the route.

Grandpa used peace and quiet to talk a bit further about himself. The conversation gave Thormon a new feeling for the forest.

The night stayed quiet and refreshing. Arzure threw a termite house on the bonfire to repel the mosquitoes. He told Thormon that insects shunned the smoke. He also discussed added details of life in the wilderness. Which fruits are poisonous, and which are suitable for eating? The importance of cutting the apical branches of some fructiferous trees. Also, how much water and sunlight plants need, when to sow certain kinds of seeds, and what kind of tree sap turns out to be edible.

Grandpa told stories about a were-pig, a man who turned into a big pig in the moonlight. That pig had eaten most of his chickens and dogs, which seemed strange behavior for a pig. He chased the pig and came about to kill it with his bow when his friend told him the man would also die if he killed the pig. Since that stood against his principles, he spared the pig. Thormon knew that it survived generations as just a superstitious tale. It blamed mythical beasts for strange happenings. But he liked to listen to Grandpa's stories. Bright and early the next solar cycle, they packed up and continued north at the fastest pace they could manage. They came upon a fork in the road: four routes going north, one going west, and one going east.

Grandpa took out his map and looked at it for a while. "Hmm. Let us wait for someone to come by. I don't know which of these roads we should take."

They waited for someone to come to their track, but nobody showed up.

"Grandpa, the night will fall soon. What should we do?" Thormon asked.

"Let's take the northern route. We ought to find the halflings."

"Grandpa, we've been riding for moon cycles, and I don't reckon any halflings live in this dense forest. Are you certain this is the track?"

"One never knows when those forests give way to grass or birches. It could be in another day or two." Arzure seemed unwilling to say that he didn't know what he was doing or planned.

Several moon cycles went by, and the scenery varied slightly. Solar cycles became moon cycles, which in turn became solar cycles—but they found nothing. Grandma's condition got worse by the day. Time passed fast, psychologically, appearing to run out, and no sign of the haven remained.

Arzure declared, "Wow! We have been traveling for too long in this forest that I think I'm seeing small trees moving."

"Do they resemble tall women?" asked Thormon.

"Yes. I guess I'm not imagining things."

Five dryads surrounded them and signaled for them to stop. They were humanoid female entities of unearthly splendor. They all had fair faces, bark-like skin, and leaves for hair. They were not bulky, clumsy trees or sweaty, fleshy humanoids. They had exceptional beauty.

"Halt there, humans!" commanded a tall dryad. Her voice sounded soft and commanding, and it echoed through the forest. Her upright, delicate posture appeared worthy of a princess.

Grandpa and Thormon stopped and looked at each other, not knowing what to do. They dismounted to show respect and faced the female entities.

"What do you seek in the heart of this forest?" she asked.

"We are looking for the halflings' haven," Thormon replied.

"Or a manner to find executioner's hood to fulfill our errand," Grandpa added.

"I have never heard of this hood of yours, but the halflings live in the Pomar. The artificially planted forest remains an extensive orchard. It seems ugly and not pristine like this one, its doom lingers imminent."

"But we need to find our pathway there. My wife stands dying, and I need this mushroom hood to cure her."

After a moment of silence, the dryad offered, "We will take you there—but only if you prove that your heart stands true. We need you to bring us the seed of Veijó, a special plant that nourishes the soil."

Arzure inquired, "But where shall we find it—and how will we identify it? We have been walking in this forest for days. I do not know how much time we have left. We cannot lose additional time. Please help us!"

"It's halfway to the haven. I won't take any more of your precious time. First, I will take you to a river. You shall follow its waters until you find a big lake. There stays the island where Veijó grows. The round seed happens to be light blue with red dots."

They mounted their horses.

"If that seed happens to be so important, why can't you fetch it yourselves?" Thormon asked.

"Hush, kid! Sometimes you must hold your tongue. People don't like to answer questions out of suspicion."

Thormon protested, "But they are not people!"

"You understood what I meant, Thormon. It befalls true for treefolk as well."

The dryad explained, "That land continues perilous to us. The ground feels hot and often catches on fire. We need someone to do that for us."

As history goes, it was typical of the dryads to ask for a favor in response to granting one.

As they followed the dryads, the vegetation opened for the female entities. The horses were a great deal wilder in the presence of the dryads. The entities had a special effect on living beings, turning them natural in every sense.

After a while, they reached the river. The horses quenched their thirst and eased their hunger with the thick grass on the shore.

The female entity cleared the muddy water with a finger's touch. It turned the water crystalline. "From here, you shall go toward the mountain—and there, you will find a lake and the island."

The river became narrower and rushed down a slope. The sky turned overcast, and a few beats of an eagle's wings later, the rain started pouring. Five blasts of thunder terrorized the horses, and lightning split an elm tree in half. The horses would not move, so they tied them up and proceeded on foot. A lot of steam seemed to loom high on the mountain, and the ground started shaking.

The older man yelled, "Hurry, kid. Let's flank the river from higher grounds!"

They climbed through a torrent of murky water that carried everything down. The water would have carried them down if they had remained on the riverbank.

The trees changed from tall symmetric conifers to contorted tropical trees. Thus, these made them harder to cross. Little by little, they were able to reach the outskirts of the mountain. Geysers spit out hot water and vapor, and the foliage gave way to bare rocks. The naked rock felt cold, tricky, and slippery, making them retreat their feet at times to gain balance. The cliffs caused Thormon to panic more than once.

Arzure almost slipped, and his outdated man reflexes would not have saved him if he lost his footing.

Thormon took Grandpa to a safer path with a less treacherous and steep slope. After the long climb, the slope leveled off.

Creatures and vegetation colonized the hilltop. The giant lagoon looked crystal clear. One could see the sandy ground and swarms of fish. Like no other, it was made of a golden hazel hue. It produced large bubbles that caught its prey, smaller fish, from below. A big goat with thick, white fur, a muscular body, and a curious gaze approached them. It stopped about ten heads away from the party and blocked the path to the lake.

The older man suggested, "Stay here. I will face the goat."

The animal's territory had been crossed, and mating season had begun. It seemed like the goat would use its horns to attack old Arzure. It had to defend its ground.

Arzure did not dare to look the animal in the eyes. "Shoo! Go away!"

The goat did not move.

"Nothing is ever easy. Why couldn't it be a simple job to find the damned halflings."

They retreated to the river.

Thormon offered, "Maybe we could cross the stream from another path."

The older man feared to traverse the water. After much coaxing, he agreed—but only where the water seemed shallow.

After going under a waterfall, they found a small cave. Thormon explored it with a torch. He saw a hollow branch and picked it up.

Arzure inspected, "Wow—that's a fossilized tree branch. It has a nice shape!"

They jumped over a small canal and found another path going uphill. Following it, they reached the lake on top of the mountain. It seemed so large that they could not see the far side of it.

The older man touched the water that was cold as an iceberg. They were unable to swim across it. Hypothermia would kill mature or young.

"We need some sort of raft," criticized Thormon.

They started to survey the hilltop, looking for wood to make a floating device. They found a big fallen pine trunk, cut the bough off with the sword, and rolled it into the water. Probing the trunk to see if it could hold the weight of an adult, Arzure found out it could only carry a small person. Thormon appeared to be the logical choice.

"Now then, my boy. It's up to you." Grandpa helped Thormon climb onto the trunk.

Thormon used his arms as paddles and thrusters to drive it to the distant side of the lagoon. As he went deeper into the lake, the water got boiling. The volcano stratified the color of the water; the cold water looked clear. And the warm water appeared dense and muddy with sporadic bubbles. Thormon only touched the cold water because he feared the acidic water.

In the beginning, it unfolded as hard to keep the trunk from rotating. After many beats of an eagle's wings, he learned to drift it. He acted with exceptional care in hot water, trying not to lose balance. His heart would accelerate. He wished the trunk would stop rotating, but he didn't have that luxury or that comfort.

On the far side, he navigated toward a small island. He anchored the trunk with a heavy stone to prevent it from rolling back into the water. It seemed like no ordinary island. The soil looked particularly rich. The lush foliage covered the ground as it paved undergrowth with soft verdant ink. Huge ferns and pteridophytes dominated the island. It appeared a lost paradise, a missing link of species long lost in eons. And as it was isolated geographically, the species could evolve.

The biodiversity appeared breathtaking here, different from anywhere else. One could see an insect the size of a cat with the body of an ant and the legs of a spider. A green amphibian the size of a dog with long legs walked on four paws like a quadruped. And a dragonfly the size of a bird that glowed like a glowworm. A bee-like humanoid bigger than Thormon flew from tree to tree, feasting on the huge flowers. He wondered if it could be hostile and how big its hive would be.

Stealthily, he looked for the dotted seed. He finally found a green, thick-rooted tree with long yellow leaves and many round blue and red seeds. It seemed not far from where he had left the tree trunk.

He sniffed a familiar honey scent and looked up. Twenty huge trees supported a hive about sixty-five heads tall. It wobbled as the bee people landed and took off. He climbed the small Veijó tree, grabbed five seeds, and returned to the trunk. He quickly made his pathway back.

On the shore, he showed Grandpa the seeds.

Arzure saw red rashes. "What is this? Your hands are red."

"It must be the acidic water."

Grandpa took a labored breath and continued, "Go wash it in the clear water!"

When he did, the rash only lessened, but it still itched at times.

They were following their timeworn tracks. They returned to where they had last seen the female entities.

A dryad stood waiting for them by the riverbank. It dozed off with thoughts one could only imagine. She moved and made herself evident to the humans.

"Do you have the Veijó seed?"

Thormon nodded, put the seed in her hand, and stepped back out of respect.

The dryad looked at the seed and mentioned, "Follow me."

She wound her path through the forest without hurting any plants. They followed her on horses, not an easy feat. They rode all night, taking only short breaks.

Finally, she pointed to a barren hill. "From up there, you can see the halflings' haven. It's about a mile away. Farewell, noble humans—and beware of these halflings. Tricksy they can be."

They set forth on the path. The tall trees gave place to grass and several angiosperm fruit trees. The villagers pruned it flawlessly. Strawberries and lingonberries climbed the round stone houses: red and green grapevines and squared-cut shrubs of blueberries, currants, cornelian cherry dogwood. Nanking cherries and serviceberries were used as boundaries between residencies. The small villagers kept the trees short and round—these were: the black walnut, black cherry, persimmon, and pawpaws.

A myriad of colorful birds chirped while feeding on the fruits. They saw a magnolia warbler and a painted bunting. Also, one could see a rose-breasted grosbeak and a vermillion flycatcher.

"Look, Thormon. I remember reading about these birds!"

On a hilltop stood a yellow cuneiform windmill with long rectangular blades. It rotated counterclockwise in a rhythm that mesmerized any observer. The houses blended well with the background. The buildings made it seem like a continuation of the elaborate landscape. The halflings had erected the village in the middle of several small, round hillocks. Those were used as a base for constructing their homes. Their holes had grass roofs with scattered flowers, round wooden doors, and small windows. The rounded walls were part of the hill and were covered with vines. The halflings laid crude welcome mats on the front doors. Flowers bordered the simple entrances. Pathways of rectangular flagstones separated the houses. The hedges gave privacy to the neighbors.

Thormon and Arzure dismounted their horses and explored the beautiful place on foot.

"Wow! I've never seen a place like this, Gramps."

"True! It seems like a true wonder, but let's not forget why we are here." The older man walked toward a house, knocked on a door, and waited for someone to answer.

A suspicious eye looked out from a small hole in the door. "What do you want?"

The older man replied, "We are looking for the executioner hood."

The round door opened, and a small, middle-aged halfling female spat, "What do you want with that mushroom?"

"Well, good morning. You see, I traveled exceedingly far to find this mushroom. Do you have any word on it?"

"Ask the villager elder. His name is Mr. Velvings. It's the green house with the tallest chimney—about a short walk in that direction." She pointed and slammed the door with no chance or opportunity to say thank you.

They walked—grabbing a strawberry here and a black cherry there, all under the watchful eyes of the halflings. The halfling mothers called their children back inside. At the same time, the human strangers passed by. These folks were not fond of any outsiders. In general, the halflings were homebodies.

To their surprise, the chimney functioned as a workplace. It sucked out all the smoke and directed it high above as a heavy smoker made circles of polluted air. The round door stood ajar, but Arzure still knocked and waited outside with Thormon.

A cranky voice asked, "What is it?"

Arzure replied, "I need some information, and a lady told me you could help us."

Mr. Velvings expressed, "Sorry. What? Is it something about a tournament you want to participate in? Come in! I can't understand a word you're saying."

They pushed the door completely open.

One could see a short tunnel with tiled floors and walls decorated with paintings of a mature halfling and his family. A pathway led to a carpeted chamber with two circular mahogany tables and a matching chair. Carefully placed stones made the floor close to the hearth, and two cauldrons were on top of hot coals. A strong scent of wine assailed their senses. At the same time, the older halfling stirred a particular ancient cauldron as he hummed a merry tune.

Arzure looked straight at the mature halfling. "Mr. Velvings, right?"

Velvings turned toward Arzure.

"In any case, you see. I am looking for—"

"Come here and have a taste of this wine." With a big spoon, he poured some wine into a wooden cup.

Arzure seemed a bit confused but still took it and sipped it.

The older halfling turned to Thormon and asked, "What about you? Have a taste of it."

Thormon smiled and took the cup from the mature halfling's hand. "No, Thormon! You can't! You're too young to have alcohol!"

"He looks tall enough to me. You humans have an odd manner of showing age. Well, it doesn't matter. And for yourself—maybe some more?"

"It tastes superb, I have to say, but I can't have a lot of it," Arzure replied.

"Hmm. How may I help you?" Velvings capped the cauldron and faced his guests.

Arzure declared, "Anyhow, as I have attempted to say as soon as I got here, we are looking for a mushroom known as an executioner's hood."

"Hmm. Interested in mushrooms, are you? If it suits you, I can take you to the right place. Let's cut a deal?"

"But what kind of deal do you propose?" Arzure asked.

"You shall see. Come quickly. Follow me. The region subsists known as the damp moors." The elderly halfling guided them in the right direction.

"OK, but what kind of deal do you want? I don't have plenty of time left. You see, my—"

"Come in this direction." The older halfling took a large gulp of wine and led them to the northwest part of the village. "Ever since I was a youngling, my pals and I would go to the damp moors to find the most delicious varieties of mushrooms and rare grapes. The grapes I liked the most were the red seedless ones. Aleatico grapes. Nowhere else could they be cultivated, only in those damp lands. Many times, we halflings have gone there and replanted fetched fruits and plants here. This beautiful landscape comes about the result of that, but the dryads did not take so kindly to us—"

"Oh! We met one of them before coming here," Thormon revealed.

The mature halfling looked at Thormon and grinned. "Good for you. Well, not really. Anyhow. Those things did not like our replanted forest. Thus, their meddlesome hands brought a dangerous vine and placed it on the damp moors. We never go near it. Therefore, our Pomar fruit forest befalls dying without the influx of new plants from the moors."

"But these trees look healthy enough to me," conjectured Arzure.

"Indeed, they do, but it just takes a slight amount of time before by chance some disease spreads and kills our planted trees. They lack the resistance inherited in the large diversity of trees we can find at the moors."

"And let me guess. You want us to defeat this hostile vine," asked Arzure.

"Well, yes! I know you will come up with something," believed the halfling.

Arzure complained, "But I am an old man—and he remains just a kid."

"Nonetheless, you are adventurers! You will come up with something," Mr. Velvings alleged as they stopped. "I will wait for you here. You two go up there but beware of the whipping vine. It stays camouflaged with the surrounding vegetation and has the element of surprise."

Thormon and Arzure climbed the slope toward the top of the pristine forest of angiosperms.

The older man put on his full-body chain mail while he turned to Thormon and confessed, "Long, I have predicted that the moment would come. When I would have to fight and face an enemy, whatever it may be. We don't know what to expect from this plant foe. Hence, be ready at all times to flee. Don't stray about—and stay behind me."

The plants were pleasant to the eye on the far side of the moorlands. The mature man took a star fruit from the tree.

"Let's save this for later."

The heat and humidity made it hard to breathe. A strong wind from the south made fruit drop everywhere.

Arzure alerted, "Be careful. The big bread fruits could hurt you. What the heck?"

A large vine had many moving plant limbs. It looked big for a human—and huge for a halfling.

With a glance, they sized up the enemy. It seemed green and yellowish in the joints, and the roots were dark brown. It moved up and down the soil, dragging the vine forward and forming a small track of lifted dirt. In contrast to regular plants, the vine seemed to have consciousness and intelligence. It seemed aware of the intruders, and it would do what it was meant to do: root out any trespasser.

The timeworn man stood his ground. He wielded a shield, and he took out a short sword. He tried stabbing the plant, but the vine disarmed the man with two consecutive slashes, making the shield and sword fly away. The vine looked like its limbs were made of resilient rope, which thinned from the thick portions attached to the main branch to the sharp pointing ends used as a whip.

Arzure fell to the ground and shouted, "Run, kid! Run for your life!"

Thormon helped the hoary man up, and they ran as fast as they could toward the halfling.

The vine whipped their butts, and they screamed and caressed their aching butts as they ran. Many additional slashes followed. With each lash, their pride became frailer and frailer. They kept running until they were far away from the moors.

The age-old halfling, trying to hold in a laugh, approached them and commented, "Vicious thing, ain't it?"

Arzure alleged, "Not just vicious. That thing will whip your ass like there is no tomorrow."

"Hmm, but you still need to get back there and end this threat. It stands as just a plant, for goodness sake."

"Oh really? Why don't you go there yourself, then?" Thormon replied.

"As I mentioned before, I am not the adventurous kind. The thrill of defeating life-endangering quests does not run in my veins!"

Thormon and Arzure stared at the mature halfling.

Arzure pondered a loud, "Hmm. That thing has no eyes or ears."

"Nor a nose or antenna," Thormon added.

"Well, I thought you guys had figured that out already. It senses you with its roots. Your weight and your disturbances of the soil alert the vine. It remains just a plant, after all."

Arzure complained, "We didn't know that. We thought we were facing a regular monster of some sort."

"You never asked me. I assumed you already knew what you were up against. You did say you were ready."

Their heads were fuming.

"Let's just grab the mushroom and leave!" Thormon recommended.

"I believe you can't do that. I'm the one who knows where it grows," replied the halfling.

Arzure gave the older halfling an angry look and mumbled, "Let's go. I think I have a plan."

"What plan, Gramps?"

"We'll enter the moors and climb a tree. From the tree, we can throw rocks to the ground to lure the vine."

"Then what?"

"I don't know. I'll come up with something. Let's cross that bridge when we get to it."

Arzure didn't sound too convincing, but Thormon followed him anyway.

They quietly made their way to the vine's domain, but the plant had simply vanished. They picked a place where the vegetation could not conceal the moving vine—and tiptoed to a breadfruit tree with a handful of rocks.

The hoary man signaled to throw the rocks at the soil, and they started throwing them one at a turn. Once they finished, they started throwing the fruit.

"This plan isn't working!" whispered Arzure.

"What now? How shall we act at this moment, Gramps?" Thormon whispered.

The older man scratched his head, jumped, and stomped on the ground.

"Come get me, you damn overgrown plant."

Thormon shouted, "It is coming, Grandpa. Get up here now!" The flexible vines were approaching at an alarming rate.

The elderly man quickly darted up the tree.

The plant stood there like it felt confused. It reached its limbs into the air and then waited under the tree.

Thormon and his grandfather grabbed the remaining breadfruits and threw them at the vine. Oddly, the plant did not react.

"Nothing seems to work!" the timeworn man confessed while equipping the crossbow.

"No, Gramps! That won't work, either!"

"Ah!" The mature man pulled the trigger, but the arrow bounced off the vine.

They remained on top of the tree. The vine played the waiting game as if time waited by its patient side.

The older man decided to change branches, but the thinner branch broke.

The plant quickly came back to life as an automaton fed with energy. And its gears were its verdant limbs and crimson roots.

Thormon had to act quickly. The older man appeared to feel hopeless that the plant would get him by surprise; he seemed at the mercy of the vine. Thormon jumped down and landed behind the tree trunk—the only thing standing between him and the vicious vine. The whipping vine changed its target and went after Thormon. It tried to circle the trunk counterclockwise and then clockwise. But the kid circled the tree and kept the trunk between him and the vine.

The vine whipped from behind the trunk and hit Thormon's shoulder. When it tried whipping again, the kid held the vine limb with his left deft hand. Another slash came, and the kid held another plant limb with his other hand. He tied every two limbs around the tree. Two by two, Thormon went around the trunk, grabbing the vine's limbs and tying them to the trunk. Finally, the whipping vine could not free itself. Its reach looked enormous, and the size could match Arzure's. And now, only its roots were free to move. It could escape if the roots kept pulling and pushing, but that would take time.

The hoary man got up from the ground and pushed and poked some branches. "Wow! You did the unthinkable! Tying this vine around this tree? You made it a true vine, which are plants meant to climb trees. Quick! Let's grab that rock!"

They rolled the big rock on top of the wrenching roots, but it still moved. They placed three extra stones over it—just to be safe.

"I didn't believe we could do it—or you could do it. Time to go back."

The longstanding halfling remained to wait for them at the moor's edge. He enjoyed and savored a fruit salad and bread with stuffing. He seemed unwilling to share that as Thormon looked at it with hungry eyes.

"Oh! You made it back? What news do you bring?"

Thormon gloated, "The plant threat stands no more—if that's what you're asking."

"At present, take us to the mushroom! It's time you kept your end of the bargain!" Arzure demanded.

The elder led them to a path that meandered through the moors to a dreadfully damp land. It seemed full of rotten tree trunks and dead leaves. The halfling grabbed a handful of mushrooms and handed it to Arzure.

"This seems to be the mushroom you asked for. It seems similar and especially as poisonous as executioner's hood."

"But it is not the executioner's hood, isn't it?" Thormon asked.

"No, I haven't seen the real executioner's hood in ages—but this mushroom bears just the same poisonous characteristics."

"But we seek the real one to heal my dying wife and by no means to use it as poison!"

"Then perhaps it will work just as fine. I can't imagine how poison could heal someone," speculated the halfling.

"Louarn was right about doubting the shaman's magic elixir," the mature man admitted.

On their way back, the halfling saw what had become of the vine. "Good job! That overgrown plant got what it deserved! I wish I could help you more, but you will always be welcome here." He offered them provisions and showed them a quicker path that avoided the dense forest. "Godspeed."

They mounted their horses.

On the route back, they realized which trail should be the right one to the halflings' haven. They saw a caravan heading west. It was destined to cross the famous Strait of Intermediary Terra. That Strait was the gateway to the Western world. When they reached the suburbs of Cicipangle, the horses' stamina depleted fast. Also, it seemed almost gone as the horses protested. They kept onward since no guard watched the area. After getting lost downtown again, they reached the west road and the gypsy encampment. The circus company looked to be getting ready to depart. The gypsies had dismantled most of the tents. They kept the animals inside metal jails on top of the large circus convoy.

Thormon's heart skipped a beat while working his way to the shaman.

Arzure's pace appeared almost jogging, and Thormon followed him. Shoving the crystal strands aside, they entered. The noise of clashing crystals alerted the shaman.

Shaman Stefan stood up and welcomed the party, "Greetings, Arzure and Thormon. I assume you brought the missing ingredient."

"Not exactly. We did bring you this mushroom with the same proprieties." Arzure placed it on the low table.

After looking at the mushroom, he confessed, "No! This will not do. I asked for the executioner's hood, didn't I?"

"But you never told us you needed a potent poison to cure my wife. Can you explain how poison can heal someone?" asked Arzure.

"Straightforward explanation. If a low enough dose of that specific poison were administered to a sick person, it would do just the opposite. It would stimulate the person's natural defenses to overtake the disease-causing agent."

"But that new mushroom would work just the same, wouldn't it?"

"You think so? If I acted recklessly. And if I gave you the elixir made with this different mushroom, disaster would result. People would die. I have seen it before."

The argument lasted an extended period, and both men were irritated.

At home, Thormon used to play the flute to ease his troubles, but he didn't have one anymore. He searched around his backpack for something similar. He remembered the fossilized wood and plucked some holes in it. He blew in it, but the noise sounded oddly muffled. He blew in it intensely and looked inside, but something blocked the air. He pushes a stick inside. "My goodness, this just won't come out."

He tried hitting the top end and decided to blow in it after a couple of tries. He took a deep breath and blew—and something flew out of the fossil. It flew all the way to the table.

The shaman and Arzure stopped arguing and looked down at the brownish thing on the table.

The shaman settled the matter, "See! Only executioner's hood would do. Your grandson knows what I need!" He grabbed the mushroom and showed it to Arzure. "Wait outside while I make the preparations."

He pushed the older man out of the tent.

"How on earth did that thing just fly out of there?" Arzure asked.

After Thormon explained, the timeworn man laughed hysterically. At the same time, tears of happiness flowed down his wrinkled face. "From here on, I shall consider you to be a boon! A godsend!"

All the commotion was interrupted by a thick mist that wafted up from the shaman's tent. They heard drums and soft chanting in a primitive dialect. A bell rang every hundred beats of an eagle's wings, and the lights inside the tent flickered.

"What on earth befalls on him in there?" Thormon tried to see what went on inside the tent, but he could not get any closer due to a line drawn on the ground across the entrance. It seemed like a magic wall blocked his path, and the energy would paralyze his legs.

A couple beats of an eagle's wings later, the shaman reappeared with his face covered in ash, blood, and white paint. He approached Arzure and handed him a glass vial with bluish liquid.

"Everyone around your wife should sip this potion before administering the rest of it to her. Take just six sips and nothing more. This elixir will drive away the parasitic evil spirit that has been bestowed upon her. And that potion will heal her within seven days. Do you understand these instructions?"

"Yes!" Arzure answered.

The shaman advised, "Now, depart in haste!"

Thormon and Arzure thanked the shaman and quickly made their route back.

Arzure seemed weary from the arduous journey. His old age seemed to catch up with him, but it appeared far from over. He held the potion like an amulet, the last hope; it would be the end if it did not work.

Thormon thought about giving some words of reassurance, but he didn't know what to say. His thoughts revolved around his grandma's fate.

Grandpa cheered, "Finally! We've arrived!"

The longstanding man rushed into the farmhouse. Thormon followed him inside.

It seemed as if ages had gone by since they departed.

Everyone in the room looked abnormally still, with an unnatural quietness. They were afraid to spoil the ritual that would soon start. No one knew what to say to them. Their mouths felt dry and unable to move.

Thormon's mother hugged him. Arzure asked about Guennola.

Suli asked, "She's still alive. Thormon, are you okay?"

Arzure demanded, "Take me to her. We don't have sufficient time left!"

Suli got up and took him to Guennola.

"It's time we did this." Arzure took out the potion, and everyone in the room stared at him while he explained what needed to be done.

"You've gotta be kidding!" Siuma expressed.

"Shut up, Siuma! We already tried everything—and this looks like our only hope!" Suli shoved the potion down Siuma's throat.

Each person in the bedroom took a sip of the elixir, and Grandpa poured the rest of it down Guennola's throat. They all stood there in suspense, not knowing what should happen.

Thormon asked with dismay, "Grandpa, was our journey for nothing?"

With tears in his eyes, the older man answered, "Maybe we were just too late."

Suddenly, they heard a weird sound—and Guennola sat up straight. Her eyes were white.

CHAPTER 20

A Magic Recovery

G uennola´s face looked like death, and her eyes were as white as the moon. Her shriek caused everyone to fall on their backs.

"Thormon, what have we done?" Arzure screamed while trying to get up.

A gust of wind filled the room, and horrific sounds echoed off the walls. The family tried to escape, but the doors were shut.

"What have you done to her?" Siuma shouted.

As everyone was in the process of trying to get up, they heard a voice. Before Arzure could say anything, another shriek caused the windows to shatter. Arzure tried to get up and help the others, but a sudden decline in temperature took everyone by surprise. When everyone thought they had lost everything, a blast of light threw everyone across the room. Then, everything became silent.

"What's going on? Why is everyone on the floor?" Guennola asked.

"You're back?" a faint voice echoed.

"I never left. What do you mean by that?" Guennola asked.

The family got up and noticed that the mature woman felt and seemed well by reading her mien. They explained what had happened.

All the symptoms went away. It probably felt as if nothing had happened to her. They guessed by her sane look. The skeptics thanked Arzure and Thormon. They said their willingness to endure despite the odds was exceptional.

The family wanted to know how this had all come to pass. They had been gone for quite a while.

Suli asked her father about Thormon's red hands, hurt buttocks, and injured shoulders. "Why in the world are you two severely filthy?"

Arzure and Thormon told Suli and Louarn about what had happened. Louarn seemed skeptical about such a fantastic tale. Suli behaved as amused by such danger.

Thormon's tale spread throughout the community. His friends started to call him Thormon, the Red-Handed Vine Killer. The nickname stuck like glue.

It was his first experience with real magic. Thormon had always believed in magic, but these days he had faith in it, sure of its existence.

CHAPTER 21

The Bards

Louarn and Suli stayed as the only family Thormon had ever known, but he knew there were more people in his family, especially on his father's side. They were not from the Eastern world.

They lived in the Western world, a wilder and more savage place.

One morning, a thin, strange young man approached Thormon and his dad in the garden.

Louarn quickly knew who it was: his brother, Gamble. Louarn ran to him, and Thormon followed, not knowing what had happened. The brothers hugged and greeted each other like old friends.

Louarn fetched Thormon, "Come here, son. This is your uncle, Gamble. He dwells in the wild western lands."

Gamble seemed a distinguished and free-spirited man who did not stay anywhere for too long. He stood as the youngest of three brothers and a peculiar character. Gamble was in Baldar by chance, and the two brothers hadn't spoken in ages.

"A son? I didn't know the family was growing. When did Suli have him? Wait for a beat of an eagle's wings. Wasn't Suli unable to have a child? You gotta tell me this miracle!"

Louarn smiled and explained how they came to have Thormon.

"Adopted? Well, if he makes you happy, then I'm happy," Gamble leisurely spoke, introducing himself to Thormon.

"What are you doing here, around these parts?" Louarn asked.

"Just passing by. Heard there were nice opportunities around these parts."

"Well, you're here—and that's all that matters! Come on in. You look tired." Louarn walked Gamble into his home.

Gamble showed Thormon his instrument and played a little bit. Thormon appeared delighted and quickly ran to get his flute.

Gamble listened to Thormon play.

"Wow, my boy. You are very skillful, but let me give you some tips." Gamble corrected the boy whenever it should be needed.

Gamble and Thormon hit it off right from the start. They would meet up at sundown and play lovely melodies and tunes. Gamble also taught Thormon how to use a sword properly.

Louarn and Suli were extremely happy that Thormon took a liking to Gamble.

After a couple of extra days, word of Gamble's arrival spread. Auntie Siuma visited rather frequently when Gamble stayed home. The adventurous, handsome man captivated her heart. Thormon liked hanging out with his uncle, but he thought his uncle appeared a bit too rough to be a bard. The bon-vivant lifestyle didn't seem to suit his uncle.

Louarn would constantly try to talk Gamble out of becoming a bard. He would ask him to go back to the way of the sword.

"Thormon has an adventurous spirit, like you, and I don't want him to become a bard. I tried teaching him my trade, to no avail. I see that he idolizes you, brother. Please be a beneficial role model for my son."

"Don't worry, brother. I won't let you down. I'll teach the boy to fend for himself," Gamble attested.

Gamble hung around for longer than anyone expected. Louarn convinced his brother to stay longer and also convinced him to accept a job offer at the ceremonial tavern.

Thormon saw that the bard did his job perfectly, receiving generous tips from men and heartwarming flirtations from women.

Gamble made many connections with bards, minstrels, and troubadours, and in one season's time, the musicians gathered at Thormon's house to practice famous music and songs of their composition.

Thormon would join in with his flute. Those were magical moments. The entire family sang along, chatted, and ate. Thormon would gather wood and build a bonfire, but the part Thormon liked most was when a bold bard would stand up and tell fantastic tales about the wondrous elf city, which united lots of bards and the like. One of the elderly minstrels even confessed that the best human bard was not fit to compete with those longstanding elves.

Everyone was amazed by the stories and tales, and soon the group began to grow outside the family. More and more people came to listen to their songs and tales. Word spread across the land that Louarn's home ought to be the right place for entertainment.

One night, a particular girl stood out from the crowd. Melissa had long, black hair, blue eyes, and a delicate bust. She seemed full of feminine curves and grace. Her smile could light up the moon cycle of a terror-stricken person on the verge of death. She was the kind of girl who every man desired. She grew up the daughter of a noble, and she blended in with princes, counts, and dukes.

Gamble had told Thormon how he had met the fair lady when Prince Hendrick hired him to perform a serenade for her. All the men in town were in love with Melissa at some point, and Gamble would be no different. Whenever she hung around, Gamble would put on his best performance. Thormon would tell his uncle in advance if he spotted her.

"Come on, Uncle. She befalls way out of your league," Thormon counted each interval she came to a gathering at Louarn's estate. He knew his uncle would not listen, but he tried anyway.

One moon cycle, Gamble decided to do something about it. He sought her in the donjon with Thormon.

"Wow, jovial Melissa, you are even nobler and gorgeous within talking distance!"

She looked down and warned, "This better be something important. I have better things to do."

"My lady, I seek you because my heart will not let me go on without making this proposition." Gamble got down on a knee.

"Humph! And what proposition would that be? Might I remind you that I am of noble birth and will not be complacent with such minor offerings?"

"I am no noble, but my love remains sincere—and my will stays strong."

"Love? Ha! You do not know what those words mean!" She behaved as if teasing him, and if it were her parents' way, she couldn't talk to peasants, and talking to Gamble would be almost an insult to her honor.

Gamble fantasized, "I am willing to become rich—or do whatever it takes—hence I can be worthy of your hand."

She smiled and replied, "So, get to it! Do a great deed. Become famous, for to greatness I am destined."

He confessed, "I am but a humble bard, but my luck might change once I venture to the elf town of Coloris. Have you heard of it?"

"I have, and your luck might change for the worse. Who knows what those proud elves have in store for you?"

The Duke of Baldar, Lord Ramon, entered the chamber. Melissa ran to him and ignored poor Gamble.

"Wow, Uncle Gamble. Why do you even try? She seems such a snob!"

Gamble gazed at the princess until he could no longer bear it. It crushed him.

"Let's go, Thormon." Gamble had tears in his eyes.

Thormon suggested, "Don't worry, Uncle. There are better women than her. You don't need her."

"True—but this will be the last occasion someone looks down on me." He crumpled up the song he had written for her and threw it on the ground.

Thormon picked it up and read it:

"Thou had hooked me up with your innocent malicious sneer,

Deep in pain and agony, now I stride into town, wounding in every way. Crashing into me the life once thought fine, but no longer.

Destined to be let down, for too much love blind even the fey.

To look at this beautiful mouth. These beautiful eyes and delicate ears.

Nonpareil among mortal women you are,

A vivid vision of perfection that makes my heart skip.

If you ever consider me, oh, Melissa the Fair,

Here, I am not as any man you know but with you.

The moment we share is divinely blissful,

Don't foil my attempts, for true desperation they might bear.

Give me a chance, oh, princess of Baldar.

You know no party is worthy without your presence. But one day, destiny shall bring you to my premises, And I will erect the highest altar."

Wow! He must like her. I've never seen him so heartbroken. Thormon trailed behind his uncle.

Gamble suddenly stopped and yelled, "No more!"

Thormon jumped back and asked, "Whoa. What's up, Uncle?"

Gamble looked at the palace and toward the horizon. "I will become rich, and every woman will desire me—and I'll show her what it means to be rejected when she comes to me for my hand!"

Thormon did not know what his uncle pondered but knew something was up.

Gamble stormed out of the palace and headed to the city to find his companions.

CHAPTER 22

The Promises of the Legendary City

F riends, I have a proposition for you all," Gamble mentioned while gathering his party of bards.

"What are you talking about, Gamble?" Miguel yelled back.

Gamble uttered, "Wait! Allow me to explain. I'm proposing an end to all of these hardships. Now, too many people are looking down on us. No further do we entertain people for scraps."

"What do you suggest? We rob a bank?" Bernard joked.

"No, the city of Coloris!" Gamble answered.

Silence struck the group.

A voice protested, "You gotta be kidding! You want us to chase a legend, the stuff we tell women just to get them to bed? Have you gone mad?"

"It's no fictitious story! How do you think I came up with this tale? Nobody told me. I read it for myself, and it occurs as a fact! It does exist."

Robert confronted, "You have lost it, Gamble. We know you came up with this tall tale, and it was only meant as that—a *tale*!"

"I didn't make it up. This is where I got it from." Gamble took a parchment from his bag.

The room went suddenly silent.

"Where did you get this?"

"It's from my brother Louarn, and it befalls as a true parchment. No tale. It happened to be sold to him by an elf needing money."

Miguel, Fabio, Julio, and Bernard were speechless.

"Did you verify its authenticity?" Robert asked.

"My brother doesn't buy any kind of nonsense. He has a specialist who checks everything. No wonder he persists as the most sought-out trader in the city."

The group suddenly turned their interest toward the parchment and started planning.

The news of their expedition spread throughout town, and word quickly spread to Louarn.

At the dinner table, Louarn advised, "Gamble, she seems not worth all this trouble. She seems beautiful. I grant you that, but this?"

Gamble replied, "I will never be looked down at again. I want to make a name for myself. I wish to be rich and famous—like you, brother."

"But I know you very well, and I know it's all because of a girl," Louarn replied.

Gamble replied, "Will you help me—or not?"

Louarn dictated, "You know that I will never partake in such a fool's errand. The answer is no!"

Gamble stormed out of the room. Louarn tried to go after his brother.

Gamble admitted, "Brother, I have never been this obsessed about anyone. If she is not meant for me, why do I dream of her every night and live in misery every day, wishing for it to end? Thus, I can dream of her again."

Louarn took the parchment from Gamble.

Louarn warned, "Don't be foolish, Gamble! One can only divine this as death and perdition. This stands as a fool's quest! You know very well of others who have gone and never returned. I will not lose a brother over this!"

The two brothers argued throughout the night and then went their separate ways.

Thormon heard the entire argument. He seemed curious about the parchment and followed his father to his office to see where Louarn would hide it. He saw where his father hid it and ran to the garden to see if his uncle was still around.

Thormon ran toward his dad. "Father, why won't you help?"

"What? Did you hear us? Stay away from that fool. There seems nothing pretty about that place!"

Louarn persuaded Thormon not to follow his uncle on his fool's errand. Thormon agreed with his father but knew he had to help his uncle.

CHAPTER 23

The Initial Journey to The Promised Land

T he promises of gold and fame spiked the bard's interest in the elf town. But with no map and no parchment, the journey would not happen.

The bards knew Thormon wanted to go on the expedition. And they tried to have Thormon persuade his father to help them.

"Father, Mother, I want you to help Uncle Gamble."

Suli affirmed, "No way! That remains out of the question."

Louarn agreed, "Your mother stands right on this. You are only a boy; besides that, I destroyed the parchment."

"What can I do to make you change your mind?" asked Thormon.

Louarn replied with a question, "Do you realize how dangerous this expedition entails?

Suli replied, "Absolutely nothing! There stays no point in arguing further! Venturing to uncharted territory? No one has ever returned!"

Thormon knew his father had not destroyed the parchment—and he knew how to get it. He decided to plot a story to aid his uncle. He thought about pretending to be at his friend's house for some period and going with his uncle to Coloris. He told his parents that he would go to the house of a friend, Daniel of Varzea, in an outlying district of Baldar. He packed up his stuff. In his mind, it would be like his grandpa's quest.

Being told to stay home repeatedly caused Thormon to become fed up. He could protect himself. In seven moon cycles, he fended off a couple of thieves who were mistreating an old lady.

I'm brave enough to defend myself. Why can't my parents see that?

For him, it was easy to go on a new adventure, and his uncle happened to be the key to freedom from boredom. One moon cycle, Thormon saw a group leaving the city for rural districts.

"Where are you folks headed?" Thormon asked.

"Away from here," someone answered.

"Where we can defend ourselves," another person added.

Thormon seemed a bit shocked, but he was not surprised. His uncle had talked about going to the elf cities, and Thormon knew he had to go along. He had heard his uncle talking about how rough the city could be, but his uncle knew how to fight.

Thormon went into his father's office to steal the parchment. And he went to where his uncle and friends would gather to play. Thormon thought that would be the key to his uncle taking him.

The six bards were playing music in town when Thormon arrived.

"Uncle, I have something for you!" Thormon handed over the parchment.

"Where did you get this?" Gamble asked.

"I stole it from Father—and now, I'm joining you on this quest," Thormon replied.

"Are you crazy, boy? I would never take you on such a journey. I will not be responsible for you." Gamble pushed Thormon away.

Thormon replied, "But I got you the map! Without it, you'd still be here playing—and you'd never be able to search for wealth."

"Thanks for the map, but you cannot come! And don't try anything dumb—or I'll tell your dad what you did. Go home."

Thormon became sad, but he did not give up on his quest.

Gamble gathered his friends and started preparing for the journey.

The following day, the bards were ready to head out. They played as they walked through town as a manner to say goodbye. Gamble played his tambourine, Miguel played his harp, and Fabio played his trumpet. Also, Julio played his drum, Robert played his button flute, and Bernard played his viola. Children and youngsters followed the band, listened to the lyrics, and sang along. Thormon took advantage of the commotion and followed them from afar.

The bards continued singing their goodbyes. And when Gamble passed Melissa's donjon, he blew her a kiss. "Wait for me—and you will not be disappointed."

The bards played until they left the city. The kids dispersed, but Thormon ran into the bushes and stealthily followed them.

Scouts charted dwarfs' abodes at the mountain's base. It was between the Prates River and the Ninmor River. Luckily for Thormon, they did not ride horses. The dense tropical forest bordering the Elder Mountains did not allow it. They needed to flank the mountain until the forest of Eslos. Dwarfs populated most of the extension of the mountain in deep underground tunnels. And the famous city of Havengar was no secret.

With no apparent trail, the only guiding clue was to go along the mountains north and east. And Thormon followed hot on their tails.

The bards did not seem like they were adventuring. It looked like they were parading and playing songs throughout the journey. Miguel's most trusted companion was a very docile hound named Medox. It seemed to be a breed between a boxer and a fox terrier. Medox followed them, jumping and barking to the tunes.

Gamble protested, "Miguel, I am worn out of that melody. Would you play something else?"

"What shall we play?" asked Bernard.

Julio suggested, "I think we should play something ampler appropriate. Something in tune with the wilderness."

After some discussion, they started to play the wild bird melody. It imitated a bird's call at times and went on like this:

"Oh, birds, by Jingo, come to cheer me up

My dear girlfriend, to say, 'Cheerio!' won't do this time.

All day and night, I have been meandering up

In great anticipation of taking away my pride,

The Whistling characteristic of a bird's call.

Bring me news, oh birds of the twilight,

Whose melody is so pleasant and pure at the gathering night,

When one calls, the next responds,

Even those of which the melody I am not very fond.

Cruel weakness could overcome a man,

If not for the appeasing wild bird tune at the dam.

They would feel the swelling sorrow of the unyielding blues.
Please, bird of paradise, bring me today the beautiful hues,
Whistling characteristic of a bird's call.
The crystalline dew of the place where you once abode,
For the job of singing brings you severe thirst.
Such as the thirst that my heart feels at this much-awaited tryst.
Oh, sweet nectar, bring me today the hummingbird to the place I once beheld."

They sang and played until nightfall. With the appeasing tune, Gamble slept at the foot of the mountain. The air felt humid with moisture on their faces and stifling. And they wore their least cumbersome clothes. Many animals cuddled by the meadow when the alluring melody drew them. Capuchin monkeys swung from branch to branch, with some settled at the tree trunk above the musicians. A cool breeze freshened up the otherwise stale dampness, and all the bards fell asleep.

The music had long ceased, and everything appeared calm. A bush moved, and Medox started barking.

Someone grabbed Thormon from behind and pinned him to the ground. "Stop! Wait! I am Gamble's nephew!"

Fabio immobilized Thormon with a headlock, bound the boy's wrists, and woke up Gamble.

"What is it?" Gamble stood up and looked at Thormon. "Kid? What are *you* doing here?"

"Uncle, I am here to help you."

"What? No! You are not coming! You are to go back to Baldar!"

"But how? I don't know the track back. I have no idea where or how I got here," Thormon answered, trying to persuade his uncle to let him tag along.

"Kid, you play a dangerous game," Fabio warned.

Gamble thought, *If I take the kid to Coloris with me, Louarn will be furious. If I send him back, and he gets lost, Louarn will kill me. I can't have any of my men escort him home. I need all of them with me. What should I do?*

He deliberated, "Tell you what, kid. If I send you on your way, you'll just come back to where we are, and if I let you tag along, I'll catch hell. I'll drop you off in the next town and have someone bring you to Baldar. I bet your parents are worried sick at the present."

The others didn't agree with having Thormon accompany them, but there was nothing they could do. So, they settled the matter almost yielding. And everyone except for Fabio and Medox went back to sleep.

When Fabio switched watch with Robert, he started roaming back and forth.

Thormon watched him closely. *What in the world is that man up to?*

Robert took something out of his pocket, looked both ways and lit it.

"What are you doing?" Thormon asked.

Robert jumped and attempted to come up with an excuse, "Nothing special—just smoking."

"Smoking what? I've never seen any smoke pipe like that," Thormon replied.

Robert's eyes opened wide, and an unnatural smile covered his face.

Thormon asked, "What in the world are you smoking?"

Robert looked at Thormon, shook his head, and offered the pipe. "Look, kid, if you keep quiet and promise not to tell anyone, I will let you smoke some."

Thormon said, "No way! My grandfather told me never to smoke!"

"Then let me smoke my pipe in peace—and bugger off back to sleep." Robert pushed Thormon away.

Thormon returned to his bedroll and slept.

Gamble woke up early, and he woke up his mates. Robert looked a bit crunchy and in a bad mood.

Once Robert shook off his drowsiness affecting his well-being, they packed up and had him lead the group through the trees with his machete.

Robert gave no heed to the branches that hit his body—and he felt no pain.

The group quickly made their route to a small town at the foot of the mountain. Fabio tried to find someone to take Thormon back to Baldar.

An elderly man was willing to take Thormon back, but he wanted to be paid upfront. Fabio tried to negotiate with the older man, explaining who the boy's father was. Also, how well this ordeal would compensate him. The hoary man agreed to take Thormon off of their hands.

Gamble commanded, "OK, kid. Now, you have to follow Mr. Clewit. He's gonna take you home."

"Uncle, I won't be a burden. I can carry my weight. Please let me go with you!"

"No! You're going back—and that's final!" Gamble handed Thormon over to the older man.

Thormon angrily followed the worn-out man. And Gamble and his group continued on their journey.

***

After days of traveling across the Elder Mountains toward the north, the men decided to rest for a moon cycle.

They set up camp and gathered around the bonfire. They started singing, telling jokes and stories, and drinking and feasting. They switched from singing to dancing to telling jokes. It came to pass a great mess, but the men didn't care.

At the end of the moon cycle, they decided to sit closer together to listen to one of Fabio's great stories and one of Miguel's jokes. They were alive and well, and they were closer to their goal.

Miguel articulated, "At this instant, listen to this, folks. A shabby-looking prostitute house I had visited before. It was known to have the price list for the services that the prostitutes could offer. The top price was for the singing fellatio, which seems appropriate for us bards who like music. The same hostess, a middle-aged brunette, always administered it in a dark room. I saved money for a whole one-third season to get the singing fellatio. But once I entered the room, I expected that the singing would be at least somewhat hindered due to the service's obvious implication. I wondered how she could sing meticulously well with my thing in her mouth. I brought a small lamp and lit it up while she sang. What did I learn?" He paused and looked at the faces of his comrades. "She was missing an eye where the hole was used for my satisfaction. Oh! Nasty eye socket.

The tall tale had a lasting effect on the boy's imagination as he couldn't help but show disgust.

The bards laughed hysterically. And when they stopped, they heard intense laughter in the wind. They quickly got up and started to search for its origin.

"Medox, go find!" Miguel pointed to the woods.

100

After a couple of beats of an eagle's wings, Robert reappeared after checking out a commotion in the tall wheat bushes bordering the trail. He appeared to be pushing a small person, and the dog jumped up and down.

Gamble screamed, "What the hell are you doing' here?"

Thormon lips were sealed, for he seemed speechless.

Gamble puzzled demanded an explanation, "I thought the older man took you back to Baldar. How—no, when—did you start following us?"

Thormon smiled and gloated, "I tricked the old man."

"How am I supposed to carry on these days?" Gambled confessed.

"We can't do much currently. We have to let him come," Bernard unwillingly confessed.

Gamble reacted, "But my brother will surely kill me. I bet he even has a warrant for my arrest."

Bernard conceded, "In any case, we'll think of something. And for the time being, the boy will accompany us."

Robert spat, "OK, but don't think you'll get off easy. You're going to carry our stuff from now on as punishment!"

Fabio added, "You'll also have to care for the food and washing."

Gamble agreed, "This instant then, it's settled—and you best not complain, or else I'll beat you silly!"

The group gave a death glare at Thormon. No one wanted to talk or tell another joke. They all collected themselves and called it a night.

Bernard pushed Thormon away. "Don't be thinking you're going to be sleeping at the moment. You will have the first watch."

***

The dog licked Thormon's face early during the day break and woke him up.

Gamble cheered, "Let's get ready to leave."

Everyone gathered their stuff and went back to the trail. Thormon aroused, not so eager to continue. As the new baggage carrier, he had his work cut out for him.

CHAPTER 24

The Path to Uncharted Territory

Their journey took them to the dark Prates River, which got its name due to the mixing of chemicals that seem to pollute the water with dirt and the side products of intense mining. The culprit comes about as the greedy dwarfs. The group looked at the river with disgust. The water looked dark and dirty, and the stench smelled unbearable.

"Wow. Who could have done such a thing?" Thormon asked while trying to carry all the bags.

"Those disgusting dwarfs," a voice stated.

"But why? Why destroy such a beautiful place?" Thormon replied.

There stood silence. It seemed like no one wanted to tell the story behind the place.

The pristine scenery took Thormon aback. Bare rocks gave way to an elaborate tunnel system that the dwarfs had made.

The voice speculated, "All of this destruction—and for what? Have no elves tried to stop them?"

Thormon didn't understand a great deal of what he heard.

All he could do was marvel at what was made as they passed by.

"Don't get so excited, boy. You haven't seen anything yet," Fabio advised.

They soon passed by a myriad of stone stairs, which led up forty stories.

Thormon could not believe his eyes. There could be no speculation of how deep the tunnels went or how high the mountain stretched.

"Wow! These dwarfs can build stuff," Thormon mused.

Robert admitted, "You gotta hand it to them. These dwarfs of Havengar are skillful with their pickaxes."

"Thormon, my boy, welcome to the Elder Mountain. This seems the location where the famed city under the mountain lies."

"Can we enter it?" Thormon asked.

Gamble stated, "No! We don't have time for that, and we probably wouldn't be allowed in any way. There are several hundred entrances, which are probably all protected. The dwarfs built this to resist an assault of any kind, and they are not the welcoming kind."

Thormon seemed amazed by the dwarfs' riding ponies. Also, they carried big two-bladed axes with big bags of gems tied to the animals. All he could do befell on imagining he was there by their side.

Robert complained, "Look at those petty dwarves. They have animals to carry them. Pfft!"

Gamble jested, "You know, it would be nearly impossible to ride those small horses. They might be a fit only for Thormon."

Bernard reasoned, "True! But we will still need some kind of animal or beast of burden once we reach the wider paths. We can't count on Thormon to be our mule for the entire trip."

Gamble rebuked, "I see. Henceforward, what do you suggest we do? Send Thormon in to steal those ponies or tame wild horses?"

"The second one," Bernard replied.

"As soon as we enter the wild pastures, we'll search for something to ride and carry our stuff," Gamble proposed.

The bards continued along the mountain until they reached the open pastures. There, they began their search for wild horses.

After a couple of failed attempts, the group finally found suitable animals for their journey. In a vast glade, they found some animal tracks.

Medox sniffed out the trail, which took them to some hoof prints.

Gamble elucidated, "If we go north, we should find a group of stallions—at least, that's where this dog seems to be telling us to go."

They went north through the pasture, which supported many large animals. Medox started barking at a group of mustangs feasting on the verdant grass.

"Quiet down, boy," Bernard demanded.

The others gathered around and mustered a plan to capture the horses.

"Stay here, kid, and learn with the bards," boasted Gamble.

They started producing a soft, calming melody that lulled five horses into a trance. Approaching closer and closer, they made sure the animals were calm and wouldn't flee. Once everything checked out, the five bards advanced while Miguel kept playing his harp. The group advanced toward the mustangs, making sure not to scare them.

Fabio approached one of the animals and took a mixture of calming herbs from his backpack; he then offered it to a brown horse.

The animal lowered its head and ate it willingly. The others soon followed. And after taming the animals, they all agreed to mount them simultaneously. They didn't intend to alarm the others.

Fabio, Gamble, Robert, Julio, and Bernard mounted the wild horses. Then, they worked the ropes around their necks. Only the big black stallion that Robert had mounted resisted the taming. It jumped forward and backward, rocking, standing upright on its hind legs, and trying to throw him off. After about five beats of an eagle's wings, the bard flew off, landing on his back and losing his horse. Everyone laughed.

Thormon laughed the loudest. "Ha! You got what you deserved!" Thormon expressed while rolling on the ground.

"Shut up, mule. You still have to carry my stuff!" Robert spat while getting up and dusting off the dirt.

"You must admit, Robert, that seeing you fly off the horse was hilarious." Julio looked like he was trying to hold in his laughter.

With four horses, they were able to continue on their journey. Lucky for them, the animals were sturdy enough for the weight of two. They all saddled up the horses and were ready to continue with Medox trailing behind them.

They crossed the wide, calm, shallow waters of the Ninmor River. They saw small fish as the group advanced.

Medox started barking and crying at the same moment.

As they touched land, Bernard asked, "Why don't we stop here and fish?"

The group looked at him, and the desire to eat something rather than rations was overwhelming. That drove the company to cast their fishing rods quickly.

"Wow! You guys didn't think twice!" Bernard laughed as he took out his rod.

They sat on the banks of the river and cast their rods, and Thormon kept watch on the horses. Moments later, the fish started to bite.

"Got one!"

"Another one here!"

Everyone caught a fish. Even Medox went in on the action and caught one.

They asked Thormon to clean the fish, and he reluctantly agreed. He held up a hazel-colored fish with white stripes. The fish seemed to be a bit off.

"Are you guys sure we can eat this?" asked Julio.

"Of course!" Gamble replied.

"But… look! The fish has a small, retractable forelimb," affirmed Thormon.

"It's nothing, my boy. Maybe that's just for steering. Maybe used for dragging in these exceptionally shallow waters," commented Gamble.

Thormon tried to protest, "But—"

"This fish sure appears weird, isn't it?" asked Bernard.

"Anyhow, Medox remains still alive. Accordingly, I believe we're safe," imagined Robert.

"He did seem happy eating it," confessed Miguel.

"Let's try it, then," Fabio offered.

"Thormon, come here! I need you to cook it and try it," demanded Gamble.

After cleaning and frying the small creature, Thormon took a bite. "It tastes like fried toad or frog to me."

"Nothing funky?" Julio asked.

"Nope!" Thormon replied.

The group jumped right in and gobbled up everything.

After they had eaten their fill, they packed up and continued their journey. There ensued no occasion for delay. They needed to keep moving.

After two hundred beats of an eagle's wings, with the motion of the horse and the late-afternoon sun, Thormon's stomach started growling. He put his hands over his stomach.

"I don't feel so well."

Gamble said, "Ditto."

"Oh my! I think I'm going to give birth to something." Julio got off his horse and dropped to the ground.

Robert confessed, "I'm OK. All I had was the—"

Medox started howling and making weird noises.

"What's wrong with that dog?" Bernard fell on his horse in agony.

Robert advised, "Quiet, fellows! We would rather not attract any attention—"

A thunderous sound boomed.

"Sorry, guys," Thormon mentioned with his hands over his stomach.

"No! That couldn't have been you!" Gamble alleged.

They all started making odd farting noises.

A voice echoed, "Halt and dismount, humans!"

"No need! We are all dying here!" Robert replied.

A figure appeared and looked at them. "Was that dog that passed by like a bat out of hell yours?"

Miguel was without words, "Well, I—"

Robert explained, "Sorry, my kind elves. My companions are not…"

A foul stench followed a loud fart.

"Is there a corpse you guys are carrying?" The elf appeared like he was trying to hold his breath.

"Oh my! I believe one of my companions seems rotting away," Robert replied.

"Hello… my… name… is… ummph… Gam—"

Medox ran back howling and farting.

There came to pass an odd silence before interruption by the sound of a flute.

"I believe a flute doesn't sound or smell that way," the elf rebuked.

"Coloris!" mentioned Gamble.

"Oh, you seek the elf city?" the elf asked.

"Dirty humans!" the taller elf told the yellow-haired elf.

"Have you no respect? What in god's name holds wrong with you?" the yellow-haired elf replied.

Robert clarified, "I'm sorry. My friends ate some fish from the river, and as you can see, I think they are dying—or something worse!"

The elves started laughing. "You foolish humans! Have you no knowledge about the fish in that river? No one can eat the GluGlu fish— unless you wish to have a dreadful experience."

"But is anything bad gonna happen to them?" Robert asked. "Besides embarrassment?"

"No! Here! Give this to them—and to that crazy dog of yours."

Robert took the herbs and handed them out to the group. They ate the herbs and quickly dozed off.

"What happened? Are they gonna be all right?" Robert asked. "Yes! Don't worry. The herbs are doing their magic."

The elves all laughed. Robert thanked the elves.

"What are your motives?" asked the taller elf.

Robert replied, "Oh, you mean Coloris? Well, we are bards—and the city of Coloris seems the place where all bards dream of going."

The elves looked at each other and nodded.

"Very well. The farting bards may pass—once they are up." The taller elf laughed and pointed in the direction they should go. "Just follow this river north. And when you find a small mound with only one tree at the peak, climb it and look east from the top of the tree. One can see the city of Coloris from there."

Robert thanked them, and as soon as the group recovered, they went off in the direction given by the elf.

Robert looked back at the elves and saw something off in their smiles and laughter. Maybe it wasn't as simple as it sounded—or perhaps they were just joking about the entire debacle.

The group followed the elves' instructions. And before long, the narrow river became wider and the forest denser.

Thormon asked Robert what the elves had told him.

Robert explained the embarrassing situation. And how the elves had named them the farting bards.

Thormon had a good laugh and jested that it did not apply to him. He was no bard.

Gamble smiled and expressed sincerely, "Of course you are!"

Thormon argued, "Anyhow, I don't know the first thing about being a bard or about the Western world. How could you say I'm one of you?"

Gamble alleged, "The Western world portrays as far too hostile. I used to travel from Pazlan to Minas Arcaika and back to Aridona. Hordes of orcs and goblins raided many small villages. And the dark elves stole what they could whenever they had the chance. My parents live in the small city of Victoria, which is where your father and I were raised. I dared not venture north to the city of Darmanan."

"And why is that?" asked Thormon.

"Currently, many dangerous humanoids roamed that territory. And they were: trolls, goblins, orcs, ratmen, and ettins. Oh, and there were rumors of a chaotic necromancer. He ruled remote lands and raised armies of the undead."

Julio shouted, "Look! The hill the elves mentioned!"

The hill appeared perfectly round. It looked like a giant orange had been hewed in half and placed face down on the ground. It was barren and yellow, only a single tree with a large bough and tiny green leaves on the top.

"How do we get up there?" Fabio asked.

The yellow rock was round and brittle. Moments later, Gamble approached the hill and mentioned, "Thormon, come here. I will give you a lift."

The slippery rock provided no support, and Thormon slipped down the slope.

They placed the biggest horse close to the hill, and Fabio stood on its back. He tried to climb it, but he failed as well.

Gamble proposed, "Let's combine all the ropes we have. If we attach a heavy sickle to the rope's end, I will throw it at the tree. It should anchor there."

After three attempts, the rope seemed finally anchored loosely to a branch.

"Hey, boy. You are light and strong enough to climb this."

They handed Thormon the rope, and he climbed the hill. Once he climbed the tree, he could see the lay of the land. Green trees covered the vast land, and no sign of the city appeared. According to the instructions, he looked east. Then, the trees blurred and dimmed, forming a glade.

Suddenly, he saw myriad of wooden buildings. Thormon couldn't believe his eyes. He saw watchtowers, wooden palaces, and spherical houses suspended over a river. Those seemed attached to huge trees like hanging fruit. Also, there were narrow wooden bridges going from one tree to another. Thormon felt as if he were hovering on top of soft clouds.

"Wow! This feels amazing!"

Fabio attempted to climb, but the rope did not hold his weight. He slipped and almost hit his head on a rock.

Thormon looked down and screamed, "You fool! How do I get down now?"

Fabio shook off the dirt and yelled, "Just slide down! I did it—you can too!"

The others tried to throw another rope at Thormon, who looked for a path down.

Gamble distressed, "Oh, crap! It looks like we're not getting another rope up there."

"You're gonna have to find a route down!" Bernard yelled.

Thormon hunkered down and slid his body down the hill. He screamed the whole way down.

The bards laughed at Thormon's funny butt slide.

Gamble preoccupied spoke, "Are you hurt, kid?"

"No, I am fine." Thormon dusted the dirt off his vest and tried to get up.

"Hmm. So, did you see Coloris?"

"Yes, Uncle!"

"Now then, which route?" Fabio asked.

"That direction." Thormon pointed toward the woods.

"You mean we have to walk into those woods?" Bernard asked.

"It's there. I saw it!" Thormon believed.

Miguel looked up to the kid, "If the kid says it's that direction, then it's that way."

Gamble decided, "Very well… let's get going."

"In any case, kid, you're gonna be our guide." Fabio pushed Thormon forward.

Thormon guided the men to where he had seen the city. "The glade should be close now!"

"Are you certain this should come to pass as the right path?" Robert asked.

Fabio stated, "He's right. We've been walking in these woods for several beats of an eagle's wings —and there's still no sign of a city."

Thormon looked at the group and assured them they were on the right path.

As the solar cycle became the moon cycle, darkness and dismay fell upon the group. Every time they would light their torches and lamps, an ill wind would extinguish the fire.

Robert speculated, "There feels like something foul dwells in these woods."

"Elfish magic!" replied Bernard.

Julio expressed with irony, "Great! At this point, we are lost! And to top it off, there befalls some kind of curse in this neck of the woods."

"I can see! Follow me," Thormon offered. The others looked baffled.

"Gamble, is your nephew crazy or joking?" Miguel asked.

Thormon asked them to tie a rope around their waists and suggested, "Just trust me!"

The bards did as Thormon asked.

"Let's just hope he knows what he is doing," Robert mistrusted.

The kid could see a greenish light afar and went after it. The group didn't understand what was happening but followed him.

The greenish light became bigger and bigger as they got closer to it.

As Thormon approached it, he asked the group to stop. "Do you guys see it?"

"See what?"

The kid knew that there was something that he alone could see. He stayed quiet for a moment and stretched his arm forward to tap the tree, but it went straight through it. He paused for a moment and then jumped into it.

"Where is Thormon?" Gambled screamed.

The rest of the group started to get worried. But before they could do anything, Gamble felt his rope being pulled.

"Whatever caught Thormon lingers immediately after me!" Gamble yelled.

"Don't be stupid, Uncle. Just come here!"

The bards crossed the magic wall one by one, and then the city of Coloris materialized in sight!

They all had blank faces. They couldn't believe that the city was hidden in plain sight.

Thormon looked at the group, smiled, and affirmed, "You guys can untie yourselves. I told you I knew the path."

The group started mumbling. They tried to find a reasonable explanation for how only Thormon could see it. The group untied themselves, sat down on a root, and wondered at the spectacular view.

Green orbs that hung from the tops of the trees illuminated the city. Each main tree had a structure resembling a wooden elevator that could take the elves up and down the treetops. The elves built a few houses over the raging waters of a narrow river. On top of the tallest trees, watchtowers were visible. Many wobbling, hollow, wooden spheres attached to thick branches had portholes. They could see a few elves resting indoors.

Gamble pointed to an area where elves entered and left the spherical houses. He declared they should head to the main branches; before long, the palace became visible. It looked like no ordinary palace. It had several conical chambers reaching skyward. The palace had many white stones stained by greenish mold that covered and colonized the arches. Also, the pillars seemed affected, giving it a touch of nature. Nature and elf lived as one.

The company traversed the city in a dream state and started to draw a lot of attention. As they passed by, elves began running away from them.

The villagers summoned guards that surrounded the bards. A rather audacious elf gave an intimidating stare, and they all went for their swords.

"Whoa! Whoa! We come in peace! No violence occurs as necessary!" Gamble raised his arms and showed his palms while kneeling.

Robert poked the others to follow suit.

The commanding elf asked, "How did you find us? What do you seek here?"

Gamble cried, "Please! We are simple musicians. Bards. We heard about the splendor of the music from Coloris and—"

The elf asked, "How did you find us?"

Gamble replied, "Anyhow, you see, we met some elves on a bridge. They gave us directions to a hill, and then my nephew sighted the city. We followed him."

"You lie!" The elf pulled out his sword.

Thormon shouted, "But I did see it!"

The elf slapped the boy's face and spat, "No human can find us!"

All the guards drew their swords.

Thormon fell back and yelled, "I'm not lying! I did see the city and the greenish light!"

That remark angered the guards even further. "Liar!"

The humans kneeled and begged for their lives.

An elf maiden approached the guards and told them to stand down. "This seems no manner to treat peaceful visitors!"

She helped Thormon stand up.

The elf commander complained, "But, my lady, I am protecting our people! These humans come here uninvited and dare to lie to us about how they got here!"

"So, you think the boy lies? Did you forget that no one can find Coloris if not aided by an elf? Yet, they arrived here."

The crowd started asking who had helped them and who had guided them.

The elf maiden turned to the group and asked, "Was it the boy who helped you all into the city?"

Yes!" Gamble replied.

The boy nodded. "Yes, madam. I have always had great vision."

She looked at the boy well and asked, "Who are your parents? This man who you call uncle is not related by blood."

He shook his head and replied, pointing to Gamble, "His brother adopted me. I never knew my real parents."

"Oh! That's very unfortunate, child." She looked at the boy, put her hand on his head, and invited them, "You are all welcome here."

The soldiers looked at her with a disagreeing gaze and left.

The bards felt relieved with an easy smile and looked at Thormon with thankful eyes.

"Thus, what now?" Robert asked.

"Please! Follow me!" The maiden elf led the bards to the central palace.

The group followed the maiden elf silently. They could feel the crowd's disapproval as they went down the street. They looked dismayed, humiliated, and broken. But Thormon walked proudly and held the elf-maiden's hand.

Thormon looked back at the stronghold's footsteps and gloated, "Aren't you glad I came along? Currently, you all owe me big time. You better come up with a perfect story to tell my dad."

Gamble smiled and said, "I'll think of something."

The maiden elf looked at them and smiled. "You owe this kid your lives. Come on. Let's enter."

The elf lords stood by three unused silver thrones in the majestic hall. The nobles and commanders all stood silent as the party walked down the hall. They were all curious about the boy who could see their city. This boy's origin seemed shrouded in mystery.

The maiden elf brought them closer to the thrones, and the elf king took his seat. The king commanded the group to stop and not to say a word. The maiden elf let go of Thormon's hand and walked over to a fancy throne. The bards did not know what went on.

Thormon looked at his uncle with a frightened face.

A soothing voice murmured, "Do not fear. We won't hurt you or any of those with you."

When Thormon looked up, he saw an elf maiden with beautiful silver hair. Her beauty matched Katrina's. Thormon felt in awe as his eyes zoomed in on the image of beauty, absorbing every detail.

She looked at him and smiled. With a sweet voice, she added, "I'm sorry about how our guards have treated you. You'd all have perished if it hadn't been for the princess."

The princess turned to the queen and king. "Father and Mother, this child seems of elf blood."

The bards all kneeled.

Gamble greeted, "Hail elf king! We are bards from the human city of Baldar. Gamble is my name, and we are at your service."

The king looked at Gamble, but he did not say a word. His interest was not with the bards. The king got up and took out his greenish sword.

Gamble opened his eyes wide and froze. It seemed like the king was going to strike him. And before he could plead for his life, the king walked past him and offered the sword to Thormon.

"What happens to be your name, young one?"

"I am Thormon, Your Majesty, but they call me Red Hands."

The king smiled and added, "That's a peculiar nickname. Red Hands? You must tell me how you got that, but first, please touch this sword."

Thormon reached out and touched the sword, and the room went silent. The sword stopped glowing. But she glowed green again before the audience could say anything.

"Oh my! My guess was right! You are somehow of royal blood."

The king took the sword back. "You see, this blade seems beckoned ever since the old ages as the Gordervith sword. It only glows in the hands of royal elves."

The bards were shocked.

Thormon asked, "Do you mean I'm a king or something?"

The king smiled and kidded, "No! Just royal—like my beautiful daughter and wife, who you can't take your eyes off."

Thormon frightened mentioned, "I'm sorry, Your Majesty. She reminds me of a dear friend. I meant no disrespect."

The king laughed and affirmed, "Anyhow, tell me about this beautiful girl you have dear in your heart. But before that, you gotta tell me where you come from?"

"I come from the harbor city of Menestrel," he confessed.

The elf-lord looked at his daughter and asked, "Hmm. Isn't that land of man close to the forest of Danith, where you once resided?"

The room stayed silent again. The king looked at his daughter and wife and ordered them to wait for him in his private quarters.

He turned to the group and praised them, "As for you, Thormon—and your friends—you are welcome to stay as long as you want! Enlgon will take you to the guest quarters."

He walked back to his throne and whispered, "As for my daughter, it appears that there ensues some explaining to do."

Enlgon led them to the outer quarters of the palace.

Walking through the crowd, the bards heard whispers about Thormon's origins.

Enlgon silently walked the bards to a separate room. Once there, he warned, "You humans better not misbehave. Even though we spared you, it doesn't mean you can do anything; you wait here. You will be called upon when needed."

The group followed the orders and entered their chambers.

Before Thormon could enter his, Enlgon stopped him. "You will not stay here with these fools. You are royalty and are to go to the finest room available."

"But where is it located, my quarters?" Thormon asked as the bards became more distant.

"The west wing," Enlgon replied.

As they walked toward the west wing, the servants greeted him.

Thormon's annoyed face showed that he felt a bit edgy and did not know what to do.

"Just be yourself!" Enlgon advised.

"Am I really royalty?" Thormon asked.

"If that's what the sword revealed, then yes. Here we are. If you need anything, a servant will be waiting for you at the door."

Enlgon opened the door, and Thormon's eyes sparkled with delight. His bedroom appeared huge. It had a soft bed with a cotton mattress and a washbasin where he could bathe and drink water. The royal architect ornamented the room finely with gold and silk. Paintings of beautiful scenery and elves hung on the walls. Thormon had never seen such a fancy place.

Elf subordinates interrupted Thormon's daydreaming to ask what he desired.

Thormon asked for something to eat and a clean set of clothes. The hardship of the travel wore him out, and all he wanted to do was relax and sleep.

In the royal quarters, the king elf, Angron, confronted his spouse, Oradeth. And later, addressed his daughter, Eledriel, also known as Minerva, in the language of man.

"Is this the so-called child you had when you adventured in the land of men?"

In tears, Minerva revealed, "He is not Camulus! I would have recognized my son!"

"But I can see you in his penetrating gaze," the king compared them.

The queen speculated, "Well, the age does not match—and our daughter came clean about her little adventure. He must be the son of Camulus! It stays only logical—unless you have another adventure you haven't told us about."

"No! It was only Camulus! I swear! I learned my lesson!" Minerva attested.

After pondering, Angron conjectured, "Thus, if he comes to pass as not your son, it still doesn't make sense for the sword to glow. One-quarter of your blood wouldn't be enough to make the sword glow. All we can conclude is that he derived from royal blood and somehow is be related to you."

"Then Camulus' mistress must have royal blood," speculated the queen, pensively walking, directing her gaze to the boy. "We have to find out sooner than later. We can't keep them here forever."

The king and queen looked disapprovingly at their daughter. So, both tried to come up with a manner to give the people an explanation of the boy's royal status. That would be the only approach to silence the gossip already stirring in the city.

CHAPTER 25

An Alternative Way of Life

The first rays of sunlight entered the window where Thormon slept, hitting his face. The warm embrace of the sun woke him. He got up and stood there with an empty gaze, listening to the birds chirping and the wasps buzzing. He couldn't recall the last occasion he had an appropriate night's sleep. Not even his comfy bed at home matched this excellent quality.

He stretched out a bit and got dressed. *Time for some answers!*

There was a knock on the door. "Are you up, Master Thormon?"

He felt slightly surprised at the title of master but opened the door. His uncle and friends were waiting for him.

"Did you get enough sleep, boy?" Gamble asked.

"Yes!" Thormon answered.

Robert boosted, "Now then, what are we waiting for? Take us to have breakfast. I'm starving!"

"Whoa! Calm down! Why didn't you guys go and have breakfast without me?" Thormon replied.

"They wouldn't allow us to enter without you. They barely let us through just to see you," Bernard answered.

Thormon looked at them and followed them to the main dining hall. His eyes sparkled with delight. The tables were the roots of the trees, and the smaller roots were the benches. He ran toward them and tried to figure out how all this had come to be.

The king smiled and asked, "Are you not hungry?"

Thormon stopped and replied, "Sorry, Your Majesty. I didn't see you there. This woodwork seems so amazing that I forgot about everything else."

"That's not woodwork, my child. The elf carpenters crafted the architecture using music itself," the king answered.

Thormon didn't know what to think or say. He just put his hand on the tree table.

"It's still alive. I know you can feel it," the king added.

"But you don't cut the tree?" Thormon asked.

"No! We never harm the forest. As you can see, we live in harmony with them. Come now! There will be moments for further questions later. At present, let's eat!" The king took Thormon to eat by his side.

The elves did everything together. Everyone sat at the table—even the guards who had almost killed them.

"Is everyone here because of us?" Thormon asked.

The king replied, "No! We live as one. We do not have what humans call currency. We do have status assigned by our elders and nobles—"

Thormon asked, "How did you become king—and how do you know what each one should do?"

The king looked at Thormon and smiled. "You are a curious one, aren't you? Well, for the present, let's eat. I'll explain how our society works later."

Thormon smiled and started to eat.

Gamble stood, chatting with some elves. An elf bard played a sweet melody on his flute. That made a thin sunflower grow taller by each beat of an eagle's wings and blossom. Once the musical work finished, he picked several sunflower seeds. He ate some and fed the rest to five frolicking parrots.

"This place feels magical," Thormon sensed.

The king turned to Thormon and answered, "This blossoms as true elf magic, you know? Only a few elves have ever mastered it. These chambers and halls never stop growing—just like that flower you were looking at."

"How?" Thormon asked.

"They are done by the power of competent elf masons and architects through the magic of music."

"That's amazing!" Thormon replied with sparkles in his eyes.

The king replied, "It truly is! The music derives from the energy the elves channel. The body and instruments are just vessels, which help, but they are not what makes it."

"Can one learn it?" Gamble asked.

"No! Are you an elf, by chance?" the king asked.

Gamble answered, "Well, with something like this, one can become rich beyond imagination."

The king looked straight into Gamble's eyes. "Why are you deeply eager to get rich?"

Gamble replied, "You can ask my nephew, but I intend to marry a very beautiful girl from the nobility. And as you know, only a noble can marry a noble."

The king smiled and confessed, "Matters of the heart are complicated. Though we think differently from humans, I know that money talks louder in the land of men. Love alone should be enough, but I know that humans don't see it in that fashion."

"I thought in that manner, too, but love won't feed us," Gamble argued.

"Love won't feed you, but it will keep you united," the king replied.

"I think she has expensive taste. That's why my uncle wants to be so rich. He wishes to pamper her," Thormon added.

The king looked at Thormon and then at Gamble, then smiled. "Bards never become rich. What are you doing here? We have no gold or riches."

"Nothing, Your Majesty. We were just really passing by. We think that fame will bring riches."

The king asked Thormon about the bard's real motives. Thormon kept his mouth shut and did not spill any information. He quickly changed the subject about his royal lineage, and they talked about how he came to be.

The day passed, and the bards and Thormon were free to walk around the city. Everywhere they went, people greeted them with respect. The bards made friends with the local musicians and soon were feasting together.

Thormon seemed happy to be around them. But he couldn't shake the feeling that surreptitious eyes were watching him.

At night, the herald summoned the bards back to the palace. The elves with the bards explained that the lords of the land were away—probably in search of answers. Thormon remained still a mystery to all.

As they approached the palace, Fabio asked the elves where they went for answers.

The elves explained that they were not allowed to say. Thormon asked, too.

Gamble advised, "Hush, boy! Do you want them to start questioning us, as well?"

The boy looked unhappy, and one of the elves offered to play with them a song that was meant as greeting the elf king and as a manner to cheer up Thormon. The boy smiled and was happy to play some music with his uncle and the bards.

The group got themselves into position to play, and music filled the hall. They were all happy to be a part of the feast.

The general of the elf army came up to the elf musician and asked him to kill the music.

The lead musician held up his hand, and the music died down. The general took center stage, and everyone's eyes were upon him.

The general glanced at the crowd and stated, "You must be asking yourselves where some of us went. Well, as you all know, the youngest of the human visitors has strong royal elvish blood, which caught the curiosity of the king and the nobles. Thormon seems of royal lineage, but we do not know who this boy descended from. His mother was not identified in the compound of elf cities either. The elf mage, Prodalus, helped us communicate with the next kingdoms. But no elf maiden conceived an elf kid in the past sixty seasons. That was even ampler curious." He petted the mage's shoulder and looked straight at the boy. "Even though the sword says you are of royal lineage, we cannot name you a prince just because of the sword. We need to know who your parents are."

The crowd started muttering about the boy's origin.

"Who is this boy?"

"Where did he come from?"

"Is he some sort of spy?"

"What is the king gonna do with him?"

The king walked toward the boy, and the room became silent. He put his hand on the boy's head and smiled. "You are always welcome to stay here!"

That comment did not sit well with the group of elves. They despised humans.

"He is not one of us!"

"They should leave!"

"The king has gone mad!"

The king took center stage and uttered, "I am the king, and you are all my subordinates. Therefore, you will obey my commands and orders! If any harm happens to come to this boy and his friends, the court will hold every perpetrator responsible!"

The crowd became silent and slowly exited the main hall. Gamble told Thormon to go back to his room.

Thormon thanked the king for his aid and left with Gamble and the bards.

A mysterious figure in a dark corner stopped them on their way back. "Nice tale of yours. Gathering money for a lady perseveres as no easy feat."

"Who are you?" Gamble asked.

The man laughed. "Someone who might help you."

The group turned, suddenly interested.

"Show yourself!" Fabio demanded.

The shadowy figure came into the light and introduced himself, "I'm Prodalus the Green at your disposal."

Bernard asked, "Who are you—and what do you want with us?"

Prodalus looked at the group and answered, "It's not what I want. It's what you want."

"And what do you think we want?" Gamble answered.

"Riches!" Prodalus answered with a mocking laugh.

"And how do you think we can acquire such riches?" Miguel asked.

Prodalus laughed again. "That depends on how much you are willing to sacrifice. Riches have a price, and are you willing to pay for them?"

"And what happens to be the price?" Robert asked.

Prodalus alluded, "Nothing you haven't done already. You made it here. You are capable of paying it."

"Very well, then. What do you want us to do?" Gamble asked.

Prodalus smiled and commented, "Right, that's the spirit. I knew you all had the fire in you, but before we can continue, let us go to your quarters."

They all went to their quarters.

Prodalus stated, "In this kingdom, we have high bounties on certain figures. We like to let outsiders do some of our dirty work."

The group did not like where this was going but opted to listen anyway.

Prodalus explained, "Well, the nymph Meliane has a lot of valuable jewelry. She keeps her fortune on the bottom of the phantom lake. Elves do not care for her, but she haggles with us to do stuff for her—and she gives hefty rewards for what we do for her."

"What kind of jobs does she ask of us?" Thormon asked.

"Nothing out of your league. You are adventurous, aren't you?" Prodalus answered.

"We try our best," Bernard answered.

"That's it? Only go and talk to this nymph?" Gamble asked.

"No. There prevails something else. The cavern of Cyclops Argus. He stands as a smith of fabulous items, and it's all for the taking—for those who are brave enough."

Robert weighed, "Thus, you are telling us to either work for a nymph or murder and loot from a Cyclops?"

Prodalus clarified, "Now then, allow me to explain. First, the Cyclops seems not a gentle kind. He has been going on a murderous rampage and—"

Fabio asked, "Then why haven't the elves intervened?"

"The Cyclops predominates as not that stupid. He only causes trouble for humans. He doesn't mess with the elves."

"And what about the nymph? Why should we go to her?" Robert asked.

Prodalus laughed. "That's for you to find out."

The group stood silently and told the druid they would need time to think about it.

"OK, humans. Sleep on it, but do not take long. I will leave this place soon."

After Prodalus left, the bards started discussing what to do.

Thormon decided to let them decide, and he followed the druid to the main hall, making sure not to be seen.

The bards pointed out the pros and the cons, and the discussion went on throughout the entire moon cycle.

Thormon rushed back to say that the druid was coming back. The group quieted down and heard a loud knock.

"Have you decided?" the druid shouted from outside the door.

"Come in, and we'll tell you," Gamble called back.

The druid opened the door and stared at the group. "Have you decided yet?"

The bards answered together: "To the nymph!"

The druid smiled and answered, "Sounds less threatening than a one-eyed monster."

The group stayed silent.

"Well, then, we leave tomorrow!" commanded the druid.

"But why not at the present?" Thormon asked.

Gamble gave each bard a task to prepare for the journey.

The druid turned to Thormon and advised, "You all must prepare for the journey. And I still have some unfinished business in this place."

He told Thormon to rest up.

***

A wild rooster announced that morning had come.

A few beats of an eagle's wings later, Prodalus knocked on the doors and woke up the bards. "Time to go!"

The group got up and quietly joined Prodalus.

The druid asked, "The elves did not whisper any word of what we are doing, have they?"

"Of course not! The elves think we are leaving the city for good," Gamble answered.

"But what about the boy?" Prodalus asked.

"They think he means to accompany us just to help us out and will return soon," Gamble replied.

"Let's go instantly! We would rather not raise too much suspicion," the druid proposed.

"But what about breakfast? We are hungry!" Fabio expressed.

"Here, have some of these!" The druid poured something into their hands.

"What is this?" Thormon asked.

"Magic berries. They have everything you need. Eat up! We have to move!"

The group ate the berries and made their way out of the city under the watchful eyes of the guards.

The druid whispered, "Thormon, you have to go out the same route you entered. They cannot know where we are nor planning to go."

Thormon took them to the green light without raising any suspicions.

After fifty beats of an eagle's wings, the druid shouted, "Stop. They cannot see us anymore. Now, let's take the real route!"

Gamble probed, "Now that we can talk, tell me about Meliane the nymph."

"She stays a very proud and narcissistic creature. Rumor says that she used to be a marine water nymph until a buccaneer presented her with a jewel. The beauty of the emerald enthralled her. And she went searching upriver for similar gems until she found one in the phantom lake. She dug for additional gems, but with that amount of dirt lifted, the lake no longer flowed freely into the river. She became trapped. Greed seems foretold as everyone's downfall!"

"In any case, but what happened to her?" Robert asked.

"With the advance of a period, her nature changed. She became mingled with the earth. Forthwith, she can no longer return to the ocean. The river stopped flowing there; it remains just the lake."

The group stayed quiet for a bit.

Thormon turned to the druid and asked, "How do you know this?"

Fabio asked, "Yeah! Not to be nosy or anything, but what kind of druid or mage are you?"

The druid smiled at the group and answered, "Well, I'm a master of the elements of nature. Nature talks to me, and I find out many interesting things and beings—and amongst them stands this nymph."

After walking all day, they reached a meadow where a trail led into a pine forest. The group asked to rest up a bit.

Suddenly, a white stallion emerged from the trees and lingered before the druid. He smiled and mounted the horse.

"I was the one who summoned this beast!" He turned to the kid and offered him a ride. "It's still a long journey ahead of us. These bards can make it on foot."

"Did you summon just this stallion?" Fabio asked.

The mage laughed and replied, "What do you think? Do you take me for a horse whisperer?"

"Maybe! You are a mage, aren't you?" Fabio asked.

The mage looked down at him and spoke, "You are a fine lad. You can make this journey on foot. You would rather not exhaust the energies of this mature warlock. You might need me to perform some magic someday."

"You should put that good magic to use and send Thormon back to his family!" Fabio replied.

The mage looked at the group and asked, "Is that what you all want?"

Before Thormon could have a say, the mage told him to be silent.

"In any case, he did help us get this far," Gamble spoke optimistically. The others nodded in agreement.

"But what about his family? They must be worried sick," Robert added. There fell an awkward silence.

"They must think I'm dead—or even worse," Thormon speculated.

Bernard disclosed, "We've all been very selfish. The boy's family must be worried sick. Heck… they might be burning money searching for this boy."

The druid smiled and summoned a dove. It flew down to his shoulder, and the druid whispered in its ears. Like magic, the dove disappeared.

"Problem solved!" the druid attested.

"That's it?" Gamble asked.

The druid smiled and nodded.

CHAPTER 26

A Contrite Sinner

T heir journey went on for a few days. The humans were visibly exhausted.

"How far is this place?" Gamble asked.

"I told you all it should be a long journey," the druid replied.

"But not this long. We have been traveling on foot in this vast forest for ages! And it feels like we are going in circles," Bernard suspected.

"You would be without me," the druid alerted.

Gamble offered, "Let's just set camp here! We can resume our voyage tomorrow."

There were no fruit trees in the forest, but Prodalus knew some tricks for generating food. He touched the closest pine tree and stepped back as if waiting for something to happen. In short, fruits fell from the tree's upper bough. Those included oranges, apples, peaches, berries, and plums. Mesmerized, the humans collected the fruit and ate it with their rations.

The bards took turns watching while the others slept.

Dripping with sweat, Robert woke up his companions. "Something means us harm by hunting us out there in these woods!"

"Calm down. What did you see?" asked Gamble.

"Some kind of beast with four arms and a hairy body! Down that direction! Come! We must leave at this instant!" He started waking everyone up and packing up everything.

The druid moved closer to Robert. "I've never heard of a monster with a description like that. Where did you see it?"

"It was there! Under that tree!"

Prodalus looked around and deduced, "There feels like something strange befalls here. I think you're seeing things."

Robert was stunned and expressed, "No! I swear! You've got to believe me."

Prodalus picked up his staff and hit the ground. Suddenly, the forest looked as bright as day. "There befalls nothing there! Look at your eyes, man!" The druid put his hands on Robert's face. "You have been smoking opium! Don't deny it!"

Robert went on a rampage, running from side to side, and yelled, "It was there! It was there! I know what I saw!

Fabio and Miguel restrained him on the ground.

"Search his backpack!" Gamble commanded.

Bernard went through Robert's pack and found a smoking apparatus made of jade. Also, a bag filled with a strange powder.

"What the hell is this?" He shoved it into Robert's face.

Gamble snatched it from Bernard's hand and threw it into the fire. "How dare you put everyone's life in danger by smoking that shit? We are in the middle of freaking nowhere! Haven't you thought of that?"

"How could you do this to us?" Bernard added.

Robert still screamed about the monster as they tied him to a tree.

"What are you going to do about him?" The druid asked.

Gamble complained, "He seems to be not even listening to us. All he keeps doing is ranting about this beast. Could you please do something to shut him up?"

The druid shoved a cloth into Robert's mouth.

Fabio sat next to Gamble. "What are we to do immediately?"

Gamble revealed, "I don't know. Let's gather everyone and see what we must do."

The group gathered around the fireplace and started discussing what to do.

Julio commented, "The story about the four-armed monster stirred something in Robert."

"We don't know how long he's been using that crap, but he never manifested like this," Gamble added.

The talks went out through the moon cycle, and by morning, they decided to keep Robert onboard. It was not because of who he was; it was so that Robert could return. They were stuck with him.

As everyone appeared packing up, Julio removed the gag and untied him. "Go eat something! We're leaving soon."

Robert did not dare to look up at his companions. He ate something and collected his things from the floor without saying a word. Everyone's gaze turned upon him.

"We can go," Robert muttered, knowing the group awaited him.

It seemed an ugly, cloudy day. They walked all day in heavy rain. The druid saw that the rain brought the morale even lower.

Several beats of an eagle's wings later, the immediate vicinity had been cleared of the clouds. It looked as if God had scooped them out with his own hands. That was because only clouds over the travelers had dissipated.

The group thanked the heavens that its entities spared them from the torrential rain.

Thormon appeared suspicious about the strange behavior of the clouds. He looked at Prodalus, and something seemed off.

Prodalus voiced, "Traveling with a mage sure has its advantages."

Thormon knew that the sudden change in the weather was the druid's handiwork.

The journey went on for almost seven days with no sign of the nymph.

The party transpired already at its wit's end.

"Are we ever going to get there?" Julio asked.

"That's right! We have been in these blasted woods for God knows how long. Even the blasted mutt feels ready to give up," Fabio added.

The druid explained, "Be patient. I know you fellows seek fortune, but from the beginning, I told you all it wouldn't be easy."

"Yeah! But you never told us it would be this difficult," Gamble replied.

The group kept strolling.

"We can't give up right away!" Thormon complained.

They all ignored him. Once they were in a small clearing, the druid extended his left arm.

A couple of beats from an eagle's wings later, a snowy white owl landed there.

The group stopped and stared at him, unsure if it was a good or bad omen.

The druid put the bird next to his ear, and after a moment, he nodded and released the bird.

"It came to my attention that the phantom lake dwells just a day away going south. I think it is very important to clarify that my task here finishes once we meet the nymph. I will be on my way."

The bards started to protest, but the mage stood adamant.

"You are the one who came looking for us!" Gamble rebuked.

The druid turned to him and disclosed, "That holds true, but don't forget that I am doing this because I was interested in your desire for glory and riches. You are not paying me anything, and I did not ask for anything."

"How are we supposed to get back?" Robert asked.

The druid grinned and foretold inquiring. "And who said all of you will return?"

And with that, the druid simply disappeared.

The bards were white with fear. They did not know what to make of the druid's words.

Gamble took a deep breath and opined, "That buffoon told us to go south. Let's just go—and not worry about his words."

The group silently agreed and made way.

After almost a solar cycle's walk, a thick fog covered them. "I believe we have arrived," Gamble acknowledged.

The fog so intense that they couldn't see their feet.

Robert screamed, "Let's stick together!"

The group slowly made their path toward the lake. A slight wind blew away the thick fog, and the water became visible. The group readied their weapons.

"Show yourself, nymph!" Bernard yelled.

There was no answer, but the group did not let their guard down.

"Show yourself! I know you are there!" Gamble yelled.

The dog started barking frantically toward the center of the lake. The group stayed on its toes. Gamble put Thormon behind him as if they were readying for battle.

A gracious hand emerged from the calm waters. And the extended arm followed until a female head with long brown hair became visible. She looked at the group and smiled.

The dog ran away with his tail between his legs.

"Stupid dog! Come back, you coward!" Miguel yelled.

The nymph arose from the water and started to walk sensually toward the bards. There was almost nothing left to the imagination. The nymph only wore jewels and gems to cover her body. The men just stared at her, not knowing what to do.

"What have you brought me, Prodalus? Or should I say who?" She continued walking sensually toward the group.

"Prodalus stays not with us!" Gamble answered.

"Then who speaks for the group?"

"I do!" mumbled Gamble.

She walked closer. Her body revealed more and more.

The bards did not know if they should fight or fall in love. On each occasion she stepped on the lake's surface, they could see the gems' glow from below.

She whispered, "What do you seek, noble warriors?"

"We are not warriors; we are simple bards," Gamble replied.

"Oh my! I haven't seen one in ages."

Gamble froze. His eyes stared directly at her beauty. Her eyes were as green as emeralds, and she looked like a goddess.

She caressed Gamble's face and gently asked, "What do you seek, my noble bard?"

"We seek riches in these lands," Gamble mumbled.

The nymph gave a sweet smile and asked, "You're not here for me?"

"My uncle seeks riches in order to marry a noble girl," Thormon answered.

"Am I not good enough for you?" The nymph caressed Gamble's face and chest.

Robert explained, "He seeks riches for a girl. Each one of us came here for different reasons. I, for example—"

"I do not care what you want. I can see that none of you came here for me," the nymph disclosed in a sad voice.

"We mean you no harm," Miguel added.

The nymph asked, "Am I not beautiful enough for any of you?"

"You are beautiful beyond words, but you are way out of our league," Gamble confessed.

"Thus, if you did not come here for me, I bet you came for what I have." Her tone of voice changed.

"Very well. I have something to ask of you. If you wish for riches, I only ask one thing of you." She switched her voice back to her seductive tone.

"And what would that be?" Thormon asked.

"You are to go south until the Elder Mountains. You'll find a dam that keeps the river Ades from flowing here. When the waters reach me, I shall give you enough riches to make you and five generations after you have a king's life."

Gamble asked, "Therefore, the only thing you wish from us means to destroy a dam?"

She smiled seductively and answered, "Yes!"

"Sounds easy enough," Fabio attested.

"What's the catch?" Robert asked.

"No catch." She started caressing Robert's face.

Thormon could see the nymph's charms enchanted the group. They were at her mercy.

"OK! We'll do it!" Gamble yielded.

The nymph smiled and added, "Great! Before you go, take this." She handed them a yellowish stone. "You will need it to break the dam."

"But what are we to do with this stone?" Robert asked.

She explained, "All you have to do is throw it hard against the wall of rocks."

Gamble took the stone, analyzed it, and asked, "Is it safe?"

The nymph smiled and answered, "As long as you don't throw it at anyone, you're safe."

That said, she returned to the lake's deepness without looking back.

At the time, the mist covered the lake. Gamble carefully put the yellowish stone in the upper pockets of his backpack. Soft clothes surrounded it as they made their route south.

The group walked for a day, following the shallow stream of muddy water where the river used to be. It felt like a calm, slow walk, which they were not used to. Medox barked at every animal he encountered.

Robert, not surprisingly, appeared not to be enjoying the walk. At each point Medox barked at something, he looked around to see what it was.

"No sign of monsters or dire beasts."

Thormon paid close attention to Robert's behavior. Robert looked at the forest as if something terrible kept on following him.

CHAPTER 27

Reconsidering Hamlet's Importance

A fter a day of walking, all they wanted to do was to sit down and relax. Medox suddenly became alert and ran toward the woods.

The group stopped and decided to follow him.

Gamble confessed, "I'm not sure, but it sounds like chatter and kids playing."

"True! There should be no one living here," Fabio added.

The group walked carefully into the woods with weapons in hand.

Thormon pointed out a light coming from a distance. "Torches, maybe? Lamps? A fireplace?"

The group made their way even deeper into the woods and found a small town.

Bernard complained, "A town here? We are in the middle of nowhere!"

The stream crossed the small village and went up the hill to a stone dam.

"The villagers built this place under the shadow of this dam," Gamble noticed.

The town consisted of about four hundred houses built in a baroque or Gothic style. A fence enclosed a herd of sheep and villagers tended vegetable gardens around the small stream.

"Wow! Who would build a town in such a remote place?" Gamble asked.

"Do you believe they were the ones who built the dam?" Thormon asked.

"I don't know. Let's see if we can find the village elder."

En route into the town, they could feel eyes upon them.

The sense of peace in the village felt contagious with mutual grooving. There seemed to be no trash, and mature ladies were mopping the floor. They only saw older people and children.

On each occasion, they approached someone to ask about the place. But the people either ignored them or ran away.

A young girl with long blonde hair and blue eyes approached them and asked, "Where do you come from?"

Gamble smiled and answered, "Hello there! We are travelers from Baldar. Have you heard about that place before?"

The girl looked confused and asked, "Where? Is that somewhere beyond the forest?"

Gamble confirmed, "That's correct! We have been traveling for seasons. We searched for the city of Coloris, but then we left, detouring to this place, which we did not know existed."

"Coloris? I've heard about that place somewhere. Maybe Grandpa will know." The girl grabbed Gamble's hand and walked him toward a house.

"Is he the village elder?" Gamble asked.

The girl smiled and led them, "Come on! Just follow me."

She led them through the park to a two-story house with many windows. The masons and construction workers filled every possible space with stylish windows. It seemed like the house of a public figure.

There was no need to knock on the door, and she just went in. "Please wait here."

The room looked like a meeting hall.

After a moment, she returned with an older man.

"Oh! These are the fellows the whole town stays murmuring about. Sorry about that. We are not used to receiving visitors. So, excuse our rustic manners. Allow me to introduce myself. I'm Ósvaldr." He smiled and showed a mouth with few teeth.

Gamble smiled. "It is all right! I am called Gamble. The others are Julio, Miguel, Fabio, Thormon, Bernard, and the one with the bad temper is Robert."

"I'm curious. What brings a group of young lads to such a place like this?" The timeworn man asked the maid to bring them something to eat and drink.

Gamble confessed, "Well, we've been traveling for seasons. We were looking for the city of Coloris."

"Ah, yes! The city where the elves live. It lingers as famed for housing riches." The older man sipped some tea.

"How do you know about that?" Robert asked.

"You are not the only ones looking for riches," the older man added.

The group turned, intrigued by the older man's answer.

"If you know about the riches, maybe you can tell us about the dam. What appears to be the use of this great dam of yours?" Gamble asked.

"Now then, you can see that about one thousand people are living here. The founders built this dam. Thus, it was already built when I came to this place. People slowly forgot the founding fathers throughout the ages. But their stone dam stands as of great importance to this town. If you climb up there, you will see a great wooden pier and many fishing boats anchored there." He stopped and looked at the men. "I am sure you did not come here just to wonder about this antiquated dam and who built it. Maybe a beautiful woman brought you here."

Gamble opined "You are right. But how exactly, right? Let me talk to my comrades."

"No problem. We are a friendly group. We do not wish or do any harm to others," the mature man walked about and instructed. "Lela, these men want to talk about our future. Let's leave them alone for a moment."

Gamble whispered, "He knows something about us. Somehow, he knows we are here to destroy the dam."

"True! But how?" Fabio asked.

"I don't know. Do you think he subsists as a seer or a diviner?" Bernard asked.

"Who knows? I only know that this dam transpires as the only thing standing between our riches and fame," Miguel opined.

"Well, we could always alert the villagers about some impending disaster. And when they look for shelter in the hills, we break the dam," conjectured Robert.

"But did you not hear the older man? They cannot thrive without fish that the dam harbors," whispered Miguel.

"That would no longer be our problem," whispered Robert.

"Yes, it would be! Don't be so cold and pretend that we are not connected to our actions and the people around us," whispered Julio.

"Then we came all this way for nothing!" spat Robert.

"We are not going to destroy this dam!" Thormon expressed. A long silence followed.

Gamble attested, "It seems not all over yet! What if we look for the cavern of the Cyclops? Perhaps it stands close by. If only I could remember the name of the cursed monster."

"I believe he goes by the name Argus," Thormon remembered.

The group decided to go after the Cyclops and called the older man. The well-worn man asked, "Have you young fellows decided what to do?"

"Yes, we did!" Gamble answered.

"I hope we can sleep safe tonight," the older man wished.

Gamble declared "You have nothing to worry about. We mean you no harm."

The mature man said, "That's great to hear. I believe you will continue your journey toward the volcano."

"Why do we need to go toward the volcano?" Bernard asked.

The older man foretold, "Now then, that's where your journey will take you next."

"Are you sure you know where we need to go?" Gamble asked.

"Aren't you going to slay the Cyclops?" the old man asked.

"Well, we are here seeking the cavern of the Cyclops called Argus," Bernard added.

"Thus, you are warriors! Do you come here to finish that man-eating monster? Or to end his mining activities that pollute all the surroundings?"

"We are only bards—not warriors," Fabio admitted. The others nodded.

The older man hoped optimistically, "But there must be something you could do. You see, the Cyclops polluted the original place we called home, killing all the fish. Today, only ruins remain in the high grounds."

"Oh my! That's terrible!" Gamble commented.

"Is there anything else you can tell us about the Cyclops?" Barnard asked.

"What else is there to say? He destroyed our homes. He made us move to the shadow of this dam and continues to mock us with his ways."

"That's not motive enough to kill him," Thormon opined.

The elderly looked at them and affirmed, "Have you noticed that only children and old ones are around?"

"Why is that? That does seem odd."

The mature man took a deep breath then revealed, "The Cyclops took our homes and polluted our waters. And he also enslaved our young ones."

He looked at his granddaughter. "Those who don't fall victim to him must leave as soon as possible."

The group trembled in shock.

The older man presumed, "I know why you came here, and I also know that a nature-bonded entity gave you another option."

The group did not know what to say.

The well-worn man confessed, "I was never strong enough to do either, but maybe you fellows have a chance to do the right thing."

Gamble explained, "As we said, we are not warriors. We are just simple bards. We have never seen real combat. We got here by chance. We would probably be dead if it hadn't been for my nephew."

The older man's face turned red. "You are nothing more than petty burglars. Just looking for the cursed treasure of Argus or the jewels from that rotten nymph?"

The long silence issued an answer in itself.

"Do what you wish, but don't you dare go near that dam. Countless lives will be lost if you do." Ósvaldr stormed away, leaving the bards alone.

The group did not know what to do.

"We hit a brick wall here," Bernard acknowledged. The others nodded in agreement.

Lela was eavesdropping, and when Ósvaldr left, she showed herself. "I overheard my grandpa. I can help you, but you must promise to rescue my friend."

Gamble came up to her and asked, "Is your friend amongst the captives your grandpa mentioned?"

"Yes! My best friend, Elisa," she replied.

"But how do you want us to help?" Fabio asked.

With tears, she answered, "I know where the cavern is located."

The group looked at her in shock.

Fabio asked, "How does such a pretty girl like yourself know the whereabouts of such a dangerous place?"

"Last season, Argus came down the mountain and raided our village. He took everything he wanted, including Elisa."

Gamble offered, "But how can we help?"

Lela said, "I followed the monster. I know where he lives!"

The group stayed silent.

Lela cried, "She was my only friend! Today forward, I am alone!"

Fabio whispered, "The abduction broke the poor girl's heart."

"I want that monster dead!"Lela snapped.

"Is there anything else you can tell us about the monster?" Gamble asked.

"What else do you want to know? He is a *monster*! Isn't that enough?"

"I apologize for the question, but we have to know what we are up against," Gamble uttered.

The group seemed shocked that Gamble had decided to help the girl without asking the rest of the group.

The girl apologized for how she had answered him and explained what she knew about the beast.

"There is no need to apologize. We are sorry if we caused you any harm," admitted Gamble.

The girl looked up at him and smiled, which melted Gamble's heart.

The rest of the group turned out feeling pretty bad. They currently did not care about anyone or anything else. The only thing on their minds had been riches.

"How are we to help her?" Bernard asked. Gamble fell silent.

"We have to do something right for a change!" Thormon tried to cheer them up.

"The lad appears to be right," Bernard reacted.

Lela asked, "Are you willing to help me?"

"Yes! Of course, we are!" Gamble replied.

Lela ran outside and shouted, "Wait here, then! I will get everything we need, and we'll leave soon!"

"She still didn't say anything that could help us against this monster," Miguel complained.

Gamble replied, "Anyhow. We still need to prepare ourselves for battle."

Moments later, she returned in sturdier clothes with a backpack. And a funny-looking goat followed her.

"I will be your guide!" she affirmed.

"Wait a moment! You never mentioned that you were coming with us!" Gamble replied.

"How else are you to get there?"

"Show us on a map or something!" Bernard replied.

She looked at them and replied, "I don't know how to look at maps."

"But you admitted it was dangerous. How are we to keep you safe?" Gamble asked.

"And to add, you still didn't tell us anything about the beast," Fabio added.

"Well, what ensues that you want to know?"

Gamble clarified, "Any information holds important. Any detail you might know will help us. As you mentioned, he means danger. And like we said, we are not warriors; hence, we must prepare ourselves."

She smiled and replied, "He is a man-eating beast. What I know is what my grandpa told me."

"Speaking of your grandpa, does he know you want to come with us?" Bernard asked.

She revealed, "Of course not! He would never allow it!"

"Are we gonna get in trouble for taking you with us?" Thormon asked.

She looked at Thormon and deduced, "In any case, you are with them—and you came through such a long track. I believe that they are more than capable of protecting me."

Thormon smiled and was about to reveal, "Well, they are here, but it's all because of—"

"Us! We know how to handle things!" Gamble interrupted.

"You are safe with us. Don't worry!" Fabio added.

The girl smiled and hugged Gamble. "As I tried to say, my grandpa told me that Argus comes to pass as a bad-tempered beast, which could be an advantage for us."

"What about where he lives? Is there anything we should know?" Miguel asked.

"His place sustains naturally occurring traps. Thus, the enslaved people could not escape, but I saw where they were. I can help you avoid such traps."

"Good! Do you have any poison?" Fabio asked.

"Why do you ask?"

"That's how we intend to take him down," Fabio answered.

The girl smiled shyly and replied, "He stays immune to poison."

The group fell silent for a moment.

"We also have that yellowish stone the nymph gave us," Gamble disclosed.

"True! If it can destroy a dam, it will definitely kill a beast," Bernard replied.

Surprised, the girl looked at them and asked, "Were you here to destroy the dam?"

"No!"

Thormon whispered, "Uncle, the explosive only works when it hits a rock."

Gamble looked at everyone and asked Lela to leave for a moment. They needed to plan what to do, and a pretty girl like her would only distract them.

The group talked for a while and planned out everything. They called Lela and stated that they were ready to leave.

As Lela walked them out of the city, the shaggy goat was gnawing on a thin branch.

Miguel asked, "Is that goat coming with us all the way?"

Lela smiled and replied, "She is my pet, Duchess."

"Oh! Did you see that hound that follows us around? That's my pet, Medox."

"Is she going to be a problem?" Thormon pushed the goat away.

"Of course not! She is our secret weapon!" Lela replied with a smile. Lela turned to the group at the stairs and instructed, "From here on out, it looks like uphill holds the only choice."

The stairs led to the vast dam's top, filling the high-altitude crater. Towering rocks fringed it like water trapped in a gigantic pan. From a distance, they could see many fishermen casting their nets.

"Just think… we could have destroyed this dam," Fabio whispered.

Miguel nudged him to stay quiet.

Lela looked back but did not pay attention to Fabio's remark. The wind got stronger as they went uphill. Cacti dotted the scenery. But the undergrowth never blocked the trail. The constant activity of the fishermen cleared it.

Lela appeared passionate and ready for anything. Gamble quickly fell in love with her cheerful and helpful mood. She was always ready to help and showed how brave she could be. No ordinary girl would dare to approach a Cyclops.

Gamble kept staring at the girl who seemed precocious and matured beyond her low twenties years of age. Her juvenile beauty was shown in her smile and her body was that of a woman, one could see.

"She's quite a looker, isn't she, Uncle?" Thormon asked.

Gamble took a deep breath. Then answered, "Well, look at those long, round, strong, perfect legs and that curly blonde hair. She's beautiful in every manner."

Thormon smiled and asked, "What about the other girl we are doing this for?"

Gamble didn't answer. He looked mesmerized, drowning in Lela's bright blue eyes.

Thormon slapped his uncle and told him to snap out of it.

Gamble smiled and soliloquied, "I've got to know this girl better. Is the goat of any assistance?"

Lela smiled and answered, "She just likes to follow me around. I've been taking care of her since she was young."

Gamble and Lela talked about each other as they made their pathway toward the volcano. Gamble appeared curious about how the people got to where they were.

The group caught up and asked her what life seemed like in such a small place. Where the youngsters who were not caught went, and how there were still children in such a place. Lela explained that they didn't always live under the dam. They used to live higher up.

She answered every question happily and then turned to Gamble. "Someone like you must have a beautiful girl waiting back home, right?"

Gamble smiled but kept unwilling to talk about his complicated situation.

Robert came about willing to explain the reason for the entire journey.

Thormon verified, "There is a nymph far from the dam. Did you know that?"

Lela replied she never heard about that.

They told her a bit about their journey and how they ended up there. "I'm pleased I got to meet you all, especially you, Gamble," she revealed.

Gamble's face turned red.

Julio asked, "Once you find your friend, will you leave the hamlet?"

She rebuked, "What will you do once we save my friend and loot some of the Cyclops' treasure?"

Gamble smiled and disclosed, "In any case, I could find a nice girl, settle down, and raise a family, but I will not lie to you. I find it difficult to stay in one place for over two seasons. I love traveling from the Western to the Eastern world and back again. In order to check out the wonders of each culture."

Julio, Robert, Bernard, and Miguel all shared similar ideas. They were all free-spirited men.

Thormon attested he didn't care lots about the treasure or riches. All he wanted was an adventure.

Lela confessed, "Well, I guess most of my long-gone friends think—or thought—the same. They all wanted to see the world and go on adventures."

Before they could add anything else, they felt a cold breeze with grinding teeth. Each breath felt heavy, labored, and inefficient. And the cold air burned their lungs, producing vapor as one exhaled.

"Are we there yet?" asked Thormon.

Lela shook her head.

Gamble replied, "I believe not, kid."

A thick mist started coming down the mountain, and Lela instructed them to seek for shelter. The trail was getting very narrow, and it would be painful to fall at that point. It should be perilous to continue under such circumstances.

"It should be better for us to stop at the ancient city." Lela pointed in the direction they should go.

As they made their route to the city, Thormon asked, "Lela, is that the ancient city that Ósvaldr talked about?"

She replied, "Yes, that's where we should go!"

The group stayed there overnight. And so, Lela took the opportunity to describe her plan. Then, she was pleased to talk about the Cyclops and everything she saw in the cave.

As they made their way around the fireplace, Lela professed, "This place was built hundreds of seasons ago. As you can see, it isn't as far from the lake as where we live currently."

"But how did this city come about?" Miguel asked.

Lela explained, "In this place, one day, a druid came to the humans and offered help. The only direction out was to go up the mountain."

"But wouldn't the centaurs or the dark lord follow?" Thormon asked.

She replied, "Well, this druid had the help of an elf and a Cyclops."

"Is it the same Cyclops we are going to face?" Gamble asked.

Lela nodded. "He wasn't always this evil."

Fabio asked, "But he helped build this place just to later run everyone out of their homes? Where were this druid and elf? Are there additional things we'll face?"

"The druid and the elf were long gone before the Cyclops became evil."

"What made this Cyclops evil?" Fabio asked.

"Some say it was because of the dam. Some unknown thing cursed him for building it. Some say that the dark lord got a hold of him. And others say that the mountain cursed the city and transformed the Cyclops."

The group's determination sank heavily like a shifting weight on their tired backs for a moment.

Gamble took her hand and looked deep into her eyes. "Could this curse affect us? I don't mean to hurt or harm you."

Lela looked at him and smiled. "It only affects people with evil in their hearts—as superstition goes."

They all looked at Robert and were a bit concerned.

Lela asked, "Why does everyone seems to be looking at him?"

Gamble inquired, "In accordance, what appears to be the plan?"

Lela grabbed a stick and started to draw on the ground. "There withstands a smaller entrance, a natural vent that leads deeper into the mountain. I have to warn you that I never had the guts to go farther than a few heads of distance into it."

Fabio shouted, "What? You mean to tell us you've never been inside that place?"

Robert complained, "But you told us you knew how to get inside and what was inside."

Lela indicated, "You see, there situates the front entry to the Cyclops' lair."

"We don't care about a front, back, or side entrance!" Miguel expressed.

Gamble added, "You lied to us! You told us you knew the place and what awaited us."

"Let's just go back." Miguel started collecting his things.

Lela started to cry. "You were the only ones who could help me save my friend! No one else will help me, and no one will come from the outside to aid us. Please! I beg of you. Stay and help!" She tried to hold them back.

The group gave her no attention.

Gamble gave her a sad look and confessed, "You could have told me the truth."

"Let's go, everyone!" Fabio yelled.

As the group started to leave, the fog stayed thicker. They could barely see a palm tree in front of them.

Gamble turned to Thormon and asked if he could see anything, but Thormon protested the mist was too thick for anyone to see.

Gamble took a deep breath and suggested, "We'll have to spend the night here. There seems no way we can return in this fog."

The rest of the group did not like the idea, but since they couldn't go anywhere, they decided to take shelter nearby.

"I do not want to stay anywhere close to that girl!" Miguel spat as they made their path to the ruins of a church.

"OK! Let's start a fire and wait this out," Fabio suggested. The others agreed.

Gamble could hear Lela crying in the distance. "Did we really need to treat her that badly?"

Miguel complained, "We are not warriors! We are just a bunch of regular men. We are bards, for Pete's sake!"

Gamble considered her side, "But still… she did this out of love. We were the only people to have appeared in this place for ages."

Thormon protested, "Uncle, we are no match for a Cyclops. We barely made it here. Imagine going up against such a beast."

Fabio concurred, "The kid has a point. We only agreed to do this because we thought it would be easy."

Gamble was still not convinced they had done the right thing and decided to go see Lela.

CHAPTER 28

Familiar Threat

I t was night, and the small party set camp inside an ancient church. Thormon decided to explore the out-of-date building. He walked around and saw many rooms. He tried to see if he could find anything interesting inside this place.

There could be hidden treasures inside this place, he thought. He continued to search until he came across a strange wall.

"This looks like an awfully thick wall between these two rooms," he checked while knocking on the wall. He noticed that the sound accused a hollow compartment. The kid called the others and told them about his findings, and they started to take notice of it.

Bernard looked at the wall and conjectured, "It looks like someone built this section later."

"Indeed, it does!" confirmed Julio.

"Do you still have your hammer?" Fabio asked Bernard.

"Yes," he replied.

"Then take down the wall!"

The noise of breaking stones sounded distinct.

"*Hush!* Remember the four-armed hairy beast that was following us? It can hear us and track us!" Robert informed, worried.

"Don't worry, Robert. There is not and never was anything following us. It was just your mind playing tricks on you," Miguel replied as they continued to break the wall.

Robert, still worried, asked, "Why did your dog start barking like crazy?"

"I don't know. The noise probably could be disturbing him," answered Miguel.

"Well, do something about it!" commanded Robert angrily.

"You do it!" rebuked Miguel, hitting the wall with the hammer.

"All right! I will quiet down that stupid mutt!" Robert got up and went outside the church. When Robert got close to the dog, it cried and ran away. "You stupid mutt! It's me! Come back here!" he shouted.

Little did he realize that a giant shadow stood upon him. He felt something strange and evil in the idle air. He turned around to a towering, ten-heads-tall monster with four arms and a foul breath. The beast opened its big mouth to full length. Robert stared at it, speechless, and then fainted without making a sound.

Inside the church, Bernard took down the wall and decided to look inside. He found a dusty wooden bookshelf with three tomes. Also, there were four wine bottles in excellent condition. This place seemed to be a small storage room long abandoned. Looking closer, they could see that all the books had the same subject but in different languages.

"*Asylum Untainted by Imaculus*. Isn't Imaculus that dark lord Lela talked about?" asked Thormon.

"Wow, this must be at least a thousand seasons old," Fabio mused.

Bernard decided to look at the fireplace and couldn't see Robert. "Where in the world did Robert go? It's tranquil at present. I'd better see if that bum didn't kill the dog or isn't drugging himself."

Meanwhile, the beast stood tired of waiting at the front hall and entered the church, one step at a turn. Unaware, Bernard was searching for Robert and the dog when he noticed a growing shadow.

"Is it you, Robert?" asked Bernard, noticing the shadow growing closer. But an awful stench alarmed the bard, who stood up to face the monster— but the beast was swift and hit Bernard's nape, putting the man unconscious.

The discovery of the books distracted the rest of the company. It was a valuable find, worth a lot of gold.

"This means these items are worth the journey. We're going to be rich with these books!" Miguel riveted.

But before celebrating, they heard a strange noise from the front hall.

"Is that you, Robert?" Miguel asked.

Before there echoed an answer, Thormon pointed in terror, "What befalls over there?"

He gestured, pointing at the big black bush close to the altar. Miguel and Fabio saw the monster crawling on its six limbs. As it perceived the glares from the party, it stood up.

"Get back, guys!" shouted Miguel, pointing his war hammer at the monster and stepping closer to the threat. He swung the hammer, but the beast countered his blow with a mighty claw. That disarmed the bard and made the hammer fly to the hall. It hit the table before falling onto the ground.

"Run! Find your uncle and Lela and leave this place!" Miguel shouted.

The monster cornered them with its four arms extended as if to catch any escaping humans.

The end is close now! If only I had my sword at the ready! thought Thormon, realizing his weapons were in his pack by the fire, like everybody else's.

But something appeared very wrong about this hairy beast, as if some high-intelligence awareness was somewhere present in its soul. That peculiarity came out as humanlike facial expressions and gestures. The giant four-armed monster let loose a burst of sinister laughter. And, in a matter of a few beats of an eagle's wings, transmuted back into the familiar figure of Prodalus.

"I got you! You should see the looks on your faces!" joked the druid, laughing uncontrollably.

"*You bastard!* It was you all along, wasn't it?" realized Thormon, trying to calm down.

"You nearly gave me a heart attack. I can barely stand up," Miguel added.

"What kind of sick joke are you playing?" Fabio asked.

"Why do you think no threat approached your way? I was merely protecting you fools with this illusion. I wanted to pay you back for what you did to that poor, sweet girl," the druid replied with a feeling of accomplishment.

Lela and Gamble came running toward the commotion and saw the bards and Thormon looking as pale as snow.

"What the heck happened here?" Gamble asked.

The group did not answer. They could hear only the druid's laughter resonating.

"Do you know this trickster?" asked Lela.

"Yes, that's Prodalus the Green," Gamble introduced the mage.

"What did you do to them?" Lela asked, looking at the druid.

"I saw how they treated you, young lady, and I felt a little bad. I wanted to teach them a lesson. Nice trick, wasn't it?" the druid answered with a smile.

"A *lesson*? You nearly gave us a heart attack. That monster could have killed us!" Fabio complained.

"Oh, please! That was no monster. It was just an illusion of one," the druid replied.

"What brings you here?" Gamble asked, interrupting the whole ordeal.

"I'm here to ensure you accomplished your errand," answered the druid as he healed and recuperated the knocked-out men with his staff.

"How do you know about our errand?" Gamble asked with a confused look on his face.

"Well, the forest creatures told me. And it got me a little worried," the druid replied. He stopped and thought for a moment and added, "But you folks are bards. You guys can't cause harm to a small ant—unless that small ant should be a lady," the druid jested, winking his eye at Gamble.

Gamble blushed and quickly dismissed the druid's words.

Thormon stepped in and contested, "But my uncle used to be a ranger!"

The druid stopped and stared at Gamble for a while. "I know those eyes. You looked quite unfamiliar back in the days," the druid mentioned, not wanting to reveal Gamble's story.

The group fell silent for a bit.

"We still have a problem!" Thormon alleged, breaking the silence.

"That's right. The dam dwells way over there. Isn't that what you came here for?" the druid asked.

"True! But we didn't know there were people around it," Gamble explained in a shy tone.

"What? What do you mean by that?" asked Lela.

The group seemed utterly embarrassed. They did not want to reveal their true intent.

The druid stepped in and spilled the beans. As he explained what he asked of them, Lela became angrier and angrier while the bards shriveled up in shame.

"How dare you lecture me about being honest?" she scolded them.

"No, no, we did not know there was a village depending on the dam," Miguel replied.

"It's true. Once we saw that there were people. We gave up on that plan," Fabio concluded, trying to explain himself.

"Anyhow, you mean to tell me that if you hadn't seen a person, you would've destroyed a dam?" Lela angrily asked.

"That's not what we meant," Miguel added.

"We are not bad people, lady. We just wanted the treasure promised. And the druid brought us to the nymph," Gamble stated.

"True, miss. My uncle and these bards are not bad people. Stupid but not bad," Thormon articulated, trying to explain his actions.

The druid looked at them and rebuked, "Don't blame me. You guys asked me to bring you there. What you decided to do was of your own accord."

Lela walked away in anger, and Gamble chased after her.

"Nice going, you dumb druid. At once, I believe you did greater harm to her than us," Fabio protested.

"You should've kept your mouth shut!" Miguel added.

The druid did feel a little bad for making things worse. "Me and my big mouth. Should've learned by now to keep it shut," he mumbled.

"Let's just hope she forgives us," Bernard said in a low tone.

No one spoke a word throughout the moon cycle. Everyone just turned around and went to sleep. On the other hand, Gamble stood out there, trying to explain himself. Lela asked him who he was and why he would want to go on such a dangerous journey and do such horrible things.

Gamble spent all the moon cycle explaining who he used to be and how he had changed his ways. And that went on throughout the night.

The morning rose with the sun upon them, and they all had a tough question: wouldn't they help the girl?

They all reunited around the fireplace for breakfast to talk.

"Thus, Druid, you came here to help us, right?" asked Thormon.

"Well, in a manner of speaking, yes," the druid answered.

"We already established that no dam is getting blown," Miguel remarked.

"And we are not going to back off on this quest," Thormon added.

The group stayed silent for a moment, but the silence broke, interrupted by Lela.

"Oh! I knew you all had superior hearts!" she praised them with a smile and tears in her eyes.

The group didn't know what to say.

"I promised her I was going to help. But thank you all for pitching in," Gamble mentioned thankfully.

At this point, the rest of the bards couldn't back out. They were too embarrassed to do so, and the druid stepped in before it got weirder for them.

"Argus consists the makings of a formidable foe. None of you would stand a chance alone," the druid advised.

"But what about you, old-fashioned man? Aren't you some kind of mage?" Fabio asked.

"Yeah! You can turn into a monster and kill him or something," Miguel added.

The druid looked at them and confessed, "If that were the case, I would never need you. You see, the Cyclops controls a power node. Something that disrupts my magic, making me as useless as you bunch. Furthermore, that specific node helps him forge magical items inside that little volcano. In other words, it's considerably more difficult than you think."

The group stared thoughtfully at the mountain, wondering what they could do to best the Cyclops.

"It would be pointless to go in daylight," Gamble opined.

"True! We have to think of a plan of action," Robert added.

They stayed inside the church, discussing the method to approach the Cyclops' lair. The druid and Lela helped out as much as they could. Throughout the morning, they gathered all the resources. And also materials required in their creepy, abandoned place.

The fire dimmed until it produced no further visible flame, just sizzling smoke. The night fell with the twilights. It was the moment to go up the mountain. The group readied themselves and started the journey.

After a couple of beats of an eagle's wings in the pitch dark, they reached the crossway to the cavern's entrance. On the opposite side of the front entrance, there was a derelict, surreptitious path leading to a vent tunnel.

"This is where we split up. Thormon, Lela, and I go to the vent; the rest of you go to the front entrance. And remember—keep yourselves safe," Gamble counseled.

They all wished each other good luck and went to their established positions. The druid hugged all of them as if he stood saying his last goodbyes.

CHAPTER 29

Alternative Entrance and Two Fronts

"Here we are," Lela whispered, pointing out the vent.

The tunnel seemed shaped round at the edges, typical of natural erosion work. The light and air penetrated both sides of the tunnel, facilitating the task. The white moonlight shone from outside and red lava glowed from inside. The temperature changed from cold to warm, and the thickness of the tunnel varied a little.

"Quick! Don't forget the layout as you crawl inside," Lela pleaded as Gamble entered, followed by Thormon.

She ushered them through an opening in the mountain. And before entering herself, she lit up an arrow. It signaled to the waiting party that they were going inside.

I hope this works. Lela thought as she shot the arrow in the air. On the other end…

The other party members arrived at the designated place. They hid behind a rock and analyzed their options. The druid went over the plan once again as they waited. He saw an open area without any structure to hide behind and, farther ahead, a big, deep ditch filled with incinerated filth. A low fire still burned deep within the ditch.

"That's probably where Argus discards his litter," Fabio conjectured.

"How could anyone get across such a pit?" wondered Robert.

The mage saw a big wooden bridge stacked against the wall on the far side.

"There remains a bridge, but on the other side." The druid paused and added, "The cyclops can withstand the weight, being the only one strong enough to move it. That's not going to work for us. We have to find something else."

"I have an idea. What if we found a long tree trunk and rolled it over the pit, much like a makeshift bridge?" suggested Fabio.

"Where would we find one? And most important, how would we carry it?" Robert replied.

Prodalus saw a long bamboo and attested, "That bamboo holds perfect!"

"Are you kidding me? It would break, even if we were thirty-seasons-old children!" disbelieved Robert.

Prodalus smiled and challenged, "I dare you to break it!"

"Hand it over!" requested the bard, and putting his full strength to the task, he found out that the hollow bamboo was as tough as an iron bar. "What did you do to it?" asked Robert, puzzled.

"Now then, let's just say it has become ironwood," the druid replied.

"But isn't your magic useless here, old man?" Fabio asked.

"It's weak here and useless inside," the druid answered.

"Our means of entry and retreat are secured," whispered Robert from behind the druid.

"Well, that would take care of the pit, but we would still be vulnerable and easily spotted by Argus," conjectured the mage.

"At the moment, we need to create the distraction," explained Bernard.

"But wait—we still need the signal," Fabio hung around as he looked into the distance. Before he could say anything else, he saw a flaming arrow fly off the horizon.

Gamble, Thormon, and Lela crawled for three hundred heads of distance. Window-like holes on the tunnel's side showed the lair's vastness.

"This is as far as I went," confessed Lela.

Looking down, they could see they were close to the ceiling of an enormous chamber. A small lake of lava was visible at the hall's center, where a massive anvil and many hammers lay nearby. On the far edge of the room, a narrow stream of churning waters crossed the lower floor, going underground.

"Such a perfect setting for a smith's workhouse. He has heat and cold and the means to shape metal," Gamble whispered.

"We must keep going. It's farther in," demanded Lela, pushing Thormon, who consequently pushed Gamble.

After about six hundred heads, the course swerved left. Then, the slope became steep, going downward.

"This ensues when we stop and wait for the commotion. We won't be able to retreat from the entrance we came in," Gamble realized, feeling tense over what could come to pass. Before he could say anything else, they heard thumps and a loud, monstrous scream.

"That's our cue!" Thormon acknowledged tensely.

Gamble, Thormon, and Lela slid down a steep slope. Gamble hit the floor hard, followed by Thormon and Lela.

"Sorry about that, Uncle," Thormon whispered as he got off his uncle.

Before his uncle could say anything, Lela came flying into him. Gamble helped himself up and then helped Lela.

"Now, where to?" Gamble asked.

Lela reluctantly pointed in the right direction. They moved out of the hole and entered a small chamber. As they entered the chamber, Lela's face became pale. Nothing took place there except dozens of skeletons piled up against the wall. Lela's heart sank, and she froze in fear.

"Are you gonna be OK?" Gamble asked while trying to calm her.

With her eyes filled with tears, she mumbled, "One of those skeletons could be Elisa's."

Thormon and Gamble looked at her and, with a sorry look, Gamble replied, "Let's hope not."

"There are additional chambers to look at," Thormon added. "Lela, we will find her! I believe she lives. The one-eyed giant captured her not long ago."

"She would not have turned into dry bone in just a few days. Those are ancient skeletons," affirmed Gamble. He tried to see things from a better perspective.

"But why would the monster kill these people? It doesn't make sense," she asked, not believing what she witnessed.

"I can only guess the slaves outlived their usefulness," answered Thormon.

Then Gamble added, "This monster needs healthy, fit, strong males for his ironwork. And females for mundane chores."

Lela did not reply. She looked around and pointed to the subsequent chambers. From here on, it was pure guessing.

They were sneaking through the chamber. They discovered it only led to a narrower hall, although high enough to accommodate the one-eyed giant. Looking at the ground, Gamble noticed smaller, fresh footprints.

"Quick! This direction!" instructed Gamble, following the prints.

As they walked down the path, the sound of a metal rattle against stone became louder. They came up to a bigger chamber and saw a number of tunnels. Its remarkable state indicated that Argus was a very ancient creature. Or that he had many extra enslaved people. In reality, though, it was a combination of both. The group became speechless, and before long, they heard the slaves speak.

"Let's hope Argus likes this alloy veins," overjoyed a coarse male voice.

"Let me see. Yes, he will probably feed us tonight if we show him this," said another male voice.

"Why won't anyone come here and help us?" a third voice asked.

The group heard a thump as if the person who said that hit hard ore.

"Shut up! You know what happens to people who think like that."

"Besides, no one in that stupid town dares to come up here. This is it. We are doomed here," another voice replied in despair.

The group quietly followed the voices and mining noises, going deeper into the earth. They soon came to a low-lit chamber. They quickly made out that these were the people they had heard. The group saw a myriad of tunnels. These wound deep into the chain of mountains in every direction and angle.

"How are we supposed to find anyone here?" Lela asked in despair.

Thormon and Gamble sneakily looked around to see if they could find any female figures.

"Maybe we should try to ask," Thormon insinuated.

"That won't be a sound idea. Look at them. They are bound to a thick metal chain connected to a massive ball. They might panic if they see us and cause a great fuss," Gamble replied while trying to think of another plan.

Before he could say anything else, Thormon went up to the nearest one in an attempt to free him.

"What are you doing?" complained the man.

"What does it look like? I'm attempting to free you!" Thormon attested, taken by surprise.

"Yes! But don't you think my pickax could break this chain?" the man replied.

"So, do it. We'll help you out," Thormon replied.

"You and who else?" the man asked.

"We have a group here. We came to rescue everyone," Thormon offered.

Before he could say anything else, Gamble rushed in and took Thormon away.

"Can't you see that if they wanted to, they could free themselves? They don't go out of fear," Gamble attested.

The people in this area just gave them a depressing look. Gamble knew what a place like this did to a person.

"There seems to be no hope for these people. Fear dominates them. They will only see freedom through death," Gamble added, quietly moving.

Before they left, they heard a voice say, "Before you go, let me warn you. There stays only one entry in and out. And Argus controls that. I am sure you already know it, or else you would not be here."

"At least Argus will have something to eat tonight," mocked the mediocre slave with a weak laugh. That indicated he stood on the edge of madness.

Gamble paid no attention to it. But he looked at Lela and Thormon and noticed they were terrified about their decision.

"There seems to be the point of no return, no going back now! You convinced us into that. You must pull yourself together," Gamble told Lela and Thormon.

Hence, they made their path through the tunnels, approaching several captured people. No one seemed keen on leaving, and Lela's friend was nowhere to be found.

CHAPTER 30

The Plan Began with Unexpected Results

The night was still young, and the bard's plan was in full motion.

"Come out here, you freak show!" shouted Bernard, running from side to side along the pit.

The sound echoed inside, and Argus quickly took notice. "Oh! I think some puny human wants to take me on. Did those villagers grow some courage to face me?" soliloquied Argus, throwing his food to the ground.

Argus stood up, stretched himself, and looked at the humans serving him. "Looks like you will cook some of your townsfolk tonight!"

With that, Argus stormed out.

The noise of thundering steps became louder by the beat of an eagle's wings. The shaking ground and ceiling produced lifted dirt, similar to consecutive earthquakes. A colossal figure appeared in the far hall. The monster had curly brown hair connecting with a full-grown curly beard. It had a round hazel eye above the nose, a stocky body, and muscular limbs. His head touched the high ceiling. With an imponent posture, Argus looked down and saw Bernard. The man mocked the Cyclops and threw stones toward him.

"Do you not know who I am?" Argus roared.

Bernard picked up another stone and threw one right at Argus's chest. "Yeah! You are some puny sissy that feeds on the weak. Come and face a real man!"

Argus' blood started to boil. "How dare you!"

Before he could finish, a stone flew onto Argus's eye. The monster became further enraged. He started punching the walls and the ground and yelled, "I will tear you apart, limb by limb!"

Argus picked up a rock and threw it at the bard, but his attempts fell short.

"You can't even throw a stupid rock. You are weak and useless!!" Bernard voiced, laughing.

Argus became even more enraged. He picked up a boulder and threw it toward Bernard, missing him again.

"You better get that stupid eye checked, you overgrown, one-eyed, fat monkey!" Bernard quickly remarked.

Argus did not hesitate to grab the massive wooden bridge, which rested against the far wall, to lay it over the ditch. "I will teach you the meaning of respect, little worm!" shouted Argus, laying down the bridge.

Bernard turned around and sprinted as quickly as he could into the woods. At the same time, Argus started to cross the bridge and gave chase. The monster passed by the druid and the bards. They could see the immense beast with a big head towering over the level of the tree boughs. He shoved trees and vegetation aside, scanning the place for the little rat of a man.

"Stay here, Julio, and keep an eye out for the beast while we go in," instructed the mage, placing the bamboo aside.

The druid placed the ironwood on the bridge. And called out for the others to walk across the bridge the Cyclops had left.

"Let's hope he trips on this," the druid coveted as the last bard crossed.

"Yeah! Let's hope he falls into this pit filled with scorching coals and filth," Robert expected.

"Oh my! The reek of rotten corpses feels just too great. How could anyone or anything live in a place like this?" Fabio added.

The group waved at Julio, showing they were ready for the next phase of their plan. Julio waved back but could not keep his thoughts and eyes away from the pit. The maggots feasting on decaying matter got him even further worried.

Let's hope we are not the next ones thrown in there, Julio thought.

CHAPTER 31

Penetrating The Belly of The Beast

Back in the inner chambers, Thormon, his uncle, and Lela left the mining tunnels. And they pressed on, going toward something that looked like better-looking quarters. They tiptoed in and saw statues adorning the hall here and there, such as the high gods from above the clouds.

"Wow! Where did he get such statues?" Lela whispered in surprise.

"I've only read about such wonders in one of my father's scrolls," Thormon replied.

The group looked around and saw many strange statues. One of them held a trident and another wore a peculiar dark helmet.

Thormon took a good look and told his uncle and Lela, "I know who and what these statues represent. And it's nothing good."

"Let's move, then," his uncle commanded, pointing to another chamber.

They quietly entered the next chamber. They found mirrors of every shape and form there—distorted, blurred, and elongated.

Lela quickly ran up to one. She took a decent look at herself and saw that she appeared prettier in that reflection. "Odd. I don't remember being this beautiful," she confessed.

Thormon took a good look around and warned, "Stop! These are no ordinary mirrors. We have to be careful. I read something about these kinds of mirrors in one of my father's books in the library. Who would've thought that they still existed?"

Lela and Gamble quickly made their route to Thormon and asked him what to do. Thormon explained some magic properties the mirrors had. From what he knew and had read, some of those mirrors were windows to various places. And others were to the soul itself.

"We have to be careful what to look for," Thormon advised as he looked around.

Suddenly, the mirror showed a reflection of their images. And it oddly changed to a big figure of a chubby humanoid.

"Good God! Is it Argus over there?" Gamble asked as dread froze him.

But the figure vanished as Thormon walked toward the image. "Where? Where do you see him?" asked the boy.

"Never mind; just a distorted reflection, like you said," Gamble replied.

But suddenly, an image of a mature man in a green robe appeared in the same mirror. He seemed to come from a different direction. The group stared for a bit, and Thormon conjectured, "I believe this mirror holds a window to the entrance."

"Is that… Prodalus?" asked Gamble, but before he could think of anything, he saw the image of Robert, followed by Fabio and Miguel. Gamble smiled and added, "Looks like they could trick the Cyclops out."

"How can we get to them?" Lela asked.

"These mirrors are windows; they probably connect this whole place. Look! There are those enslaved people we passed by," Thormon made evident, pointing to an enthralling mirror. Gamble and Lela realized that each mirror showed a chamber.

Thormon looked around for a small mirror. "From what I read, there seems to be one mirror that connects everything. Help me find it."

Lela screamed out for Thormon. She happened to be holding something that looked like what he had described.

"Quick! Let me check this. Lela, go to an eye-mirror and see if you can find me," Thormon requested.

Lela ran around the place until she could find Thormon's image. "That's our communication window," Thormon realized. He quickly explained how everything worked.

"OK, Lela, you stay behind and help us out," Gamble instructed while plotting another plan.

"Yeah! I'll keep track of who passes by and inform you if Argus returns," Lela replied.

Thormon and his uncle nodded and worked their route to the next chamber. The round room had a giant metal throne, big enough to accommodate the one-eyed giant. And it had an enormous table with metal legs and thick glass. No need for lamps, as a big hole in the high dome-like ceiling let through the sun's light at its zenith.

"Someone comes this way!" warned Gamble.

Thormon turned to the mirror and asked who it was. Lela replied it was one of the slaves.

"Anyhow, where should we go?" Gamble asked.

"I don't know. There are too many mirrors to keep track of. But from what it looks like, if you continue in that direction, you are bound to run into them," Lela replied.

Thormon and Gamble continued their route quietly toward the directions Lela had given.

***

With the druid's group, Prodalus and company walked through a kitchen. Next, they saw a big cauldron and a poor young woman. She seemed chained next to the big metal pot. Miguel approached her and, without hesitating, hit his ax on the chain, freeing the enslaved woman.

"What have you done? You have brought doom to me," complained with dismay the shabby girl.

"You do not wish to be free, young one?" asked Prodalus.

"You don't understand. Argus has eyes all over this place, and the punishment for escaping entails cruel death!" she granted, terrified.

"Argus is not here. We lured him out. I think we'll have enough time to get everyone out," Miguel hoped for the best.

"Don't worry; we also have a mage with us!" added Robert.

"What do you seek here?" she asked, not wanting to leave.

"Well, we are trying to rescue a girl and whoever else we can," affirmed Miguel.

The girl stared at the four men. Her gaze shifted from Robert to Fabio and lingered on Prodalus. At the same time, she perused their faces and gauged their reasons. "A group of men like yourselves wouldn't just come here to rescue a girl."

"They are here for the gold. As for me, I'm here to save anyone I can," Prodalus replied.

The additional men were a bit embarrassed. And the look the girl gave them made them feel even further ashamed.

"Enough of chitchat. We need to hurry. The monster will soon return!" warned Prodalus, concealing his agony.

She nodded her head and agreed to follow Prodalus.

Thormon and Gamble made their pathway across the chambers. They tried to convince the slaves to go with them but to no avail.

"Let's just leave them here," Gamble suggested.

"I hope Lela's friend shows a different mental condition than these slaves," Thormon added as they made their route.

"Quick, Lela, check where the support group stays," Gamble demanded.

Lela quickly ran around the room, trying to find out where the other party should be.

"I don't know! I lost them!" Lela cried out.

Before Gamble could say anything, he bumped into Prodalus. "Hail, Prodalus!" greeted Gamble, getting up from the floor.

"Good to see you're still alive, but what about Lela?" Prodalus asked, helping Gamble up.

"You know Lela?" the girl asked, surprised.

"Yeah! She was the one who convinced us to come here," Gamble replied.

"Wait for an instant! Are you Lela's friend?" Miguel asked, surprised.

Prodalus interrupted everyone and asked again, "Where dwells Lela?"

The group quieted down and looked at Prodalus. Then, Thormon explained what Lela was doing.

"Oh! I see. Give me that mirror!" Prodalus demanded, taking the mirror from Thormon's hand. He looked at it well, but before he could communicate through it, Lela came in, screaming, "Argus returned this direction, he could be here soon! It looks like he stopped chasing that weird guy."

The bards stayed in silence. That could mean only one thing—he either ran away or fell killed.

Before anyone could say anything else, Lela screamed, "You found her!"

"Leave the reunion for later! At present, we have to leave!" Prodalus ordered, killing the mood.

"But before we leave, we cannot go empty-handed. Where are Argus's riches?" asked Robert.

Elisa answered while trying to contain her happiness. "Well, Argus always lingers in this room. Always counting something and then pushing something away."

"That's rather peculiar," noted Prodalus, pondering, trying to use logic to find the solution.

"If I were the giant beast, what would I do?" Thormon tried to interpret as he looked around. He saw a bulky seat with massive plates concealing something like a box.

"Quick! We don't have much time!" Lela pleaded in a panic, endeavoring to hurry everything up.

"Sit there, Uncle!" Thormon requested, pointing to the throne-like seat. "OK!" agreed Gamble, running toward the seat. He knew Thormon was up to something, and as soon as he sat there, both heard a clicking sound.

The group ran around the room, trying to find where that sound originated. When Prodalus shouted, pointing to an opening on the edge of the round wall. Thormon ran toward it and set out to push it open; the others also followed him.

Lela, still in a panic, screamed, "Hurry up!"

The group pried the door open and saw that there were many rooms in this place.

"Do you believe that this seems a route out or a way to the treasure?" Gamble asked Elisa.

Before she could answer, an imposing ranger came running, then screamed, "We have to leave right away!"

They heard a loud thump and then a scream that echoed, "I know you weaseled into my domain, you rat!"

The group froze in terror.

"We won't be able to go out that direction!" Prodalus conjectured in a panic. "Quick, everyone, into this secret room!"

The group quickly rushed inside and pushed the door shut before Argus entered the room.

"I know you are in here! I will find you and eat your bones, as I did with your friend!" Argus shouted sarcastically.

The group didn't know what to say or how to react. Prodalus quietly hushed them inward under Argus's thumps and screams.

The secret passage led to a narrow tunnel inclined downward, going to the center of a volcano. The central chamber was the forging room. Where it was, the small lava lake fed the needed heat. And the small underground river fed the much-needed cold. They spotted the small vent holes on the high wall, close to the ceiling where Thormon, his uncle, and Lela had come through.

"That could be our route out," Gamble quietly suggested, pointing to the ceiling.

"But how on earth are we supposed to get up there?" Fabio replied, showing the height and the impossibility of getting there.

"Let's look elsewhere," Julio reckoned, pointing to something. It looked like a different chamber.

"Yeah! I'm melting here," Gamble replied.

They entered a tunnel. It led to another big, square chamber with gigantic metal shelves. Glittering items were placed, reaching fifty heads high. The group didn't know what to say.

"Well, you found what you were looking for," Lela complained ironically, knowing they wouldn't be cornered in this place as if they had just left instead of attempting to find the treasure.

"You mean to tell me they came here looking for this?" Elisa replied angrily, punching one of the bards.

The group didn't know what to say or how to reply.

"All of this will be worthless if we die here today," Prodalus sadly said with a tone of finality, he remembered once being in this same position, a Deja Vu. He looked around the room for some sort of weapon.

The group started looking around. The treasure meant nothing to them anymore. They went everywhere, kicking away the gold, silver, and precious gems in order to find anything they could use as a weapon.

"Look! It seems like Argus means to build a whole new chamber at the far end," Lela speculated as she went inside, followed by Thormon.

Lela and Thormon felt renewed with hope as they saw a collection of items. There were shields of all sizes, lances, spears, swords, maces, and unique items. On the far wall were many armor pieces such as helmets, plate armor, chain mail, iron boots, and trousers. On the next wall were many staffs, wands, gems, gold, and jewelry inside steel chests.

Thormon quickly ran out and told everyone he had found what they needed. The group ran inside and saw that maybe today was not the day they'd perish.

The group started to go through which items they might need. Prodalus told them that those weapons were not ordinary. He seemed surprised that they still existed and that the Cyclops could get his hands on such weaponry.

"These are from the legends of Windor the Anarchist and the city of Tenebra," Prodalus said in disbelief.

At the same time, he went through the weaponry. Coming upon what he wanted, his eyes shone when he found the famed thunderbolt staff with a diamond on its head.

"I can't believe this exists!" He examined the staff and added, "This staff could grant us some leverage against Argus."

The group gathered what they could and started arming themselves. Prodalus helped Lela, Elisa, and Thormon find the best protective gear. Robert grabbed a massive, round golden shield. It seemed filled with items rich in diamonds and an odd-looking sword next to it. Fabio took possession of a platinum-closed Norse helmet. It seemed ornamented with a single blue stone on the forehead. And then, something that resembled a pitchfork. Miguel put his hands on a solid gold candelabra. Gamble chose a mighty silvery trident and ornamented golden armor.

"You guys are not going to fit yourselves in any type of armor?" Gamble asked as he looked at his friends.

"We can't move inside any of these. We don't know how to fight like you," Fabio replied.

Prodalus, hearing that, handed them some brass plates. "At least Argus won't be able to rip your hearts out. Your limbs, on the other hand, are a different story."

As the group readied to leave, they heard a threatening deep voice. "I see that it's not only one but an entire group. Did you think you could outsmart me? You sealed your fate once you decided to come to my domain," Argus intimidated them with a sinister laugh.

The group tried to find out where his voice came from. Elisa pointed in fear to the mirror. "He knows where we are!"

Thormon threw the mirror across the chamber, breaking it into several pieces.

"We don't have ample time," Gamble complained as he finished his preparation. He sighted the beast about to cross the bridge over the water stream.

Before they could do anything, Robert saw the terrifying giant skidding to a halt as one eye focused on the company of intruders.

"He's here!" shouted Robert.

"Return my items at once, and I shall grant you a painless death, or, if you prefer, I shall smash your skulls as I did to your friend!" Argus yelled in a coarse and powerful voice.

"Just try it, and you'll see who's gonna be crushed!" Prodalus yelled back, trying to gain time.

"Green worm, you have no power here. I made sure of that. That stick won't do anything for you!" warned the Cyclops as the weapon caught his attention. "Hand it to me, and I'll let you live."

"You take me for a fool, Argus? You know very well what this staff can do!" Prodalus replied.

"Your magic won't work here!" spat Argus, walking forward daringly.

The druid released the trigger and raised his hand. "Please don't make me do this. You know very well what this does!" Prodalus screamed as the monster came closer and closer.

The druid had no choice but to use the staff. He spun it manually and then released the trigger. The gears rotated in the opposite direction. The spinning gear hit the diamond at the tip of the staff. The impact discharged a spark that formed a lightning bolt.

"Stay back!" the druid screamed at the group and the monster.

Argus jumped away, grabbed a big lance from the shelf, and quickly struck it on the wall. The lightning ray hit the metallic lance that worked like a ground wire, missing him completely.

The monster got up, giving a devilish smile and look. "Give up!" shouted the cyclops as he picked up a round shield and threw it like a giant Frisbee, aimed at the druid.

The old elf parried the giant shield with the thunderbolt staff. The impact drove the staff off his hand and into the ground, and the shield ricocheted toward the wall. That threw the druid against the shelves, striking his nape as he hit the boards. Lela quickly ran to his aid, and the rest of the company awaited what to do next. Thormon looked at Prodalus and then at his uncle. Gamble raised his sword and looked at Argus.

"You weaklings. You have no chance against me!" Argus gloated at the group and did not acknowledge Gamble much. "Who will deal with me now?"

"You deal with me this instant!" Gamble rebuked him with his sword raised.

"Oh! It looks like we have a wannabe hero. You dare to confront me with that twig!" gloated the cyclops, laughing at his challenger.

"That's not my intention, but if need be, the nymph will come to our aid," Gamble replied, gripping his sword more tightly.

"It's not going to happen. How on earth would she even come here?" Argus replied, showing a slight air of worry.

"Who do you think made us come here?" Gamble replied.

Argus stopped for a moment and lowered his arms. "Go on. I am listening. What does the nymph want?"

"She still blames you for the dam. But she wishes to barter a passage with you," Gamble replied, hoping Argus didn't discover his bluff.

"If that were the case, why didn't you just say so? Your friend would still be alive," Argus speculated, starting not to buy Gamble's bluff.

Gamble looked at Argus and then at his company. He took a deep breath and replied, "We needed to lure you out to see what you have to make an exchange."

Argus got confused. "First, you mock me, then you enter my home like thieves, and then you take one of my slaves."

The Cyclops chewed on some hard root. "You also tried to murder me. And let's not forget you have my prized possessions on you." He stopped for a bit and looked at Prodalus.

Gamble didn't know how to reply. Fabio looked at the stream and then back to Gamble as if telling him to talk about the stream.

"Well, everyone stated—even the nymph herself—that you were never one to talk to. You always resorted to violence. So, we were afraid to come straight up to you," Gamble replied as he pointed to the stream.

Fabio quietly walked toward Gamble and got his bag.

The Cyclops stayed quiet for a moment. But soon saw that the group orchestrated something surreptitious, getting ready for it.

"But I still don't understand. Why go through all this trouble?" Argus wondered as he prepared himself for something.

"Now then, we needed to check for ourselves if there were water streams inside your lair," Gamble replied. He noticed that Argus was not buying his story anymore.

"This stream isn't big enough for her," Argus mentioned, rebuking Gamble's story.

The group helped Prodalus up.

Argus, seeing that, jested, "That worm has no power here. Don't tell me he has been the one you brought to summon that witch."

Prodalus composed himself and walked toward Argus. As he made his route there, he whispered, "Get the explosives ready."

"You see, my wicked old friend, I may not have magical powers. But I can still conjure some kind of water magic. Which, you see, remains the only kind of magic you didn't lock," Prodalus bluffed as he made his way closer to the stream.

Argus looked confused by what the druid discussed and added, "What do you mean, I haven't blocked everything? The power node channeling I made confirms that no magic exists here."

The druid smiled snidely and replied, "It seems you gave your soul away to that dark lord for nothing."

"What are you doing, old man?" Argus yelled as he saw that the druid was up to something.

"What I came here to do!" the druid replied as he raised his arms.

The mage spun his hands, waving and muttering something inaudible. The group stood back and readied themselves for what was to come. Argus froze in fear, and before he could react, the druid yelled as he threw something.

"Take cover!"

The yellow explosive from Gamble's backpack was handed to the druid. When Argus seemed unaware, he cast it against the walls of the thin water stream.

There sounded a loud blast, throwing the druid and Argus in opposite directions, along with rocks flying everywhere. The ground started to shake. The group helped Prodalus up.

Trying to recover from the blast, Argus yelled, "What have you done?"

"The nymph is on her way. Prepare yourself!" the druid replied as he readied everyone to escape.

The stream started to get bigger and broader. It ended up destroying the bridge between Argus and them.

"There goes our route out!" Robert confessed in dismay. "In no time, the water will flood the entire place."

"We have to jump into the stream!" Gamble commanded as he saw that Argus was also trying to escape.

"Can't you do something, druid?" Julio asked in fear.

The druid looked at them with a smirk and then pushed Thormon into the stream. "That's our path out," he indicated.

Gamble and the rest were surprised by what the druid did but knew they had no choice. The place was coming down. They all jumped in and let the stream take them. Argus saw that and decided to run toward where the stream led—the old dried lake in the ancient city.

As the druid jumped in, he heard Argus's words: "I'll catch you all!"

The group floated down the treacherous stream. It ran from up the mountain to all the paths down into the archaic city.

Thormon washed up on the muddy lake. He looked around and saw that the lake was filling up, but there was no sign of the others. He took a deep breath and jumped back upstream to look for the others. One by one, he brought them to the shore.

"I knew you would save us," the druid mentioned as he caught his breath.

"I don't care what you know. Help me with my friends," Thormon appealed.

At the same time, he saw that Gamble, Julio, Fabio, Robert, Lela, and Elisa were out of the water but still not safe.

"They swallowed a lot of water. Help them!" Thormon added as he shook the druid.

The druid recovered his magic and emptied their lungs of water. The group caught their breath, but the ground shook before they could thank him.

"He's not going to let us go!" Elisa expressed fear. "Quick! We need to leave this place!" Fabio added.

They heard a scream before anyone else could say anything, "No one enters my home and lives to tell the story. Not without my permission."

The group froze in fear. Prodalus, in contrast, appeared boosted with further confidence than ever.

"What are you doing, old man?" Gamble asked.

"Trust me!" Prodalus replied as he readied himself.

The thumping stopped. Everyone turned their eyes toward the distant side of the newly formed lake.

"Do you see anything?" Elisa asked, still in a panic.

"No, only trees," Lela replied, holding Elisa's hand tighter. There was silence.

All of a sudden, birds started flying toward them as if they were running away from a predator.

The trees started to tumble over, and the one-eyed giant was soon visible.

"It will not be that easy this time!" Prodalus shouted back as he raised his staff. "Stay behind!" He unleashed his staff's power and a wall of earth rose, towering over all the fighters, blocking Argus from his prey.

"Do you think that puny wall will stop me?" Argus screamed.

"Quick, everyone! Follow me!" Prodalus shouted to the group as he made himself up the wall.

The party climbed the wall, and from up there, they had a bird's-eye view of the entire valley.

"What's your plan?" Robert asked

"Just watch!" Prodalus answered as he raised his hand and staff and chanted some words.

The group looked down and saw voluminous water coming from the volcano.

"You mean to drown me, old man? That's all you can do?" Argus shouted as he ran toward higher ground.

More and more water came down, flooding the valley, isolating the bards and their companions as if they were standing on an island in the middle of the lake.

"How on earth do we get out now?" Julio asked, surprised by how much water gathered there.

"Trust me!" the druid replied with a smirk.

The group stuck closer together and started to search for Argus.

"Do you believe he drowned?" Thormon asked

"We're not that lucky," Fabio replied.

Before anyone else could say anything, Gamble shouted, "Look! It appears that the ugly beast put himself up a tall tree."

"It looks like he's holding on for his life," Thormon replied, focusing his eyes on the giant.

The druid mumbled something, and a wall of water rose on this occasion. It formed a massive tsunami wave that crashed into the Cyclops. The monster tried to hold on to the tree. But the force of the water was too intense, making the giant spin back and throwing him down a slope.

"I believe this means the chance to escape or stay here. It's up to you this moment," the druid put them on the spot. At the same time, he raised mud banks that created a makeshift stairway down the receding water.

They jumped from mud bank to mud bank until reaching the flank. As soon as Elisa and Lela were on firm ground, they cornered the druid.

"You need to kill that man-eating monster!" Elisa demanded, pushing the druid back.

"Someone must stop him!" added Lela.

"He won't bother you anymore. We destroyed his den. With all that water, he can no longer forge anything," the druid replied, trying to calm the girls down.

"But he still lives. We need to stop this madness!" Lela replied, showing the druid that the monster's behavior would never cease.

"In accordance, he will need even extra people at present. We destroyed his workplace," Thormon added. He was concerned as well with the outcome of their actions.

"I believe he will never return if we destroy the volcano," the druid replied.

"But haven't we done enough damage? What have we done?" Thormon replied with tears in his eyes, knowing very well the fool's errand they were on—also, the high cost of what they'd done.

The group stayed silent as they saw Thormon rip out his armor, throwing it to the ground.

"I hope this was all worth it," Thormon commented skeptically as he walked away from the group.

Gamble looked at the girls and his friends. His heart sank. He sat down in deep thought, turned to Julio, and asked, "What have we accomplished here?"

"We saved Elisa," Julio replied in a sad tone.

"Let's hope she's worth the price we paid," Fabio added, looking at the girls with deep hatred.

Prodalus, seeing what went on, tried to soften the outcome. "The people inside the cave were husks of themselves."

The girls, still not accounting for what had happened, continued to worry about the Cyclops. They asked Prodalus to finish him off.

"He will try to repair his lair!" Elisa kept saying.

"That will take very long, and if it turns futile, he will have to leave his volcano and look for a new lair," conjectured Prodalus.

He attempted to keep everybody's mood up, but he saw that the group fell distraught. Before he could say anything, he felt something strange in the water.

"Brace yourselves! The nymph means to be on her way as I summoned her!" Prodalus shouted and reached for support. The others did the same.

It seemed as if the nymph came as soon as the water from this lake escaped into the ancient vacant river course. The water ran through the valley into the old dried river until reaching the phantom lake, where the nymph lived.

"I have to commend you on a job well done! As I promised, you may have a wish. I believe it was wealth and richness you all desired. I have lots of treasure," the nymph said sensually.

The group stayed silent.

"Will you not demand your reward?" the nymph asked as she looked around.

"We didn't defeat the Cyclops yet. We simply threw him somewhere. However, we did not destroy the dam. All we did was cause death and destruction," Gamble replied with a hopeless look.

The nymph smiled. "What I asked you to do was to create a route for me to leave my prison. How you came to it is none of my concern."

The girls were in awe at what was going on, and soon they shouted, "You need to destroy Argus's house. In that manner, he will have to leave, and we'll be free from that monster. The village will flourish and become prosperous."

The nymph looked at the girls with a disapproving and threatening glance. "How dare you demand something from me! Nobody gave you this task. From what I see, you have no say here. It's their choice and their choice alone!"

"We want the riches and treasures! Did we come here in vain? Bernard stands dead. Did he die for nothing?" asked Robert.

"Is that what everyone wants?" the nymph asked.

"We need to oust the monster. Money stands as nothing in comparison anymore. Look at what we did and what we lost. Isn't that enough? Not even Thormon stands here to give a say, and he has a pure heart, which I destroyed," Gamble realized sadly. He tried to do the right thing after all the shame and destruction they had done.

"Decide promptly, for to me, the volcano befalls as winning the battle against water, and soon, Argus will return. Decide now," requested the nymph.

"Destroy the volcano." The bards confirmed, one by one, in a sad tone.

"Is that really what you all desire?" asked the nymph. She wanted to make sure of their request.

Gamble nodded, and the others stayed quiet.

The nymph took a good, hard look at them and decided, "So be it."

She raised her arms and reversed the river upstream and into the volcano. The waters filled the tunnels, causing the lava to lose its battle. That made the entire lava hotbed turn into solid rock, killing the volcano.

Lela and Elisa jumped joyfully, but the group showed no signs of happiness. Soon afterward, they shrugged the girls away.

"We threw away our only chance of richness," Fabio complained. There fell an eerie silence.

The nymph looked at the group and departed without saying a word. But a thunderous scream echoed throughout the ancient village before she could leave.

"You puny rats! What have you done? I no longer have a home or booty! I'll rip you all apart!"

Thormon ran back, and as he caught his breath, he alerted, "Argus the giant is swimming and diving. He's coming in this direction!"

The nymph stopped then attested, "That old green fool you have with you will be no match for that monster, and neither will any of you."

"Please help us!" Thormon pleaded.

The nymph looked at them arrogantly in disdain. "Why not? You all freed me from my prison and did not ask for any of my treasures. I could help you. I will scare that monster away."

Before she could add anything else, Argus returned and saw that the nymph was aiding the bards.

"What do you do here, witch?" Argus asked with a frightened tone.

"I'm here helping these fine men. You see, they freed me from my prison, one that, I believe, you built!" she replied in a threatening tone.

Argus did not know what to say. He knew he was no match for the water witch; thus, he mentioned, "It was not only me who built your prison."

"But you were not the one who freed me, and I don't wish to be trapped again," the nymph replied. She raised her hands and commenced a wall of water to turn into ice. "If you do not leave this valley immediately, you'll make it your final resting place!"

Argus was hence afraid that he did not dare to face the nymph. He quickly turned tail and ran away.

The nymph laughed and gloated, "Run, you fool!" She threw ice spears at the giant, hitting him multiple times as he escaped. The nymph turned to the group. "That thing won't bother any of you ever again."

As Thormon tried to thank her, she disappeared into the mist.

"Well, that was fun," the druid alleged sarcastically.

"No, thanks to you," Robert replied.

The group soon gathered and talked about what to do next. Gamble took the girls and Thormon back to the hamlet while the druid and the bards looked for Bernard's body.

"Well, everyone, we'll meet at the hamlet and decide what to do next," Gamble instructed as they parted ways.

The journey back to the Hamlet felt like an eternity as it was filled with hardship. Gamble and Thormon were reluctant to say a word to the girls. All they did was walk quietly and in thought.

Meanwhile, the bards and the druid went back up to the forthwith dead volcano in search of their friend's body.

"This is not how we expected this to end," Robert realized, pushing some of the bodies of the dead slaves out of his path.

"Shouldn't we at least bury these people?" Fabio asked as they passed.

Before anyone could answer, they were taken aback as they saw a lake full of dead bodies.

The druid looked at them. "This seems to take longer than we thought."

CHAPTER 32

Freedom from Rogue's Dominium

A s Gamble, Thormon, and the girls approached the village, they could hear fireworks, music, and laughter.

"What are those fools celebrating?" Gamble asked in a tone of disapproval.

"You freed us from the monster!" Lela replied, trying to lift his spirits.

Both Gamble and Thormon did not wish to answer her. They received a hero's welcome as soon as they entered the hamlet.

"Where stands the rest of your party?" the elder asked. Gamble did not answer.

"They will come down soon enough," Lela answered.

The people gathered around Gamble and Thormon, repeatedly screaming, "Behold! The saviors of our hamlet!"

Gamble and Thormon shrugged them away and only asked for a place to wash up and rest.

Lela and Elisa praised them and asked everyone to let them rest; subsequently, the Hamlet did. But there seemed to be no manner to contain the place's happiness. The community celebrated throughout the solar and moon cycles. And the rest of the group had returned by dawn.

"Come, brave warriors! Dance! Drink! Feast! You all earned this victory!" a rather stout villager mentioned.

"Where befalls our companion?" Fabio asked, not wanting to partake in any of the festivities.

A single villager pointed to the elder's home. And thus, they made their route there, elbowing the villagers.

Gamble and Thormon heard a knock and answered the door. The bards and the druid were back.

"We found Bernard dead, with his limbs broken off his torso," wept Julio sadly as he entered.

Gamble let his emotions flow and cried, "I won't have the courage to tell Bernard's father that his only son happens to be dead. All this for nothing."

Lela tried to comfort Gamble. "You saved my friend, Elisa."

Gamble did not care what Lela had to say and asked the group, "What took you guys so long?"

"We spent most of the day burying the poor souls we doomed when the place flooded," Miguel complained angrily. He pushed one of the villagers away who was trying to attend to him.

"Bodies. Bodies everywhere," Fabio mumbled as he sat on the floor.

The villagers present did not say a word.

"They were all far gone from this world. Husks, I tell you!" a villager mentioned.

Thormon, listening from a distance, rebuked: "Husks? They were people! Your people. Your brothers and sisters! And this ensues as how you all react? You are all as evil as Argus!"

"They were not well in the head. You did them a favor!" the elder replied, trying to step in and minimize the situation.

"Nothing, any of you, will pay for what we did. We buried your dead. We drove your monster away. We brought peace to this hellhole. Nothing you say can or will help us. We lost our only chance of riches; hence, you all could have this stupid party. I demand payment! Make your stupid villagers go back there and recover our lost treasures," Robert requested in a fit of rage.

The bards and the druid did not agree or disagree with Robert; they were silent.

"The treasure is cursed!" the elder replied.

"We do not care! For what we went through and lost, this curse means nothing," Robert replied.

The elder took a nuanced look at the group. Not knowing what to say, he simply replied, "Well, you didn't die, and surely, you showed Argus a lesson."

"He is right. Argus learned the hard way not to mess with these men," Prodalus attested, trying to lighten the mood.

The bards didn't want to say a thing.

Prodalus tried to break the somber moment. He turned to Thormon and asked, "How did you hold your breath and dive very well with scarce air in your lungs? It must be at least one thousand heads of distance from the mountain to the lake."

"That's right. We never thanked Thormon for saving us from the flood you caused inside the lair," Lela added.

At the same time, attempting to break the mood, Gamble speculated, "He probably didn't need to hold his breath. This kid seems so full of surprises. I wouldn't be surprised if he claimed he had some kind of mermaid lineage."

"I know nothing about mermaids," replied Thormon, surprised at how far his lineage could go.

"Hm, the mystery about your elfish blood has been revealed. You see, merfolk and elves lived like distant cousins," Prodalus conjectured.

"But elves can't breathe underwater!" Gamble contrasted, interrupting Prodalus.

"Wait! Let me finish. You see, their kind split a long epoch ago, going into different habitats. It's possible that, by chance, your biological father and mother were descendants of some kind of royalty From these two different splits. Hm, what are the odds of that?" Prodalus currently was intrigued about whom the boy turned out to be.

As Prodalus discovered Thormon's roots, the group looked at the boy with new eyes.

"Indeed, this young man remains a mystery," the elder noted.

"Let's not lose our focus here. You guys are still getting me that booty," Robert demanded, showing that he couldn't care less about the boy.

"True! I want my share!" Fabio replied.

Prodalus looked at them with disgust. "All you care about transpires to be the booty left behind. Mysteries and wonders—you guys do not care."

"Those won't make us rich!" Miguel replied, showing that this fool's errand fed him up.

Prodalus smiled. "You are the real fools here. Have you not noticed that you are all wearing valuable armor? You do not care for mystery, but you are all wearing a part of one."

The room stayed silent as everyone looked at each other.

"What do you mean, valuable?" asked Robert, intrigued by why these armor pieces were precious.

"These were all part of a forgotten city, one only told in tales," Prodalus replied. He showed that mystical forces clouded their quest in even greater mystery.

"What city are you talking about?" Thormon asked.

"The lost city of Tenebrae," Prodalus replied.

Gamble seemed taken aback. "My brother became extremely rich with just one item from that place."

The bards were all surprised at what they had with them. The elder appeared instantly intrigued by how Argus had come across such items.

"Argus had more tricks and secrets than we'd expected," Prodalus added. At the same time, he saw that everyone was straight off interested in what they had.

"Let's just stay with our spoils, then. We have enough here to last many lifetimes," Gamble concluded.

At the same time, he talked to the group of bards. He tried to convince them to forget about the treasure left underwater.

"Now comes what I want," Prodalus confessed as he stood up and faced the kid.

"What do you mean, what you want?" Gamble replied.

"Do you all think I'm leaving empty-handed? You all got what you came for. As for me, I still didn't get what I wanted," Prodalus replied.

"And what stands as your part of the deal, old man?" the elder asked.

Prodalus smirked. "I had it in my hands, but unfortunately, I lost it in the stream, which seems presently under the lake. Only Thormon can retrieve it for me."

"Why didn't you ask the nymph?" Robert asked.

"Why didn't you ask her to retrieve your treasure?" Prodalus rebuked him.

The group fell quiet for a moment, waiting for Thormon's answer.

"How would I find it? You saw how big the lake became," Thormon replied.

"Oh, trust me, boy. You'll know," Prodalus replied, shrouding the topic into even further mystery.

"Can I say no?" Thormon asked.

"You all owe me your lives. I did get you all out of that place, didn't I?" Prodalus replied.

"I thought you were helping us out of goodness," Robert protested.

"Did you all help these people out of goodness?" Prodalus replied as he put everyone in their places. "You all had your reasons, and I had mine."

Thormon had no choice, and thus the group convinced him to go back.

Thormon seemed not thrilled but also knew he had no say here.

There was no need for the entire group. Hence, Prodalus asked only for Gamble to come along. Feeling bad about what had happened, Lela asked if she could come along. They agreed, and all four of them made their route back; the rest of the bards stayed behind and rested.

The journey up was a short and somber climb. Lela stuck with Gamble and tried to talk to him on the path up. She showed Gamble how caring she could be. Lela slowly won back Gamble's admiration.

"This seems to be the place!" Prodalus confirmed, pointing to where he wanted Thormon to dive.

"How will I find it?" Thormon asked.

"Once you swim down, as you look around, the closer you come to it, the shinier the orb will get. That's how you'll find it. Go immediately, boy!" Prodalus answered.

Thormon nodded and jumped into the lake.

Prodalus looked at Gamble and Lela. "This might take a while. You both can wander off a bit, and when Thormon finishes, I'll summon you back."

Lela thanked Prodalus, grabbed Gamble's hand, and took him for a walk.

Both talked about what had brought them to this place. Gamble talked a bit about his past—how he'd met the bards and what he wanted to do after this ended.

Lela couldn't hide her admiration for him; the more he talked, the closer she got. In a moment of thought, she asked Gamble for forgiveness. Gamble smiled and acknowledged that she had nothing to apologize for.

Gamble plotted and implemented this whole mess. Before he could add anything else, Lela shut him up with a kiss.

Gamble became love-struck. He did not know what to do. Before he could say anything, Prodalus called for them.

"Well, how did your walk go?" Prodalus asked, knowing already what had happened.

Both just smiled and said it went well.

"Your nephew has retrieved the staff. This boy stands out as a real jewel," Prodalus praised him, holding the staff proudly. "You completely redeemed yourselves, your debt stands no more. Currently, go back to the hamlet. I believe everything ensues as ready."

Before they could speak, the druid walked into the woods and disappeared.

When they returned to the hamlet, the villagers supplied the adventurers with food. And they gave them horses for their journey home. Fabio kept the mysterious book, they had found at the ancient church, inside a wooden coffer just for safekeeping. But he commended that Thormon continued to be more than welcome to read it. The rest of the bards packed the armor they used so they could sell it later.

Gamble, however, refused the horse and supplies.

"What are you doing?" Robert asked.

"I have found what I looked for all along; my heart stays no longer void," Gamble replied, holding Lela's hand.

The bards just smiled and wished him the best. Thormon, on the other hand, inquired about how he would return and whether he would ever see him again.

Gamble smiled. "I've had too many adventures in my life. I've finally found peace, and I know this stands out as what my brother always wanted for me. Tell him I have found my treasure and that I will now settle down. He'll know what I mean."

Thormon cried and hugged his uncle.

"This means goodbye, then, Uncle. How will we get back without you?"

"You were the one who brought us here. You can bring everyone back." Gamble smiled as he put Thormon on the horse and waved goodbye.

The voyage back felt long. The bards weren't as cheerful as when they had started their journey. Soon, they arrived at the dwarf city of Havengar, where they sold their horses and resupplied themselves. They continued toward the border of the Elder Mountains on foot. The forest seemed very dense from that point onward.

The bards did as promised and brought Thormon to his parents. Before long, they were in Baldar. When Suli spotted Thormon at the gates, her eyes filled with tears. She quickly ran toward her son, hugging him midway to their house.

Louarn eased his worried appearance and patted his son's head. "You are far too smart for your own good," he reprimanded.

"We will ground you for one-third of a season, and be thankful I'll let you leave the house ever again," reprimanded Suli.

"By the way, I didn't see your uncle with the bards. Where is he? I must have a word with him," Louarn snarled while his wife shook her head in disapproval.

"He stayed behind. He mentioned that he had found his treasure and would promptly settle down," said Thormon in a sad tone.

Louarn smiled and hugged his son.

Soon after they settled, Thormon told his parents about his journey. They were eager to know every scrap of detail about where he'd been for the past couple of days.

CHAPTER 33

The Young Ages

Two seasons had passed since Thormon last saw his uncle. Thormon chose not to tell anything to Louarn or Suli about who he was or what he had found out. And the bards also promised to keep Thormon's lineage a secret.

Thormon's parents kept him on a tight leash. They rarely allowed him to go anywhere except to work at the shop with his father. On rare occasions, his parents would let him go to the river and let him swim. Thormon knew he could remain underwater for as long as he wished, but he would decide not to. He did not intend to scare his parents more than he had to, for they might think he was drowning. Nonetheless, he could not help but wonder what Prodalus told him—things about his biological mother since only mermaids can hipnotize with melodious songs, he could bet she was Triton's daughter, the renowed king underwater, but he was no diviner.

What would my parents think about me having royal blood? They would not understand, Thormon thought each moment he dived.

On seven days, Thormon went to the usual place where he could meet his friends, Logmar and Sveinn, at Onion Hill. Of course, parents and servants supervised the boys.

"Is the captain still not letting you off the hook?" Sveinn joked to Thormon.

"No! I still have many seasons on my sentence," he replied, laughing, knowing his dad didn't care.

They sat down, looking over the city. And they were about to start talking about their moment together when Louarn asked the boys what happened to Ormr.

Logmar smiled and asked, "Haven't you heard? Ormr entered the knight's guild, probably due to his noble ancestry—at least, that's what they said."

"Wow. Who would've known? Hey, Thormon, didn't you defeat him with a sword?" Louarn asked.

"True! That means you should also be allowed to become a knight!" laughed Logmar.

Louarn frowned and replied, "No way, Thormon! You better get those ideas out of your mind! You've had too many adventures lately." His friends laughed, and Louarn confessed, "I wish it were that simple."

"You know, my father told me that anyone can become a knight. That entails, if you know the right people," articulated Mark, looking toward the distance.

"Well, my brother got his knighthood initiation as a gift from Lord Vermundr. It seemed like something to do with my old man's diplomatic help," mentioned Sveinn.

"Hm. My cousin also got in. I think it also had to do with my aunt's habit of currying favors to some rich folks," opined Mark.

Louarn, surprised at what the boys were saying, opposed them, "Don't expect any favors from me. You're not getting into this knighthood. You will be a merchant like me."

The kids were surprised and tried to convince Louarn of the superior deeds knights did but to no avail. He stayed set on never letting Thormon become a knight. Even Thormon tried to persuade him otherwise. But it only made him angrier, and thus he stopped the discussion and returned to the city.

Back at the Thours' market, the next solar cycle, Thormon heard rumors of a great knight making his route to Baldar, which stirred the crowd downtown. Thormon appeared eager to see him and pestered his father the entire time to go to the square. At that place, he should meet the renowned knight.

"I said no! For the last time, you will not meet this knight! We have a lot of work to do. These items you and the bards brought and sold are an extreme rarity. And we have to catalog and price them accordingly," Louarn mentioned in a tone of rebuke.

Thormon tried every kind of argument, but Louarn shot him down immediately.

From a distance, Thormon could hear the crowd cheer.

"Hail, Magnusar!" the peasants cried out.

With each ovation, Louarn got angrier and angrier. But the sound kept getting closer and closer.

"I hope he doesn't make his path here," Louarn mumbled.

"But Dad, don't you want his money?" Thormon replied, hoping that the knight would make his route into the store.

Louarn just looked at Thormon and told him to go to the back of the store to fetch some items that a noble had ordered. But before Thormon could go, the knight arrived at the store with a company of warriors, towering over the others. Magnusar looked at least a head taller than most men.

Magnusar turned to the warriors, saying, "Please keep these folks out of this place while I see if it has the famed items the nobility talks about so much."

Surprised by what the knight expressed, Thormon and Louarn welcomed him.

"How can I help you?" Louarn asked and then told Thormon to return and finish his task.

The knight removed his helmet, smiled, and offered, "Let the boy stay. I can see it in his eyes—he wants to help me."

Louarn agreed and asked the knight what he intended to search with purchasing as the underlined goal.

The knight looked around. "I heard that your son and some bards brought back items that shouldn't even exist. Also, common knowledge passed on generations attest those items are long-lost for ages."

Louarn cleared his throat. "How did you learn of such things? Weren't you away on some quest?"

"True! Some of the quests I go out on are in search of such items as you possess. I am intrigued by how simple folks like you are strong-minded. And how could you have come across such wonders," the knight replied in a calming tone.

"Still, you haven't answered my question," Louarn replied. "Why are you here?"

The knight smiled and repeated the same statement. But on this occasion, he inquired about the boy present.

Louarn did not like the direction of that conversation. "This is my son, and he has no business with you. He still needs to finish a chore I set him to do!".

The knight looked at the father and the son and kindly suggested, "Then maybe I could help him. We are servants of the people, and it's not polite to refuse a knight's aid."

Louarn did not know what to say. He just murmured, "What is it you want?"

The knight smiled. "To help the boy with his chores."

And with that, he went out back with Thormon to set aside the order.

"Anyway, Thormon, how old are you?" the knight asked.

"Fifteen, sir! I'll be sixteen in a season," Thormon replied.

"Wow! Such a young age and with so much baggage. It reminds me a lot of when I was young. Of course, I couldn't find such treasures," the knight commented, surprised.

Thormon looked up at the knight and smiled. "These aren't the only adventures I've been on. I've already stolen treasures from pirates and fought off some crazy monkeys."

The knight interrupted him. "Wow! Monkeys? Did they have horns on their foreheads?"

"Yes! How did you know?"

"I've already been to that island, and those monkeys are no small business. How on earth did you survive such a feat?" the knight asked.

"Well, I think I'm somewhat special, something like a knight. I even saved a girl from drowning," Thormon boasted.

The knight and the boy spent the rest of the afternoon talking about their feats. And with each story, the knight grew increasingly surprised at what the boy had done. Louarn, in contrast, appeared unhappy that the knight kept talking to Thormon and befriending him.

At each point, he tried to interrupt them and give Thormon another task, and the knight would follow. Louarn finally gave up. He asked if he would buy something since the knight's companions blocked his business.

The knight kindly asked, "How much gold do you make in a day?"

Louarn replied, "It varies. On average, five hundred gold coins a day."

The knight took out a pouch and threw it to Louarn. "Well, I believe there is about five days' worth of your time."

Louarn did not know what to say. He became utterly embarrassed.

I completely misread the knight, Louarn thought. Then he had a heart-to-heart, "I apologize for mistreating you, but my son has been wanting to be a knight. I believe that, by what you heard of his adventures, he worries us too much. His mother almost went crazy at the thought of losing him. He happens to be our only son."

The knight looked at Thormon. "Did you put your parents through all those hardships?"

Thormon looked down and nodded, but then added, "Those people needed my help."

"True! But you should never let concern befall the ones you love! Family always comes first!" the knight replied, putting his hands on the boy's head. He turned to the father and complimented, "I see this boy stands out as free-spirited. The further you try to hold him back, the farther he escapes."

Louarn nodded, knowing that they did try to keep Thormon fenced. "What do you suggest we do?" he asked the knight.

"Well, who can fetch me a sword?" the knight joked.

Thormon quickly ran toward the items he'd brought from his last journey. He picked out a magnificent sword that one of the bards had encountered while they were in Argus' den.

"Stop, Thormon! That sword is not for giving out of charity. We haven't even cataloged and appraised it yet," Louarn yelled.

But Thormon held the sword high, showing it to the knight, who could not believe they had come across such a wonderful item.

"Is this one among the things you brought back from that hamlet you told me?" the knight asked.

Thormon nodded and handed it to the knight.

The knight took a good look at it. "If you want an appraisal, I can tell you this sword shouldn't exist. It's part of a legend, and holding it in my arms, I can feel its power within it. Good job, kid!"

"Well, I sold a staff once to the mayor, and it made me amongst the wealthiest merchants in the city. It was also an item from legend," Louarn mentioned, trying to come up with a price.

"You just became the wealthiest man in the nation!" the knight attested, standing up and handing him some precious diamonds and rubies.

Louarn did not know what to make of it; he seemed dumbfounded.

The knight turned to the boy, saying, "You have a unique gift, and you need to perfect it."

Thormon and his dad stood there silently, not knowing how to react.

"What do you mean? Did you mean he needs to hone his abilities?" Louarn asked, not wanting to know the answer.

The knight looked at the boy. "It's amazing and quite a feat; he remains in one piece after all those adventures. He does have the makings of a knight!"

Thormon's eyes sparkled with those words, but Louarn quickly shut him down once more.

"I told the boy, and I'll tell you once again. He remains expected to become a merchant, like his dad!"

The knight smiled. "Why don't we discuss these matters over dinner? I just made you the wealthiest man in the land. The least you can do seems to invite me to your home. It would be my honor to dine with you and your family."

Louarn did not know how to react. Having a knight as a guest stood as one of the highest honors one could have. That will elevate his standing in society, so he agreed.

The knight thanked him and exited the shop, through the crowd, and toward the palace.

Louarn turned to his son. "Is that what you want, son? A life of reckless risk and killing as a profession? Not being able to marry or establish a family? Bound to the code of chivalry and honoring only your king?"

Thormon did not listen to his father's words. All he heeded befell on the people's admiration when the knight walked toward the horizon.

People would respect me. Gleeman will write songs about me. People will remember me everywhere. That would make me immortal in their eyes. What more fantastic thing could I ask for? imagined Thormon.

"It's not a life I want for you. And by the way, we must prepare the invitations and our home for the knight," added Louarn.

CHAPTER 34

The Meeting

L ater that period, after one solar cycle, the period came for the feast. Louarn's entire family, except his brother, and Suli's were present. The dinner became the talk of the town. Louarn had an ox killed for the occasion.

The hosts set up the table for royalty. They used the finest silverware and the best platters and dishes from the land of the halflings were on display. Louarn also invited the bards to play at the estate. Even though they did not need the money, they went anyway.

Guennola and Arzure welcomed the knights. They were flattered by such presence. Never in their lifetimes did they expect to dine with such renowned companionship. Magnusar also brought his good friend Teodor, a knight of the highest honor. Thormon could not believe his eyes, two of the greatest knights in the kingdom were there. They introduced themselves to the family. Louarn took the opportunity to make a speech.

"Dear friends, family, and noble guests, we are honored to have you with us this evening. Please accept our humble welcome to this feast in your honor."

Teodor raised his hand and uttered, "No need for pleasantries. We are all equals here. Let's sit down and enjoy this feast!"

Everyone looked surprised and relieved. They saw that the knights were as humble as they were. And subsequently, everyone sat down and started enjoying their company. Thormon quickly ran and sat in between the two knights. Guennola complained a little but sat beside Magnusar, and Arzure sat beside Teodor. The rest of the family wanted to sit as close as possible to the knights.

The feast went on for several beats of an eagle's wings. Thormon got the opportunity to talk to both knights, and his grandparents were in awe. They'd never expected knights to be surprisingly humble. And accordingly, they talked for many beats of an eagle's wings. Guennola told stories about

Thormon's exploits and riveted about adventures with his grandpa to save her. The bards also pitched in with their adventure with the boy and how he saved them. Throughout the feast, everyone talked about Thormon's crazy adventures.

Teodor smiled, turned to the grandmother, and asked, "Have you or the boy ever been to the castle?"

Guennola smiled and shook her head. "I always wanted to go there. And I believe the boy wants to, as well."

"It dwells just a few hundred beats of an eagle's wings going west. I will take you there tomorrow. You'll love it there," the knight added. He also discussed having the boy see how the knights trained and worked.

This invitation did not come as a surprise. Guennola had always dreamed of having a knight take her to a castle and see what they did in their everyday lives. On the other hand, Arzure stayed a bit jealous, but he knew very well what the knight attempted to do. He understood his wife's wish.

Suli looked a bit startled. She had no words on the matter. The more she tried to gauge this situation, the more petrified she became. She knew that the knights were trying to recruit the boy.

"Son, will you ever leave us behind, this life that we offered you in exchange for trying your luck at a brute's lair?" Suli knew of the knight's intentions very well.

The knight also turned to Suli and extended the invitation to the mother. "You and your entire family are invited to go with us."

"But I do not want that kind of life sweeping away my son. He will start entertaining ideas of becoming a knight himself!" Suli commented.

"My fair lady, the boy stands out as a knight in the makings. Look at all he has done without any kind of training, whether you like it or not." The knight laughed.

Guennola looked at Suli and advised, "You can try to keep him all to yourself. But the more you try, the more he will distance himself from you. Over there, he can become a noble knight, something grand and honorable for him and the entire family."

"I am the mother, and as long as he remains underage, he will follow and obey me and Louarn!" Suli replied, shutting down her mother.

Thormon turned to his dad. "Dad, Mother will not let me go to the castle. Please talk to her and tell her that it would be good for me."

Louarn replied, "You know your mother is stubborn. She will not listen to me, and since you are not going anywhere without her blessing, it is better to get used to it." He paused and added, "But you have your grandmother's blessing. I believe you are halfway there."

Thus, Thormon asked his grandparents, Guennola and Arzure, to talk to his mother.

"Don't worry. I will convince her. No doubt about it," Guennola remarked.

Thus, the feast went on until daybreak. They'd never had that much fun with such illustrious company.

Before leaving, the knight turned to the father and the mother, giving them a sealed paper. The father opened it and saw his son's name written beside the squire's. It appeared signed by the knighthood and the king himself. The mother started crying. Guennola quickly came to her aid.

"You knew this should ensue in the end, my darling."

"But if it makes a difference, know that it would be an honor to have him as a member of our community," Teodor declared.

The father did not know how to react. All he could think of befell on his wife's cry, and his heart felt heavy on letting Thormon go; he became instantly stern.

The knights kneeled in thanks and affirmed they would be back to pick up everyone to go to the castle; then they left.

Guennola took Suli into the house. She talked to her about all the positive things that would come for her and the entire family.

"Who will represent us in court? Who will protect us if there does not exist a single knight in our family? Opportune destiny chose the boy for this! Let him get proper training, for destiny means everything in a man's life."

In that manner, she convinced Suli to let Thormon go to the castle.

***

The next solar cycle, bright and early, the knights were there to take the family to the castle. The women and the grandfather got into the chariot with the knights. But both father and son decided to ride their best horses, which could rival any of the palace's horses.

Louarn took the opportunity to have a heart-to-heart with his son on the route to the castle.

"Therefore, I guess your days at the market are over," exclaimed Louarn mournfully.

"It's not like that, Dad! I promise you that I will always come by," compromised Thormon.

His father looked at him, knowing the promise would be impossible to keep. "Whatever you do, know that your mother and I are proud of you. Do not hesitate to leave if things aren't going well."

Thormon nodded in agreement. The mysterious gaze on his face and the mysteries and adventures ahead of him seemed evident. It turned out to be Thormon gauging his motives and advantages of becoming a recruit at the castle. His father pondered about the toughness of the castle. Next, he mentioned the training and the hardships he would need to undergo. And the loneliness he would feel when being away from his loved ones. Thormon heard every word and agreed with his father. But he stayed headstrong in following his wish. They talked for several beats of an eagle's wings, and soon, they could see the palace on the horizon. It stood as a grand place, with five towers and two domes gilded with gold and silver, surrounded by a deep moat ditch. Archways adorned countless buildings, and gardens and high walls fringed the adornments. A retractable bridge remained as the only way to enter the castle. The women and the men were in awe at the sight of such beauty. Guennola came to pass as happy as a child at a candy store. She turned to the knight and asked to be taken there like a princess. The whole group laughed, but the knight agreed.

Magnusar poked his head out and called out for Louarn. "My dear friend, you heard the lady's request. Would you mind if we switched places?"

Louarn laughed and agreed to do so accordingly.

As the knight got on the horse and put Guennola on it, he turned to the boy and stated, "You are a squire, my boy. Go on ahead and announce our coming."

Thormon nodded his head in excitement and galloped quickly toward the bridge.

A pike man, blocking the path, saw the boy on the horse rushing toward him. He extended his long weapon, crisscrossing another pike held high by a second guard, and yelled, "Halt there! Who are you, and what is your purpose here?"

I am Thormon, the knight Magnusar requested me to announce his arrival. Thus, here I am," assured the youngster.

The guards looked at the boy and asked, "Where is he?"

Thormon pointed to the horizon where a chariot and a horse carrying two people made their route closer and closer.

The guards took a good look and asked, "Very well, but who is that mature lady he is carrying?"

Thormon smiled. "That's Princess Guennola!"

The guards looked confused because they'd never heard of such a princess, especially one at such an advanced age.

As custom dictated, the lead servant announced their arrival. "Open the gates for Knight Magnusar and Princess Guennola!"

Upon hearing the announcement, Guennola laughed hysterically. And everyone inside the chariot couldn't stop laughing.

"Well, my fair lady, you got your wish! You are, at present, a princess!" Magnusar said jokingly to Guennola as he helped her down from the horse.

The guards still did not know what to make of it but went along. "Please bring your horses and chariot to our stables, and take yourself into the castle."

The group did as the guards told them and soon crossed the bridge.

They saw several knight trainees practicing with dummies as they entered the castle. Sometimes, they faced one another. And the clash of swords produced sparks and metallic noises. Soon, they stopped as they noticed a group of commoners enter.

A tall, slender guy went toward them and introduced himself. "I'm Naglfar, and that is Gunnarr and Arnkell. This young lad must be the new guy you were referring to."

Magnusar and Teodor introduced the party and presented Thormon as the new squire.

Thormon appeared a bit taken aback and afraid, feelings transparent in his edgy face. It seemed too much and too fast.

His father, noticing how his son looked, turned to him and assured, "Don't worry. I am sure you will be all right here. After all, this remains what you want, and if you get bored of it or don't fit in, come back home."

Thormon smiled and raised his hand to the small crowd. "I am Thormon. Glad to meet you all."

The three knights shook his hand and welcomed the boy.

Gunnarr turned to him and asked, "Are you Magnusar's or Teodor's squire?"

Teodor raised his hand and promised, "I will teach him the ways of the knight!"

Thormon was absent-minded and thus unaware of what the knight mentioned.

Gunnarr smiled and asked the boy, "Do you have any questions?"

Before the boy could ask anything, Magnusar turned to the group and suggested, "Let's leave the boy here. He needs to get acquainted with his new surroundings. In the meantime, let me take you all to see the inside of our beautiful castle. When we finish, we'll meet up with them again."

As a result, the group parted from Thormon, leaving him in the company of Naglfar, Gunnarr, and Arnkell.

Gunnarr turned to the boy and tried to make things clear, "Before I got interrupted, I asked you if you had any questions."

Thormon replied, "Yes! I have many, but the first one is how the knighthood apprenticeship works?"

"Well, it is not too bad in the beginning. We have to run laps around the castle in the morning. Help the real knights with any assignment they might have. Do some push-ups in the afternoon. Practice fighting while mounted on horses. Learn how to use lances, melee weapons, swords, and maces; parry with shields. You know, the basic stuff," explained Naglfar.

"But you don't have to worry about these things at the present. Right now, you are a squire. And as a squire, you must help the knight don his armor and hand him whatever weapon he might need," informed Gunnarr.

"All that works is helping the knight to fetch what is needed and that means for you to get acquainted with the weapons and armors. Being a squire is the first important step in becoming a knight. As you may know, every knight stood once as a mere squire," added Arnkell.

"You are right. Everyone here was once a squire—everyone but Ormr," discredited Gunnarr. He pointed a finger to a gloomy guy training with swords by himself at the far side of the Central Park of the palace.

"Keep yourself fit, and don't overdo it with the food, my boy, and you'll be fine!" Arnkell commented.

The poor lad had gained some weight. And he looked at least one head taller than he was the last time Thormon had seen him at the Onion Hill.

"We still need to show the boy around. Enough of chitchat, and let's get to know the boy's new home," Gunnarr verbalized.

The three knights took the boy around. They showed him the training quarters, sleeping quarters, and the cafeteria. Also, there was the castle's outskirts which would serve as his training place. Finally, they met the others in the palace, where he would finally say farewell to his family.

"Gunnarr, my friend, did you show the boy around?" Teodor asked.

"Yes! And he looked quite impressed, might I add," Gunnarr replied.

"Good to know! I hope you like it here. We'll give you the best training in the entire eastern realm," Magnusar added.

With that said, Arnkell told them to go to the dining hall of the palace. The castle chef and butler prepared a feast for Thormon's family—an exception for the new wealthiest family in the land and the soon-to-be nobles.

They dined and talked for several hundreds of beats of an eagle's wings, but soon came the moment to say goodbye.

They bid farewell to each other and advanced each to their distinct destinations. One could not see it, but a tear ran down Louarn's and Suli's faces as the entire family left, leaving Thormon behind.

Louarn turned to Suli and revealed sadly, "A new chapter in our boy's life seems about to begin. When we see him again, he will not be the same sweet boy we remember but a brand-new man."

Suli looked back and waved her last goodbye. But before Thormon could make his course to his new quarters, Suli rushed toward him and gave him her final hug and kiss goodbye.

"Please! Always be that same sweet, helpful boy I know you are!" remained her final words lingering and echoing in the air.

CHAPTER 35

Routine

T he next day, inside the palace's guest room, Thormon was woken up bright and early. An older knight with a long white beard and pointy mustache was dressed in chain mail. He had the responsibility to guide the new youngster in the practice area.

"Young one! You are the new squire, aren't you?" he asked.

"Yes, sir—lord, I mean," Thormon replied, somewhat confused with the proper titles.

"Hm. Then you need to come with me. I need to take you to your new quarters," the old knight mentioned as he ushered Thormon to a big cottage.

Inside, he saw many rooms. Some doors were open, and Thormon could see some young men either praying or resting. Other doors were closed, though. He followed the old knight down the hall until they reached the last room.

"Here we are! This room will serve you well as long as you reside here," the old knight guaranteed as he looked for a key to open the door. The old knight pushed the door open and shoved Thormon in.

"It's not palace material, but it will suit you," the old knight affirmed.

Thormon saw a small room with a small bed covered in thatch and straw. It looked like one-fourth the size of his bedroom back home.

Nonetheless, it suited him well, for he had brought scarce luggage and needed no furniture.

The old knight gave him a key and a list of instructions and revealed, "Welcome to your new life, squire. May the gods bless you and watch over you." With that, the old knight departed.

"At least I have my own room," Thormon soliloquied after the older man had left.

Thormon walked around the small room. He realized that the inner walls did not go all the way up to the ceiling but halfway. He heard a soft rattle of snoring from the adjacent room.

It looks like I'm not alone here, he thought as he explored further. *On the other hand, at least it's well-ventilated. I can get some fresh air from outside.*

He lay down and pretty much shut down. His chores wouldn't begin until later that day.

Time flew, and before he knew it, a voice barked at him.

"Wake up, lazy ass! It stays now as the time to gather at the main square! Didn't you hear the bell ringing, you worthless kid?" asked the old knight, shaking his arm.

Thormon woke up, somewhat alarmed. "What? Who?" Then he realized what had transpired. He had forgotten about the castle for a moment and thought of home. "Oh, I guess I was more tired than I realized."

Thormon jumped out of bed and rubbed his eyes to shake off the sleepiness.

"Let's go, squire! Here—take this! You don't want to be late, not at Lord Vermundr's speech," warned the old knight, treading out of the cottage.

Thormon followed him, changing his clothes as he walked.

The vassals of Vermundr gathered at the main square. It seemed an extensive clearing fringed by several buildings and most of the palace veranda, where the speech should be delivered. Thormon jumped up to get a better view and saw women for the first time inside the castle. They dressed in stained clothing, lips without rouge, and hair unkempt with no braid done—also, a rude demeanor—the characteristics of female servants.

Guards ordered the crowd into groups. The hierarchy divided the people. There were servants, plebeian employees, squires, knight apprentices, and full-fledged knights. And ladies and lords. Everyone knew their proper place. Thormon made his route toward the squire lot. There were around forty of them, teenagers and shabby-looking. In contrast, the knights, with trimmed, oiled hair and well-dressed attire brought within themselves a posture demanding respect and admiration.

"Ladies and gentlemen, I present to you, Lord Vermundr!" bellowed the herald as the lord showed himself at the top of the high balcony. The giant banners of Vermundr's family coat of arms extended from the elevated porch down to the ground.

The bronze bell on top of a tower rang three times. A few crows took off from the high roof as he walked out. The yellowish sunlight came straight from the setting sun. Its shine on top of the building blinded whoever looked up at the monarch. Burning incense produced massive amounts of smoke, bringing a sweet scent. The nickname "the misty" seemed evident forthwith.

"My dear folks! I call you all out here to welcome our newest squires, who will undertake the hard training and practice. Hence one day, they shall become knights." The Lord looked upon the squires and added, "May you all welcome them as a part of our family. Know that these young lads have left everything behind to serve the land, king, and country. May the gods bless you all!"

The present crowd cheered and welcomed the young boys. Once the lord concluded the boys' welcoming, he, the lord of the land, continued his speech. He spoke of trivial things, nothing that concerned Thormon much. And once finished, everyone made their route back to their quarters. Tomorrow would be a brand-new day.

***

For the next two seasons, Thormon trained fiercely. Such training and hardship should isolate him from the rest of the world. His heart remained focused on being the best squire he could be. His master pushed him to his limits.

"I need you able and ready for the tournament," Thormon heard a knight tell his squire. It reminded the boy of what was needed to be the best.

His efforts were not in vain. The lord of the land and the body of knights admired Thormon's grit and toughness. Some knights would sometimes come to the supervisor and ask if Thormon could be their squire.

But before that came the days of the games.

"My people! I, Lord Vermundr, am here to open the ceremony of knights' games! As tradition dictates, we are to promote the interexchange of warriors every decade. It includes every major city of the Eastern world. Don't get overexcited just yet, for the tournament won't start until the full moon.

"For the present, we'll be receiving champions from various cities. And for that, I would like to request your best and warmest reception. Of course, our champion, Magnusar, will represent us! I have a firm conviction that he will live up to his reputation and our expectations. The gentry came up with the festivities to bring people together. After all, what means better than to consolidate our big family? Let every knight prove his valor in these games, and let the festivities begin!"

The crowd cheered as the herald presented the knights to the public one by one at the main square, where a band of hired bards produced loud music for the crowd. Also, female servants served food in enormous trays. Thormon's family went wild after the orator introduced him alongside Teodor. The boy seemed a bit shy, but after spotting them, he waved back.

After the formalities, the squires were allowed some intervals off. A bunch of them took over the far side of the square. Most were either too shy or afraid to make themselves noticeable. But they still took the opportunity to wager among themselves. Others just drank beer while talking, not paying much attention.

Thormon took the opportunity to meet with his parents and see how they were doing. They talked for a while and caught up on what they were up to. Soon, another boy came up and presented himself.

"Oh, I see that you are Louarn and Suli's son! You are from Baldar, right?" the squire asked.

The couple turned to the squire and introduced themselves and Thormon.

They found out that the boy derived and grew up in the harbor city of Menestrel. He was called Einarr and had the opportunity to introduce Kettil the Barefoot. Both boys, Thormon, and his parents talked for hundreds of beats of an eagle's wings. Soon, a boy named Sigmundr joined the conversation. Thormon's parents asked if he had any girlfriends they should know about.

Thormon blushed. And before he could say anything, Sigmund commented, "Did you see small Eira, the daughter of the chief cook? Man, she seems very easy on the eyes, but her father is a hard-ass and never lets her out of his sight."

Louarn laughed and asked, "Who is this girl you're talking about?"

The boy raised his head and looked around. Once he found whom he searched for, he pointed toward her.

Suli smiled and disclosed, "I believe that looks like someone I know. She does look familiar."

"That's too bad. In that manner, that will foil my plans," conceded Halldórr, cousin of Logmar. The resemblance between them seemed obvious. Only Halldórr looked a bigger, stubbier version of his relative.

"Shut up! Your lack of skills would foil your plans even if her father were to be a pimp!" joked Sigmundr, and the others laughed.

"I like girls from Eritrea way better. They are tall and slender brunettes with dark eyes," declared the short Kettil while changing subjects.

"Is that where you come from?" asked Thormon, making small talk.

"No. I come from Victorn, a place farther east. That's where my hometown is located," replied Kettil.

"Hm. Never heard of it," replied Thormon.

"It's not a very famous city, but it stays a fine place throughout the ages nonetheless," Kettil added.

"My uncle spent most of his life in the Western world," boasted Thormon.

"I heard Western fighters are a fearsome lot," confessed Kettil.

"With all the orcs and hostile beasts lurking around, they must be," added Sigmundr.

Thormon didn't say lots. He barely knew about his uncle's past. Before anyone could say anything more on it, Sigmundr changed the subject.

"Look, Halldórr, if you are eager to learn how to court girls, just look at Gunnarr in action. He's a real ladies' man," commented Sigmundr, pointing at Gunnarr, who appeared to be courting a beautiful female servant.

"Hm, interesting," Thormon conceded.

"Yeah! That stands as the traditional knight combo—politeness followed by courtship," added Halldórr.

"Ha-ha! It almost sounds like you know what you are talking about," mocked Sigmundr.

"*Pfft*! All right, there definitely exists a manner to settle this matter. Do you see that girl over there? She looks all by herself. Why don't you go talk to her, Halldorr?" defied Einarr, smirking.

"As a matter of fact, I will! I intended to do that, anyway," revealed Halldórr, puffing up his chest.

"OK! Just don't make a fool out of yourself," remarked Sigmundr.

Halldórr gathered his wits and plodded toward the lonely girl. She appeared to be drinking quietly and unaware of the approaching predator.

"He looks too unnatural—heavy and awkward," commented Kettil. He directed that to the others. At the same time, he observed Halldorr's moves.

Halldórr approached her, and the next thing they saw coming to pass was Halldórr being anxious, his increased heart rate and labored breathing indicated it. He sprinted like he had stolen something, and the guards were hot on his tail.

"Whoa! What happened there, charmer?" asked Sigmundr.

"When I tried to say hi, using all my charm, she turned to me and told me that she was married."

"To whom is she married?" the group asked, intrigued.

"To Sir Absalon. Can you imagine that? And she threatened to call her husband if I pestered her," confessed Halldórr.

"You are such an imbecile. Knights don't marry servants or plebs," Sigmundr reprimanded.

"You are an idiot! She would say anything, even that she is married, just to get rid of you. You approached her aggressively," revealed Einarr.

"Wait—that means she is not married?" asked Halldórr.

"What did we just tell you? Knights don't marry commoners. That's only a mistress, not the wife, you dumb imbecile," rebuked Einarr.

"Why didn't you warn me?" asked Halldórr.

"We just wanted to see if you had what it takes. It's not our fault that you are incompetent," Einarr replied.

"*Psfutt*. Why do the knights have so many women and we, not a single one?" questioned Kettil neutrally.

"Ha! Speak for yourself, Barefoot! I got myself a girl," declared Sigmundr.

"Yeah, yeah. Sure, you do. The only thing remains, she lives thousands of heads away. Only God knows if she exists," mocked Halldórr.

"She *is* real, more than any of you could ever handle," Sigmundr retorted.

The night went on, full of small talk about girls, battles, and glory. It happened to be an easygoing moon cycle with no caretakers or supervision. The boys were free to do what they wanted. They drank, danced, and, whenever possible, flirted with the girls, but without success.

***

A voice in the distance screamed, "Wake up, you lazy maggots! It's the moment for you to ready yourselves at the courtyard!"

A loud thump on Thormon's door woke him.

"Oh, my. What a hangover!" complained Thormon.

"Get up, you useless scum!" the caretaker barked as he banged on the door.

"I'm up," Thormon moaned as he worked himself out of bed and into his uniform.

Thormon made his course to the hall and met up with his companions. They all slithered toward the courtyard. When they arrived there, the sun punctured their eyes. And the words of the caretakers thumped in their ears about how discipline was a must-have in the castle and that at the crack of dawn, the squires were supposed to be up and running, ready for training.

"Yeah! Yeah! We know. We know," Halldórr moaned as they all got together.

They followed the flow of individuals to the big wooden table, where they found wooden chairs and waited for the cook to serve their breakfast.

"Don't forget—we are beneath the knights. We sit back there," Sigmundr moaned as they dragged their way toward the back.

Young pageboys brought trays filled with bread, eggs, and bacon. They served milk in big glass gallons, distributed over the long wooden table. So, one could pour oneself a drink without bumping into each other.

"I believe you need water instead of milk, you dead beats," a young pageboy murmured as he saw the state of the squires.

The boys didn't say a word. They just nodded their heads and accepted what the pageboy suggested.

The food didn't taste that great, maybe due to their state. The stench of booze seemed shabby. It reeked intensely about whoever inhaled the air nearby. Their eyes could barely stay open. It turned out to be a sad state to be in.

"Why did we drink so awfully much last night?" Thormon murmured.

"It seemed like a good idea last moon cycle," Sigmundr replied, trying to keep his head up.

"Yeah! It always seems like a fair idea. That is, before anyone does something stupid," the pageboy sniped. At the same time, he refilled their cups with water.

The boys shrugged the pageboy away and told him to mind his own business, but the kid just laughed and lectured them "Grow up! What kind of image are you fools showing to the people here? Especially to the beautiful women across from you?"

The squires quickly tried to compose themselves. And Thormon looked around to see where these beautiful women were seated.

From afar, Thormon glanced at four pretty, young girls. They sat at the farthest side of the table, close to the kitchen.

"Wow! Who are those beauties?" Thormon asked.

Halldórr picked his head up, looked around, and asked, "Where?"

"There! Close to the kitchen," Thormon replied, pointing toward the girls.

"Are you crazy? Don't make it so evident that we are checking the girls out! I know where the kitchen is positioned inside the palace," Halldórr alerted as he grabbed Thormon's arm and put it down.

The boys, in unison, saw where Thormon directed his index finger. He seemed to be pointing and making evident the unaware girl. As a result, many nodded in agreement, "You have good taste!"

"Those are the servants' daughters. Quite pretty, aren't they?" Kettil replied with a smirk.

"Probably not out of reach for the likes of you, Thormon," Einarr added.

Thormon glanced at Einarr and asked, "What do you mean, not out of my reach?"

Halldórr smiled and answered, "You have quite some things to learn, Fresh."

"After all, this is still just your third day of the season," Kettil added.

Thormon shrugged those comments away. And a bit later, he complained, "None of you has provided me any information of value. For example, their names."

"Thormon, you dog! You just arrived, and you want to know the servants' daughters' names," Halldórr commented. He put his hand on Thormon's shoulder and then continued. "Well, which one would you like to know?"

"The one in the middle!" Thormon answered.

"Ah! The chef's daughter. You do indeed have good taste. That's Eira." Kettil had jumped in to answer before Halldorr could give the name.

"She is beautiful, but don't go barking up that tree. Her father is like a hawk. And even if you do muster up the courage to talk to her, her father does not want a pretty thing like her meddling with the likes of us—mere squires," Einarr added.

"True! He will chop us, cook us, and serve our remains to everyone else as a meal," Kettil kept on elaborating.

"But didn't you say those girls were within our reach?" Thormon inquired.

"True! But you went out of your way and chose the only one to whom we cannot get close. Why didn't you ask about the less attainable girls?" Einarr complained.

Before Thormon could say anything, a firm hand smacked his and Halldorr's shoulders. They looked up. Halldorr, Einarr, Sigmundr, and Kettil turned as pale as death.

A strong, low, thundering voice followed. "I saw you bums pointing at my daughter and overheard your comments. You four deadbeats know your path around here, but this other fool doesn't. Thus, I'll only say this once: *take your eyes, thoughts, intentions, or anything your filthy mind can muster off my daughter*!"

Thormon swallowed; his throat felt dry, and the saliva descended heavy. "I meant no disrespect. I only acknowledged your daughter's beauty. You won't deny that she stands out among the crowd." He took a deep breath and continued. "I've been here only three days. I'm still getting used to the rules and norms of the house. Please forgive me."

The father squeezed Thormon's shoulder. "At least your friends had the smartness to tell you she is out of your league. And for that, I will not poison your food—for the time being. But I'd watch what you eat forthwith."

"We are truly sorry, sir!" the boys replied.

The chef took his hands off Thormon's and Halldorr's shoulders and chastised them, "Good to know." He paused for a moment, looked at the boys, took a wooden spoon out of his apron, and smacked each boy on the head. "That's just a taste of what will come if you boys don't stay in line!" The chef walked away.

The pageboy came to pick up the dishes. "Hope that cured your hangover," he lectured, witty, as the boys passed their hands over their heads in pain. "Hope y'all learned your place."

The boys just gave the pageboy a harsh look and shrugged him away.

***

As routines went, the squires had their duties after breakfast. Believe it or not, only some apprentice knights knew of Thormon's master. The squires were ignorant to that matter, as was Thormon by the dull look on his face. He completely forgot the name of his knight. He had alcohol-induced amnesia; hard drinking can have such an effect on a teenager's mind.

"Now then, Thormon, who is your knight?" Halldorr asked as they went to the barracks.

"Believe it or not, I don't remember his name. I think it's Magnusar. But I'm unsure about the details or procedures," replied Thormon. He felt stupid for not exactly realizing a squire's role.

"Magnusar already has a squire; as a result, I'm almost sure you won't go to him," Haldorr cogitated.

"Didn't they tell you when you arrived? They normally do. That's the procedure," Sigmundr added.

"I don't know. Everything took me aback exceedingly. So, I paid little attention to that," Thormon replied, embarrassed.

"Everyone, upon arrival, is designated a knight; just ask around," mentioned Kettil.

"I'm Sir Ragnar's squire. Haldorr serves Sir Daven. Einarr over there serves Sir Jakob. And Kettil serves Sir Hemming," Sigmundr explained.

"I know I have a master knight, but I don't remember his name," confessed Thormon.

"Come with me, and I'll help you find who you'll serve. I'll use my wits," Haldorr offered as he and Thormon parted from the remaining boys.

"How will I find out?" Thormon asked, worried.

"Leave it to me," Haldorr replied as he stepped inside one of the quarters.

Thormon stayed outside. He heard Haldorr scream, "I need to talk to that good-for-nothing squire. The new one that we call Thormon. He knows nothing. Who is that useless squire's knight?"

The young boys in the quarters quickly ran around to find out who it should be. As they ran, they also got the answer.

"It's Teodor! It's Teodor!"

Haldorr looked at the young boys there, threw a sword to the floor, and commanded, "Good to know! At the moment, go polish and sharpen this sword!"

The young boys ran off to obey him.

Haldorr threw his head out the window and whispered to Thormon, "Did you get that? At once, go—quickly!"

Thormon ran to Teodor's barracks, and the caretaker met him upon arrival.

"Finally! I thought you would never show up. Now, you are here. Listen up, boy. Always obey and do whatever the knight asks of you without question. You must always keep his armor and weapons clean and polished. Always walk on the right side and two steps behind him. Never speak unless spoken to. Treat women respectfully. You must be the first one up and the last one to bed. And for heaven's sake, go to the library and study the chivalry code."

Thormon nodded and followed him to the barracks.

Thormon stopped at the door, turned to the caretaker, and asked, "Before I go in, where can I find Sir Teodor?"

The caretaker looked around and pointed to a lonely knight on a stool. "That man sitting at the round table. He can help you."

Thormon shyly walked toward the man and mustered a question. "Are you Sir Teodor?"

The man took a good look at Thormon and smiled at him. "No, young sir. I'm not that short of a man. Maybe you can't see him. Let me help you." The man took a deep breath, looked around, and screamed. "Teodor, you dwarf! They finally assigned you someone who can carry you on his shoulder!"

Then a scream replied, "We'll see who's small when the tournament comes!"

The man put his hand on Thormon's shoulder and instructed, "He's all the way back there. You'll know who it is by the size and, forthwith, by how angry he stays."

Thormon thanked him and ran in the direction the man told him. Upon arriving, Thormon looked at the man and asked, "Sir Teodor, now I remember you from the feast back at home. Glad to see you!"

"Yes, Thormon, likewise! But I believe you are late. Aren't you the squire who was assigned to me by Magnusar? Have you forgotten?" replied the knight.

"Yes! Magnusar assigned me to be your squire; I only forgot your name. Thus, I did not know where to go," Thormon eagerly replied.

Teodor looked at Thormon from top to bottom and declared, "Let's just hope you have what it takes to handle a knight like me. I am tired of going through squires like wine. It comes to pass the time one was strong enough to handle me."

Thormon just nodded.

"If you could tell me a little about yourself while you start fetching my armor over there—Magnusar gave me great praise about you." The knight pointed to the far corner where a plate of armor seemed placed flat on a table.

Thormon told Sir Teodor about his history, background, and where and what he did.

Teodor turned to the boy and praised him, "You can be quite useful!"

Thormon smiled, but a frown quickly put him in his place. He stayed quiet for a moment. He told Thormon what his superiors, including himself, would expect of him. The knight transpired as the one doing the talking.

Not very different from the work I did back at the Thours' market, thought Thormon as he went through the armor.

"No! Boy! It's the other one!" were the screams he heard.

Thormon brought the ones he thought were right. But Teodor burst into anger. And the knight yelled at the boy, "I overlooked your lateness and sheer appearance of a hangover. But stupidity, I won't tolerate."

"I'm sorry, sir. I don't know what I need to do. The quartermaster sent me to come here to learn," Thormon replied shyly.

The knight looked at the armors and murmured, "It seems a bit difficult to figure out which is which. And I only told you to fetch an armor, but I never told you which one." Teodor looked through the armor and started explaining a bit of what filled up today's schedule. "The armor for the occasion today stands as jousting. Therefore, the armor should be cumbersome, with extra shielding on the jouster's side. You have no idea which side is mine. I'm left-handed. Hence you should get the armor with stronger padding on the left."

Thormon looked through the armory and brought Teodor the correct one.

"OK! You got that right. Currently, let's work with the rest of the armament." Teodor explained as he tried to hide his impatience.

As Thormon prepared the knight, Teodor told him a little about himself. Of course, he was interrupted frequently to guide Thormon properly. But Thormon learned that Teodor had just moved from Cicipangle. And he took a liking to Baldar and its people.

In the following days, Thormon learned in depth about the different kinds of plate armor. Also, he studied functions and how a blacksmith should work the tempered steel so that a full armor could weigh less. He also took his moment to read up on the codes and conducts. He followed all the rules to the letter.

Teodor took a liking to the boy. He seemed humble and quietly withstood all the abuse and rudeness thrown at him.

Throughout the seasons, Thormon became quite well known. The caretakers and the masters of the castle took a real liking to the lad.

Thormon met other knights and squires, and a bond consolidated.

CHAPTER 36

The Winter Tournament

It was the most awaited event of the decade. Knights from all over the kingdom came to test out their might. At the castle, everyone hung about in a frenzy.

One-on-one, the squires gathered up close to the fireplace. They talked a bit about how they had been doing and their opinions about what seemed to be on the verge of coming to pass.

"Thus, Thormon, we no longer have enough spare time. How are you handling the crazed dwarf knight?" asked Haldorr.

"It hasn't been easy, but I've learned a lot," Thormon replied.

"You should have. That man is a real ball-buster," Sigmundr gossiped.

"Yeah! Especially the instance you joined the squires. It wasn't the best of it," Haldorr added.

"Why? What do you mean by that?" Thormon asked.

"You know about the tournament that seems about to commence, and there is a lot at stake here," replied Barefoot.

"We've been squires for many seasons, and you, only for a few seasons," Sigmundr added.

"How do you expect to compete with us?" Barefoot asked.

"What do you mean?" Thormon asked back.

"You are going to go up against squires and seasoned knights—those who are as one with each other. Heck, we know even when our knights need to piss," Haldorr replied.

Thormon looked at the boys with a blank face.

"The court's inscriber published the list of who befalls fighting who," Barefoot added.

"Yeah! The fights will commence tomorrow at the main square. Only the best gets to go to the castle and fight," informed Sigmundr.

"Thus, you need to fight in order to fight?" Thormon asked, confused.

"In a manner of speaking, yes. But the first round of this tournament remains for the plebs. And it's also a good way to separate the wheat from the chaff," Haldorr answered.

"Thus, everyone is in it and betting on these fights, right?" Thormon asked.

"That's it! Today, you are starting to get it," Haldorr replied.

"I heard that Sir Wiking's brother stands matched up against Sir Absalon. And, as you know, only one of them will make the list," informed Sigmundr.

"Teodor will go through the same thing, right?" Thormon asked.

"Yeah, but I'm interested in seeing Absalon get his righteous ass kicked. I still cannot shake that whore of a mistress he has, a real doggone cocky girl," Haldorr replied.

"You mean the one who blew you away at that party a few days ago?" Barefoot joked.

The group laughed, except for Haldorr.

"I can't believe you are still holding a grudge," Sigmundr announced.

"My apparent demeanor meant without a doubt that I felt humiliated in front of you guys. And later, my knights found out and mocked me," Haldorr replied angrily.

"Well, changing the subject from Halldorr's love life to the tournament—could you tell me about it in detail? How come Magnusar ensues already at the castle phase and does not need to compete at the square?" Thormon asked.

"You see, he stands in for the local champion. I mean, the kingdom's champion," replied Einarr.

"Every kingdom's champion does not fight in this first phase. They go directly to the castle's brawl," Sigmundr added.

"Therefore, Sir Teodor seems enrolled in the tournament's first phase, right? I don't know sufficiently. Teodor does not tell me any confidential information. With him, it's just work and work," Thormon confessed.

"Hm," the group let escape a guise of sympathy and pity.

Halldórr broke the awkward silence. "We know who transpires fighting whom from the list. Which the quartermaster gives on the day of the fight."

"If that's the case, how do you know who's fighting Absalon?" Thormon asked, confused about the whole thing.

"I have my ways. I've been a squire longer than you," Haldorr replied.

"That's why you know exceedingly about this damned tournament," replied Thormon.

"My cousin is experienced as one more of the guests in one of these knights' games a while back in Eritrea. However, he couldn't give stuff away. He told me stories about it. Which made me want to become a squire," Haldorr added. He ensured that he did not share private information.

"And how did it turn out? How did your cousin describe it?" asked Barefoot.

"A duo of knights from Cicipangle got the first place and the victor's reward. That's all I can say," replied Haldorr.

"That's it! You'll only tell us who won and nothing else?" Thormon asked, intrigued and wanting to know further.

"I can't give you all the details. We will have our knights face each other. That is, if they can get far enough," Haldorr replied, wanting the upper hand.

"Hm, stop being exceedingly cheap. You have a slight advantage. None of us ever saw or had anyone tell us how it went," Sigmundr replied angrily. "Well, at least Sir Ragnar is not competing. The task would put me to the test as a squire. Less work for me; extra work for you all."

"Wait a moment! Is your knight not competing? Why the heck not?" the group asked.

"I am more of a caretaker. Sir Ragnar is quite old," Sigmundr revealed, but he got interrupted by Haldorr.

"True! That man is old! He is doing us a favor by not competing. The only thing you'll be helping him with remains his walking stick," joked Halldórr.

Sigmundr looked down on Haldorr and shrugged his comments away. "Sir Ragnar can still put up a good fight. He just doesn't feel the need to waste his strength on such tournaments."

The group looked at Sigmundr for a while.

Haldorr added, "In any case, you'll never experience the tournament firsthand. What a shame. From what my cousin told me, it's amazing!"

The conversation continued throughout the day. And as the place got further and further crowded, that's when further concerns came to light about the knights' games. Everything from public humiliation to death could take place. Knights could lose their knighthoods. Squires could be humiliated and cast out—nothing happy or cheerful. That was not something expected. By the solar cycle's end, the boys returned to their quarters rather fearful than hopeful.

The next day, Sir Teodor woke up and got ready early. A pageboy came to the cafeteria and told Thormon that the knight expected him at the barracks. Thormon quickly stuffed the rest of his bread in his mouth. And he worked his path through the castle and into the military facilities.

At the time, he entered the courtyard. He saw the short knight in the distance, sharpening his sword, almost at a constant pace, with a refined technique while whistling an appealing tune. His head seemed set on his task, occasionally broken up by swinging his left leg back and forth. Thormon approached the knight, but before he could say anything, the knight looked up and said, "Hm. You are finally here. Help me don my armor, if you will."

"Good morning, sir!" confirmed Thormon.

The knight just looked at him and pointed to where Thormon should start. Thormon walked toward the chest and started rummaging through it. He realized that the armor looked different. The blacksmith's logo attested that he made each piece of satin-polished carbon steel. It had a pleasing sheen. Something hard to miss. The breastplate had an ornamental golden lion etched on it. The gauntlets were unique in design. It had the wrist piece embossed with bronzed steel and the rest made of burnished steel.

"Wow, I've only seen something like this once—at the Cyclops' booty," Thormon commented lushly.

Seeing the amazement on the youngster's face and hearing his words, the knight commented, "This armor comes to pass as my family's most valuable heirloom. I will wear it for the first time in honor of my late father."

"I know you'll make him proud," Thormon reassured his master.

"Let's hope I do. He was a knight himself. He died from old age, not in the manner every knight should die. Which means in battle and not in a bed," Teodor had a heart-to-heart as his appearance reflected his inner sentiments. Then he shielded it and became stern, "It doesn't matter much nowadays. Hurry up with the armor. I need to find out whether it fits me well."

Thormon helped strap on the armor. The knight moved his limbs to see how well the armor suited him.

Thormon looked at him and smiled, "Sir, it fits you perfectly!"

The knight looked at the polished silver mirror and got the impression he saw his father's ghost. He mentioned in a somber tone, "The spitting image of my old man, a chip off the old block." He stood there for a moment and then turned to Thormon. "Grab that wooden sword and the iron one!"

Thormon fetched both swords and handed them both to the knight. The knight grabbed the wooden one with his right hand and told Thormon to stay with the iron one.

"Try your best to hit me," Teodor staged a slight frown.

Thormon reluctantly advanced and took a stance. But before he could say anything, the knight swung his sword toward Thormon. He forced the boy to either defend himself or fight.

"Let's see if you are knight material!" Teodor held his stance as he readied himself for another swing.

Thormon realized the knight did not jest. He raised the sword, and they started the duel. The youngster avoided hitting the knight, which angered Teodor.

"Stop defending yourself! I need you to try to hit me! Gunnarr declared you were quite the swordsman."

"But, sir, I've never had the proper training with swords," protested Thormon after receiving a painful blow to the chest.

"That never stopped you from helping your uncle and friends," Teodor mentioned with sarcasm. He tried to provoke Thormon.

"But, sir—" Another blow hit him.

"Stop whining and attempt to hit me! Don't you want to be a knight? Consider this your first lesson!"

Thormon looked seriously at the knight and started to wave off his attacks. Three strikes later, the wooden sword had been broken in half by Thormon's counterblow. And once he had the opportunity, he attacked the knight. Surprisingly, Thormon got a few shots in. But the knight outwitted him, even though he was not equipped with a proper sword. He managed to throw Thormon to the ground.

"You have potential kid. All you need is a brain. Always watch your opponent. Anticipate his movements. Even though I was unarmed, I managed to beat you. At least this armor can handle damage," Teodor attested, helping Thormon up. "Do not put too much strength on each blow, for you will lose your balance. Be careful with your swings. Instantly ready yourself again, and take some swings at me. I will not block them. I will stand my ground and decide whether this armor remains in proper condition."

Thormon started with weak strikes but increased the strength of each blow. Thus, he could figure out how much the armor could take. Thormon hit the knight in different places so that the knight gathered all the required information.

"Very well, Thormon," the knight eulogized as he parried Thormon's last blow, taking the sword from his hands.

Thormon fell to the ground. The knight helped him up again.

"You gotta watch your footing, as well. Now, help me out of this armor."

Happy with his new armor, Sir Teodor asked Thormon to polish it and set it on the wooden table, piece by piece. Once the work had ended, he should be free to leave.

"Sir Teodor, you are in the tournament, right? I can't help but wonder since you seem intensely focused on training," Thormon asked curiously as he prepared to leave.

Teodor gave a small smile. "I believe you already know the answer. The thing is, do you think we have a shot?"

"To tell you the truth, I've never seen you fight, and the way you move amazes me," Thormon replied.

"Let's hope so. You are in this with me. We are a team. Never forget that," Teodor replied, showing Thormon his somewhat humane side.

Thormon smiled and left the barracks. As he walked out of the courtyard, he heard screaming and cheering from a crowd. He quickly followed the source of the sound. And moments later, he stood on the main square, where two knights dueled, circling and sizing each other up. Both boys recognized Thormon. So they opened a path for him to enter the inner ring of people, very close to the dueling knights. Among the crowd, he found Sigmundr and Halldórr.

"Where have you been? We've been looking for you the entire day," Haldorr asked sternly.

"I was with Sir Teodor," Thormon replied.

"Oh, OK! Let me give you the rundown. You see, those two squires have provided sword and mace about two times now. No horse or lances were included in this duel, just a pure melee contest," informed Sigmundr breathing laboredly.

"Do you know those knights?" asked Thormon.

"I told you already about today's fights. At least you made it to the most important one today—Sir Wikings' brother and Sir Absalon. That tall yellow-headed one appears to be Wikings' brother. I keep forgetting his name. And the other one with the thick beard seems to be Absalon."

Thormon started cheering as well, but soon, he heard something odd. It appeared not to be in the common dialect but something elfish. Thormon looked around and saw, from the opposite side of the crowd circle, a white knight. He looked like he was muttering something while eyeing Sir Absalon. Thormon fixed his eyes not only on the man's mouth but on his hands as well. He shook Sigmundr's shoulder and asked if he saw the man in a white robe, and he told Sigmundr to pay attention as well.

"Look! On every occasion, the white paladin says something inaudible and gestures symbols. So a boost of energy and an increase in morale takes over the losing Sir Absalon, who suddenly is able to give a big, bold attack, almost overcoming the much younger and stronger Sir Wikings' brother. But look—the blessing wears off quickly. That forced that white knight to mutter the magic words nonstop." Thormon pointed his fingers toward the man in the white robe.

"Where does this old dog get this unending energy? He seems relentless," confessed Halldórr, referring to Sir Absalon.

"Tell him, Thormon," Sigmundr requested.

Thormon pointed his finger toward the man in the white robe and asked, "Who is that white knight on the opposite side?"

"Oh! I see him. He looks rather odd. Everyone stays cheering, and he is just there, standing in a trance-like state. And look at the dragon symbol on his body banner. Wait a beat of an eagle's wings —he stands as an emissary from Cicipangle!" Haldorr gazed hard at the white knight due to his poor eyesight.

"Hm. Just wondering. Nothing to it," Thormon concluded.

He saw that the others did not share his suspicions. Therefore, he just kept on observing. The fight went on. Clearly, the underdog had the upper hand. Sir Absalon struck the rival knight with his mace, knocking the opponent's sword away. That gave him an opening and finished his tired adversary with a hit on the chest. The knight flew back, falling hard on his back.

The crowd cheered in a frenzy.

The grounded knight fought to get up but couldn't. Sir Wikings stepped in on behalf of his defeated brother and shouted, "It is over! My brother's adversary defeated him!"

Sir Absalon composed himself and nodded in agreement. Sir Wikings thanked the knight for the match. He picked up his brother and shouted to Sigmundr, "Come here, Squire, and help me!"

Not only Sigmundr went there. Also, several squires dragged the yellow-headed knight out of the ring and into his quarters.

As soon as both knights left, the crowd dispersed.

"I believe that's our cue to return to our quarters," Haldorr concluded, surprised by the fight's outcome.

Thormon nodded, and both walked back quietly. Thormon did not want to comment on the oddities he'd seen, and Haldorr did not wish to comment on the lost sure-win fight. Both boys saw a familiar face as they entered the castle's gate.

"Hey! Isn't that your love interest?" Thormon joked as they approached the lady.

Halldórr stopped and replied, "Yeah. Isn't she Absalom's wife?"

"I believe not," Thormon replied as they passed by and saw a look of disdain for Absalon and his embracing real wife, which reflected on the young girl's face.

Haldorr stopped and, with a smirk, tormented the woman, "Your husband won. Thus why aren't you there celebrating with him? Don't let that other woman take your knight."

Haldorr smiled. The lady just ignored him with a nasty, scornful facial expression.

"Well, don't let your husband treat you like a mistress. These knights discard their mistresses like trash."

"Bug off, you creep!" the lady replied as she walked away.

"Damn, Haldorr! That was cold!" Thormon acknowledged, and both boys chuckled.

"He-he! I have to see how much I lost," Haldorr jested. He changed directions, walking toward a gathering of people.

"Aren't you coming back to the barracks?" Thormon asked.

"This stands as another part of the fights that you need to know. This is where we make or lose money. I'm not rich like you. Therefore, I need to find alternative ways to make money," Haldorr replied.

It intrigued Thormon. Hence, he decided to tag along.

It seemed that a lucky Cicipangleman had won a large sum, placing all his money on the underdog, old Absalon.

"Look at how lucky he is—if I'd only had that kind of luck," Haldorr complained as he saw that he had lost everything.

Thormon knew that, somehow, the man had known the result of the fight beforehand. When he saw the man celebrating with the people from Cicipangle, he knew something fishy seemed to be happening.

Could that mage have something to do with it? he thought.

"Don't you think it's odd?" Thormon asked Haldorr.

"What's odd? Losing all your money? That man had a hint on whom to bet, that's all," Haldorr replied, shrugging away Thormon's suspicions. "Let's just get to the barracks. I bet our knights want to talk to us or demand our service."

And in accordance, the boys headed back.

CHAPTER 37

Beginning of the Tournament

I t was nearly dawn. The sun hadn't risen yet when a company of six wearied by travel, wayworn elves from Coloris entered the castle.

The elves had ceremonial armors and a banner symbolizing the High Elves of the East. Their equipment set them at an honorable position in Lord Vermundr's account.

The quartermaster awoke Thormon and told him he should welcome the elves.

"I'm not their welcoming committee. Why should I bother?" Thormon asked angrily.

"You have lots to learn! At the moment, get up, and do what I say!" the quartermaster replied as he hit Thormon on the head.

Thormon complied and did everything that his superior should ask of him. At the end of the solar cycle, the knight summoned him.

"In any case, how did it go?" Sir Teodor asked.

"Being their servants all day long and not training? What do you think, sir?" Thormon replied, showing that he wasn't pleased with what had happened.

"You know, their king asked for you personally to be their aide here," Sir Teodor replied.

"That means nothing. I've met that race before. And while I'm with them, the elves, it takes precious time from training with you," Thormon commented. "

Oh, do not worry. We'll have plenty of time. You see, I was put into another position in return for your services to them. I'll fight way up on the ladder before the interspecies combats. Thus, time stays what we have."

Thormon did not understand a thing of what Teodor kept on saying, but he nodded and mentioned, "If you say so. At least tell me when we'll be able to train."

"Soon. Until then, you need to stay put. And who knows? You'll learn something important. Those elves spoke highly of you as if you were one of their kin," Teodor replied.

Thormon looked surprised and comprehended the strategy Teodor undertook here.

"Being a knight means not only training or fighting. Sometimes, getting to know your enemy seems even reasonably more important. At this point, that's the lesson for today. Tomorrow, meet me here, and we'll talk about the chivalry and philosophy of the knighthood. You see, training comes in all kinds." Teodor winked and sent the boy off to his quarters.

Thormon went on helping the elves, and at night, he met with his master. The tournament's ruckus barely impacted the boy. He seemed to be learning much from the elves and his knight.

Seven days later, another company entered. This time consisting of dwarfs from Havengar, no less grand than the elves. They were at the castle as guests of honor. They were to fight in the tournament as well.

However, Lord Vermundr placed the competitors at the greatest distance from each other. Thus, one company dwelled in the left wing and the other in the right wing of the palace.

The elves and the dwarfs had always arrived at the beginning of the tournament. So, they studied their competitors' fighting styles. And then, they had to follow suit with the proper protocol. It stayed as the custom throughout the ages.

***

After nine days, everyone involved in the tournament came to attend it. Thormon had already been released from his duties with the elves. And he undertook training with Teodor at full pace. The contest thinned out the fighters with every passing day. And soon, it was the occasion to put Thormon's knowledge and Teodor's fighting skills to the test.

All the knights who had made it this far were to dress up and report to the arena. The official announcements of the fights for the second phase were slated to happen.

Trumpets and coronets announced what was to come. The beginning of the second phase of the knights' game. The knights walked into the arena and lined up, facing the crowd.

There the bothersome background noise fell to silence. The herald stood up and announced, "Ladies and gentlemen. I am proud to present the competitors for the Eastern World Top Championship contest. The names are being assorted and sorted out as I speak, and, in moments, we'll know the second round of fights. Winners progress to the next round, and the rules oust the losers from the competition."

A beautiful woman approached the herald. She held a golden bowl with the names of the knights. Later, the results of a lottery with the names assorted chose the fights by chance.

"In front of us, we have our matches. Our fights will begin tomorrow at sundown, and only one fight per day. The first fight of the tournament stays—Sir Daven faces Sir Absalon!"

The crowd cheered.

"Our second fight is—Sir Hemming faces Sir Nikolaus! Our third fight is—Sir Erland faces Sir Kennet! Our fourth fight is—Sir Pontus faces Sir Joakim! Our fifth fight is—Sir Mikkel faces Sir Ulrik! And our last fight of this round will be—Sir Arvid faces Sir Teodor!"

Sir Teodor turned to Thormon and mentioned with relief, "Lucky for us, we have enough days to train and observe. The gods are in our favor."

The next day, Thormon got up early and trained with his knight throughout the morning. Also, into the afternoon until it went nigh the time for the first fight.

"We need to watch every match, Thormon. I know you have a good eye. Hence, keep watch!" Sir Teodor requested as both were en route to the arena for the fight.

"The first fight appears to be Sir Daven against Sir Absalon. He is the bald, older guy, right?" Thormon asked as they sat.

"That's right. He doesn't look the part," Teodor replied as he focused on the fighters. "Somehow, he managed to make it this far."

"I remember I saw something off when he stood fighting." He got up and started to walk around the arena. "Let me see if I can confirm something," Thormon suspected something was wrong.

The fight started, the commotion fired up the crowd, and soon, it was difficult for Thormon to walk around.

Wow! These people get riled up! I must make my way closer to where Sir Absalon remains, Thormon thought as he pushed his way forward.

He tried to get as close as possible, but there were too many people. Thormon could not have cared less about the fight. His focus remained on the crowd, and soon, his troubles did not go to waste.

"It's the same guy," he noticed quietly. "I need to approach him."

Thormon got as close as he could. He noticed a man in a white robe muttering something ancient. He couldn't understand the meaning due to the crowd's noise, but he understood one word: "luth." Thormon quickly turned to the ring and saw Sir Absalon take back the fight with renewed energy. He overpowered his adversary, winning the match.

Those words the man muttered—I know where they are from. Maybe the elves can help me, Thormon thought as he followed the crowd out of the arena. He met up with Sir Teodor.

"Where did you run off to?" Sir Teodor asked.

Thormon explained what he'd seen the first instance he went to watch Sir Absalom's fight. Now, he mentioned that he wanted to talk to the elves. Sir Teodor thought it seemed nothing. And that they should concentrate on their training and strategies. But he did tell the boy to watch for anything suspicious.

"Go on, then. Have a quick word with the elves, but I'm expecting you back before the dinner bell," Teodor paced back and forth.

Thormon thanked him and ran to the palace's rearmost wing.

"Well, hello, Thormon! Good to see you here! What did you think about the fight? It seems to be your first occasion watching one, right?" one of the elder elves asked.

Thormon smiled. "It's the second time but with the same fighter. That's what I'd like to talk to you about."

The elf cleared a table and had Thormon join them as a guest.

"I cannot stay here for long. My knight wants me back by dinnertime."

The elves nodded, and Thormon went straight to the point. They took in all the information he provided, what he'd seen and thought of both fights.

The elves were intrigued by the information given. And they explained to Thormon that it would be a weighty accusation. It remained forbidden to even speak elfish during the tournament. It had words of power, and everyone there must fight as equals.

Thormon assured the elves that what he had heard was elfish of old, but again, they asked him to be careful not to judge. They explained how the tournament worked and all of its rules and duties.

"Wow! The squires never told me anything like this," Thormon realized in awe.

"True! We never want to overwhelm anyone, but that's how serious this tournament appears to be," the elf replied with a smile.

Thormon thanked them and promised to be vigilant and wiser about what to say and accuse.

The thought of the true responsibility of such a tournament made him anxious. Could Teodor win this tournament? Anxiety crept in, and he found himself walking back to the barracks, where he went for training. There appeared to be Sir Teodor, collecting his armor.

"How did it go with the elves? You came back oddly quick."

Thormon just gave him a weird smile and picked up his armor and gear. "Where should I put this?" he asked.

"Carry this chest to the main square, and wait for me once you get there," Teodor responded.

Thormon nodded, dragged the heavy gear to the main training area, and sat on it.

I didn't think this tournament was rooted in this kingdom's political landscape, Thormon thought. *But how can I prove what I saw?*

***

The following daybreak at the tournament, Thormon went to see Barefoot, who stood already there, next to Hemming, preparing for the fight.

Barefoot saw Thormon approaching. With a smile, he asked the people to make way for his friend. Thormon hugged Barefoot and wished him luck.

"Did you notice that Sir Daven lost to Sir Absalon? Halldórr seems quite pissed off," blurted Barefoot.

"Yeah! I went there! I saw it," Thormon replied.

"How is that old man still winning? How can he?" Barefoot asked.

"Barefoot, my boy," Sir Hemming smiled interrupting the boys. "Help me don my armor."

"Hold on, Thormon. I need to get this. Meet me at the courtyard after the fight," Barefoot offered.

Thormon patted him on the back and found a spot to sit and support his friend.

The thrill of emotion riled up the crowd for this one. The cheering got wilder and wilder. Thormon blended in, and at this interval, he decided to go with the flow. The next thing he knew, the fight seemed over. And Sir Hemming celebrated next to Barefoot. He lifted his sword and shouted in the middle of the crowd.

"Bring it on! I am ready to dispatch anyone you throw at me!" Hemming screamed to the public after winning in record time.

The next solar cycle Thormon found Sir Teodor sorting through his armor and weapons.

"Thus, how went the fight yesterday?" Teodor asked as he handed a sword to Thormon.

"It ended pretty quick," Thormon answered.

"Did you find anything suspicious on this one?" Teodor asked.

"No, why do you ask?" Thormon replied while preparing the mill to sharpen the sword.

"Just wanted to know. I didn't see you there. Hence, I thought you were looking for something within the crowd," Teodor replied.

"I stood next to Barefoot," Thormon informed as he fed the horses.

"Today, Sir Erland faces Sir Kennet. I'd like you to pay close attention to Sir Kennet. He seems off. Maybe you can tell me why." They both finished their chores and headed out to the arena.

Sir Erland faced Sir Kennet. Thormon did as Teodor asked and paid good attention to Sir Kennet, who, unfortunately, lost.

After the fight, Thormon talked to Teodor and asked him why he wanted him to pay closer attention to Kennet. Teodor explained they dressed Sir Kennet's horse. And he had a feeling that it would mean his loss; he was proved right. Teodor talked to Thormon. It was about the importance of paying close attention to every piece of detail. And that something so simple could mean the difference between defeat and victory.

Teodor fetched the horses the next daybreak then turned to Thormon and demanded, "Dress the horses with armor immediately. Here—I will help you."

Thormon got the steel plates and placed them around the horses. It ensued a bit difficult. A stubborn stallion wouldn't stay still.

"Why did you bring both horses? You'll only need one," Thormon asked as he finished strapping the last piece of armor.

"To see which one handles the armor best. It's not something we look into on the day of the fight," Teodor replied. He mounted one of the horses and asked Thormon to mount the next.

Both tested the fight patterns, such as strategies, abilities, and commands. Thus, they each picked the best horse for the tournament. When they finished, a pageboy arrived and requested Sir Teodor's presence.

"OK, boy! Feed the horses, and send them back to the stable. Once you finish, you can go watch today's match. It looks like I won't be able to be there," Teodor recommended as he followed the pageboy.

Sir Pontus faced Sir Joakim.

Thormon went to the match but felt too tired to care much about it. His eyes were closing. He slept through the entire match, waking up only when a cleaner told him to go home.

"Who won?" Thormon asked the cleaner.

"Buddy, if you didn't want to watch it, and dared to sleep through one of the best fights in the tournament, I'm not going to tell you. Try to figure it out by yourself." The grumpy cleaner kicked Thormon out of the arena.

Teodor woke Thormon to the next solar cycle.

"How went yesterday's match? I heard it was one for the history books. I bet you couldn't even sleep with excitement," Teodor mentioned enthusiastically.

Thormon scratched his eyes, looked up, and smiled shyly at Teodor. "I have to go to the bathroom!"

Teodor held him down. "No, you are not! You gotta tell me who won!"

Thormon smiled. "Another underdog won!"

"*What?* Neither of them happened to be an underdog! One matched the might of the other. They were evenly matched," Teodor replied angrily.

"Well, it transpired amongst the best fights ever," Thormon replied.

"That, I already know. All I want to know is, *who won?*" Teodor asked again.

"Ask the caretaker. I'm so lost in words that I can't explain how the fight was," Thormon replied.

"I'm not concerned about the fight. Just tell me who won!"

Thormon got up and projected, "Isn't it time for us to have breakfast? We have a huge day before us, and our fight is tomorrow. Therefore, let's focus on that."

"But who won?" Teodor cried out as Thormon walked out of his barracks.

■■

Thormon did as his master told him throughout the day. And when the moment came, he went to the arena for the last fight; he knew it would test him.

This time, he didn't sleep but paid close attention to Sir Mikkel and Sir Ulrik. It seemed not one of the best fights he had ever seen, but it turned out to be a good match nonetheless. Sir Ulrik was the winner of this one.

After the match, Thormon went straight to his barracks and meditated on the ensuing fight. In this instance, he would be center stage, along with Sir Teodor.

The next solar cycle, Sir Teodor woke him. "Get up, boy! It now stays as time for action! Let's go, boy. We have many things to do before the fight." Teodor shoved Thormon out of bed.

Thormon felt extremely anxious—that seemed clear on his face.

"Swipe that look off your face, boy. You don't want to appear weak," Teodor advised as they were en route out of the barracks and into the arena.

In the arena, the feeling did not go away. Thormon looked around and dreaded that he would freeze up when the moment came. His perception of the arena ensued differently from what he had seen. On this occasion, he stood located at the front and center.

"Come help me organize these gears," Teodor demanded, interrupting Thormon's thoughts.

Thormon nodded and walked toward the knight. But he looked like a child among the circus' magical charm.

"Snap out of it, boy! We have a lot to do!" Teodor yelled, snapping his fingers and taking Thormon out of his trance-like state.

When the time came for the start of the fight, adrenaline kicked in. That gave Thormon unbearable pain in the stomach, hyperventilation, elevated blood pressure, and an abnormally palpitating heart. Also, a feeling of worry mingled with excitement. The boy was sweating like crazy.

By noon, they finished all preparations. Sir Teodor told Thormon to grab something to eat and then rest. The servant would summon him in three hundred beats of an eagle's wings.

"Come, Thormon. It's the moment," the caretaker tried to give Thormon enthusiasm as he uttered softly and soothingly.

Thormon got up, took a deep breath, and made his course to the knight to prepare for protocol.

Thormon and Teodor exited the castle and made their path toward the arena.

"Wow, that's way more scores of people than I expected!" Thormon realized.

He became pale with anxiety.

"True! There are more people here than in the preceding fights. There are not enough places for everyone. We will have to go through the crowd," Teodor replied. He tried to calm Thormon as they approached the arena's fighters' entrance.

The crowd opened a way for them, making a corridor where the people attempted to shake hands and give them moral support. Upon entering the arena, both Thormon and Teodor looked around in awe.

"Even the elves are here in this instance," Sir Teodor remarked with a fearful tone. He raised his hand, greeting the crowd, and told Thormon to fetch the horse.

Standing on the opposing end of the track, Sir Arvid looked fearless.

"Don't let that menacing look scare you. He is doing that for show," Sir Teodor told Thormon. He mounted his horse, and Thormon handed him the lance, along with a dagger, sword, and shield.

Both knights circled the arena, greeting the crowd, nobles, and plebs. Both went to opposite ends and sized up each other with respect. The public became silent. Each cavalier at each end of the footpath raised their lances and awaited the signal. They proceeded with each step of the rules of engagement.

A beautiful maiden, followed by a high-ranking lord, descended to the stands. The beautiful maiden held out a handkerchief. She looked at both knights, smiled charmingly, and dropped the handkerchief. The horses shrieked. The sound of the pounding hooves of the heavy destriers against the earth became louder. That was, until both lances made contact, throwing both men in bulky metallic armor to the ground. The crowd went wild as shields and wooden shrapnel flew into the air. Teodor fell on his back against the dirt. He lifted himself and looked around to see if he had managed to send Sir Arvid to the ground, but a massive cloud of dirt blocked his view. He went for his sword but noticed that someone had broken it.

Confused, he turned to all directions and yelled, *"Sword!"*

Thormon darted toward the knight and handed him another great sword and a new shield. The other knight was already picking himself up with a Viking sword. Neither of the knights had the advantage related to the jousting contest.

Sir Teodor could not make out what Thormon kept on screaming at him. He removed his helmet and threw it to the ground, but the noise sounded still muffled.

The crowd continued experiencing the fight in a frenzy.

Both knights drew their swords and approached each other.

Thormon noticed Sir Arvid's unnatural recovery and quickly scoped the crowd. Soon, he saw a commotion. A white paladin pushed his way through the crowd, then began an odd muttering, never breaking his gaze from Sir Arvid, who launched an audacious combo of cuts and thrusts, hurting Sir Teodor's arm.

That man is meddling and interfering with the fights! I need to do something promptly, thought Thormon. He tried to call the attention of the elves.

Thormon saw that Commander Enlgon of Coloris appeared to be analyzing the fight. That happened as he had told Thormon.

Thormon ran into the ring with a mace in hand but got pushed back by Sir Teodor.

"I never asked for that!" he screamed.

The elf focused on Thormon, wondering why he would do such a thing.

Here, it seems to be my chance! Thormon thought. He noticed that he had caught the elf's attention. He made a sign showing the elf where to look.

Enlgon circled the arena. He stood between the white paladin and the fight in a manner that blocked the view.

"Move! You are in my way!"

But as soon as the paladin got blocked, Sir Teodor overcame his opponent. He threw the opposing knight to the ground.

The paladin angrily yelled at the elf, *"Move!"*

"I am entitled to position myself anywhere in this arena!" Enlgon replied as he stood his ground and called out for the rest of the elves.

"Stay closer to your privileged area!" replied the paladin, who seemed already angry as he had noticed the knight was losing the fight.

Since Enlgon would not move, he decided to push away the people next to him. But more and more elves came and blocked the paladin's view.

This commotion worked in favor of Sir Teodor, and with a powerful blow, he disarmed his opponent. Before any more unexpected bursts of energy should happen, he stepped forward, placed his great sword in the fatigued knight's throat, and screamed, "Yield! The fight is over!"

The knight nodded and accepted defeat.

Thormon looked at the crowd and smiled at the elves. He saw that one of the elves confronted and rebuked the angry paladin's curses and provocation. Enlgon nodded in respect for Thormon's quick thinking.

He looked around at the battleground. As the crowd cheered and the guards picked up the losing knight, Thormon ran toward Sir Teodor.

"Good job, Master! Let me carry your sword."

Teodor nodded. "OK, but next occasion, be attentive to a greater extent about what I ask you. Please also pick up my helmet and put it with the gauntlets."

The knight, very tired, walked back to his quarters. Thormon stayed behind. He told Teodor he would join him as soon as he finished. The crowd dispersed, and Thormon noticed that the elves did not budge. Thormon waved to them, and Enlgon nodded back.

"Let's talk out back!" Thormon screamed. Enlgon nodded and made his route out.

Once Thormon finished storing all the armor and weapons. He made his path to the back of the arena, where he met with Enlgon.

"Good to see you came, Sir Enlgon," Thormon greeted politely the elves bowing down.

"You were right about the meddling, but still, it's not enough. I will send scouts to spy on the winners and watch the next fights closely," Enlgon informed. He shook Thormon's hand and then walked with him toward the palace.

Thormon and Enlgon plotted how they'd get to expose the paladin's plight. And how they needed to do it before the fights got to the cross-human battles. Thormon got interrupted by Barefoot, congratulating him on the fight.

"Man! That turned out incredible! I thought Teodor would lose for sure!" Barefoot scratched his forehead and raised one eyebrow.

Thormon looked at his friend, surprised, and smiled.

"I'll leave you to your friend. Catch up with the knight and commemorate the victory. You all deserve it!" Enlgon praised as he parted.

"Whoa! The high elf was talking to you? Didn't think they had any kind of interest in these fights," Barefoot confessed surprised.

Thormon reminded Barefoot that he stayed with them before the fights. Since the time they arrived, the elves showed interest in Thormon personal life for he was royalty that transpired as frequent meetings and brief talks.

"Oh yeah. I completely forgot about that. Why on earth did they want you?" Barefoot asked.

"I have my connections, too," Thormon replied sarcastically.

Barefoot smiled. "Yeah, right! What did you do? Polish their shoes when you lived on the streets?"

"No, I've been to their city," Thormon replied.

Barefoot opened both his eyes, and his jaw dropped. "What do you mean, *been to their city*?"

"Yeah! I've been there. How do you think my uncle and his bards became rich and famous?" Thormon smiled.

"I thought you were joking or something. I never expected it to be true. No normal being can reach it," Barefoot replied, baffled.

Thormon smiled again. "Well, by the looks of it, I'm no normal being."

Before one could say another word, the friends interrupted them, congratulating him on the victory.

"I hope we are not to face each other on the next rounds of fights," Barefoot remarked sincerely.

"Indeed," Thormon agreed.

And before the group of friends could say anything else, Teodor looked angry. "Break it up. I need to have a word with Thormon!"

Thormon waved bye to his friends and walked with Teodor. "Don't doze off the manner you did, kid. Concentrate on the fight and not on the crowd," Teodor demanded firmly.

"Sorry, sir. I had to try to—"

The knight cut him off. "No excuses! I could have lost the fight! Just follow my lead next time." Teodor then complained about how Thormon behaved during the fight. "Oh, I don't want you to talk to the elves. They could be our potential adversary."

Thormon gave Teodor an angry look. He knew he couldn't just accuse anyone of meddling without proof and nodded to the knight. He shrugged off his hand and bid good night.

"Aren't you going to join me in the dining hall to celebrate my victory?" Teodor asked.

"It was your victory, not mine. And like you mentioned. I could have made you lose. So, I'd be just dead weight." Thormon, a little frustrated, returned to the dorms.

He thought *I helped him out, and all I get ensues as a speech on how to be a squire.*

***

The next solar cycle, a commotion of a company of knights from Eritrea awoke Thormon. At the time, they arrived at the castle. They carried a banner of a great white shark with menacing teeth. They were from the harbor community. And they worshiped marine animals and considered them as lesser gods.

Thormon ran to the barracks door and gazed upon them.

"Weird set of fighters. Right?" the quartermaster asked as the group passed.

"I've never seen that banner or those people before," Thormon replied, surprised.

"They live on the sea, or so I've heard. They are also half man and half water creatures. I'd stay away from them if I were you." The quartermaster pushed Thormon back to the barracks.

"I've been everywhere, and not once have I heard about them," Thormon appeared sincere.

"That shows that you haven't been everywhere. This land seems full of surprises and oddities, man. You must hear the stories some people say about the far west. Stuff that'd give you nightmares," the quartermaster added, before being interrupted by a pageboy.

"Sir Teodor wants you at the practice arena," the pageboy passed along the information.

Thormon nodded and went right away.

"Now then, you are finally up," Teodor reprimanded the boy as he went through some wooden swords.

"I woke up early. I just thought you wouldn't be practicing today," Thormon explained.

"Yesterday's fight showed me that I cannot undermine any adversaries. And at this point, when a group of fierce warriors has arrived. And more will arrive, coming from the west. We still have a couple of solar cycles until the heralds announce the new arrangements for the fights." Teodor threw a wooden sword to Thormon and went on to practice.

Days went by. Teodor and Thormon trained in metal-plate armor, wielding real, blunt swords—all with the lingering thought of when and who they'd fight next.

"The way I see it, only Sir Hemming should be my match. The others are much less dangerous in combat."

"Do you think Sir Absalon could pose some threat to you?" asked Thormon.

"No. To tell you the truth, I am surprised that he even made it this far. I've fought him before, and he stands out as a joke of a knight," Teodor replied.

Before somebody could say anything else, a pageboy interrupted them.

"Come quick! All fighters are to go to the arena. The herald will announce the matches!"

Teodor and Thormon both made their route toward the arena. There appeared to be quite a big crowd, and some fighters from the West were also present.

"Will you fight any of those guys?" Thormon asked as they walked to the makeshift podium.

"Not yet. They will join only later on," Teodor replied.

Soon, every knight slated to fight, along with their squires, were aligned.

The king's herald arrived, giving each knight a numbered plaque. "These are your respective call signs. We will raffle them and choose the order and who each will fight," he instructed.

And in accordance, the fights were arranged and scheduled.

"My dear people, we are getting closer and closer to the real meat of the festival. Soon, we will see the actual battle. All including both man and beast, elves versus dwarfs, and demons versus angels. What we came here to watch!

"But now, let us narrow down, sieve these fine knights, and see who remains worthy to face the next phase. We have Sir Teodor against Sir Arvid. Sir Absalon against Sir Hemming. Sir Erland faces Sir Kennet."

The crowd cheered as the nobility picked the fights, and soon, the herald announced the dates.

"Let's begin with Sir Absalon and Sir Hemming two days from today. Sir Teodor and Sir Arvid will fight the following solar cycle. And Sir Erland against Sir Kennet, the solar cycle after that."

Teodor looked at Thormon and had plain-spoken, "Well, boy, our luck appears set. If everything goes well, we'll face either Sir Hemmings or Sir Absalon. And by the looks of it, Sir Hemmings has this one in the bag."

The crowd and the fighters dispersed, and soon the final stages of the fights would commence.

That same night, a messenger from Enlgon came to Thormon. The message was that they would watch the fights and look for proof of Thormon's accusation.

The day of the first fight came. Against all odds, Sir Absalon beat Sir Hemming and soon faced either Sir Teodor or Sir Arvid. The elves did not interfere. But they gathered enough information on the paladin who used magic.

The second solar cycle came. At this point, Thormon concentrated entirely on the fight. He knew that the elves would be watching over him. Sir Teodor won the fight with relative ease, and currently, only Sir Absalon stood in his way.

The third day of the fight came, and Sir Erland won and had to face the reigning champion, Sir Magnusar.

Today the contest staff set the fights—the battles between Sir Absalon versus Sir Teodor and Sir Erland against Sir Magnusar.

During that moon cycle, Enlgon visited Thormon.

"Listen, I suspect that the same paladin, the one from Cicipangle, somehow influenced many of the fights," Enlgon told Thormon.

"I know! But I thought you already solved the problem," commented Thormon, open to Enlgon's solution.

"Not only with Sir Absalom's fights but on additional knights from the order. He always remained there, muttering enchantments to bless the knights," Enlgon noted.

"But you insinuated that it should be a serious accusation. You asked me not to say a word. You believed that you would see first why the knight from Cicipangle would risk exposing himself."

Enlgon looked at the boy and replied, "My spies went around and dug up some interesting information. As you know, no wizards or paladins are allowed present in any of the fights."

"Not even in the main ones?" Thormon replied, surprised.

"Have you seen any wizards walking around?" Enlgon replied in defiance.

"No. Only those shady characters that I told you were present during the fights."

"Stay with me at this moment, young one. The paladins from Cicipangle can easily meddle with any fights they want at this point. Making the worse fighter win and, in that manner, helping his order. Remember you chattered that Teodor told you that Sir Absalon was a joke? Yet, he won every match."

"But if wizards or paladins are not allowed, how do they control the use of magic during the fights?" asked Thormon.

"Every land signs a decree and lists every paladin and wizard under one roof. You see, boy, we know who uses magic in this land—and none of them seems located here," Enlgon replied, scratching his head.

"Then how do you explain the paladins in the city?" asked Thormon.

"Leave that to me. I will talk with this Sir Absalon. Let's see how much he knows." Enlgon opened the door, turned his head, and added, "Let's just hope your knight wins, for we cannot interfere."

Standing at the palace in the Baldars' quarters, Enlgon inquired about the company of six knights sitting together by a round table.

Enlgon smiled, pulled out a chair, and sat with them.

The knights looked at him in surprise. One of them spoke up. "What are you doing in these corners? Your place is not here."

Enlgon smiled at them and replied, "I know there befalls interference with the fights. I will not tolerate this kind of cheating going on in this castle. You know this city does not allow magic during the tournament."

They opened their eyes wide, and Sir Absalon stood up angrily. He asked rhetorically and daunted, "Who do you think you are to come here and throw these unfounded accusations at our faces? If you weren't who you are, I would dispatch you. You know damn well that those accusations can eliminate your entire company. Not to say that all our magic users are far from here."

"I indeed have no proof of any illegal practice of magic yet. Only whispers, but know this: I already sent news to the ministry. Thus, a wizard will be present at the final stage of the fights. If the magic wielder tries anything again, guards will punish him," Enlgon replied.

"You are wrong. Nothing stays happening as surreptitious meddling. We all would have seen or felt it," shouted a second knight.

Talk spread around the palace about this accusation. It defiled the reputation of Sir Absalon, but most did not know what to think about the whole mess.

Later that season, Thormon learned from Enlgon that he happened to be bluffing concerning the wizard. Enlgon explained to Thormon that no magicians were allowed in the city, even under such circumstances.

"All I need seems to pretend a wizard will be in the arena. Make them believe that. I will ask one of the elves to dress like one. Best-case scenario— if he turns out involved, he will know that it came from me and we can restrain the cheater," Enlgon elucidated wandering around anxiously. "We have to be very careful. If one discovers any irregularities, the tournament could be compromised and jeopardized. The losers like Sir Hemming could request the right to compete again. That means you could probably not be in the finals right this instant. That information could put not only that, but the entire tournament is in check, in serious danger, or could even be canceled. You might be too young to understand. But the implications could go deep into our political climate. Thus, know this, young one. If the paladin there uses magic, we cannot interfere without concrete evidence."

Thormon nodded but disagreed. Thormon understood that there were bigger things at play. That forced him to accept it, for he could not prove anything, nor did he have the power to challenge the entire system.

***

Finally, the day came for the fight. People were lined on the streets of the main square and in the windows of their houses. It was the very final fight of the first part of the knights' games. There looked like no extra room remained in the arena. The first fight of the day had Sir Magnusar as the victor, and now it was the turn for Sir Absalon against Sir Teodor.

The proper armors fitted both horse and Sir Teodor. He acknowledged that getting used to the armor would do him good, just like the animal. The contest board blunted the lance and the sword according to the rules. The other weapons were fitted according to the specifications. Thormon and Teodor were waiting for the inspector to give them the go-ahead.

"Be calm, boy. Just do what we trained. After all, I'm the one who's going to fight," Teodor reassured, trying to calm the boy.

Before Thormon could reply, an emissary from the elves visited them.

"What gives us the honor of your visit?" Teodor asked.

The elf smiled and indicated that he needed to talk to Thormon privately. Teodor thought it seemed a bit odd but complied.

The elf explained the plan to Thormon and told him to focus solely on the fight. Thormon nodded and thanked the elf.

"Never saw that before. Those elves must like you," Teodor commented after the elf left. "Oh, look. I believe it's time!"

Immediately, it applied the protocol for the contest. Thormon ran toward the chest, where guards kept the weapons and spare armor parts. Teodor strolled in front, waving to the public, while Thormon dragged the chest into the arena. Both could hear cheers and cries of happiness. At the time, they crossed the gate and entered the battleground. Thormon settled down on one side and started polishing the weapons. He looked up and saw that the arena was overcrowded. Not even pigeons had a place to play around, not being able to eat bread and leftovers.

Wow, what a turnout, Thormon thought. He looked around for the elves, the paladins, and friends, and soon he spotted Barefoot. He waved at him and ran toward where he was sitting.

235

"I am glad that at least one of us made it to the final. Even though I expected Hemming to face Teodor," Barefoot shouted.

"Thanks! Where are the others?" Thormon shouted back.

"They are—" The crowd's noise rang so loud that it muffled his answer.

Thormon just smiled, pretending he understood, then ran back to his designated area to await the beginning of the ceremony and then for the fight to commence.

Teodor knew his opponent to be weak. Sir Absalon seemed the clear underdog.

And so, the jousting commenced.

Teodor hit Sir Absalon with a lance in the stomach, throwing him off his horse. He hit the ground hard. Teodor circled Absalon and then dismounted his horse. Absalon, with his back against the ground, looked like he was already defeated. He could not move.

"Call it, you fool!" Teodor screamed, knowing that Absalon had lost his will to fight and seemed defeated.

But all of a sudden, Absalon raised his hand, pulled himself together, and stood up.

Amazingly, Teodor asked surprised, "How can you stand up after that blow?"

Absalon, still shaken up, grabbed his sword and lifted it. Teodor quickly charged against him, but the old dog moved fast and evaded the blows. At the time, it became clear that he could no longer parry any additional strikes. And Teodor kicked his shaking legs, taking away his opponent's balance. Without means of support, Absalon fell face down to the ground.

"I don't understand how you got up, but stay down and yield!" Teodor screamed. "Where seems to be your infinite endurance that you had in other fights?"

Suddenly, Absalon stood up. His eyes were tired, but his body had life renewed within it.

"How could you still stand up?" Teodor asked, surprised.

Absalon raised his sword and went berserk. A vicious swing of his sword disarmed Teodor. And then Absalon side-kicked Teodor's stomach, throwing Sir Teodor to the ground. He could not breathe and tried to pick himself up. Thormon quickly ran toward Teodor, bringing another weapon. But he got kicked hard and thrown to the ground.

Teodor saw Absalom's eyes were not the same; they were angry red.

"What has gone in you?" Teodor screamed as he evaded Absalom's blows. He ran toward Thormon, lifting him and sending him to his corner. But Absalon was there as soon as Teodor turned around. Absalon struck his sword onto Teodor's helmet, making it fly across the ring and making him dizzy. The knight tumbled down to the ground.

"Do you give up?" asked Sir Absalon. When no answer came, he pummeled his opponent several times in the face. Sir Teodor writhed.

The crowd looked in awe. Thormon tried to intervene but got wounded and thrown to the ground.

"Do you give up, forthwith?" repeated Absalon.

With a bloodied face, Teodor looked at Thormon, who stood also bleeding and wounded. He raised his hand and nodded to stop the fight, but Absalon rushed toward him again and hit him even more.

The entire arena remained in silence. The knight was in a rage state that they'd never seen before. Thormon ran toward the knight but got beaten to a pulp. Even Absalom's squire couldn't stop him. The guards ran onto the arena to restrain Sir Absalon and take Teodor and Thormon to the healing room. The crazed knight went at it toward anyone who approached him. He would be there with bloodied eyes and a shriek of death.

After several unsuccessful tries, one of the royals in the arena screamed out to get a bucket of cold water. They threw the cold water at Absalon, and, like magic, they kicked him out of the trance. And so they could subdue the crazed knight. Absalon looked up and saw what he had done. He could not believe his eyes.

"What have I done?" he asked as the guards carried him away.

The individuals did not hold feasts or victory celebrations during that solar cycle. No one could make out what exactly had happened in that arena.

CHAPTER 38

New Acquaintance

That moon cycle, sir Magnusar came to see his colleague.

"What in the world happened in there? Once you have healed up, come and see me. We have lots to discuss," Magnusar recommended and then turned to Thormon. "Thormon, my boy, I called for a special healer for you. Ormr, fetch those herbs and put them on Thormon's face."

Thormon opened his eyes and asked, "Who is he? I've never seen him around the castle. Is he a squire as well?"

"Indeed, I am!" Ormr replied.

"The word spreads around that you never became a squire," Thormon murmured.

"That's because I sleep inside the palace, eat with the knights, and practice indoors. Some privileges I have, though I am a squire nonetheless. At present, hush and let me treat your wounds," mentioned Ormr. He walked toward Thormon. "From this moment on, you will sleep in the palace's guest rooms. By that approach, we will better take care of you."

Thormon gave a shy smile in acknowledgment. The caretaker put his hand on the boy's forehead, murmured a blessing, and then left. On his course out, he saw the elves standing outside the infirmary.

"Is it OK for us to see the boy now? Though against the rules, we brought a mage to help the boy," Enlgon inquired.

The caretaker seemed surprised that the elves had such interest in the boy, much less bringing a mage. They knew very well it was forbidden. He nodded and mentioned that they could see the boy.

Enlgon entered the room with the mage. Magnusar quickly stood up and demanded answers.

Enlgon calmly walked toward the boy and relieved the boy, "Do not worry. We have him, but we must mop this mess this instant."

Magnusar, still not knowing what happened, angrily questioned, "I'll ask you again! What is going on here? You know damn well that no magic is allowed within the city walls. Why on earth do you bring a mage here?"

Enlgon looked at Teodor and asked, "And how stays your friend?"

"You still didn't answer my question!" Magnusar rebuked him.

"I will, in time, but first, we must heal these wounds. A berserker caused them the injuries. And you should know that something seemed amiss in that arena today. Let me help them, and then I'll answer your questions." Enlgon calmly asked Magnusar to step outside.

Magnusar reluctantly agreed. And once he stood outside, Enlgon closed the door behind him. Magnusar looked at the elves and asked, "What in the world is happening?"

"Check with the knight who won, but don't go to his quarters. Go to the dungeons. He stays locked up there for his own good. You know his condition matches as that of a spellbound creature," one of the elves calmly replied. The others opened a way for him to go.

As he passed the last elf, he grabbed Magnusar's arm and pledged, "Do not worry. The boy and the knight will be fine. Meet them tomorrow at the high sun in their new quarters inside the palace."

Magnusar, surprised, quickly ran toward the exit and into the dungeons.

***

Thormon woke up in a beautiful room. He looked around; at the door, he saw Enlgon with someone from the court, he presumed.

"Enlgon, what happened?" Thormon asked as he tried to get out of bed.

"Don't get up! You still need a little more healing," Enlgon answered as he ran toward the boy. "Do you see the man with me? His name is Axel. He is the person responsible for the enforcement of the rules in the tournament. He is here to ask you some questions. Is it OK?"

Thormon nodded. "He can ask me anything."

"Hello, Thormon. I happened to be at the arena when Absalon beat you and your master to a pulp. Something that has never happened before. First of all, we'd like to apologize for letting such conduct of a gruesome nature occur to you. We let your parents know that you are fine and that we will make up for it monetarily. As for the knight, he decided to become a ranger. He appeared so ashamed of what happened that he couldn't face himself ever being a knight again," Axel informed candidly.

"He did not know what happened. And now, what about Sir Teodor?" Thormon asked.

Axel smiled. "Well, my boy, I'll get to that, but first, let me tell you what happened while you were asleep. Your suspicions were correct, as Enlgon pointed out. You were able to spot and pinpoint something that not even our best eyes were capable of finding. You also handled the matter in a manner that belies your age. Very commendable, might I add. You took to the people who are connected and knowledgeable. And with their help, we could arrest the ring of cheaters who infiltrated the fights." Axel paused momentarily. And he then confessed, "You know that this can never leave this room. But the official story stands out as that Absalon got called to help out a city thousands of heads from here. Henceforth, he has taken the mantle of the ranger. Since he quit, Teodor inherited his spot. We are still weaving the details into how badly beaten someone could still fight and compete. But that's not for you to worry."

"But what is it you want to ask me?" Thormon asked.

"Right to the point." Axel turned to Enlgon and admitted, "I like him!" Then he continued. "We would like to know exactly when you first saw the paladin—which fights."

Thormon scratched his head. "It was against the Wikings brothers."

"Hm, interesting. And how could you pinpoint and determine that there occurred meddling?" Axel asked.

"I saw a constant murmuring and fixed gaze, and whenever I intervened, things went bad. I knew, then and there, that something was off."

"Interesting. And, at first, did you tell anyone?"

"I told a friend, but he thought it should be just my imagination," Thormon replied.

"What did you do then?"

"I saw other fights. Oddly enough, I couldn't find meddling, only the ones with Absalon," Thormon replied with a questioning look.

"You know that Sir Absalon was the ultimate underdog. If you were to bet on him, you would certainly lose money." Axel turned to Enlgon and asked, "What were the odds—a million to one?"

Enlgon smiled. "Something like that. All I know seems that whoever bet on him made a lot of money—which, by luck, not many people did."

Axel laughed. "Which made our job easier."

"What about the paladin?" Thormon asked.

"Oh, presently, you have a question. First, let me finish the questions I have. Enlgon pronounced that you took this news of the paladin to Teodor, right?" Axel asked.

"Yeah, but he didn't believe me. He hinted that it was a grave accusation. Hence, I went to Enlgon for help. That's when he got involved."

"Intriguing. From that point on, I already know; thus, I won't have to bother you anymore. As for your question, we take cheating very seriously here. This tournament remains an opportunity to gather different races and folks. And we cannot have something like this tarnish it. There exists a strict code that we cannot slay paladins, but we can ensure they never do any greater harm. We cut off his tongue and hands; we muted and crippled him for life. As for those involved, if it suits you, you can go to their tombs. The looters and the king retrieved the money." Axel answered.

Thormon looked surprised by the outcome. He stayed there, taking in what had happened.

"See, boy? That's why I told you to be extremely careful of your accusations. If none of that had panned out, you would face wrath," Enlgon told the boy.

Axel smiled and winked at the boy. "At the present, you know a little further about what goes on behind these walls and what we do to maintain order."

Axel left the room, leaving Enlgon inside.

"Now that everything stays in order, I suggest you rest up. The next phase starts in one-third of a season, and I believe that by tomorrow, you'll be fine to get up and see Teodor. For the present, Ormr is here to help you," Enlgon sat down and rested his head against the wall, then he signed for Ormr to enter the room.

Thormon asked Ormr where his friend-squires were. But due to the circumstances of what had occurred, they could not hang out together anymore. This fact forced him to make new acquaintances and friends; Ormr became one of them.

CHAPTER 39

New Home

After a few days in the palace, Thormon could leave the room and get to know his new home. At first, he pondered with a hand resting on his head, showing that he had reached a resolution. He needed to be nice to everyone around him. After all, they helped him recover. Ormr helped him out throughout his initial days and when the time came. He could visit Teodor, who recovered amazingly fast, just like Thormon had. And it seemed hasty to return to practice.

"Teodor hangs around in the hall past the red carpets. He wishes to speak to you," Ormr informed as he returned to his duties.

"Thanks. I'll go see Master right away!" Thormon replied anxiously, walking toward the direction Ormr gave.

Everything felt new and exciting and resulted in an easy stance. This side of the castle looked nothing like he'd ever seen. It housed greater than forty thousand individuals. He calmly walked down the corridors, taking it all in, looking around like he should be a child in a candy shop.

I never knew this place could house so many people, he thought as he wandered around.

Then he met and recognized a familiar face.

"Good to see that you are up and about!" Enlgon complimented, smiling.

"Sir Enlgon! It's pleasant to see a familiar face! I'm completely lost here. I've been to the palace before, but never to this side. Would you mind helping me find Teodor's room?" Thormon asked as he looked around in wonder.

"Sure! I'll take you to him," Enlgon replied as he called Thormon's attention to follow him.

Enlgon touched on the matter of the conversation they'd had. At the same time, Thormon slept in his straw bed, which reminded him of the promise he made about secrecy. Thormon nodded, showing Enlgon he knew what he signed for. Enlgon changed the subject and started talking to the boy about this part of the tournament.

"Not all the fighters have arrived yet, but soon, everyone will be here," Enlgon said with finality.

"Wait! There are still more people to come?" Thormon asked, surprised.

"Oh yes! For example, there are some colossal fighters from Makake Island," Enlgon informed.

"Wait! Those guys are here?" Thormon asked fearfully.

"Yes! We have to test the best fighters; the only way to do that without going to war seems to be using this tournament. Do you know anything about these beasts from Makake?" Enlgon asked.

Thormon stopped, took a deep breath, and confessed, "Yes, I had a run-in with them a while back. A friend of mine lost his hand. It was unpleasant."

Enlgon looked at the boy. "Good to know. They stay in that aisle there; therefore, I suggest you don't wander off there."

Thormon looked pale as he asked, "Is there anyone else I should know?"

Enlgon laughed. "There are some pirates, as well."

Thormon's face became even paler. He stopped for a moment and looked around. "Is it a good idea to have me in here?"

Enlgon looked surprised. "Don't tell me you messed with these pirates, as well. My goodness, boy, is there any creature whose toes you haven't stepped on?"

Thormon swallowed dry. Then admitted, "I do like adventure, but please, I do not like quarreling with people or things."

"Hm, nice to know. I'll let the staff know; they will not put you in the same vicinity as these folks—just for safekeeping," Enlgon mentioned.

Thormon nodded and thanked him, and they both continued walking.

"Here we are," Enlgon expressed as he knocked on the door.

"Come in!" a voice offered.

Enlgon opened the door and greeted both Teodor and Magnusar. He left Thormon there and gave his goodbyes.

Thormon smiled, nodded a hello, and sat on a chair. Magnusar turned to the boy and asked about his new quarters. Thormon told both men how he felt and how he was feeling about the latest batch of fighters. The ones that had arrived and those who were still to arrive.

Both knights laughed and joked about it. But they assured Thormon that he needn't worry about anything. After all, it appeared like the occasion to compete, fight, entertain, bet money, cheer, and win glory!

"For this moment, we need to follow protocol. Everyone needs to gear up and meet at the main hall, where we will all be introduced formally. Then, there will be the schedule for the following solar cycles of the tournament," Teodor notified. He and Magnusar put on their armor.

The group geared up and went to the main hall. A huge crowd gathered as the fighters aligned. An older man raised his hand. The entire crowd stayed silent. The old man quietly and calmly walked toward the throne, stopped, looked around, and sat on it. He called for a scribe, who handed him a scroll. He opened the scroll and started talking.

"We are all gathered here under one banner and one common goal. Many seasons ago, our forefathers made a pact after a brutal twenty-season war. And that we will never again measure strength by such means. Consequently, we created this tournament to see which of us was the strongest, without the need for bloodshed. Creatures, beings, humanoids, and many others are allowed to partake in our tournament. We witnessed the first part. Sir Teodor and Sir Magnusar were crowned champions of the Knights of Men, who will represent the civilized world of high men." The king stopped for a moment and called both knights forward. "And here they are—your champions for this tournament that will commence!" The king looked at them and added, "Make us proud!"

The crowd cheered. The king raised his hand, and the room stayed silent once again.

"Straight away, allow me to introduce to you all that this realm and the realms beyond have to offer. Come forth, mightiest fighters!"

One by one, the fighters came forth. And the king introduced them and gave them his blessing. There seemed companies from pirates to barbarians, elves to night beings. Also, intelligent beasts. This soon became the most intense part of the ceremony.

The room stood quiet when an ape with a golden Viking helmet walked forth and spoke for his company. "We have come a long course to be honored to fight in this tournament. My name is Grooach. We come from the mystical island of Makake."

"Yes! I've heard about it. And I've also heard that there are fierce beasts there," Lord Vermundr replied.

"Do not fear! Although I am the only one who can speak the tongue of men, my warriors will not mess around while alongside me. It is only I who represent them. Fear not. My warriors are now harmless toward the people and will not pose a threat," Grooach guaranteed. At the same time, he showed respect toward the king.

"Well, Grooach, men in Menestrel know you as the red gorillas but tell a bit more about you. After all, today stays as the solar cycle of introductions. And you are the most intriguing of all the contestants here today."

"Men in Menestrel know us as the red gorillas. But among ourselves, we, apes, call ourselves BongKong, meaning king of apes."

"Why at once? Why only now did you decide to participate in our knights' game? It has been around for ages, yet not one of you showed up here before," inquired Vermundr.

"That is true. The people here would like to know. And I shall give it to you. A ruthless brute ruled our island; the alpha Kong. He ruled, imposing fear, and cared not for fellow humanoids. If not for adding them to his diet, he would have prevailed as a fearless cannibal. When I overthrew his kingdom of terror, things started to change."

"Interesting. You look very scholarly, yet your companions do not. Why is that? Can any of your companions speak?" asked King Vermundr, looking at the rest of the apes.

Grooach's appearance became stern. "Isn't it enough that I speak for them?"

"I couldn't care less, but this fight includes only intelligent beings. No dumb beast shall enter it—unless that is, one speaks. You know that fighters can be paired up, but in your case, you will have to fight alone against two opponents."

Grooach looked not cowed or dismayed. He huffed in the air and proudly boasted, "Great! I can fight for two! As you know, my companions can't speak, but they are loyal to me, and I will keep them close if I may."

"You may do that, but make sure you follow the rules of the castle and tournament," replied King Vermundr.

The ape bowed and accepted, "Agreed, Your Majesty."

The king smiled and blessed the ape and assigned them bigger quarters. The introductory protocol soon ended, and everyone returned to their quarters. The fighting would commence in fourteen solar cycles.

***

As the moment grew closer to the fights, thus did the tensions. Thormon stayed as far as he could from the pirates' and the apes' wings, always hiding in the kitchen during meals and passing through there. At the time, he needed to go to the training grounds. Also, the master cook thought it seemed odd that a squire with somewhat of a history would scurry like a scared mouse into his kitchen. But apparently, by his kind smile, he felt it was all right, overlooking the matter.

One solar cycle, Thormon crashed into the kitchen. And into a beautiful blonde, blue-eyed girl.

"Watch it! You brat!" the girl screamed out in anger.

"Shush! They will hear you and know that I'm here," Thormon mentioned softly. He put his hands over her mouth and waited a bit for a mean-looking pirate to pass by.

The girl angrily took Thormon's hand off her mouth and retorted, "What's wrong with you?"

Thormon stayed quiet for a bit while looking over his shoulders, waiting for an opening, to be precise. Once he saw no trace of the pirate, Thormon sighed in relief. He apologized and explained to the girl what went on.

"Oh, that's why I see you always running into the kitchen. My dad and I were starting to wonder. Whether you always run in here to see me or grab something to eat," the girl replied in a relieved tone.

"No! No! Nothing like that. I just needed somewhere to hide. Ever insofar as the kitchen seems located between where I need to go. It became the perfect place," Thormon replied. He still looked around to see if the coast looked clear.

"Well, since you are here, you can help me clean the mess you made. Help me grab these things from the floor and take them to the trash bin," the girl replied, still a bit angry.

Thormon calmly helped clean up the mess he'd made. And when he finished, he apologized once again and started to walk away. But the girl screamed, "Aren't you going to at least ask for my name? I know who the hell you are. Everyone here knows who you are, Thormon. Teodor's squire. I thought he taught you to have manners around a lady."

Thormon blushed in embarrassment, lowered his head, and replied, "I'm sorry, ma'am. I'm concentrated on training and keeping myself from not being killed by the pirates and apes. I forgot to be chivalrous around such a beautiful maiden."

The girl blushed and extended her hand to greet Thormon. "My name is Eira, daughter of Emerand, the main cook of the palace."

Thormon knelt, gently took her hand, and kissed the palm of it. Also, he replied, "A pleasure to be in your presence, my fair maiden."

The girl felt utterly embarrassed and gave a small, girly laugh. Thormon smiled, stood up, gave her a wink, and ran off to where he needed to go.

Throughout the entire ordeal, the father stood in a corner, watching. Once Thormon left, he quickly went to Eira.

"I don't want you talking to that boy. He is nothing but trouble," the father retorted.

The girl nodded and went back to her daily routine.

***

As solar cycles went by, Thormon became further interested in Eira. Every instance, he would run into the kitchen and chat with her. But always under her father's watchful eyes. She looked strong-willed, and soon they started to meet outside the kitchen.

Their safe place stayed as the castle's garden and then the cemetery, where Eira often placed flowers on her mother's tombstone. It came to be the only period they could be alone and talk.

"Eira, I understand why your father never takes his eyes off you. He lost one of his precious, dearest loves and won't risk losing the other one," Thormon confessed. Then, they calmly strolled through the garden.

"When you look at it in that fashion, it doesn't sound entirely bad. The truth is, sometimes I covet leaving and being free. You know, to do whatever I wish and never worry about my father's eyes on me."

"If you ever did that, it would be the death of him, and that's not counting all your friends," Thormon replied.

"Which friends would miss me?" she asked, surprised.

"I bet you have many friends," Thormon insinuated.

"As a matter of fact, you are the only friend I have. My father keeps everyone away from me," she replied in a somber tone.

Thormon hugged her and soliloquized. "I would like to be more than a friend."

Eira blushed, and with that, she smiled a special smile full of grace and kissed his cheek.

Thormon felt extremely happy, and that emotion reflected on his face. It felt cozy, like a nice getaway from his worries and duties as a squire. He cherished every moment spent with Eira. That was because he knew everything would be chaotic around the palace once the fights started.

***

Finally, the solar cycle came. People gathered around and went to the arena. Fighters from all over were there to test their might. Teodor and Magnusar were scheduled to fight on the third moon cycle, against the Black Knights from Cicipangle. For the first two solar cycles, the quartermaster commanded Thormon to observe and report the fights to Teodor and Magnusar.

***

The first fight seemed slated to happen between the elves and the dwarfs. Enlgon and Alrod were in the ring.

The dwarfs were no match for the elves, who quickly subdued them in a fast and elegant match. Alrod was the tallest of the elves and the strongest, as well. The responsibility and the role as a fight mate chosen to make up the duo befell on Commander Enlgon, who wielded a scimitar and a round shield.

***

On the second day, the fight finally got slated, accordingly to the Wheel of Fortune. And that between the barbarians from Menestrel against the pirates from Eritrea. One big, bearded barbarian stood at least eight heads tall, and the companion was bald and albino. The pirates wielded cutlasses. And they had black bandanas and little armor, only silken clothes. It turned out to be not an elegant fight. Both sides fought dirty, almost on the brink of breaking tournament rules. But the barbarians emerged as the victors.

***

Finally, the big day came for Thormon. Teodor and Magnusar were facing the Black Knights from Cicipangle. As they went through protocol,

Thormon looked around to see if Eira hung about there. And there she appeared, hanging out with the Thours, his father, and his mother.

Both sides were assigned a place to stay, and the fighting commenced.

The Black Knights had different colored eyes (heterochromia), superhuman strength, and agility. Their baleful eyes carried a magnetic scanning gaze that gauged the opponent's very soul. Not only that, but there seemed to be something very sinister with them, something unholy. Magnusar struck first, swinging his sword overhead. But the Black Knight caught it within the palms of his hands. Everyone looked baffled. How could someone simply catch a sword like that?

Teodor saw his partner's agony and ran to the aggressor, leaving his opponent behind, but all were in vain. His blows were also parried and evaded. The other knight walked around and watched both men agonize against one opponent.

"You are no normal human!" Magnusar remarked with increasing dread.

"You mean we are beyond human?" the Black Knight, who patiently watched, replied with sarcasm.

Both men tried to fight one knight, and that knight kept on parrying and mocking both men. The other Black Knight just strolled around the battlefield, observing.

"Neither of you are human. What kind of foul beast are you?" asked Teodor as the enemy pushed him aside toward the one observing, gauging.

Thormon and Ormr stood there. They seemed surprised that both knights were no match for one of these Black Knights.

"We have to do something. Open the chest!" Thormon screamed to Ormr.

"What for? They already have the best weapons with them. And they did not ask for more," Ormr replied.

Thormon shoved him. "I came across something similar to this once. No conventional weapon can hurt them, but I read that a special silver alloy and brightness can hurt them. Help find something that matches that," Thormon demanded as he overturned the chest. They could search for a much-needed weapon.

As the boys looked for the weapon, Teodor and Magnusar fought fruitlessly. It looked as if both of the Black Knights were mocking them. Both Black Knights closed the distance between Magnusar and Teodor.

One of them smiled and jested, "This bores me. Let's make it a tad easier for them."

One of the Black Knights threw both men across the ring. Then, asked the observing one, "How do you suggest we make it easier?"

"We don't need this heavy, clumsy armor. Let's remove it and give these mortals a show they'll never forget," the observing knight suggested.

As Magnusar and Teodor got up, the Black Knights stripped off their armor with evil looks on their faces.

Magnusar readied his sword, turned to Teodor, and asked, "What are these two up to?"

Teodor looked around and saw Thormon frantically going through their weapons. "I wonder what those two are up to, as well. They've gone mad, these Black Knights."

The Black Knights of Cicipangle attacked from opposite directions. There stood both Baldarians in the middle, back-to-back. But they weren't attacking; they were mocking the Baldarian knights. They were somewhat like children, playing with their food.

Sir Teodor saw the way the fight went on. To change the odds and fight plans, he told Magnusar, "These two are just toying with us. Let's split up!"

Both knights started running around, thinking they could confuse the Black Knights. But all it did only appeared to make it a little more challenging for them.

Thormon stopped looking through the chest and gazed at the fight for a moment. He turned to Ormr and asked, "What in the world is going on?"

Ormr, with a confused expression, replied, "I have no idea. The Black Knights aren't fighting. They are just making Teodor and Magnusar look stupid. These Black Knights are showing off how superior they are."

"They think that this seems just a stupid show-off. Teodor and Magnusar look like headless chickens! Their swings pose no threat," Thormon realized as he returned to look for the weapon needed.

Ormr looked at Thormon and asked, "What are you looking for, exactly?"

"Anything silver!" Thormon replied as he continued searching.

"You idiot! You won't find that here! Look for it in the barracks! Under fine ornaments!" Ormr commented. Before he could add anything else, Thormon just got up and left.

The entire arena and both Baldarians did not know what took place. For their strategies were not working. The audience fell silent when confusion spread virally throughout the site. A young noble stood up from the king's cabinet and yelled, "Just finish the fight already!"

Both Black Knights looked toward the sound of the shout, gave a smirk, and replied, "We will finish when we want! In here, we are our own masters!"

Once that gloating speech sounded across the arena, Teodor swung at one of the distracted knights, cutting him. The knight flung Teodor across the field as if he were a fly. The Black Knight showed no pain. As Magnusar helped Teodor up, Teodor looked at the knight and confessed, "There ensues no way he could not have felt that. It seemed a mortal wound, and he didn't even flinch."

The crowd stood in horror at what they had just witnessed. The crowd screamed, "Demons!"

"Devil incarnated!"

"Demon of the night!"

The wounded Black Knight looked around and yelled back, "I'm beyond human! Those playthings cannot harm or hurt us!"

The crowd looked in complete panic as they saw the wounds simply heal in front of their eyes.

The nobles and representatives all started to panic as well. They turned to the king and asked, "How could you let these demons enter our tournament?"

But among them, a young nobleman from Cicipangle calmed everyone.

"There seems no need for panic. We are here to show our might and nothing further. If beasts are allowed, why can't our best fighters participate? The king knows who we are."

The king stood up and ordered everyone to silence. He walked toward the ledge and ordered the Black Knights to stop mocking the fights. But the Black Knights couldn't have cared less. It was their playtime. "Make them take this seriously. Or they will forfeit this fight," the king demanded as he turned to the Cicipangle noble.

The noble calmly made his path down to the arena. As he walked down, the crowd made way. Everyone had fear in their eyes.

The nobleman entered the arena and called both of his knights, who reluctantly yielded to his call.

"You have no domain over us in this place!" one of the Black Knights gloated.

"But I do have domain over you! You will obey your master!" the nobleman replied.

"We have only one master! And it will never be you!" the other Black Knight replied.

"Do you wish the same end as your kin?" the noble commented angrily.

Both knights bowed their heads in fear and submission and asked, "What is it you need from us?"

"Take this fight seriously, and show them the proper respect that your lord demands of you. Do it quickly; it's almost high noon. And don't forget—he also has high plans for this place." So, the nobleman finished. He saw a young boy running frantically towards the Baldarian knights. He had weapons in hand.

The Black Knights calmly walked toward their chest and picked out their best swords.

On the near side of the arena, Thormon deliberated quietly. He then explained to the Baldarian knights what they needed to do.

"We can turn this around. Use this silver sword and shield, and soon, sunlight will be your aid. Those dumb knights played around so much that they forgot that the shade here does not go on forever," Thormon swaggered as he handed the weapons to both knights.

The taller Black Knight walked toward Teodor and started a series of attacks. But Sir Teodor could parry all his blows.

The shorter knight used his weapon more agile and skillfully. Thus, he could land some blows on Magnusar.

So both knights faced each other. They noticed that the weapons Thormon had given them did affect the Black Knights. All of a sudden, a ray of sunlight crossed the arena, causing both Black Knights to retreat toward the shade.

"Drive this foe to the sun!" Thormon screamed out.

Teodor and Magnusar decided to change tactics. Both knights would stab and walk backward. That was until the Black Knights stopped chasing them. Then they would stab again and walk backward again. In this manner, they'd be able to lure the Black Knights to the far arena, where the sun's rays had started to grace the place. But only a small portion kept on bathing the arena. Try as they might, the Black Knights would not cross the threshold into the sun.

"What's the matter with you? Why won't you come to fight me at once?" asked Sir Teodor.

The crowd started to boo when the lack of action in the arena became clear. The Baldarian knights called the Black Knights to fight, but all they did was retreat. This ongoing fight fed up Sir Magnusar, and his look of agony showed that he felt obligated to please the crowd. He charged toward one of the Black Knights. Meanwhile, Sir Teodor took his polished silver shield and directed the sun's rays like a mirror onto the Black Knight in Magnusar's reach. It hurt the Black Knight, unbeknownst to the crowd and Sir Magnusar, who could damage him further with cuts and thrusts of his silver sword. No one but Thormon and Sir Teodor understood it, the reason why the non-armored Black Knights showed weakness in the melee. The other Black Knight threw his sword to the ground and yielded, and out of nowhere, the Cicipangle noble hit the table and yelled, "We yield!"

In that fashion, the fight ended. And the Black Knights walked away, one being not mortally wounded but injured. And the other in shame.

The crowd cheered but booed at the same instant. It resolved as an overly long and bland fight.

Thus, the Baldarian knights and their squires made the route out of the arena. The nobleman from Cicipangle walked toward them to congratulate them on their victory.

"You bested my knights. I gotta ask, though, how did your squire know what to do?" the nobleman asked.

Both knights bowed and permitted the nobleman to talk to Thormon. The nobleman walked toward Thormon, smiled, and greeted the boy.

"You are quite an interesting fellow. I have to say. You surprised me with the knowledge of the Nosferatu warriors." The nobleman came closer to Thormon's ear and asked, "How did you come to such knowledge? I hid it carefully from everyone."

Thormon looked at the nobleman with surprise. Thus he replied, "I came across some texts and weapons from a lost city. Tenebrae, I believe."

The nobleman looked even more surprised and asked the boy, "I haven't heard about that place for quite a long spell of research. You are quite remarkable. I would like you to be a guest of honor at one of my parties. I would also like you to be a royal guest at my side on the king's and nobles' cabinet in the arena."

Thormon looked surprised and excited. He mentioned that he would ask his master and that it would be an honor to consort with the nobleman. The nobleman smiled and asked Thormon to go to his master at once and ask him.

Thormon agreed and started to run but then stopped, turned around, and asked apologetically, "I'm sorry, sir, but I never asked your name."

The noble smiled at the boy. "Luc Simau!"

CHAPTER 40

Continuation of The Tournament

T he last solar cycle of the fights drew closer, and one of the most awaited fights seemed about to occur. Early that day, Thormon heard a knock on his door. When he slowly opened the door, a strange-looking fellow greeted him.

Thormon took a good look and asked, "May I help you?"

The man bowed and stretched out his hand. Thormon looked at it and saw that he stood holding a letter. Thormon took it and thanked the man, but the man simply disappeared before he could ask anything else.

Hm. That's odd. Where did he go? Thormon thought as he looked around.

He walked back into his room and opened the sealed letter. It was an invitation to watch the Makake Island warrior fight, but it befell on him to accompany Luc to the king's tower. He would have the best seat and view of the fight. Thormon apparently felt quite surprised but excited at the same instant. He quickly dressed and ran to Teodor's room to tell him the good news.

***

The moment came for the most-talked-about fight. Thormon seemed equipped with his best clothes. And his posture showed that he felt proud to hand the guards his invitation. Soon, he stood at the noble's side of the arena. It appeared like something he couldn't have imagined. Food and drinks were served at will; music lingered, heard in the background.

Is this a fight or a party? he thought as he walked around, trying to find his host.

Somebody tapped him on the shoulder. He quickly turned around and saw his parents alongside Luc.

Luc smiled and greeted Thormon, who was thrilled to see his parents.

"I knew you hadn't been able to see them for a while. And this is the least I could do for a boy who outsmarted my best fighters," Luc acknowledged as he put his hand on the boy's shoulder.

Thus, Luc walked him around the balcony. Luc told Thormon that he had been to his parents' shop and bought many artifacts that he and the bards had brought for their journey. He also made an offer to Thormon's parents—one that would make them well off for many generations to come. Luc seemed happy to say that they'd accepted it. Thormon felt delighted that he did not need to worry about his parents anymore. So, the boy eased his semblance but he looked immensely interested in the fight more than anything else.

Luc saw that the boy had no interest in politics, money, power, or wealth. And that the fights were the only thing he focused on. Luc started talking about the upcoming fight. He looked interested in seeing how the beast would fight. Thormon, on the other hand, told Luc about his run-in with the beast and that they were vicious things. He also confessed he'd been hiding from them since they arrived at the palace. Luc had a good laugh and assured the boy that nothing bad would happen to him. At the time, before he could continue the conversation, a trumpet sounded, indicating the fight was about to begin.

Everyone took their seats and waited for the fighters to enter the ring.

Grooach entered the ring wearing the golden helmet and wielding a tremendous heavy sword as if holding a light rapier. That showed his superiority. The crowd was in awe.

Luc turned to Thormon and whispered, "How was a run-in with him? How did he become exceedingly intelligent? We all know that they are incapable of it. I know you've seen it for yourself."

Thormon explained to him about the golden helmet and that maybe that had something to do with it. Then, the noise of the crowd cheering sounded extremely high that he had to stop speaking.

A pair of Victornian swashbucklers entered the ring. Both men were boasting how agile and strong they were, mocking Grooach, who paced around in a rage, waiting for the fight to commence.

"I also know that you had a run-in with the pirates," Luc whispered into Thormon's ear.

Thormon looked at Luc, surprised, and asked, "How did you know that?"

"Your parents told me. Moreover, I know you've been hiding from them, as well. That beautiful cook's daughter told me so," Luc joked.

Thormon gave a shy smile. "You are well-connected. No one knows I'm seeing that girl. Please don't tell anyone. Her father would kill me."

Luc laughed out loud and replied, "My boy, I will help you out. That is, if you tell your tales of the Makake Island and the run-in with those pirates."

Thormon smiled and agreed. But before he could say anything, they heard a loud screech, followed by a battle cry.

The fight had commenced!

Both pirates took defensive positions as the ape pounded on his chest, screaming.

"What kind of devil is this?" the swashbuckler in blue asked.

"Devil, you call me? You will meet the devil soon, insolent worm!" shouted Grooach.

Then he charged toward the one dressed in red. But the agile swashbuckler kept circling, preventing the ape from closing the distance. The one in blue decided to test his opponent's might by launching a sequence of attacks. His sword looked two times smaller than the ape's, but he showed greater skill at swordsmanship. The ape did not care and just blocked the incoming attack until one finally landed. Grooach stepped back and pretended to be hurt in the stomach. The blue fighter, thinking he had an advantage, went in for the kill. But once he entered Grooach's range, a powerful side blow hewed him in half.

The entire crowd was in shock at what had just taken place. Grooach's diabolical laugh sounded threatening and surpassed any other noise.

Dread filled the red swashbuckler as he saw his partner cut in half.

"Now it is just one-on-one!" swaggered Grooach, laughing.

The red pirate looked horrified. He was presently alone, facing an enemy twice his size and many times stronger. He stepped back and considered quitting the fight but decided to take one last try. He threw a desperate blow at the big primate, but it did not work. The ape just shrugged it off as if it were a mosquito.

"His fur seems too thick!" somebody shouted.

Grooach raised his hands in a show of dominance and shouted, "Yes! I am invincible! Nothing can hurt me!"

Amid the commotion, Luc turned to Thormon and asked, "Is that true? Is he invincible?"

Thormon looked at the panicking pirate. He turned to Luc and mentioned, "He is strong but not invincible."

Before anyone could say anything else, they heard the pirate scream, "Curse you, Lord Vermundr! Why allow such a beast in this contest!"

Grooach laughed and replied, "I am more civilized than you! And yet, you call me a beast!" He stopped for a moment and saw how scared the pirate appeared and then added, "I will let you live. No shame in it. Just throw your sword to the ground and walk away."

"You think I am a coward? I will not throw my sword away, nor will I give up. I need to avenge my friend!" the pirate swore to himself as he restored his strength.

He stepped back and analyzed the best approach. And he launched a combination of attacks at full strength. But the beast blocked the left, right, and overhead blows. The pirate fell back but plunged again. And this turn, the beast failed to parry the one on the thigh, getting the sword stuck on him.

"Congratulations! Now it's my turn!" Grooach screamed as the pirate tried to recover his sword.

The beast kicked the sword away with one leg, sending it flying toward the crowd. With one of his hands, he pummeled the pirate hard that the blow killed him before he even hit the ground.

The entire crowd seemed in shock.

Grooach raised both his hands, celebrating. He turned toward the tower where the king stayed and yelled, "No living thing can defeat me! Are you satisfied? Or do you need me to fight more?"

The king raised his hand, ushering silence. He stood up and replied, "You are truly a talented and formidable fighter. I do believe you are no match for any of the fighters."

Grooach smiled and replied, "Then crown me your champion!"

"The rule says that you must defeat a group of fighters one at a time--"

Grooach interrupted the king. Then he gloated, "Not even all your fighters together could best me." This boasting comment prevailed as if an offense to all envoys at once. In that manner, he would show his superiority.

The king pondered for a moment and acknowledged that a pair of fighters would be no match for the ape.

"The objective of these fights comes about as a way to show the mightiest of the nations. There is no need for death, but your power holds unmatched. I cannot allow any more deaths. Since I will not allow duels against you, I will crown you the champion —only they can accept your challenge. Since you challenged them all to one fight, I will consult them and see. If they accept, you will have a final fight. If not, you will be crowned champion."

Everyone looked in shock at the turn of events.

Luc turned to Thormon. Then he affirmed, "It looks like the fight will test your knowledge concerning the ape if the fighters accept."

Thormon looked at the ape, resulting in a cold chill down his spine, showing dread.

Luc put his hand on the boy's shoulder and advised, "Go to Teodor. He will need to know what you know. I will consult the others and help you all as best as I can."

The air of uncertainty lingered everywhere. The crowd dispersed, and the nations currently had to decide what to do.

CHAPTER 41

The Beginning of the Corruption

The leaders of the three remaining nations decided to meet on the fight's outcome. They conversed endlessly.

"No fighter alone can defeat that ape. All of you would be foolish to let only a couple of warriors fight against that thing," Luc revealed while he slowly walked across the room.

"That much we know! But what advice would a defeated nation give?" asked the representative of Menestrel sarcastically.

Luc stopped, turned to the one who questioned him, and replied: "Knowledge! My friends, something you all lack for such a decision."

"You mean knowledge you never gave your fighters?" Enlgon asked with irony in his tone.

"Those fighters were too proud. They needed to be taught a lesson. And that came from a young boy; how humiliating," Luc replied calmly.

"You let your fighters loose. Hence, they could learn a lesson?" A Baldar noble asked.

"In a way, I wanted to show you all my kingdom's power. And you were all afraid of it, that is, until my fighters' pride took the best of them," Luc replied.

"True! But they still lost, no matter what, and to two mere knights," Enlgon replied sarcastically.

"That is also correct. But don't forget the vampires would have won if they hadn't been so cocky… and completely undermined their opponent. A valuable lesson learned there," Luc warranted looking away at nothing at all.

"Enough of this pissing around! You came here uninvited and implied you have a solution for us; tell us already," the noble from Menestrel snarled.

Luc stopped, smiled at those present, and pulled a chair to sit down. He called in one of his trusted servants and showed them something terrifying. Luc somehow could foresee outcomes, something that scared everyone present. And the grasp of such power could tip the balance. Luc explained to all that they needed to fight the ape as in a battle royale. That this meeting would be for nothing if not done so.

The leaders were in a frenzy. They did not know that anyone could possess such power. But they had more questions than answers, and they still heard what Luc had to say.

The meeting continued throughout the night and by the following solar cycle, the lords of the land arranged a new and different match. Coloris, Menestrel, and Baldar joined to fight the Makake opponent.

News of this "new" arrangement spread like wildfire throughout the kingdom. Something like that hadn´t happen before. But since the opponent accepted, the fight was scheduled.

***

Thormon appeared anxious due to the upcoming fight. He did not know what to make of it. All three nations together, his mind ran wild about what could happen. Teodor looked at the boy and, seeing how trouble befell him, finally decided to talk to him.

"What's on your mind?" Teodor asked

"This doesn't seem right; the ape represents a formidable opponent. He has some powerful tricks up his sleeves. I ran into him already, not something pleasant, but I still outsmarted him. Why, then, must six fighters go up against one? That doesn't feel right. All one needs to do happens to stay cautious and witty; that way, one can outsmart the ape. Although he embodies a tough opponent, there seems no need for this kind of arrangement."

"Nonsense! That ape is unbeatable! He symbolizes a monster for our darkest nightmares. Someone needs to take him down!" Teodor replied

"But at what cost? If I, a simple person, could outsmart him, imagine what you could do. Skilled fighters with the knowledge that I possess," Thormon presumed.

"Nonsense! You know damn well there is no possibility we can defeat it; he stands double our size and triple our strength. You could never defeat him; just run away," Teodor confessed what he truly believed.

Thormon nodded, knowing it wouldn't make a difference what he said. He seemed like nothing in this cog. It ensued as if all took place already in a plan coming to motion.

The solar cycle finally came, and the once-in-a-life fight occurred in a planned manner. The night progressed, getting close, and everyone gathered. People packed the arena; they were basically on top of each other.

The fighters presented themselves in the central arena, bowing and showing off. They were the champs from Coloris, Makake, Menestrel, and Baldar.

The seven finalists arranged their fight stances. Thus, six of the three remaining nations were on one side, and the ape was on the opposing side.

As they readied, Magnusar turned to Teodor and suggested, "Let's have the elves attack the big monster first and follow right after."

Not afraid of the monster, the taller elf ran forward. The elf acrobat tried to stab with his spear at the primate monster. But the beast stepped back and deflected the blow.

"Watch out for the sword, my friend," screamed Commander Enlgon, but there was no opportunity to deflect it.

Grooach thrust his massive sword towards the acrobat, who quickly dodged and jumped onto the sword; jumping again, he got very high up, reaching for the head of the ape. He struck Grooach's ear with a side blow of his spear and landed a foot in the beast's chest, staggering the beast.

Seeing this opening, with a boomerang in hand, the big barbarian looked at the ape, stepped back, and threw it toward him. But Grooach caught it with his right hand and quickly spurned around. Next, he threw it back at the barbarian, knocking both of them down.

"You call this a weapon?!" Grooach mocked.

Teodor and Magnusar saw an opening and ran toward the ape. But Grooach quickly swung his arm, throwing both knights backward.

Grooach gave a loud screech and threw away his massive sword at Enlgon, who happened to block with his shield, but it threw him back due to the weight of the impact. The acrobatic elf tried to run toward the ape. But the deflected giant sword hit him at the tip, resulting in a scar across the chest.

Now all six fighters had their backs against the wall. Each one needed to pick themselves up and decide on a new approach.

"I need no weapon to fight against you puny things! My bare hands will do!" Grooach gloated as he scratched the ground. He showed the public he slowly sharpened his claws.

The acrobatic elf recomposed himself. And he frantically ran towards the ape, throbbing his spear at the ape. But Grooach's free hands were quick and parried each strike. The elf stepped back and ran to the alternative corner of the arena.

Teodor looked around and shouted, "We all have ganged up on him, let's rout it out now together while we still can."

The five warriors picked themselves up and surrounded Grooach, closing the distance. They all approached like a dwindling circle.

Grooach saw that five fighters were closing in while one ran around in a manner of distraction. He swung his arms and shouted: "If that's how you want to fight? Like cowards! I am forced to scream!"

"Scream all you want! I never thought someone your size would end a fight screaming like a little girl!" taunted the albino barbarian as the others closed in.

Grooach pounded his chest and shouted: "You will see who is the little girl once I tear off your limbs!"

When the five fighters, along with the acrobatic elf, came in for the kill, Grooach gave a loud shriek, paralyzing the five warriors and throwing the acrobatic elf to the ground. The sound paralyzed the entire crowd, as well. Grooach looked around and calmly walked towards the albino barbarian. He grabbed him and squeezed his neck until blood dropped in gusts. The ape threw him aside as if he meant nothing to him and walked towards the remaining four. And incredibly that barely killed the man when he could recover mobility, he tried to run from the ape. But Grooach had no hurry; in fact, he had all the time in the world. He slowly walked to the big barbarian, who still recovered, grasping for air, grabbed him with one hand and broke his neck, ensuring he lay dead.

The entire arena seemed petrified. Grooach showed the public how strong his constitution was. The remaining fighters saw how sinister and evil this beast was and dreaded this moment. The elves looked around and tried to work on a strategy. Enlgon parried with his shield, made of a special alloy that blocked sounds. He raised it and had the taller acrobat elf get behind him and strike at will with his far-reaching spear.

Grooach saw the elves closing in and gave the loud shriek once again. But the shield blocked the mechanic wave from the primate's scream.

They got closer and closer and attempted their plan. But Grooach's quick hands deflected the attack, and with a swift move, he grabbed the spear and split it in half. Both elves retreated. Grooach punched the ground and pounded his chest. But he did not scream this time, for he saw that it also affected the crowd, causing panic and disorder. Lord Vermundr became exceedingly alarmed, and Grooach noticed it.

The four remaining fighters regrouped and needed a new plan. But oddly enough, Grooach never attacked them. He transpired as only defending and enjoying the moment.

Grooach turned to the Lords, then asked, "Do you wish me to end at this point? Or do you want me to let your remaining fighters recompose themselves before I defeat them?"

The lords were silent.

The natural light subsided. The servants brought several torches to illuminate the central arena.

Thormon ran towards Teodor and reminded him of his story.

"The eyesight! Of course!" Teodor shouted as he ran towards one of the spectators. He grabbed a drink from the man's hands and extinguished the torch.

The public did not know what to make of it. But Thormon, Ormr, Teodor, Magnusar, and the elves soon ran around the arena. They grabbed the spectators' drinks and extinguished the torches.

Grooach realized what they were doing and quickly got a hold of a lit torch.

"What a cowardly tactic!" Grooach screamed.

He waved the fire from side to side, bringing terror wherever he went. But even though his eyesight seemed limited, the arena's illumination seemed sufficient for him to fight the others. Hence, only the lamps at the far edges of the arena were kept lit.

Darkness engulfed the place.

"Show yourselves and fight, cowards!" the ape kept on shouting and searching.

Sir Teodor and Magnusar ducked down and rested in the dark places. Meanwhile, the elves with night sight roamed stealthily. They tried to figure out how to overcome the beast.

"At this instant, the tables have turned!" A noble mentioned to another.

Lord Vermundr started to enjoy the turn of events of the fight. He turned to Luc and confessed that his speculation of the contest's outcome ensued to the fore wishing.

The beast started to go nuts and, losing patience, stroked everything it could find. Grooach accidentally killed at least two observers. Also, he injured dozens in his pursuit to find the fighters. The ape heard the cries and pleas and decided to stroll toward the center of the arena. He noticed that people were running away and leaving the stands.

The intelligence inherited from the helmet won the battle against the instincts. Rage gave place to cunning. Grooach gave his terrifying screech and paralyzed half of the crowd. That mobilized the fighters.

He turned to where he thought the king and nobles were and screamed out: "I will not continue! I can't fight what I can't see! No one involved in this needs to get hurt! Did you little cowards hear me?"

The voice from the crowd replied: "Consequently, you wish to forfeit the fight?"

Grooach looked back and replied: "I fight for glory; I have no desire for rewards!" he bellowed for all to hear. Then he hinted: "If you fight like true warriors, I will fight, too."

Grooach pounded his chest. He showed his anger and continued: "This denotes not what I expected for this civilized tournament. I did all that you asked, and still, you resorted to cowardly tactics. Come fight me, Enlgon, Alrod, Magnusar, and Teodor. You call yourself knights and fighters, but here you are, running away!"

Grooach, noticing that the advances stopped, placed both his hands on his waist. "What emperor would risk himself by his own choice? What emperor would leave his throne to fight in the front line for any tournament? And yet here I am, the emperor of the Tropical Island of Makake, doing all that! I do not wish to forfeit, but if you don't show yourself right now. It is something I will have to do; I will not hurt another innocent soul for your entertainment. I declare myself the winner! No warrior here is brave enough to face me in the clear!" But the silence stood as the only answer. Thus, the big ape pounded the ground several times and stormed to his quarters. Enlgon looked at Teodor and Magnusar, not knowing what to make of what just happened. This act broke the will to fight. Therefore, the contest ended without a true winner. People lingered in the dark, expecting to hear from lord Vermundr on the matter. But the lord of the land gave no statement or resolution. And as a result, people left back home, booing the lack of actions taken that night.

Enlgon turned to Teodor and concluded: "I guess that makes us the winner."

Teodor looked down and then around, commenting: "Well, the big ape left. Thus, I believe we are the winners. But at what cost? No one expected this outcome."

The fighters gathered their things and left for the palace; en route, they ran into Grooach. Four servant apes were carrying him. He was inside a fully covered cabin of bamboo with four rod handles. There were two apes in the front and two in the back carrying the load. The fighters stopped, giving room to Grooach.

As Grooach passed by them, he signaled the apes to stop. There stayed dread of what the ape might do. But he looked at them in disgust and confessed: "I hope you enjoy your false glory; none of you earned it."

The fighters readied their weapons, thinking the ape would lash out. But nothing happened. The ape just looked away and signaled the carriage to proceed.

"That came about a close one," Thormon declared.

"Yeah! I thought he would attack us," Teodor replied. Then he added, "Carry the wooden chest to the barracks and let's call it a night; go see your parents or do whatever you want. We'll meet tomorrow at noon. I believe we won't celebrate today nor hear any announcements, but the king will want to see us tomorrow, so be ready."

Thormon nodded and took the chest to the barracks.

He opened the door and tried to find something to light the torches, but he couldn't find any. Hence, he sauntered in the dark towards where the chest was stored. He sat on it and started thinking for a while, when he noticed someone entering the barracks and strolling towards him.

"Who is it?" Thormon asked.

"Won't you guess? Can't you see in the dark?" the voice softly replied.

"Eira, is that you?" Thormon replied.

"Of course it is!" She smiled and asked, "Did you win?"

"Didn't you hear the booing and the ruckus?" Thormon replied.

"I did, but I thought it occurred as part of the show," Eira replied and then added, "Come with me. I want to show you something!"

"Ok! Let me just finish up here," Thormon affirmed as he completed his task.

Once finished, he turned to Eira, held her hand, and left the barracks. As he closed the door, he asked, "By the way, where did you want to take me?"

She smiled and replied, "Come to this path."

She led him to several buildings in the direction of the castle. She took him through the gardens and onto the outskirts of it. As they both ran, they bumped into Sir Teodor.

Teodor stepped forward, picking up his pace, turned around, and asked, "Thormon, is that you?"

Thormon, surprised to see him there, replied. "Yes! And sorry to ask, but what are you doing here?"

Teodor put his hand on Thormon and replied, "I'm just thinking… What a horrible showcase. Now I have to see what we must decide…"

Thormon looked at Teodor and asked, "Well, did you have a chance to talk to Enlgon?"

"No, he went directly to his quarters. He remained not in the mood in this instant," Teodor paused for a bit and added, "What a big mess! That's what! But I have hope that we and the elves will split the prize."

Then he added, "But be careful now, I thought you were going to see your parents and not your girlfriend. You know, it is not safe here tonight. People from everywhere came here to watch and bet. But without a clear winner, the unfortunate ordeal spoiled the bets, and the folks are a bit aroused."

And with the mention of being girlfriend and boyfriend, both Eira and Thormon blushed, and Thormon replied, "Ok, we will!" and both bid Teodor farewell and left shiftily.

***

The next solar cycle…

Thormon met with the knights and the elves at the designated place.

"So, Enlgon, what have you decided to do?" Magnusar asked.

"What have you and your friend decided?" Enlgon responded, throwing back the question.

"We thought of splitting the prize. Don't you think it's fair?" Teodor added.

Enlgon looked at both men and, with a harsh tone, answered, "Fair? Would you say the result occurred fairly concerning what we did to the ape? We broke the tournament rules to adjust to your king's whimsical wishes. In the end, not allowing a beast to be crowned champion."

Both knights looked surprised and asked Enlgon to elaborate on the matter.

Enlgon asked both knights to follow him to the hall of knowledge. Once there, he asked a keeper to fetch him the Book of Champions.

Enlgon opened the book and started talking to both knights. "You see, here, we have the rules and knowledge of the tournament. There is a reason why magic and the like are not allowed within the city during the tournament. We even punished those whom Thormon brought to our attention, but you all know this. What I want to get to is in this chapter."

Enlgon explained what had happened and how it conflicted with the rules and even broke them.

"But you also agreed to the fight!" Teodor accused Enlgon.

"True! But a strange presence of dread and fear blinded me in the king's chamber during the meeting. Didn't you feel something off, too?" Enlgon asked as he tried to make sense of why he and the others would break the consecrated rules of the tournament. His thoughts lingered on godlike Luc.

Both knights were speechless. Teodor stood up and tried to make sense of it. He went looking for alternative books related to the tournament. Magnusar grabbed the book from Enlgon and attempted to skim and find an answer to their question.

Enlgon, saddened by his own decisions, seemed hopeless. He stood up and articulated, "My kind and I withdraw from this decree and treaty of this tournament! We will not be a part of it, do what you want, but the elves are no longer a part of the treaty!"

Magnusar did not know what to say and let Enlgon storm out of the hall of knowledge.

As he left, he bumped into Thormon and warned, "Be careful, boy; something dark is brewing here. You know where to find us if you ever find yourself in trouble."

Before Thormon could say something back, Enlgon stormed away.

"What is his problem? What did you find?" Thormon asked.

Teodor and Magnusar closed the book he held, and the latter said, "This entire outcome stays a sham."

Thormon, not understanding what happened, asked again, "What do you mean, a sham?"

Teodor came strolling and replied, "Grooach should be considered the champion… but the king won't allow it."

"The elves do not want to participate in this. Enlgon and Alrod will follow protocol. But they will not accept any prizes or glory. Enlgon made clear we did not earn this shameful victory."

The air of doubt and uncertainty lingered about as both knights left the hall of knowledge. They then made their route to the palace's court. This maelstrom stayed as not something one could fix.

End

PART 1